BON VOYAGE

Bon Voyage

(SECOND EDITION)

JB Williams

Stephen Zimmer

JB Writes Stuff

Contents

Many Thanks!

Many thanks to my editor, Stephen Zimmer. He took the mess of *Bon Voyage* and made it far better than I could ever do. The second edition would be nowhere without his help.

1

The Hook Line

Planet: OROS
System: AMAZON
Sector: PORTUGUESE INTERSTELLAR
Date: 28-FEB-2428

Ethan João Rifts hates space. In fact, he imagined his life going in a completely different direction when he was a kid, and it did not involve space. He imagined himself growing up, growing old, and dying on Oros, with an animal sanctuary in his name.

But that never happened.

Like many Orosians, he hopped from one job to another; from retail, to grocery, to fast food, to retail, to grocery, to fast food, and so on. Then, a series of unfortunate events by a combination of his and other hands forced him from one situation to another, and now he is on a bus, resting his head against the back of a seat with his bag on his lap.

In the bag are the last of his clothes, a few possessions, and some papers inside a sealed folder. He sold his possessions, closed his bank account, and purged his online accounts. For added security, he is wearing a gray hat to hide his dark red hair, and he has sunglasses to conceal his green eyes. He cannot do much about his pale skin, but without the hat and sunglasses, he would stick out like a sore thumb, which is the last thing he wants.

The inside of the bus is white with a blue band streaking across the length that connects to the Federation of Sol Systems symbol: a golden Sculptor constellation surrounded by a golden wreath. Advertisements of vaccines, military service, universities, and movies run along the length of the bus, but they are covered in graffiti, ranging from squiggles to an actual gang sign of three machetes stacked over each other, like a crossed-out equal sign. The largest symbol is painted on the back of the bus, and it is an entwined tree with its roots and branches twisted to hands reaching up and reaching below. Written in a circle around it is "Ramos do Vazio. Sementes da Árvore."

Ethan does a lot to ignore that symbol, and someone spray painted crosses around it and over it.

Choro music is playing over the bus's speakers, others on the bus talk among themselves, and Ethan believes he saw some of the passengers look at him, but he pretends not to notice. The bus passes a scarce amount of people, despite it being a sunny day, and the buildings range from high rise apartment complexes that look like bricks and steel, to glass monoliths with corporate logos; with the absolute tallest belonging to a company called Arx Corporation, its logo is simply a sharp "A."

The towering obelisk makes sure everyone knows their motto: "Building the Future. Together."

The bus passes statues of warped proportions in front of the Museum of New Rio, advertising an exhibit for a long extinct race that used to live on the planet. Near the cultural center is a franchise restaurant with enticing holographic projections of burgers, drinks, and snacks. The most notable of the eateries is a Klumsy K's, with a 1920's architecture design and full parking lot.

At one point, the bus stops at the local mall, too. The mall is the Green Roof Mall because of its green glass roof, and while its arches and pillars and exterior masonry give it a mediocre appearance, the interior is hollow and boring.

The bus picks up some more people from the mall bus stop, and Ethan keeps his head down as the newcomers file on, each sliding their pass across an orb at the top of the stairs. Once the new people are on, the bus resumes driving, and no trouble comes.

The longer the bus drives, the less urban the area becomes, replacing the tall buildings with short, rundown buildings such as diners and fuel stations, a row of abandoned houses being retaken by trees, grass, and vines, and the smooth roads degrading to cracks and potholes.

The road continues on and expands into a six-lane interstate with sparse traffic that slowly spreads to their own exits, while the bus continues straight. The road is nudged between two walls with electric fences and lampposts that would activate at night to give plenty of light to anybody driving, and the roads that split from it get the same treatment. The walls guard the infrastructure from the overgrown plant life, and the Orosian farmers must use terrariums to protect their crop and livestock, lest they want the pollen to kill their livelihood.

Thick, twisting trees, tangling vines, and heavy shrubs cover Oros, and no amount of projects could clear normal colony sizes, because the plant life grew too fast. There are even rumors that the Federation resorted to a combination of fire and "salt bombs" to clear areas for settlers to build, but even keeping the cities, settlements, farms, and infrastructure operating is a monumental task because of pollen storms and the rapid growth of the plants.

During pollen storms, people need to seek shelter to avoid getting buried or lost in the thick clouds. After the pollen storms end, cleanup crews must act fast to sweep the pollen off the streets and clean the generators, which leads to frequent power outages. The fences do nothing to stop the pollen, either, but they stop the other plant life. But that brings the question: Why would anybody settle on Oros?

For that, the answer is simple. Economics. Oros (and the Amazon System in general) has a lot to offer with lumber, minerals, agriculture, cattle, tourism (which is fueled by their expansive forests and the ruins of a long-dead alien race), and businesses and guilds use its location as a hub. Oros' location is excellent for connecting to other sectors in the Federation of Sol Systems.

To the North is the Anglosphere; to the East is the Prospect Sector; South has the Latin Planetary Republics, and West is the Expanse Colonies, with the Sol System tucked behind it and surrounded by other regions in the Federation. Regions such as New Africa Territories, Grand Khazar Frontier, and the New Sun Conglomerate. Greater Arabia was also part of their Federation at one point, but a war with their neighbor did not end well, so it is no longer theirs. All this knowledge is courtesy of the public education system and the local library Ethan used to visit when he was not sneaking into the zoo.

The bus Ethan is on drives for another hour, dropping off most of the people along the way at other stops scattered along the interstate. When it reaches its destination, it stops at a sharp gate and a large cement brick wall with razor wire on top. In front of the wall gate is a large sign with "Fort Mirror" in bold white letters, and below the name is the Sculptor of the Federation, and next to it is a sailboat on top of a star with "AATS" inside said star.

This is the acronym for "Association of Assisted Transport and Security." Their headquarters is in a city called Blackwell, which is on Americana, the crown jewel planet of the Anglosphere. Ethan briefly remembers that place, but only leaving it with his parents to head back to his father's home world of Oros.

With the bus stopped, a burly man in a red suit and black vest approaches the bus; his partner, who is considerably smaller, follows him, but Ethan does not like the way he always keeps his hand on his holster. The driver opens the bus when the two guards approach, and the large guard gets on, while the smaller one stays outside.

"Good day, Jerry," says the guard.

"Good day, Luiz," replies the driver, far from enthusiastic.

"How many are on the bus today?"

"Four this time."

"Any contraband?"

"Ask them. I don't know."

"Do you have any contraband?"

"You serious?"

"Don't get mad at me. I'm just doing my job."

"No. No contraband, this time."

Luiz smiles thinly and slaps the driver's arm with his folder as he walks on the bus.

"Fico feliz em saber," says Luiz.

Jerry rolls his eyes, and once Luiz is on the bus, he looks at everyone. His eyes are cold and black, sweat reflects off his dark tan skin, and his fingers tap on the clipboard. As he strolls down the aisle, his partner walks after him.

Each step is heavy and precise, and everyone tries to avoid eye contact as Luiz's large shadow looms over them. Unfortunately for Ethan, he is the first in line, and Luiz looks at him and motions him to remove his hat and sunglasses.

"Nome?" asks Luiz.

Ethan reluctantly takes off his hat and sunglasses and pulls out his wallet (filled with colorful Federation bills called "fedos") and shows his ID. *"Ethan Rifts, senhor. É meu primeiro dia como membro da AATS."*

The guard looks at the ID, and then at Ethan, saying as he returns it, *"Qualquer contrabando?"*

"Não, senhor."

Luiz snatches the bag and sifts through it, pulling out clothes, sniffing some of them, and running his fingers along the seams. He also pats the bag a few times and ends with ordering Ethan up and frisking him. When he finishes, he forces Ethan to sit down by pressing his hand on his shoulder. After that, he moves on.

"Você é bom. Boa sorte para você," says Luiz.

Ethan watches Luiz go to the next person on the bus, and he sighs, returns his sunglasses and hat, and bangs his head against the seat while the guard searches the rest of the passengers.

A little while later, the bus pulls to a stop in front of a row of block-shaped buildings, all with one door and one window. In front of the line of buildings are three flag poles. The middle, and tallest, is the Federation flag with a blue background. The second one is the Oros flag, which is a tree with roots gripping a blue orb and a white background. The third and smallest is the AATS flag with a black background, and the plot of grass surrounding the flags is thick and green.

Beyond the buildings are blocks of hangars with air towers placed at equal distances. The pavement is covered in pollen, which is being vacuumed up by trucks with large hoses and tanks. People wearing magnet boots are on roofs, using brooms to brush off pollen from the structures.

Ethan and the three others get off the bus and immediately start sweating with the hot, wet atmosphere that is mixed with the smell of grass and fuel. The other three walk towards the row of buildings, and the bus drives off.

Ethan looks over his shoulder, watching the bus go until it rounds a corner, then he swallows, takes a deep breath, and walks towards the row of buildings. They are each numbered, starting at "01" and ending at what Ethan can only guess is "10."

It is fortunate that Building 01 has two men sitting outside at a table and chairs, all bolted down with a fan plugged in and blowing cold air over them, as well as a radio playing. One is sunburned and muscular, with blond hair and blue eyes, and the other has dark hair and eyes with copper skin. Both are wearing gray jumpsuits with dark sweat blotches around their necks and armpits, and the suits have fishhooks stitched on their backs and shoulders.

"-A polícia distribuiu uma recompensa de trinta mil fedos por informações sobre o tiroteio em massa nos Apartmentos Luxuosos do Rio Rise. O suspeito ainda é desconhecido e solto."

Hearing that brings Ethan to stiffen and bile surges as he wonders if this place knows what he did. Sure, the radio claims they have no information, but the media lies. Maybe the police have secretly passed the information on to the AATS?

"Are you serious?" says the blond man, bringing Ethan out of the paranoia trap.

"Yeah, I can't find them," says the dark-haired man, who is searching through a backpack.

"How could you forget the cards?"

"Don't bite my head off."

"Getting the cards was your one job!"

"I can always go back to the ship and get it. No big deal."

"Too late. We're already here."

"Excuse me," says Ethan, feeling sick and gripping his bag with white knuckles as the radio continues its broadcast.

The pair look at him.

"Yeah?" asks the blond.

"I'm-" Ethan swallows, "-looking for Captain Brown of the *Hook Line.*"

The dark-haired man jabs his thumb at 01's door.

"Right in there," he says.

The blond kicks his shin. "Hey, we don't know who this guy is… So, who are you?"

"I'm Ethan Rifts. I'm new."

"Oh, okay. Get in there."

Ethan blinks. "Uh…"

The blond gets up and opens the door. "Get in there. Captain's waiting."

Ethan takes a deep breath and goes inside. Upon entering, the door slams shut, making him flinch, and then he takes off his sunglasses, removes his hat. He goes to the only desk in the room, passing fans and quickly getting acquainted with the stuffy air.

When he reaches the desk, he lays his bag by his feet and stands awkwardly with his folder in hand. In front of him is an elderly, dark-skinned man with gray hair, deep wrinkles, and gold eyes, wearing a navy-blue suit with gold bars, a black belt, and black shoes; he also has a damp rag around his neck, and his head shines with sweat.

He is sitting behind the desk, and next to him is a lean woman, also sunburned and sweaty, with snow-white hair with blue roots and intense blue eyes; she is a head shorter than Ethan. Like the two men outside, she is wearing a gray jumpsuit with a black belt, but she also has a black vest and a gray hat, with a black brim and decorated with the fishhook. She has a pistol holstered on her belt. She is partially sitting on the table with her arms folded across her chest, one leg over the other, foot towards Ethan, and her eyes locked on him. She also has three diamonds tattooed on her hand.

The old man stands up and holds out his hand, appearing disinterested. "Papers."

Ethan gives the old man the folder, and he skims through it before taking out a few sheets and putting them in a folder of his own on the desk.

"So, you're Ethan Rifts," says the old man.

Ethan nods. "Yes sir. I am here for the *Hook Line.* AATS said you were the only one available."

"Your application sucks."

Ethan shifts in his spot and looks down, and the old man puts the folder down on the desk.

"But you are the only one available, so let's cut to it. I am Captain Abraham Brown and this-" he points to the woman, "is Marian Dartmount. She is my right-hand gal."

Ethan glances at Marian again. She furrows her brows slightly, and he quickly puts his attention back to Abraham when he talks again.

"Before we get too far, I want to make something clear," says Abraham. "I did not want you on my ship, but Federation and AATS regulations say that I need a medic on board before I can go anywhere, so you're being hired on as a medic. We've been stuck on this forsaken planet long enough and we're about to lose a lot of money if we don't get moving now."

Ethan blinks. "But I only have veterinarian training, sir."

"Your point?" says Abraham.

Ethan swallows nervously. "Different biology, sir."

"Do you want off this planet or not?"

"Yes sir. I want off, sir," says Ethan timidly.

"Alright then. Shut up and listen."

Marian snorts laugh, and Ethan's eyes briefly flick to her with a flash of annoyance, but quickly looks back to Abraham when she returns the glare.

"Veterinarian training is still medical training that I can work with. But if it makes you feel better, we got textbooks, a test dummy, and simulations, as well as the game Operation. You can learn human biology as you go," says Abraham. "Now I run an easy ship. You do your job, do it well, and you get a raise. Do it poorly and your ass is transferred to another ship. We all clean, we all cook, we all rotate for inspections, and we have game night every three days. Unfortunately, we don't get television in space travel, so you'll have to watch or listen to whatever disks are on board or read what we have in our library. If you want to fight anybody, keep it in the commons and do not wreck the furniture. Are we clear?"

"Yes sir," says Ethan.

"Good." Abraham returns the folder to Ethan. "Marian, show our new medic the ship and crew while I finish getting us prepped for launch. I want the engine hot and ready when I get on. We've already wasted enough time waiting for a replacement and I do *not* want that contract to expire."

Marian gives a quick salute, slips off the table, and walks past Ethan while slipping on a pair of sunglasses she had in her pocket.

"Follow me," she says, her voice being rough, but oddly pleasant.

Ethan puts on his hat and sunglasses, picks up the bag, and then follows Marian out while he puts the folder in his bag.

When they get outside, Marian says, "We're going to have to make this quick. Captain got the word you were coming, so we started the resupplying early. That means all we need is the captain to come back with the exit code and we'll be out in space."

"Yes ma'am," says Ethan.

Marian points at the large blond man. "That is Roger Whirling." Then she points at the dark-haired man. "And that is Calvin Darwish. You two, this is Ethan Rifts. He's taking Julius' slot."

The two do not stand up, but Roger extends his hand.

"Hello again. Looks like you're the lucky winner after all," says Roger.

Ethan awkwardly shakes it. "I...I guess so."

Calvin mimics Roger. "You'll like it on the *Hook Line*. We're like a big happy adoption home."

Ethan shakes Calvin's hand. "That's... nice, I guess."

"Cool. That's done. Time to go to the *Hook Line*," says Marian.

Ethan follows Marian around the side of the building, and even though she is walking fast, he keeps up with her. Their steps, plus the wind from passing vehicles, kick up clouds of pollen, and men shout orders in the distance.

"So why do you want to go to space?" asks Marian, having to raise her voice because of a passing vacuum truck making a path in the carpet of pollen.

"I just need to get away from Oros," says Ethan. "With my mom buried I have no reason to be here, and I've seen enough of this place."

"I can understand. This place sucks. I don't speak a lick of Portuguese, and yet I can tell plenty by the news."

"Really?"

Marian nods. "Gang wars. Mob hits. Shit like that. Hell, earlier this week the news was blasting about six guys who got capped in a fancy apartment. From what I could tell, it looks like the cops and locals are bracing for a mob war. I'm glad we're leaving before that happens."

Ethan feels sick again. "Yeah, I definitely don't want to be around when that happens."

And that is where that conversation ends.

Marian leads Ethan towards a massive hangar marked "01," and inside is a large ship that is, from what Ethan can tell, two hundred seventy feet long, one hundred seventy feet wide, and eighty feet tall. It has a round center, and two stubby wings with long, thin engines, a rectangular nose, and smaller exhaust ports dotting the nose and running along its sides. The ship is standing on braced wheels and chained to a truck on treads waiting to pull it out.

The windows on the bridge are tinted, and on the nose is "*Hook Line*," with a fishhook next to it. Next to the *Hook Line* is a long truck (also on treads) with workers removing empty to half-empty fuel canisters and replacing them with full, glowing green canisters that are eight feet tall and four feet wide. The side of the *Hook Line* is open, and the workers are using an inclined conveyor belt and straps to guide the canisters inside. There is another truck with a massive air tank on its back that has a hose going inside the ship, and lastly is yet another truck that is parked near the back.

There is a red-skinned man with long black hair, dark brown eyes, and a bead necklace, wearing his jumpsuit open at his waist so his white shirt (wet with sweat) is exposed. He is signing the paperwork on a clipboard for a driver who is next to a robotic cart with orbs on its corners and bands of digital screens on its sides. After the paperwork is finished, the driver and his cart leave, and the red-skinned man looks at Marian as she and Ethan walk up.

"Hey Marian, we just got the supplies reloaded. Can we please leave this planet now? Or is the captain still waiting for the replacement?" he asks.

"We finally got our medic, so we can go within the hour," says Marian. "Ethan, this is Moon Stone. Moon, this is Ethan Rifts. He's going to be our replacement medic."

"Really?" Moon looks up and down Ethan, with his hands on his hips and his brows scrunched. "Where'd you study?"

"*Nova Faculdad Comunitéria Do Rio,*" says Ethan.

"The hell is that?"

"A community college."

"Great. What kind of degree do you have?"

"I minored in business and majored in animal hospitality, which included veterinarian training as a mandatory elective."

"Nice." Moon smacks his lips and glares at Marian. "Nice. Julius' replacement is a dog doctor. What kind of horseshit is that?"

"Take it up with the captain," says Marian. "And stop being dramatic. It's not like Julius is dead. He just changed crews. You can always write him a letter if you miss him that much. Maybe you can send him a dick pick, too?"

"The captain should have hired someone with **human** medical training, and you know it. This guy doesn't even look like he can take care of himself. How's he supposed to take care of us?"

"Take it up with the captain, Moon." Marian shakes her head and walks up the *Hook Line*'s ramp. "Come on, Newbie."

Ethan follows Marian up the ramp, and after making the mistake of looking at Moon, his steps quicken to get away from the glare.

The interior of the ship is cooler and not as bright, so the two take off their sunglasses. The first area is wide with a metal floor and metal crates tied down, as well as a robotic cart with orbs on its corners and bands of digital screens on its sides. It is strapped it down, and it beeps and whirs when Marian waves at it.

"That is HL-0001, but we call him HL," says Marian. "HL, this is Ethan. Say hi, HL."

HL-0001 beeps and rocks back and forth in its straps as green bars scroll across its screen, and Ethan quietly waves. After he greets HL, Marian continues walking, and once they exit that room, they enter a hallway with lights that are spaced evenly down the hallway, which has labeled doors going down their length. The walls are sleek and have wood panels with pictures of various landscapes. But one section is a large, locked case, holding various certificates and inspection reports. The floor has a thin red carpet stained with black footprints, and it leads to a door down the hall.

"Armory. Locker room. Fridge. Freezer. Dry storage. Broom closet. Back there was receiving," says Marian, pointing at each room with snapping motions, while muffled noises travel beneath their feet. "Down there is the engine room, which you shouldn't be down there without explicit permission from either Captain Brown, me, or our engineer, Aiden Parsen."

She kneels and pulls open a latch that reveals metal stairs and a room down below that is brightly lit, and the commotion of refueling and re-airing with talking workers floods out. Ethan cannot see anything much down there besides the stairs, metal walls, and a calendar of… He squints his eyes… The calendar has a canine, girl… humanoid… thing in a skimpy bikini leaned over a beach ball on a sunny beach with white sand.

Ethan leans back and looks at Marian, who is giving him a knowing look.

"Aiden is a veteran of the Aarde Conflict," says Marian. "That's his calendar."

"Is he… Is he into that?" asks Ethan.

"He married an Aarden, so, yeah, he's definitely into it."

Ethan wrinkles his nose, but Marian slaps him on the back of the head.

"Don't make that face," snaps Marian. "His wife is sweet. Her English is terrible, and her accent is thicker than a milkshake, but still. She's sweet."

Then the door at the end of the hallway opens, and a man with a mountain of height and sheer muscle mass enters. He has thick dark hair with streaks of red on his temples, and there is an orange tint in his hazel eyes. When he sees Marian and Ethan kneeling by the engine room, he smiles and strolls towards them.

"Hello, Mary. Who do we have here?" asks the man.

"Aiden, this is Ethan Rifts. Ethan is going to be our medic. He also peeked at your calendar," says Marian.

Aiden shrugs. "Not like I hide it." He looks at Ethan. "Medic, huh? What kind of training do you have?"

"Veterinarian, sir."

"Well, you'll fit right in. We're all animals around here in a way. Now, if you'll excuse me, I have an engine to prep."

Aiden slips between the pair and squeezes through the doorway, and he goes down the stairs.

"Better hurry. The captain is already getting the clearance for lift-off," says Marian.

"The engine will be hot and ready when he pulls up," says Aiden. "Also, stay out of the bathroom for a while. I left a present for Taksheel to clean up."

"You know he'll get you for that," says Marian with a grin.

"That's future me's problem."

Marian chuckles, closes the latch and motions Ethan to follow her. They go through the door Aiden came from and enter the commons. It is a circular area with a kitchen in one portion, a dining room in another, and an area with couches and love seats, a mounted TV with an entertainment center, and a full bookcase. The commons have doors, more wood panels, and lights, and in the center is a large, thick door with "Bridge" above it. Off to the side, at the far end, is another door, white with a red center, and above it is "Infirmary." Next to it is the community bathroom and showers. The community area had been decorated with the paraphernalia of fishing equipment, taxidermy of fish from various worlds, pictures of fish and fishing boats, and a blue-print of a crab fishing boat.

"Infirmary is where you'll be most of the time," says Marian, while Ethan studies the décor. "The bridge is where we'll have our meetings, and everyone is paired in their rooms. You get to bunk with Moon."

Ethan looks at Marian with worry, but she ignores him and walks to a room marked "Moon + [Reserved]."

But before she can open the door, another door marked "Taksheel + Aiden" opens, and a light gray, slender man with a wiry build, curly black hair, and stone-gray eyes walks out wearing black boxers. When he sees Marian scowling, and Ethan giving him a blank look, he stops and nods upward a bit.

"'Sup," he says.

Ethan's eyes flick up and down the man's odd body, completely silent.

"You better be auditioning for an underwear commercial," says Marian sourly.

"No, I'm banging Riva. Or was. We're done now. A little victory session for completing our tasks." Taksheel ends with a click and a wink.

Marian scoffs. "Pig. Ethan, this is Taksheel Iyer. He is a failed underwear commercial actor, now resident conspiracy nut. Taksheel, this is Ethan Rifts. He's our new medic."

Taksheel holds out his hand, and Ethan reluctantly grabs it and finds himself not liking how Taksheel locks his arm in place, squeezes his hand, and peers into his eyes.

"You're not Section 0, are you?" asks Taksheel.

"I... What?" Ethan looks at Marian and then at Taksheel. "What are you talking about?"

"Knock it off, Taksheel," says Marian.

Taksheel's cold eyes warm up, and he smiles and releases Ethan's hand. "I'm just trying to protect the crew. You know, these Section 0 guys are bad news. I got all kinds of shit on them if you want to see my wall." He counts off with his fingers. "I got maps, pictures, articles, leaked memos. You name it, I got it, and I am gonna make a screenplay about it one day. Starring me, of course, as my big comeback after being blacklisted from *lotion* commercials. Aiden's going to help, too, with his experience in black ops and all."

Ethan scrunches his brows and Marian sneers.

"You actually have to have talent first, Taksheel," says Marian.

"Says the gender quota hire," retorts Taksheel.

Marian narrows her eyes, and Ethan's eyes dart between them. Then Taksheel's door opens, and an elegant woman shyly pokes her head out. She is fair-skinned, and she has brown eyes, like melted chocolate, and messy dark hair with thick lashes, and she is covering herself with a sheet.

"Do we have a new person?" asks the woman.

"Yeah, this is Ethan. He's replacing Julius," says Taksheel.

"Thank God. Julius gave me the creeps." The woman leans out slightly and extends her hand, which has three diamonds tattooed on it. "Hello Ethan, my name is-"

"Whoa, stop! I'm doing the introductions!" interrupts Marian. "Ethan, Riva Bonnevue. She is our computer specialist. Riva, Ethan Rifts. He is going to be our medic. And do not shake her hand. You don't know what she's touched."

Ethan drops his hand, and Riva retracts hers with a shameful blush.

"But I do," says Taksheel with a smirk.

"Put some clothes on! Both of you!" yells Marian. "We'll be leaving within the hour. As for you, Ethan." Marian opens Moon's door and points inside. "Make yourself at home."

Ethan walks into the small room, finding two beds, two dressers (one with hair care and candles), two little lamps above the beds, and one large light in the center of the ceiling. He sees one bed is tidy, and the other is messy with a dream catcher and marked calendar above it. So, he puts his bag on the tidy bed and looks at Marian, who is leaning against the door frame, watching him closely.

"Excuse me, Marian," says Ethan.

"Just Dartmount. We aren't on a first name basis yet," says Marian.

"Yes ma'am. But will we be gone a long time?" asks Ethan.

Marian stares at him critically for a few seconds. "Yeah. The captain hates this planet. No offense."

Ethan waves dismissively. "None taken."

"But we'll be doing what we've always done," continues Marian. "Help a stranded ship, do some resource delivery, serve as security or taxi. It all depends on the contract. Right now, we're going to the Prospect Sector on a taxi job to pick up some guy at Onyx Station. The pay is great, but Julius ducking out on us put us in a bind, so the captain is grouchy now. Your arrival probably saved our commission, but we'll have to double time it now."

Ethan feels a bit of relief come in, but it is not about the commission. The Prospect Sector is not only the newest addition to the Federation, but Onyx Station is in the Peace System, which is the farthest system in humanity's interstellar empire. He will be far from trouble out there.

"What is the route after we're done?" asks Ethan.

Marian stares at him again, only longer this time, with her finger tapping hard against her wrist. "We'll head down to the Latin Planetary Republics, drop the guy off at Isabella Station, and then we'll cross through the Expanse Colonies, pass through the Anglosphere and New Sun to get to the Aarde Union. Then we'll spend some time on Aarde so Aiden can see his wife. You won't see this place for a long time."

"That's fine by me."

"You also came at a good time because we have a vacation coming up for the *Hook Line*, and if we're lucky, the vacation will take us to Winter 9," says Marian, her eyes drifting right.

"That is a specific planet," says Ethan.

Marian shrugs. "Winter 9 has some amazing slopes and…"

Marian's voice drifts off, and a few seconds later, she taps the door frame and walks off.

"Never mind, chitchat is over. Get set up quick," she says, her voice carrying in the ship. "We'll be having a team meeting when the captain comes back."

Ethan watches her go, and after she is out of sight, he blows a puff of air and begins unpacking.

The Signal

Association of Assisted Transport & Security Log
Date: 14-APR-2428
Ship: *HOOK LINE*

CPT. Abraham Brown Transcript:

Captain's log, April fourteenth, twenty-four twenty-eight; contract number one-oh, one-four, two-zero, zero-eight, client name is Harvest, he refused to give his first name, but the pay was too much to pass up.

We are currently two weeks behind schedule due to Julius Steinven leaving without notice, but we are en route to Onyx to pick up a man named Dr. Arcos Rock at Onyx Station. Julius's replacement, Ethan Rifts, is an animal doctor, so I have him cooped up in the infirmary studying human biology. I've been watching him, and he seems like a nice kid, but there is something off about him. Marian also told me about his questions. That boy is hiding something, and he keeps watching us, especially Marian. If what he is hiding endangers the crew or if he tries anything against Marian, then I'll dump him off at the next outpost. Or launch him in space and label it a workplace accident. But if he is good, then we will give him the privilege of knowing more about our vacations.

As for this Harvest guy and the small fortune he is willing to pay for us pick up Dr. Rock? Well, I do not like it either. I looked up anybody with a name of "Harvest" with Riva's help and everything that came up did not match who we met. And when we looked up Dr. Arcos Rock, we found he worked for Arx Corporation's weapons research department before switching careers to the Federation Department of Xenobiology and History.

So, I have a weirdo in my crew, and we are going to be picking up another weirdo to drop off to a shady weirdo. It's all strange, but the pay is too good to pass up and my crew knows it. That is all for now.

This is Captain Abraham Brown, signing off.

*****

Ethan Rifts hates space. It is an endless black coldness, with far and few beauties. Stars are but distant twinkles, and most of the planets and moons humans have colonized needed to be altered drastically with terraforming or colony domes. Or, in some cases, living in "cloud cities" orbiting gas giants, or living in habitats hovering around other celestial bodies not fit for human living, but great for research or mining.

But that is not all.

Every new planet or moon discovered and colonized is a petri dish of bacteria, germs, diseases, and viruses, and those microscopic demons have variants in relation to the regions of their planet or moon, which means humans need to develop a constant supply of vaccines to keep them at bay.

Then comes the other prices of colonizing other worlds and moons. Human forms and skins change because of their climate and gravity. Some develop a strong immunity to one thing but have a fatal weakness to others. Strong bones, weak bones; thin muscles, thick muscles; tall, short; thick skinned, thin skinned. All these variables need accommodating when the Federation does its bureaucratic or military or medical affairs.

Humanity has been spreading across the cosmos for hundreds of years, and the cosmos has gradually twisted humans as payment for encroaching on its domain. And while Federation propaganda sends out a constant supply of "Diversity Is Strength," and "Unity Through Differences," and "Building Together," and many other happy slogans, the distances and differences between each planet, each moon, each system, and each sector in the infinite expanse of space has created rifts, and the only reason that the Federation is held together is because of the chains they impose on the colonies.

But even beyond the borders of the Federation of Sol Systems, there is trouble with the neighbors, and they must protect themselves plus their vassals from them. The only common ground that humanity has with the rest of sapient life populating the galaxy is that space hates everyone with equal malice.

However, nobody cares about this when they are inside the *Hook Line*, protected by its metal hull and the wood panel walls covering the metal. This sentiment is strongest in the commons, where Ethan is playing cards with Marian, Riva, Aiden, and Moon.

The group is sitting at the round table, and in the middle of the table is a mix of gum, bite-sized candy bars, little spaceship-shaped crackers, and small candy packs, plus a row of three cards. Everyone has two cards in their hands, and everyone is wearing white jumpsuits with gray pads trailing their shoulders and limbs, as well as black boots with Velcro straps covering the zippers. Everyone also has a thin computer pad on their wrists that is measuring their pulses and keeping other information stored for ease of access.

The table is brightly lit by the ring of lights above it, and near the table is the fridge, a counter, a sink, an oven, and cabinets full of rations and dishes. Hanging on the wall for ease of viewing are the Federation and AATS flags, but Aiden is the only one who pays any respect to the Federation flag. He salutes it every morning, or stares at it from the couch for hours at a time, without saying a word or moving. To everyone else, it is just colorful fabric.

"I'm in for three gum and a candy bar," says Riva. She has her long, dark hair tied to a ponytail and is wearing light-brown eye shadow to complement her eyes and thick lashes. She tosses in her bet. "Next."

Riva smirks at Ethan, even though he is not next, and Ethan scratches his red hair as his green eyes look at his cards, which are a king and an ace. He looks at the table and sees a king, a two, and a ten. Next to Ethan is Marian, and she shakes her head in disgust as she studies her cards. Over the past two weeks, Ethan has frequently glanced at her and sits close to her just as much, like today, for example, but he blames that on the size of the ship, rather than an unknown force determined to make him odd.

"This is the worst hand I have ever seen," says Marian; she still matches the bet, though.

"Not my fault," says Aiden.

"You're the dealer."

Aiden smirks, and Marian jabs her thumb at Ethan.

"Your turn, Newbie," says Marian.

Ethan tosses his cards in. "I fold."

Marian's jaw drops, and Moon snickers and matches Riva's bet.

"Keep folding. It makes the game easy," says Moon.

"You've folded every hand so far," says Marian.

"I don't have good hands," says Ethan.

Aiden puts down another card. It's an ace.

Ethan frowns.

Then the door opens and Taksheel walks in. He passes Marian and exchanges a quick kiss with Riva, before taking a seat next to her. Ethan notices the glare Marian is giving the pair, but he also thinks he is the only one that notices because nobody reacts to her expression.

"What did I miss?" asks Taksheel.

"Aiden's shitty dealing. What's the update?" says Marian.

"Well," begins Taksheel.

He reaches for a pack of candy in Riva's stash, but he stops when she grabs his hand and gives him a phony angry stare.

"Don't eat my money, dear," says Riva.

Taksheel pulls away. "Roger and Calvin are almost done with the inventory check."

"Timetable?" asks Marian.

"Just a few more minutes."

"Good. We'll be touching down soon, and Aiden has an announcement to make."

The group looks at Aiden, and he waves at the table.

"Toss in something," says Aiden.

Taksheel looks at Riva's cards, looks at her, she nods, and then he shoves her entire bank in the pot.

"She's all in," says Taksheel.

Marian and Moon immediately throw their cards in the pot, and Riva cheers and claps while Taksheel grabs a bowl from the cupboard. When he returns, Riva sweeps her winnings in the bowl, and Marian snatches Ethan's cards before Aiden can grab them. When she sees what they are, she glares at Ethan.

"You folded with an ace and a king?" says Marian.

"Really?" says Riva.

"I didn't think they were good," says Ethan.

"Oh my God, you suck," says Moon.

Ethan looks at Moon with a slight desire to stab him in the neck.

"Maybe I can give Ethan some pointers next time we play?" suggest Riva.

"No, that's alright," says Ethan.

"Nah, it'll be fine," says Taksheel. "She can teach, and I can play her hands."

"I don't think it will be fine," says Ethan.

"Hey, go for it, Newbie. You can use the help, because if your medic skills are as good as your card skills, then we are boned. Hell, we'd die from a common cold under your watch!" says Moon.

Ethan's hand tightens, and Aiden flicks a two of clubs at Moon's face.

"Knock it off," orders Aiden.

Moon tosses the card back, and Marian slams her hand on the table.

"Hey, I'm in charge here!" barks Marian. "Moon, knock it off. Aiden, shuffle, and deal better."

"I'm good, I'm good," says Moon.

Aiden shuffles, and Riva stands up with her bowl of winnings.

"Well, it has been lovely, but I am going to enjoy my winnings for a bit," says Riva. "By the way, Ethan, my offer still stands."

Ethan nods, and Aiden casually tosses the cards to Ethan, Marian, and Moon to start the next game; Riva and Taksheel take the love seat and turn on the TV to watch a cartoon; and around twenty minutes later, the door opens again, and Roger and Calvin enter the commons.

Roger goes to the fridge and grabs two bottles of soda, gives one to Calvin, and they take the seats previously occupied by Riva and Taksheel.

"Deal me in," says Calvin.

Aiden tosses him two cards, and then he looks at Roger. "You want in?"

Roger shakes his head, and Calvin leans to Ethan.

"Hey, slide me some cash," says Calvin.

Ethan gives him half his bank, and after Calvin thanks him, Marian looks at Aiden.

"Okay, the group's here. Spill the beans," says Marian.

Aiden takes a deep breath, and then calls everyone to attention. Once all eyes are on him, he speaks.

"Ladies and gentlemen, it has been a privilege serving with you, but this will be my last mission," says Aiden.

The group exchanges confused looks, but Marian keeps her eyes on the cards, while Ethan locks his eyes on Aiden.

"Why are you leaving?" asks Moon.

"I've just had enough of this life," says Aiden. "I'm going to be settling on Aarde with my wife and we're going to open a dairy farm."

"So, you're going to abandon us like Julius?" Moon looks at Marian. "Did you know about this?"

"Me and Captain Brown knew about it for months. His pensions from the military and AATS are all set up," says Marian. "He agreed on five more jobs, and this is the fifth one. When we're done with this job, we'll cut straight to Aarde, drop off Aiden, and then it's vacation time."

"On Aarde?" asks Calvin hopefully.

Marian's face sours.

"Or somewhere else?" asks Calvin slowly.

"It is up to the captain," says Marian.

"Maybe the captain will allow me and Ara to go with you guys on a vacation?" suggests Aiden. "I know she'll love it. She's the adventuring type."

"Yet she wants a dairy farm?" says Taksheel.

"More my idea than hers," says Aiden.

"We can talk more about vacations when the job is done," says Marian. "Other than that, give him a hug, everybody."

"Oh no, don't hug me, I don't deserve it," says Aiden, holding up his hands with a strained smile.

"Nonsense! C'mere you!" Taksheel goes to Aiden's side and hugs him tight. "I'm going to miss my conspiracy buddy!"

The rest follow Taksheel's lead, forcing Aiden to stand, and he returns the hugs and handshakes, but Ethan stays in his chair, watching the scene with a distant look. He watches Riva wipe tears from her eyes. He sees Marian and Aiden exchange quick hugs and kisses on the cheeks, and Calvin shakes his hand. After Calvin finishes shaking Aiden's hand, Roger grabs his hand and they both flex their arms, getting amused chuckles from the group. Once that is done, the intercom turns on with a crackle.

"Attention crew, this is your captain speaking. We will exit warp-jump in five minutes. The bridge is now open for the show," says Abraham.

The bridge's door flashes green, and Marian leads the group to said door. When she opens it, the group files in and sees bright streaks of blue and white zipping past them, like lights of a tunnel. The tinted windows do a lot to dim the light, but Ethan remembers that instant blindness is guaranteed without the tint. So, seeing that is unnerving.

Watching the lights are three people: Captain Abraham Brown and the two pilots, Han Greqir and Yuriv Vulki. Ethan met those two after he finished settling in, and the two pilots are wearing red jumpsuits with yellow bands that trace their limbs and collar.

The bridge is spacious, but also almost empty. There is the captain's chair and the two pilot seats, each with its own consoles and steering mechanisms. Even the Captain has one, but it is strictly for emergency use. At the back of the bridge are folding chairs locked against the wall with bars, and an orb-shaped projector hangs from the ceiling and its lens is pointed at a blank white section of the wall. Then there is HL-0001.

He, as Ethan was reminded plenty of times, is next to Abraham, and when *he* sees the team, his screens flash green and he rolls towards them. HL-0001 circles around them, beeping and whirring, and after Marian kneels to rub one of the sensors on his corners, he circles her and then goes back to Abraham's side.

"How soon, Captain Brown?" asks Marian.

"Soon," says Abraham. He looks at Aiden. "You want to sit on the bridge with me and the boys and look at the scenery? It'll be your easiest job yet."

Aiden smiles. "They might need an engineer."

"I doubt it. It's only a taxi job."

Aiden shrugs. "You never know."

"Touchdown in one minute," says Han.

"Starting exit sequence," says Yiriv.

Yuriv types on his terminal and the *Hook Line* rumbles and hums with swirling yellow lights reflecting off the walls. The team braces themselves in their own way, and after a long moment the exterior lights disappear and in its place is a dark planet with a small moon and a distant blood-red sun. Seeing this sends a shiver up Ethan's spine, and Aiden whistles impressively.

"There she is," says Aiden. "The edge of human civilization."

"Um, Captain Brown, we got a problem," says Yuriv.

"What is it?" asks Abraham.

"We are not getting any signals from the Onyx Station. No code requests, no ship signals. Nothing."

Marian furrows her brows and goes to the window, and Yuriv types in a command, turns the dial on his panel, and points at his screen.

"All I am getting are two signals, and only one is clear, but weak," says Yuriv.

"Play it," orders Abraham.

Yuriv types in another command and the team looks at the speakers around the room when the signal starts with the screaming of a terrified man in tears, evacuation alarms and screams in the background.

"This is Captain Junjie Ding of the Bon Voyage! *We have been overrun! We need-"* The audio suddenly ends, and then it repeats, *"This is Captain Junjie Ding of the* Bon Voyage! *We have been overrun! We need- This is Captain Junjie Ding of the* Bon Voyage! *We have been overrun! We need-"*

"Turn it off," orders Abraham.

"This is Captain-"

Yuriv turns it off, and the room goes silent. Ethan looks around at the team, feeling a cold sweat rolling inside his suit. Marian keeps looking out the window, while Abraham rubs his brow slowly.

"What is the other signal?" asks Abraham.

"It's encrypted with something I have never seen before," says Yuriv. "This one is also a little stronger than the distress signal. Neither of those signals will leave the system, but somebody really did not want people hearing *Bon Voyage*."

Abraham motions Riva next to him, and she follows with Taksheel close behind.

"What do you make of this?" asks Abraham.

Riva studies it for a moment, and then shakes her head and looks at Abraham.

"I don't know. Not yet anyway, but it appears to be live, so someone is still transmitting," says Riva.

"Should we investigate?" asks Taksheel, quickly adding, "Actually, yeah, you know what, we really should investigate those signals.

Something is going on over there, and as AATS members, we must help those in need. Unless something's changed in the charter."

"How about we don't do that," says Moon.

"*Bon Voyage* is calling for help," says Aiden firmly.

"That is not our contract. Our contract is to pick up Dr. Rock and leave," says Moon.

"But we can't leave *Bon Voyage*," says Aiden, his voice getting heavier.

"We don't even know what the distress is for!"

"We should avoid it, but not for Moon's reasons," says Roger. "Whatever it is, it sounds bad, and we did not bring enough for a security or rescue mission, or even medical and ration supplies for extra bodies. We have enough for just us and our ship's defense."

"What if we just skim it? Figure out wherever *Bon Voyage* is, assess the damage, and then call for backup?" suggests Calvin.

"Like a scout mission?" says Roger.

Calvin nods. "Yeah."

"You can't be serious," says Moon.

"We have to do something," says Riva, getting a nod of approval from Taksheel.

Then an argument breaks out without Ethan's involvement, and while the team bickers, Aiden goes next to Abraham, standing mere inches from him, and covering the captain with his shadow.

"Captain, we cannot leave *Bon Voyage*," says Aiden, his voice dark and heavy.

Abraham sighs and turns to face Aiden. "How's our fuel?"

Aiden hesitates. "Without the station to refuel us, we have enough to jump back to Oros. Every other system is too far."

Ethan's gut clenches, and Abraham looks at Ethan for a moment, before looking back at Aiden. The two have a staring contest, but soon the captain's eyes break away, while Aiden's remains locked in place. Abraham sighs again and paces around the bridge. This brings the others to simmer down on their arguing, and after a moment of silence from the captain passes, he looks at Marian, who is still looking out the window.

"Any sign of Onyx Station?" asks Abraham.

Marian turns to Abraham and shakes her head. "No sir. But there is a ship not too far from us starboard side."

Abraham looks at Ethan again, which brings the team to look at him. This causes Ethan's legs to lock and his eyes to flick over everyone with growing panic. After that, Abraham looks at Aiden, who is the only one not to look at Ethan but keeps his eyes on the captain.

"Seeing as how Onyx Station is missing, it is safe to assume that the contract is void," says Abraham. "That means there will be… problems for us."

Moon groans and slumps against the wall, and the others sulk, but nod in understanding.

"However, as members of the AATS, we must investigate distress signals," continues Abraham. "We will investigate *Bon Voyage*'s signal, and the encrypted signal, as well as circle Onyx for signs of Onyx Station." He takes a deep breath and rubs his hands together. "If we find Onyx Station and Dr. Rock, we will refuel and continue our original path. But if we do not, we will have no choice but to return to Oros."

Aiden nods approvingly and Taksheel pats his arm with a smile, while Roger and Moon show quiet disappointment.

"Suit up," orders Abraham.

Marian swiftly motions the team out the door.

"Alright, you heard the captain. Time to suit up!" says Marian.

The team files out, and once the last person leaves, the door slams shut and flashes red.

3

Bon Voyage

Ethan is last in line as the group quickly makes their way to the armory with the bangs of their heavy steps bouncing around inside the hallway. When they reach the armory, Marian holds her wrist-pad to the orb next to the door. The orb glows green and two thin green lines slide along her band.

After that, it beeps and the door slides open, revealing locked cages occupied by rifles, pistols, ammo, and knives. Near the cages are lockers with everyone's names above their designated locker, with Ethan, Riva, and Aiden having special footlockers for their gear.

Ethan goes to his locker and holds his pad next to the orb. The pad is scanned, the locker clicks open, and he repeats the same process for his footlocker. The whole time his hand trembles, even though Marian drilled him on it twice already. Everyone else is swift and fluid with putting on their gear, but Ethan fumbles around. He is even the last one done, but nobody really notices since they are grabbing their weapons from the cages.

Ethan's suit is a white jumpsuit with red pads and stripes connecting the pads. His only defense is a pistol (his holster is currently empty), and on his belt are a few pouches containing a quick stitch kit, medical foam, burn gel, gauze laced with disinfectant, pain pills, and adrenaline shots. Ethan's suit also has a unique medical device called the Medical

Assessment Device, or MAD. It is a small square that rests on top of his hand with wires going into the suit and three orbs of different colors on its front, with a micro-holographic projector in its center.

As Ethan finishes up, he looks at the next closest person. That person is Aiden.

Aiden has a padded blue jumpsuit with small metal plates stitched on them, protecting his limbs, chest, and spine. On his back is an air tank, and his helmet is full-face covering, with a tinted slot for his visor. He is also carrying a large amount of gear in a backpack and on his tool belt, and he has a holster for his pistol. But his helmet is open, so his face is showing all his determination right now.

Ethan looks around and sees Riva walking away from a cage, holstering a pistol.

Her suit is light gray with thin white padding and a small computer taking up her forearm, which is connected to a battery pack on her back. Her belt has a few cases of small tools for computer repair and diagnosis, as well as a holster for her pistol. Unlike Aiden, Riva is displaying some anxiety, and Ethan briefly pauses his touch-ups to watch her turn away from the group and rest her head and hand against the wall, her free hand balling into a fist and rubbing her heart while panting. When she sees him looking at her out of the corner of her eye, she pauses, straightens out, and then approaches him. When she in front of them, the two are quiet, until Riva flashes an unconvincing, and somewhat pained, smile.

"Don't worry, it is just *kriettejs*," assures Riva. "I get them every mission."

"What's crate-ish… esh? What is that?" asks Ethan.

"Jitters."

"Okay, no. That… I'm sorry, but that does not look like jitters," says Ethan. He looks at Marian for a second, before looking at Riva. "Does Dartmount or Captain Brown know?"

"Of course! They know it is just *kriettejs*. I get them every time. It is pre-mission anxiety."

"Riva, that's not jitters. That's something-"

"Ethan!" snaps Riva, slamming her hand in the locker just past Ethan's face and staring hellfire into him, with her chest heaving from heavy breathing and some sweat moving down her forehead. "I know you're trying to be a medic, but you're not there yet. I am fine, and don't... Don't get Marian, the captain, or Taksheel worried over nothing. Please."

Ethan sighs. "Riva, I-"

"What is going on here?" says Taksheel lightly.

He walks next to Riva and Ethan, wearing an armored suit comprising a helmet and thick red jumpsuit with metal plates stitched on the arms, shoulders, shins, and thighs, and a metal vest with armored gloves and boots. There is also a slender tube with cables that connect to a headset that is clipped to his ear, with the tube latched on his shoulder. He also has an ammo belt with his pistol holstered and knife sheathed, and he has his rifle pointed up, without the magazine in the magazine well.

Taksheel looks at Riva, who backs away from Ethan. Then he looks at Ethan, who holds his hands up.

"Nothing happened," says Ethan.

"Of course nothing happened. You got it backwards," says Taksheel. "Ethan, *you're* supposed to trap Riva against the locker and Riva is supposed to be helpless against your aggressive flirting."

Ethan scrunches his brow while Riva balks, and Taksheel chuckles and lightly slaps Ethan's shoulder.

"But next time, try it with Marian. She'll love it," says Taksheel.

"I need to..." Ethan glances at Riva, she shakes her head, and he looks at the weapons locker, "... finish setting up."

Taksheel grins. "Of course. You better hurry, you're the last one."

Ethan nods and slides past Taksheel and worms his way past Roger, Calvin, and Moon, who are wearing the same suits as Taksheel. When Ethan gets to the cage, Marian is standing there, holding a pistol out to him, grip first with a stern frown. She is wearing a suit like the others, only she has a golden "C" in a white circle over her heart.

"You're the last one, Newbie," says Marian.

Ethan takes the gun and holsters it. "Sorry, ma'am."

"We'll be doing more drills to get your speed up after we get back," says Marian. Then she hurries away. "Let's go. We're burning time."

When the team returns to the bridge, the *Hook Line* has almost reached the ship Marian saw not too long ago.

Abraham is watching the black mass get closer with an intense look in his eyes, and Han is carefully guiding the *Hook Line*, while Yuriv is speaking in the radio.

"*Bon Voyage*, this is the *Hook Line*, responding to your distress call. Do you read?" says Yuriv.

Static plays over the speaker.

"*Bon Voyage*, this is the *Hook Line*, responding to your distress call. Do you read?" repeats Yuriv. "Still nothing, sir."

Abraham grunts, and HL-0001 beeps and bumps his leg lightly.

"We're ready to go, Captain," says Marian.

Abraham nods and goes to his seat with HL-0001 following him. Now, they are next to the derelict ship. The enormous ship's hull takes up the entire view, with more expanding above and below, and the captain orders lights on.

Two enormous lights on the *Hook Line* flash on, bathing the massive ship's hull and smaller wings with engines on them; but the engines are dim. The light reflects off the white hull, and as the *Hook Line* travels along the side, the words "*Bon Voyage*" appear, and they are painted in gold letters with the Federation symbol next to it.

Gold bands run horizontally, and as they travel, the white hull loses its color. Burn marks, jagged gaps, floating debris, and corpses scar the ship, and sparks pop out of the openings, while lights flicker in observation balconies.

HL-0001 beeps and whirs, and its screens flash to red as it rolls backwards.

"What the hell happened here?" asks Moon.

"Pirates," says Aiden.

"We really shouldn't be here. This is beyond a pirate attack," says Roger. "This is-"

"We already agreed we're going in," interrupts Taksheel.

"How about we do a scouting mission just on the outside?" says Calvin. "I mean, look at that ship! That is one hell of a mess for our little crew."

"We're going in, regardless," says Aiden sharply. He looks at Marian. "Right?"

Marian nods, and Aiden looks at Abraham.

"We're going in," affirms Abraham. "So, no more griping or there'll be hell to pay."

"I'm just saying there are alternatives," says Calvin.

"Bathroom duty for three months. Who's next?" says Abraham.

The team goes silent and watches the scene unfold with growing tension.

The *Hook Line* passes a gigantic dome with a green substance on the glass, and they circle up and shine their light on a communications relay poking out of another observation dome. Then, the *Hook Line* travels higher so the team can see the *Bon Voyage's* elongated shape, and when they reach the back, they see four cylindrical exhaust ports that are also dark. Three are in good condition, but the fourth is popped, leaving a gaping hole in the back of the ship, which has a cloud of twisted and melted debris around it.

"Find us an emergency entrance," says Abraham.

Han and Yuriv nod and begin their search. The *Hook Line* gently swoops down, and its lights slide along the hull until they find a yellow and black circle with red "Emergency Entrance" above it.

"Bingo," says Han.

Yuriv types in a command, and schematics and a menu appear on his screen. A minute of typing and menu sifting later, a jet of air ejects from *Bon Voyage* as the yellow and black door opens. Once it is all the way open, a tube slowly extends until it is rigid at twenty feet. Han then turns the *Hook Line* to its side and uses precise, controlled bursts and micro-flicks of the controls to inch their ship to the tube.

"Steady as she goes," mutters Han.

Ethan braces himself as the *Hook Line's* side creeps, centimeter by centimeter, to *Bon Voyage's* emergency entrance. Then the ship rattles, and the tube and *Hook Line* lock together with a loud ding, confirming the connection.

Han takes a deep breath, wipes his hands, and smiles. "You are free to move around the ship."

Abraham looks at Marian. "In and out, like always."

"Yes sir," says Marian. "Let's go, team!"

The team leaves the bridge in a speedy yet orderly fashion, while HL-0001 beeps and flashes green. They go to the receiving area, and as the door opens, the team slips their magazines in. Aiden adjusts his gloves, and Ethan swallows a lump in his throat while looking at Riva. She is leaning against the wall and looks at Ethan with worry.

Before Ethan can approach her, she goes forward with the rest of the team, leaving Ethan to be the last one. He follows them to the receiving area and stops at the clump they made with Taksheel and Marian up front by a door with a swirling red light above it.

"Everybody ready?" asks Marian.

"Yes ma'am," says the group, some louder than others.

"Good. Punch it, Taksheel."

Taksheel pushes a red button on the wall and the door slides open. The team sees a blue-tinted tube with a retractable metal floor. There is also one bright light shining at the end. The light is over a round door with an orb next to it, and a black orb with a red band is in the corner. There is a faint buzzing down the hallway, too, and just looking at it makes Ethan's gut tighten.

"Alright," says Marian after some hesitation. "In and out. Let's go."

Marian goes first, followed by Roger and Calvin, and the rest stay behind, watching them travel down the tube. When they reach the door, Marian holds her pad to the orb and... Nothing.

Ethan looks around anxiously, and Marian tries again. And again. After the fourth time, she returns and motions Riva over.

"Riva, I'm going to need your computer powers," says Marian.

Riva goes with Marian, and Taksheel taps his trigger guard and paces in circles. It is a tight fit for Riva with Roger and Calvin. She plugs in her wrist-top computer, and after a minute of typing, the emergency entrance slides open to a dark wall. Roger and Calvin slip through and their lights shine in the dark, briefly revealing steel and walkways as they sweep the area.

"Alright, team. Move up," says Marian over the radio.

Taksheel is the first to go down the tube, followed by Aiden, then Moon, and lastly, Ethan. Once all of them are in, they activate the flashlights on their weapons and shoulders and sweep the area.

Their lights illuminate blood on the floor and walls, as well as bullet casings on the floor, scattered tools, wrecked escape pods, and a severed arm near a broken vent. At the far end of the docking bay is a broken door with light shining through it, and the light illuminates a broken cart tipped on its side with luggage spilled on the floor.

"Move up," orders Marian.

Ethan shines his light on an escape pod, seeing it has been torn open. Then he moves his light and sees another vent grate, and generators lay in pieces, with metal burnt and twisted and covered in fire suppressant foam.

Ethan shudders and follows his team to the door. All of them are creeping towards it, and when they reach it, Roger and Calvin take either side, while the others remain hidden in the dark.

"AATS! Anybody there!" shouts Roger.

Silence.

"AATS! Any friendlies! Respond now!" says Calvin.

Nothing.

Roger looks at Marian, and she nods.

"Be careful," says Marian.

Roger nods, then he nods at Calvin, and the pair slips through the broken door. The next room is dim, so Ethan can see their lights sweeping the area. When he hears heavy breathing, he looks to his side and sees Aiden is next to him, tense with his hand on his pistol.

"Pirates rarely stay around after an attack," says Aiden. "But when we find them, Hell will be comfortable when we're through with them."

"Clear!" barks Roger. "But brace yourselves. This room is fucked."

Marian orders her team forward, and when they enter the next area, they fan out, each slowly becoming more worried and horrified by what they are seeing. The lobby can easily hold one hundred people, and usually they are brightly lit with pleasant music and the occasional announcement.

But this lobby is subdued, with dim orange lights and pockets of red emergency lights swirling over the doors and benches. There is no announcement, but a buzzing is playing through the speakers. The message boards that are not shot out are showing the same message.

Sec. C Carry Pod 01- Status- DELAYED

Sec. C Carry Pod 02- Status- DELAYED

Sec. C Carry Pod 04- Status- DELAYED

Sec. C Carry Pod 05- Status- DELAYED

Sec. C Carry Pod 06- Status- DELAYED

The team keeps walking, passing bloodied clothes, scattered luggage, broken benches, and pillars with gashes ejecting sparks. Black orbs with red bands are also placed in equal increments, which bring the hair on Ethan's neck to stand, and a cart with red screens and luggage strapped to it is roving across the lobby.

When Riva tries to approach it, it releases a shrill whine and zooms off into a corner, just to repeat the noise and speed off to another section when Moon walks towards it. Then the cart stops by a locked door, spins in a circle like a panicking animal, and drives off.

"I am officially creeped out," says Moon.

"Yeah, can we go? Just screw scouting, screw this ship. Let's just go," says Calvin.

"No, we have a mission to do and we're doing it," says Aiden.

"Hey, I'm in charge!" snaps Marian. "And yes, we're still doing the mission."

"Oh, come on! Look at this place!" yells Moon. "There's no mission here! This is a vanity run now! All this does is give us brownie points on the report, but I can tell you right now this is not normal! There is something evil here, and we need to get out while we still can."

"Moon, shut up," says Marian harshly.

Ethan ignores their confrontation and looks around some more. During his search, his eyes lock on a mural of *Bon Voyage* flying through a starry space dotted with colorful worlds and painted over the mural is a poem written in blood. That poem is:

One by one we go

When it stops, we don't know

One by one we go

4

Section C

One by one we go.

Ethan cannot take his eyes off those words. The gruesome display leaves a knot in his gut, and his eyes slowly trail a streak at the "o" that leads to a poll of dried blood that stretches to a broken vent, like someone took a brush to the blood and dragged it across the floor.

Ethan's throat clogs, and his hands shake while the team explores. He can hear them talking, but he cannot understand their words. The buzzing has also gotten louder, and a strange, foul smell is in the air. He can't put his finger on it, but whatever it is, it is not a good mix with the stale atmosphere, and it is leaving him nauseous.

But despite the distractions of smell and noise, Ethan spots thin green strands hanging from the vent opening. Ethan scrunches his nose, kneels, and peers into the vent. The streak of blood disappears into pitch-black darkness, but with what little the light offers at the opening, Ethan finds more of the green strands on the vent's surface, so he runs his finger across it. It breaks easily, but it is also sticky.

Then, the buzzing suddenly pops and an automated voice booms over the speakers that makes everyone jump.

"Please remain patient! Flights will resume momentarily!"

The message echoes in the empty lobby, and Moon mutters a comment while Marian walks towards Aiden, who is by Taksheel and Riva. Meanwhile, Ethan retreats from the vent and looks at the blood under the poem. He sees it is not only fresh, but it's laced with a faint orange tint and green dots. He touches the blood and slowly rubs his fingers together and then pulls them apart to study the anomaly, all while the message repeats over the speakers.

"This is a weird pirate attack," says Taksheel.

"I've never seen one like this before," says Aiden.

"This was not a pirate attack and we need to get out of here," says Moon. "Right guys?"

Roger and Calvin nod, but Taksheel shakes his head and paces around a vent grate with his rifle aimed at the dark opening in the ceiling.

"The AATS doctrine is clear. We need to help these people," says Taksheel.

"What people? There's nobody here!" says Moon.

"We don't know that," says Aiden. "This is just one lobby. We have much more to explore."

"No offense, Aiden, but I don't think there's anybody left," says Roger.

"Yeah, we scouted the ship, and it is dead. There is no recovering from this," says Calvin.

"We need to call the navy. Let them handle this," says Roger.

"Taksheel is right," says Marian. "The AATS doctrine says we need to assist ships in distress in any way we can, and we're going to do that."

"Oh, come on," grumbles Moon.

Marian turns to Ethan and furrows her brows when she sees him inspecting the blood. "Newbie, what are you doing?"

"There's something in the blood," says Ethan. "I don't know what it is. None of this was in the reading material."

Marian approaches Ethan. "What do you mean?"

Ethan shows Marian the tainted blood, and she grimaces while the rest of the team surrounds Ethan to look at the gore. All have various expressions of confusion. The only one not in the group is Riva, and when she arrives, she takes a deep breath before speaking.

"All the doors require a Captain's Override," says Riva.

"Oh, looks like we're trapped. Time to go," says Moon.

"Newbie, wipe that crap off," orders Marian, and then to Riva, "Can you override the lock?"

Ethan wipes the blood on his pants leg, and Riva nods.

"I can do it. It will take me a few minutes, though," says Riva.

"Alright." Marian looks around for a moment before pointing at a door labeled "Sec. C Main Hall." The letters are dimly lit, and a ring of red lights up the center of the door; the orb next to the door is also red. "Unlock the door to the Section C Main Hall. We'll work from there."

Riva nods and goes to the Main Hall door with Taksheel following her closely, and Marian orders the rest to form a perimeter. The team obeys, but Moon and Calvin begrudgingly cooperate while Roger and Aiden do it with more discipline. Ethan tries following Aiden's lead but fails as a copycat.

"Please remain patient! Flights will resume momentarily!" echoes the message.

Riva plugs her computer into the orb, sits down, and begins typing away. As she types, the cart cautiously travels across the lobby with its stack of luggage poking over the benches. Ethan, Aiden, and Marian watch the cart, and when it is concealed behind a pillar, it stops moving.

"Something spooked that cart bad," says Aiden. "And from the looks of it, someone didn't want anybody leaving."

"But where are the bodies? There should be lots of bodies!" says Moon.

"We'll look for a security room and have Riva pull the logs," says Marian.

"Understood," says Aiden.

Suddenly, an audio box appears in front of Marian via the communicator on her shoulder.

"Status report," says Abraham, the audio waves fluctuating in the box with his voice.

"None of the escape pods were launched, and the lobby is a mess," says Marian. "Aiden believes that someone trapped the colonists and massacred them. But there aren't any bodies."

"Pirates?"

"No sir," says Aiden. "This is something else."

There is a ding, and the door and orb turn green. Riva unplugs her computer and opens the door, revealing a dark hallway with patches of dim red lights. The lights buzz, some flicker, and all of them reflect off the metal walls and floor with the darkness heaviest in the corners. There are also lights from signs for shops and services, all of which read "CLOSED."

"Riva got the door open, Captain Brown. We're proceeding to the Section C Main Hall," says Marian.

"Keep me posted," says Abraham.

"Roger that. Dartmount out." The projection disappears and Marian turns on her flashlights. "Lights on. Move up."

The team turns on their flashlights and creeps into the darkness with their fingers on their trigger guards. As they go down the hallway, their lights sweep over the scenery. They find streaks of blood, bullet casings, and a broken vent cover.

Off in the distance, sparks burst out of the black, prompting the team to look at the source, which is a shop gutted by fire. The steel is black; the materials are ash or warped, and a twisted body lies on the floor, shriveled, with their skin black and flaking, their bones cracked, and their eyes and tongue burned away, with the remnants of their suit melted to their body.

"Vishnu hamaaree raksha karen," says Taksheel quietly.

Riva falls behind, and Aiden's breathing becomes heavier and his hands tremble as he sweeps the area. This brings Marian and the others to look at him with worry.

"Are you okay?" asks Marian.

Aiden takes a deep breath and closes his eyes. His hand grips his pistol tight.

"Aiden? Buddy? You alright, bro?" asks Taksheel.

"Stop!" snaps Aiden.

Marian, Taksheel, and Riva recoil, and Aiden takes another deep, shaky breath before he opens his eyes. His hardened orange and hazel eyes shine in the dark like a predator.

"This is the Vagsten Tunnels again," says Aiden.

"Oh," says Marian.

"What's the Vagsten Tunnels?" asks Ethan.

"The Battle of Vagsten was the last major battle of the Aarde Conflict," says Aiden. "But it wasn't a conflict. It was a full-scale war that destroyed the entire planet. Vagsten was the last stronghold to fall, and beneath it was a tunnel system. My unit went in there and burned everyone alive."

Ethan is too shocked to say anything, and he does not move when Aiden travels forward with speed.

"We need to find survivors," says Aiden.

"Right. Keep moving everyone," says Marian.

The rest move forward, save for Ethan, but when the lights shrink, he jogs after his team. As he jogs, he sees a broken door at the end of the hall, and he hears a light humming.

"*One by one we go... When it stops, we don't know...*" says a faint female voice.

The team skids to a halt and frantically sweeps the area with their lights.

"Did we all hear that? Or was that just me?" asks Moon.

"Should we bust out the Ouija board? Do some EVPs?" jokes Roger nervously.

"There's a survivor! Find them!" says Marian. "Taksheel, you're with me. Calvin, you're with Roger. Moon, you're with Newbie. Aiden and Riva. There's a security station somewhere around here. Find it and pull the logs."

Aiden and Riva leave in a hurry, as do Roger and Calvin, but Moon stares in disbelief at Marian.

"Why am I with Newbie?" asks Moon.

"Because you're a pain in the ass. Now get going!" says Marian. She then activates her communicator. "Captain, we heard a survivor and are pursuing."

"Good. Keep me posted on the updates," says Abraham.

"Yes sir. Dartmount out." Marian disconnects and sees Moon and Ethan still standing next to her. "What are you two doing? Get moving!"

Moon backhands Ethan's arm and nods towards a door labeled "C-3." It is unlocked and has a domed camera watching it. The pair approach the door, and after Moon holds his pad to the orb, it beeps, and the door slides open.

The hallway beyond the door is dim with flickering orange lights and a row of locked doors and dark windows with signs above them. Some windows have large cracks in them, and others are riddled with bullet holes. The walls are damaged with dents, shrapnel cuts, and large gashes, and a mist sprays from a broken pipe above with streaks, splatter, and dots of blood staining the area.

"Great. More blood," says Moon. He then takes a deep breath, adjusts the grip on his rifle, and walks forward. "Well, let's go, Newbie."

Ethan trails Moon. Their footsteps echo in the dead hallway, and after a minute of walking, Moon stops cold, causing Ethan to bump into him.

"Watch it," hisses Moon.

"Sorry, sir," says Ethan.

"Better be. But listen."

Moon holds up his finger, and Ethan listens. There is electric humming, but there is also metallic scraping. Moon's finger gradually shifts to pointing to the source, and Ethan squints his eyes when he sees a silhouette down the hall.

The swirling orange light briefly reveals the figure scraping the wall in one-second increments. The two cautiously approach the figure, and the closer they get, the more they hear his muttering and the clearer his form becomes.

When they are only a few paces from him, they shine their lights on him and see that he is a colonist judging by his uniform: a blue jumpsuit with yellow cuffs, black boots, and a small pad on his wrist.

"I'm here. You're here. We're here," mutters the colonist. He scrapes a jagged piece of metal along the wall, where an entwined tree is carved in. The metal has cut his hands, and it's scraping echoes in the hall, bringing Ethan and Moon to cringe. The colonist brings the jagged piece up, and right as he presses it down, he stops, stiffens, and then turns to look at them with yellow-tinted eyes and a wide grin that tears his cheeks. "I'm here."

5

───

One By One

The colonist steps back from the wall and sways in his spot, giggling and twitching. His brown eyes are tainted with thin yellow veins. Orange veins bulge under his clammy skin, where they wrap around his neck and trace the side of his head and sweat drips off his nose and soaks his head and clothes. The colonist giggles and taps the side of his head with his crude knife as he walks forward.

"You're here," says the colonist.

"Hey, don't come any closer!" shouts Moon.

He and Ethan take a step back, and the colonist stumbles forward, holding the blade down and his eyes bulging, with his arms pulsing and shoulders jerking from his heavy giggling.

"We're here," says the colonist. "The ship. The home. It is ours. Ours. And I'm here. I'm home. Home!"

"Newbie, scan him," says Moon. He shines his rifle light on the colonist's eyes, which causes him to turn away, hissing, and holding up his hand. "Yeah, stay back!"

Ethan raises his MAD and the vent above rattles with something large and heavy scraping it. They risk glancing up, but quickly look at the colonist when he walks towards them again.

"Hey, stop moving!" screams Moon. "Stop moving or I'll blow your brains out!"

"Sir, just relax, we're here to help," says Ethan. He activates his MAD and keeps talking, as the lines crisscross on the colonist. "Can you tell us where the rest of the colonists are?"

The scanner beeps and projects a display of vitals; racing heart, high body temperature, some improperly treated wounds, an unknown infection needing blood work to identify, and a brain scan that is consumed by red and blue flares.

"I'm here," says the tainted colonist.

Then, the Tainted opens his mouth wide, his cheeks tear, and a raspy, airy scream leaves his throat as he charges Ethan with the crude knife raised. Before Ethan can react, bullets tear into the colonist's chest.

His orange-tinted blood sprays on the floor, and he gurgles as he stumbles into the wall and slides down, leaving thick streaks on the surface. The pops of gunfire echo down the hallway, and the familiar stench of spent gunpowder lingers in Ethan's nose as he looks with wide eye at Moon, who is walking past him with smoke rising from his rifle.

He stops by the Tainted, who is making raspy breaths, and he puts another three rounds into his head. Then he brings up Marian through the audio box projection.

"Hey Marian, we came across a survivor, but he tried killing Newbie, so I shot him," says Moon.

"What! Why? What did Newbie do?" says Marian.

"Nothing!" says Ethan defensively.

Moon holds up his finger and inspects the blood. "The guy was nuts, and his blood is like what we found in the lobby."

"But where did it come from? They sanitized these ships and everybody on them before they let them go anywhere," says Marian.

Another audio box appears with Roger's name. *"Hey, we got a problem. Me and Calvin had to kill three colonists. They attacked us and one of them bit Calvin."*

"He's going to have to go in quarantine," says Ethan quickly and shakily. "Then we need to find a Federation medical ship or base and have them look at him and this ship."

"Newbie, shut up. I'm on the comms!" snaps Moon.

"I'm just saying that nothing on our ship has anything for whatever *this* is," says Ethan, pointing at the dead colonist. "Calvin needs to be quarantined."

"Hey guys, I'm fine. Really," says Calvin, his box appearing next to Roger's and the other shrinking down to provide space. *"It was just a scratch, not a bite."*

"How about we just shoot Calvin and get off the ship?" suggests Moon.

"Moon, you sick fuck, we're not doing that!" yells Marian.

"Thanks, asshole. Love you, too," says Calvin.

Moon turns to Ethan and meets his horrified look with a shrug.

"It was worth a try," says Moon.

Ethan shakes his head slowly, and then he hears tearing and notices movement out of the corner of his eye and looks down.

"Moon might actually have a good idea for once, and Ethan is right. We don't know what it going on and the infected already tried killing us, so we should put Calvin down before he goes nuts on us," says Taksheel, his audio box appearing and causing the others to shrink.

"You shut up, too," says Marian.

Ethan's eyes widen again, and he steps back and taps on Moon's shoulder. "Moon."

Moon looks at him from the side. "What?"

Ethan points at the Tainted, and when Moon sees what he sees, he freezes. The Tainted's sleeves have ripped, and his arms have torn open with bloody tendrils that look like vines curling and swaying, and the body is twitching with ragged gasps and bloody bubbles coming from his mouth. Gunshots ring out from the audio boxes, and Moon and Ethan back up.

"Newbie... Run," says Moon.

Ethan and Moon bolt down the hallway, and the Tainted shrieks and chases after them. Its warped scream, their heavy steps, and the gunshots in the audio boxes echo in the hallway.

"We're getting out of here right now. Fall back to the Hook Line! *Captain, we need to leave* Bon Voyage *right now! Aiden, Riva, wrap up what you're doing and get back to the* Hook Line *immediately!"* orders Marian.

"We're on our way," says Moon. He disconnects and turns to shoot a few more rounds into the Tainted, dropping it and leaving it twitching on the floor. "Let's go, Newbie!"

Ethan runs past Moon, but then a vent grate breaks off and something lands between him and Moon. They turn around, and three claws rip through Moon and pop out of his back. Ethan freezes as the creature lifts Moon off the floor.

Blood drips from the claws, and the blood trails down Moon's chest and legs and drips to the floor. Moon's gasps are weak and wet, and his rifle clatters to the floor as his mouth and chin become soaked in blood. The creature makes stuttering clicks as it stares at Moon with its large, bright yellow eyes, and Ethan steps back, hyperventilating, and unable to blink.

"Ethan," gasps Moon. "… Ethan."

The creature throws Moon against the wall, and he crumples to the ground, limp with a pool of blood spreading around him. The creature looks at Ethan, making the stuttering clicks as it marches towards him.

The creature is wearing a tattered blue jumpsuit stained with dark red blotches. The black boots have torn, revealing three long claws, and their fingers have fused and elongated into three talons. Patches of bark-like chitin cover their hands, forearms, shins, neck, chest, and head, and sharp bark protrudes from their shoulders. The exposed skin is bulging from muscles and orange veins, and its cheeks have ripped all the way, exposing jagged teeth.

Ethan raises his pistol with shaky hands and steps back, his vision blurred and breathing heavy.

"Stay back!" cries Ethan.

The creature's back pops open, sprouting vine-like tendrils, and its clicks turn to a shriek as it rushes towards Ethan with its arms stretched to him. Ethan also screams, and he pulls the trigger as fast as possible.

Bullet after bullet rips into the creature, pushing it back and puncturing a circle of holes all over its chest and shoulders. These don't stop it, but when it is on Ethan, his last shot strikes it in the head, blowing its skull open and leaving an oval of gore on the wall, thus causing the creature to crumble to the ground.

Ethan's breathing and vision are still shaky and foggy, and his quivering hands can barely hold his pistol when he discards the spent magazine and slips a new one in.

The tendrils - the vines? - on the creature's back are slithering and coiling around on the floor and in the air, each following Ethan's movements as he slides along the wall, keeping his pistol trained on the abomination. When he reaches Moon, he hears sporadic gunfire echoing in the distance, and he steps around the blood and shakes Moon's shoulder.

"Moon?" says Ethan with a cracked voice. He looks at the creature again and gives Moon another shake. "Moon. Are you okay?"

Moon is silent, and Ethan swallows and turns his partner's limp body to see his entire face is pale and soaked in blood, and his eyes are wide open. His communicator is flickering colored pixels with no shapes on the wall, and garbled words flow through the speaker as the gunshots get more chaotic.

Ethan wipes his face and falls against the opposite wall. He looks at the creature and the Tainted not too far from him, both with vines searching their limited area and giving off a putrid scent.

The gunfire continues, and Ethan takes a deep breath and reaches for Moon's rifle but stops when the vines of the dead creature all turn to him. He remains frozen for a few seconds before he snatches the rifle and scrambles up and aims it at the bodies.

He flicks the rifle between the two corpses, and then reaches for Moon and grabs the spare magazines from his ammo belt. Then, an audio box suddenly appears with sharp jagged wave lengths and Marian's terrified voice, making Ethan jump.

"*Rifts! Respond!*" yells Marian; there is gunfire and Taksheel cursing in the background.

"I'm here, ma'am," says Ethan, flicking his focus back to the bodies when he hears shifting, just to see the vines still looking at him.

"*Where's Moon? I can't get a hold of him!*"

"He's gone, ma'am," says Ethan, walking backward. "Something attacked us and killed him. It used to be a colonist, but I … I don't know what it is now."

"*Fuck! You better get your ass back to the* Hook Line*!*"

Roger's audio box appears.

"*We've got the dock secured!*" says Roger. "*But you better hurry! We can't hold it for long! They will swarm the ship if you guys don't hurry up and get here!*"

"*Ah, shit. I'm low on ammo!*" says Calvin in the background.

"*Are you serious right now!?*"

"*Rifts, get your ass moving NOW!*" orders Marian. "*Riva! Aiden! Report!*"

Ethan runs, but he doesn't get far when he hears snapping and banging. He turns around, right as Riva's audio box.

"*We got cut off, but we're circling around the outer hallway to get back to the lobby,*" says Riva, her voice trembling and cracking. "*Don't leave us behind! Please!*"

"*Nobody is getting left behind,*" says Marian, "*but you need to run!*"

While this goes on, Ethan watches in horror as the vines from the two dead creatures pull their bodies to Moon's corpse. The vines burrow themselves into Moon's flesh, making his body shift in sharp motions with his back arching, his fingers bending, and his arms and legs twisting.

The vines pull their limp bodies on top of Moon, like three dolls being stitched together, and their chests split open, turning the ribs into teeth. The large teeth sink into Moon's chest, and that is enough for Ethan to run down the hallway.

His boots bang on the metal floor, while flesh and bone rip and snap, and seconds later, there are two raspy screams, followed by thrashing and then heavy footsteps banging after him.

Ethan runs faster, and right as he is about to reach the door he and Moon came through, it slams shut and locks.

"No-no-no-no-no!" cries Ethan.

He slams into the door and presses his pad against the door, but "Captain Override" appears, and he screams and bangs on the door. The banging footsteps rapidly approach, and Ethan turns, and swears and ducks, narrowly avoiding enormous claws that break the orb and get stuck in the wall.

The vines on its back whip around, with some grabbing Ethan, but he pulls away and runs down the hallway, heart racing, and eyes and throat burning. He passes the blood puddles that marked the three bodies, and a moment later, metal snaps, and the overlapping roars echo in the hallway.

Ethan slams into the wall before taking a sharp turn in a random direction. The flickering emergency lights reflect off the walls, and he sees an open door with faint light pouring into the hallway. He ducks into the room, and closes and locks the door, and then runs towards the only desk in the room and slides behind it. He crouches down low, turns off his communicator, and readies his rifle.

After that is silence.

Ethan's breathing is heavy. His heart is racing, his hands shake, and he looks at the only window in the room while his ears listen for the danger. The light reflects off the window, blotting out the outside darkness, and then he hears the heavy steps outside. He completely freezes and tenses up. No breathing, no shaking.

The steps get closer, and when they are outside the door, Ethan squeezes his legs against his chest and tightens his grip on his rifle. The footsteps keep going, and the two screams echo in the hallway.

The noise slowly fades with the steps, and when all is silent, Ethan waits another minute before he exhales. After that, he activates his communicator.

"This is Ethan, is there anybody out there?" asks Ethan quietly with a trembling voice.

Nothing.

"Is there anybody out there? Somebody, please respond!" says Ethan.

Still nothing.

Ethan presses the rifle against his face, trembling and breathing heavily, with sweat trailing his cheeks. Then there is a bright flash of light, a rolling rumble and rattling, and a violent jerk that throws him to the floor. The lights flash off and warning alarms ring in the room and out in the hallway, followed by an automated voice.

"Warning! Hull breach in Section C! Evacuate immediately! Warning! Hull breach in Section C! Evacuate immediately!"

Ethan jumps to his feet and runs to the window. He sees twisted debris spinning in space and more of *Bon Voyage's* hull has been torn and warped. He also cannot see the *Hook Line*.

"What? No! No, no, no, this is- This isn't happening!" Ethan activates his communicator, even though he can barely hear himself over the alarm and the repeating message. "This is Ethan Rifts! Can anybody hear me! Please respond!"

Marian's audio box appears. *"Rifts? Rifts is that you? Can you hear me?".*

"Yes ma'am. I'm here," says Ethan, pacing in circles and scratching his head. "I...I can't- I don't know what happened!"

"The Hook Line *exploded,"* says Marian. *"We lost the Captain, Han, Yuriv, HL, Roger, Calvin. They're all gone. It's just you, Aiden, Taksheel, Riva, and me."*

Ethan's heart drops, and he falls to the chair. "How? How did it explode?"

"I don't know. The ship passed inspection before it left... Those things must have swarmed the Hook Line *and killed everyone. We need to get out of here.*

We need to get off Bon Voyage*! Meet us at the Section C Transit Station, Ethan. Then we'll go to the bridge and figure out what to do from there."*

"I...I don't know where the Transit Station is," says Ethan.

"I downloaded a map of Bon Voyage *when I was searching for information. I'll send it to you,"* says Riva in the background.

"Can't I just meet you in the lobby?" asks Ethan.

"The explosion gutted the dock and lobby. You'll need to find another route," says Marian.

Ethan groans and slumps in the chair, and Aiden's audio box appears. *"Ethan,"* calls Aiden.

Ethan looks up, half expecting to see Aiden's face.

"You'll be fine, I promise. But we need our medic, and you need to be brave. Do you understand? This nightmare won't end unless you walk through it," says Aiden.

Ethan nods. "I... I understand."

"Good. We'll see you at the Station. Stay safe," says Aiden.

Ethan's pad beeps, and an envelope icon appears on the corner of his wrist-top computer screen, which is currently taken up by his sharp vital signatures. Ethan swallows, and he hits the envelope icon, which brings up a message.

From: Riva Bonnevue (rivaluvsbonbons4evr@aats.com)
To: Ethan Rifts (riftsethanj@aats.com)
Subject: Bon Voyage Map

Ship map attached. Stay safe.
-R. Bonnevue

File: BonVoyageMap.zip

Ethan downloads the file, and the pad beeps upon completion, and Ethan looks at Marian's audio box.

"I have the map," says Ethan.

"Good. We'll see you soon. Dartmount out," says Marian.

Marian's audio box then disappears, leaving Ethan alone in the room.

6

The Stitcher

Ethan stares at the area where his commander's audio box was just a moment ago. After a deep sigh, he stands up, checks his weapons, and when he finds they are good, he pulls up his map on his wrist pad.

After he finds the Section C Transit Station, he marks it on the map, which leads to the map zooming in on his position like a GPS. After that, he cautiously approaches the door. Once at the door, he stares at it, chest heaving from his shaky breathing and his skin itching from the sweat trickling down his face.

"Warning! Hull breach in Section C! Evacuate immediately!"

Ethan swallows and opens the door with the emergency message looping over the speakers. Whirring and banging echoes in the halls, and he quietly steps out with his rifle raised.

He checks his map again before going down the correct direction. His steps are quick, and his eyes dart around as the lights from his weapon and shoulder flashlights bob. His heavy breathing and racing heart clogs his ears, and his boots make faint taps as he walks. The shadows stretch and condense as he sweeps the area, and a mix of rolling rumbles and traveling electric hums stalk him from every direction.

Soon, Ethan reaches a green-lit door, and when he opens it, he gasps and jumps back. Then he swears under his breath, shakes his head, and walks past a colonist laying on the ground in a dried pool of orange and red blood.

The corpse is surrounded by pollen and green film, her torso is torn open and one of her arms is severed, with a splatter of blood on the wall, ceiling, and floor. Thin vines are curling around her spilled, torn organs, and snaking in and out of her skin. Her mouth is wide open, with her remaining arm standing straight up with roots spreading from her elbow and across the floor. Her skin is covered in bark, and her eyes have grown into open bulbs with pollen sliding out.

Ethan shudders and walks as fast as he can, leaving footprints in the film and pollen. After he crosses the body, he brings up the map again and flicks his eyes between it and the intersection of the hallway. When he sees where he needs to go, he turns his walk to a jog and-

"One by one we go... When it stops, we don't know..." sings a female.

Ethan stops and swings his rifle around.

"Hello?" calls Ethan. "Hello? AATS!"

"Hello? I see you," giggles the female, her voice in the vents and having a faint hiss to it.

Ethan aims his rifle at the vent. The grate is still in place, so he can't see much, but between the metal slits he can see two beady, yellow-tinted reptilian eyes staring at him and gloved fingers poking through. This is a spliced human. Ethan has seen plenty of them on Oros. They're always weird to observe, but at this point, Ethan is happy to see any kind of human on *Bon Voyage.*

"Do you want to be Gary's friend?" asks the female. "Do you want to be my friend?"

"Um... Yes?" says Ethan.

The female giggles. "Let me get Gary. Gary needs friends!"

The eyes and fingers disappear, and her scraping and shuffling travels over Ethan's head and goes down the hallway. He then activates his communicator and follows the stranger.

"Commander, I'm trailing a survivor. She's in the vents, and she says she has another survivor," says Ethan.

"What is she doing in the vents?" asks Marian.

"I don't know, ma'am. Maybe she feels safer in them?"

"Or maybe she's nuts like the others."

The stranger turns, and her noise goes over a locked door, where her noise rapidly fades from Ethan's ears. Ethan presses his pad against the orb, but the same locked message from earlier appears. Ethan tries again, but to no avail.

"The survivor went through a locked area. I can't pursue her," says Ethan. "What are your orders?"

"Leave her and keep going to the Section C Transit Station," says Marian. *"We need to regroup and get to the bridge. Once we get to the bridge, we can call for reinforcements and get help for the survivors."*

"Yes ma'am."

"Dartmount out."

Marian's feed cuts out, and Ethan sighs and paces in a circle. He looks at the locked door, then up at the vent, and then behind him, and he sees a vent grate. He stares at the grate and mentally weighs his options.

On the one hand, he found a survivor, or rather a (hopefully) friendly survivor found him. The last survivor tried to kill him, and Moon died shortly after. However, the survivor - or the Tainted - was infected. *However,* this survivor did not even try to kill him. Loopy, yes, but she has not tried harming him. She also has a potential survivor with her. And as a member of the AATS, he has an obligation to help those in distress. But he cannot get to this survivor… But she can get to him, and she can bring the other survivor with her.

Ethan goes underneath the vent grate, looks side to side, and then focuses on the dark slits and waits for a few seconds for any signs of her or a creature.

"Ma'am!" calls Ethan.

Nothing.

"Ma'am, I can't reach you! But I am going to the Section C Transit Station! Meet me there! Again, Section C Transit Station!"

Ethan waits a few moments, and when nothing happens, he sighs and resumes walking down the hallway towards his destination. As he walks, he passes through a broken door labeled "Section C Transit Station" and enters a room of near total darkness. There is another light in the far end, revealing a set of stairs with the same message as the sign above the door he went through, but this light is dim and fading in and out.

Ethan stares at the pulsing light for a few seconds, and then continues into the dark. But as he walks, he hears a new set of heavy steps trailing him, plus a pair of stuttering clicks. He stops, turns, and sees a shadowy silhouette not too far from him. Then four yellow eyes open, and the silhouette roars with two voices and rushes Ethan.

"Shit!"

Ethan runs towards the light with the screams, heavy steps chasing him. Within seconds, a solid mass rams Ethan, and he crashes into the wall beneath the light.

Ethan twists on his back and kicks the creature away, and he barely gets up when it lunges at him again, slamming him into the wall near the stairs. Ethan's foot slips off the top step and the two roll down the stairs.

The flashes of pain and swirl of colors batter Ethan, and when they land, Ethan coughs and pushes himself up with blood oozing from his head. He sees his rifle has slid away from him.

The creature thrashes on the floor, screaming and slashing and whipping the air with its claws and tendrils, and Ethan dives for the rifle and rolls into the kneeling position with his weapon aimed at the creature's chest.

The creature twists itself upright as this happens, and Ethan sees Moon's head hanging crooked next to the first Tainted's head. Thin vines have slithered through their necks and out of their mouths. Their eyes are blank and yellow, and ribs and vines serving as teeth and hooks and stitches attach their torsos.

Their legs and feet have also been mutated by the vines, and one of Moon's and the first Tainted's arms have crossed over each other on the bulky chest. Moon's remaining arms have three sharp claws sprouting from their wrists with his hand fused to it, and the other arm has mutated into one large, curved claw, and patches of its skin have hardened into sharp bark.

"Ethan," wheezes Moon's voice.

"I'm here," says the second head in a raspy voice.

The creature Moon became, the Stitcher, runs towards Ethan, and he screams and unloads his rifle as he runs backward. The explosive stream of gunfire leaves Ethan's ears ringing, and the bullets rip into the Moon Stitcher, making it stumble back as blood and bits of flesh and bark spray off.

With the last bullet fired, Ethan reaches for a new magazine, but the vine from the Moon Stitcher's back grabs him and slams him against the wall, causing him to drop his rifle.

The impact leaves his head throbbing and ears ringing, and he chokes for air as the tentacle tightens around his throat. Darkness bleeds into his vision, and the Moon Stitcher stands up on shaky legs and aims its claw at Ethan.

Ethan draws his pistol and rapidly shoots the arm of the enormous claw. The shots shred the flesh and break the bone and bark, and its claw falls off right as it goes for the kill. Ethan then spends the last bullet in the magazine to shoot the vine that is choking him.

As he does this, the vines whip him with stinging results.

He keeps going, and he grabs his rifle and runs down the hallway. He does not get far before a vine grabs his leg and yanks him down. The impact knocks his vision out of focus, and while he is dizzy, the creature pulls him across the floor. Ethan turns on his back with his rifle in hand, and he screams in pain as the claws pierce his right shoulder.

The Moon Stitcher leans forward, and the two heads growl with thick, sap-like slobber, green dots dripping down on Ethan while blood pumps from his wound. Ethan grits his teeth, presses both of his legs against the Moon Stitcher's torso, and uses all his might to push.

He screams through his teeth as the claws pull out, tugging up his flesh with it, and when the claws pop out, the creature loses its balance and falls to the side. Ethan then turns on his side with his rifle in hand, slips in a new magazine, and shoots it in the torso.

The two heads screech and the Moon Stitcher thrashes as its chest explodes in a shower of gore. Its orange blood spreads towards Ethan, and he pushes himself up, stumbles against the wall, and uses it for support as he hurries down the hallway, leaving a thick streak of red behind.

When he reaches the next area, he finds an elevator with a directory on it, which includes his destination. Watching the elevator is another black domed camera with a red band.

The elevator is green, so Ethan hits the down button and slumps against the wall while aiming his rifle at the Moon Stitcher. The creature is laying in the same spot, twitching with the vines occasionally snapping towards the severed arm.

While Ethan watches the abomination, his arm shakes, his wound throbs, and his head feels like it is loose. Then the elevator dings and slides open, and Ethan peeks inside. He sees nothing, save for a sign that says, "I AM NOT INFECTED." The sign and walls are splattered with blood, and a brown trail leaves the elevator.

The elevator closes, and Ethan slips inside. He falls against the wall and turns to face the hallway. Before the doors close, he sees the Moon Stitcher try to stand up. The door closes with a mix of a crackle and a ding, and Ethan sees a bloody handprint smeared at the base of the door.

After it clicks shut, Ethan pushes the button for the floor he needs, leaving a bloody fingerprint on the button, and he collapses into the corner as he rubs his face. When he pulls his hands away, his face is red, and he takes a deep breath, grabs his medical gear, and gets to work patching himself up as he descends further into Hell.

7

Gary

The humming and clanking of the elevator drown out Ethan's wince as he tenderly unzips his medical suit and peels it away from his bleeding shoulder. Strings of blood stretch and snap on the formerly white suit, and dark red gashes mark his right shoulder with lighter red blood oozing out with every beat of his heart.

Ethan shakily removes a can of medical foam and awkwardly sprays it against the wound, making a sloppy mess of white that quickly turns to pink from the mixing with the blood and then turns into a shell within seconds. The searing pain causes him to drop the can, and he bangs his head against the wall.

There he remains, silent and trembling, with only the sounds of the elevator to keep him company. A moment later, he reaches into his pouch and pulls out a Quick Stitch Kit; or the QSK. To the untrained eye, it looks like a staple gun with pincers, but Ethan knows that the small silver block device is pain in a shiny package.

Ethan positions the QSK pincer against the tip of his wound, takes a moment to collect some courage, and then pulls the trigger.

SNAP!

The pincer snaps in and out of Ethan's skin, leaving a thin wire that tightly binds the edges of his wound. The pain causes him to drop his device, swearing up a storm.

The elevator comes to a sudden stop, and Ethan sees he is on the floor he needs to be on, but before the doors can open, he hits the emergency stop button, thus sealing him inside. Ethan collapses against the wall and slides down to the floor, breathing heavily and clutching his wound with his face soaked in tears and sweat. Long seconds pass before he musters the courage to grab his QSK and press it against his wound.

SNAP!

Ethan almost drops it again, and his vision is clouded with tears.
SNAP!

Ethan grinds his teeth, takes another deep breath, and-
SNAP!

He leans over, chest heaving and sweat dripping off his nose, and he takes another deep breath, presses his back against the wall, takes a few more deep breaths, and then goes for it.
SNAP! SNAP! SNAP! SNAP! SNAP! SNAP!

Ethan cries painfully, drops the QSK, and falls to the floor with his good hand pressed against his wound. His other arm throbs with the worst pain condensed around the new stitches. Sharp tingles run all the way to his fingers like barbed maggots.

He can feel the bumps on his flesh and the tiny metal strings holding his shoulder together. He stares at the blood splattered on the door and now notices sharpie writing on the wall next to the door: *"Hang in there. Love- Gary"*

Ethan winces and pushes himself up, and with shaky hands, he clips the QSK back on his belt and opens the elevator door. He really doesn't want to, because he felt safe in there, but his team needs him, and he really doesn't want to die in space. If he's going to die, he's going to die with dirt under his feet. Space be damned!

With the elevator door open, Ethan steps out with his rifle raised and his two lights aimed into the room. The room is dimly lit, its walls are covered in pipes, and at the far end is a set of small stairs with a door at the split level. Above the door is a sign reading "Sec. C Transit Station."

The elevator shuts behind Ethan, cutting off its light, which makes the room even dimmer. As he walks forward, his foot kicks away a sharpie. He watches it roll away and jumps when his lights shine on a corpse propped against a cart with broken screens and orbs. The cart and the corpse are covered in scratches, and the cart has "Skipper" written on it, while the corpse is wearing a gray jumpsuit with "G. Salamiin" on the tag.

The corpse's skin is covered in bark, and his muscles are bulging as branches breach the skin. His mouth is wide open with vines hanging from it, and his eyes have open bulbs with pollen covering his chest and legs. Roots have broken out of his hands, feet, and back, and they have spread across the floor and wall, and covered the cart.

The vines snap to Ethan when his lights shine on them, and he curses and jumps back, but the body does not move. He keeps his rifle trained on the body, and he steps to one side. The vines, while wiggling like worms in the air, follow him. He steps to the other side, and the same thing happens.

As Ethan does his experiment, he notices a workstation with various tools, all marked with the Arx Corporation logo. Next to the workstation is a wall with two lamps shining on it. The wall is covered with names, dates, and ages, and beneath the writings are melted candles and scattered sharpie markers. The last names on the wall are: "Skipper + Gary Salamiin APR-07-2428 (28 mos/31yrs)."

Ethan goes to the workbench and finds a bloodied note taped to it. He takes it off and reads it.

Dear Carmen,

I'm sorry Skipper and I couldn't make it. We tried getting one of the escape pods to work, but they attacked us. I need you to find another way off the ship.

Don't go playing hero. Everybody else is gone, and you'll go mad like Harold and or jaded like Arnvin trying to save the rest. Find Bitson. He can help you get off this ship. Live for us while you still have a chance.

Love always- Gary

Ethan rereads the note, then looks at Gary's corpse with a cold tingle running up his back as he remembers the survivor talking about a "Gary." He looks at the corpse for a few more seconds before he gently puts the note down.

Then he goes to the door, while casting a wary eye at the vines stretching towards him. But when he reaches the door, his heart sinks. Not only is the door dim, but its orb has been smashed. Its wires dangle, and bits of its lens, shell, and chips lay in pieces on the floor.

Hoping for the best, Ethan presses his pad against its dangling sensor, but nothing happens. He holds the sensor steady and level and presses his pad against it.

Still nothing.

He rubs his pad against it.

Again, nothing.

Ethan rubs his pad hard and alternates between strained slow and frantic fast, and when nothing changes, he curses and whacks the sensor against the wall, causing it to snap loose and fall to the floor.

Ethan scoffs. "Great."

He paces in front of the door and prepares to contact Marian, but he stops when he sees a vent in the middle of the ceiling. Then his brain registers the crates scattered around the room, all with the Arx Corporation logo stamped on them.

So, he begins his work by pushing them together. The first two are heavy, so for the third one, he hastily empties the contents of the crate on the floor, while occasionally looking at Gary's corpse.

The vines are watching him in a way that makes him feel like he is a monkey in a circus. After he gets the third crate emptied, he puts it on top of the other two crates, which are positioned beneath the vent, and he stands on top of it.

With some struggle, Ethan pulls the vent open, wincing as it creaks. Then he pulls himself in. Just that simple task strains his arms and core, and when he is inside, he finds that there is enough room for him to crawl on his hands and knees and to turn around, too. He also finds that the vent is lined with little lights and panels with ascending ID numbers, all starting with "Sec. C."

Ethan takes a deep breath and begins crawling. His hands and knees thump and his feet scrape on the surface as he makes his way down the vent to a nearby vent grate, but he pauses when he sees a thick vine at the far end slither by an opening. He freezes, and watches as the slimy plant moves along the vent, and when its tail end of mandibles disappears from view, Ethan is trembling and hyperventilating. He stays motionless for a few more seconds before he goes to the vent grate. Once there, he peers through the slits for any signs of trouble.

When he does not spot any signs of danger, he frantically pulls the interior latch on the vent. After it falls open, he jumps down and stumbles because of the shock on his shins and knees, but he quickly regains his composure, moves away from the vent, and sweeps the new area with his rifle.

His lights streak over hissing and shaking pipes and scratched on the floor is a message written in English, Portuguese, Mandarin, Spanish, Hindu, and Arabic, in black paint with elegant strokes. Each line is the translation of the one above.

Oh Lord, lead us from unreal to the real

From Darkness to Light

From Death to Immortality

Guide us to You

Amen

Around the message are handprints made from black paint with empty paint buckets nearby, and the prints lead to a sealed door marked "Trash Incinerator." Religious symbols surround the door, ranging from crucifixes to crescent moons and Oms, as well as a symbol of recent creation in the Federation; a religion called Unity, which is symbolized by a sun with wings. On the wall across from the other symbols in red paint is the entwined tree; it is larger than all of the other symbols, like a god looking at lesser beings.

The panel next to the door with the handprints is green and has a bold message saying, "Process Complete."

Ethan shudders and hurries down the hallway with a wet lump in his throat. The pipes hiss and shake, and the lights flicker on and off, making the shadows dance against the walls.

He passes through another door, and after doing a quick sweep of the area, he takes a deep, shaky breath and cautiously moves forward. Once he enters the new area, lights flash on with a hum, and crackling music that is supposed to be soothing plays over the speakers.

The sudden activity brings Ethan to a halt, and he frantically scans the area. He does not see any danger, but he sees that the room is long with wide windows.

The room has destroyed carts scattered about. Some are carrying luggage and others are carrying food and supplies. The food has long expired; the supplies are trampled, and on the wall is a broken screen displaying a message in a frantic flash of colors and pixels that bathe the room in a disorienting rainbow.

Please Remain Patient. Transportation Will Resume Shortly.

Ethan stares at the message, then looks down the length of the room to see another door waiting to be opened, and finally, he looks out the window and sees Marian's group on a platform across a chasm with a rail network. Marian is standing at the edge, looking at him. Aiden and Taksheel are patrolling the area, and Riva is sitting against the wall with her computer plugged into an orb by a door.

Ethan looks left, then right, then he looks at a vent nearby and half expects either a monster to jump out or the crazy lady he told his destination to. But the seconds tick by, and when he is certain nothing will come after him, he activates his communicator and brings up Marian's audio box.

"Rifts, are you okay?" asks Marian.

Ethan sees Aiden turn around and look across the way at him.

"I'm okay, ma'am," says Ethan.

"You don't look okay to me," says Aiden. *"Ethan, how badly are you injured?"*

"I'm fine, sir." Ethan looks down at both ends of the rail. "Where's the trolley?"

"That's what we're trying to figure out," says Marian. *"We called the trolley, but nothing is coming. Riva is trying to figure out why."*

"From what I can see, the transit system is at an emergency stop. One trolley is blocking the rail, so they have put the entire system at a standstill," says Riva.

"Great…" says Ethan.

Riva stands up, carefully unplugs her computer, and goes to Marian's side.

"Ethan, the good news is that the block is on Section C, and the Section C Transit Hub is a couple of floors above you overlooking the rail," says Riva. *"If you can get there and get to the administrator's computer, I'll be able to hack it from here and get the whole system back up."*

Ethan frowns. "Can't I just break the window and climb across?"

"Unless you sprout wings, you are not getting across," says Marian. *"Besides, the transit system will be the quickest way to get to the bridge."*

Ethan's shoulders slump. "Right."

"I can go to Ethan," says Aiden.

"That's good. Ethan can use the help. Just be careful out there," says Riva.

Marian glares at Riva, and Aiden nods and is about to leave, but Taksheel steps in front of him and holds his hand out. While Ethan cannot hear Taksheel very well, due to him being in the background of Marian's feed, he can hear enough.

"That'll take too long," says Taksheel. *"The direct path is no good, and this place is a demented labyrinth. We'll be here waiting for hours for you two to meet up and do the thing when Ethan can just get it done in a few minutes."*

Aiden looks at Marian. *"Mary, we can't leave him alone."*

"Rifts, can you do the task on your own?" asks Marian after a long pause.

Ethan's heavy heart races, and his throat tightens as his eyes glaze over, staring at his team across the chasm. Marian's expression is a mix of worry and sternness, while Aiden's and Riva's all worry, and Taksheel is standing stiff by the door.

"I'll take care of it, ma'am," says Ethan. "Aiden, I'll be fine. And Riva, don't work too hard. Rifts out."

8

The Voice

Ethan disconnects before Marian can say anything, and he goes to the door at the end of the room. Beyond the door is an empty hallway with emergency lights, a buzzing intercom, and a body lying in a pool of pollen and dried blood with their head missing, their limbs severed, bulbs sprouted, and roots spreading from the gaping wounds to the wall, floor, and ceiling.

Vines wiggle in the air. When Ethan makes his way past them, they reach for him, with one wrapping around his ankle, but one quick tug is all it takes for him to break free.

His spine tingles as he goes down the hallway. When he reaches the end, he finds a ramp leading to another area.

Ethan checks his map and finds that to get to the Transit Hub, he will have to go down the ramp, pass through a spacious area, then go through a couple more spots before taking an elevator to his destination. This convoluted path does a fantastic job of annoying him, and after a deep sigh, he proceeds forward, shaking his head.

"Hey, Arx Corporation, we need you to build a ship," says Ethan.

"How would you like it done?" asks Ethan in a unique voice.

"Ridiculously complicated! So, when people are stranded and fighting for survival, they get lost and confused and die alone!"

Ethan finishes with a punch to the wall, which he immediately regrets, since now his hand is hot and throbbing. He seethes and shakes his hand, but keeps walking, and when he reaches the bottom, he opens a door.

As soon as the door opens, the stench of rot, mold, and decay rush Ethan like a landslide of garbage, and he gags and steps back, holding his nose and his eyes watering. A moment later, he forces himself to move forward, and the door closes behind him when he is out of its sensor's range.

The new area is barely lit with bands of failing light, and the intercom is spotty. The room has destroyed barricades made of crates, tables, desks, and chairs, and the floor is littered with weapons (both military and crude), garbage, spoiled food, bullet casings, blood, broken bones, and ripped flesh. Most of the doors are welded shut, save for one in the distance, and it is dim and partially open.

He walks towards the door, passing a severed limb here, a broken bone there, but there are no bodies of the crew and colonists, and from what he has seen so far, he knows why.

"Good afternoon, survivors!" says a jovial male voice suddenly over the intercom, bringing Ethan to stop. The odd voice echoes in the room, and it appears in the area Ethan just came from, causing a slight overlap. *"We are on day twenty-one of the* Bon Voyage *survival challenge! Many have failed, some are holding on, and the new contestants are finding out how difficult this really is! But the new contestants have also taken* Bon Voyage *by storm with incredible teamwork and resolve. Sooooo... Will. They. Maaaake it? Let's find out! Don'tforgettolikeandsubscribetoStuckOnASpaceBoat."*

The voice is replaced with the instrumental of the Federation of Sol Systems' anthem, and Ethan sneers at the intercom.

"What the hell?" says Ethan. He activates his communicator. "Commander, did you hear that message over the intercom?"

"Yeah," says Marian, with the anthem also playing on their end. *"It looks like we have another nutty survivor on our hands. He must be on the bridge. That is the only way to use the wide scale intercom system."*

"And all the more reason to get there quickly," says Taksheel. *"If that guy's there, then there might be more survivors with him."*

"Agreed. Let's just hope they don't maul us when we get there. As for you, Ethan. Hurry it up. The quicker you get done, the quicker we can go home. Dartmount out."

Marian's feed cuts off, and Ethan smacks his lips and continues to the door while the anthem echoes around him.

"I should have taken my chances on Oros," says Ethan.

When Ethan reaches the partially opened door, he finds a lot of blood and bullet casings, and in front of the door is a security officer surrounded by dried blood. The officer's head has been pulverized by something that blew a hole through his face out of the back of his head.

Ethan shines his light through the door opening and sees more hallway and rows of dim lights and a locked door at the far end, with a body in a gray maintenance suit in front of it. Ethan tries forcing his way through the door, but it is too narrow, so he grabs it and starts rocking it.

The door wiggles a little, so he braces himself, presses both hands and a foot against the door, and begins pushing. His muscles strain, and the loud screeches of metal drown his grunts as the door slides on its rail bit by bit.

The screeching gets louder and longer, and his limbs stretch further out. Soon the door is open enough for him to go through and he stumbles into the hallway and checks his map as he takes a moment to catch his breath.

The map shows he needs to go up a flight of stairs near the locked room, so he hurries down the hallway, but stops by the corpse in front of the locked door.

The corpse is torn open, and their shoulder and neck are mangled. Splinters of white bone poke out from the dark red and orange blood. Vines have grown from the gashes, while their skin has hardened in other parts.

Ethan grimaces and is about to continue his trek, but he stops himself when he notices the corpse has a red and green striped band with a golden key icon and a white orb next to a small screen. The vines twitch, but the body doesn't move.

Ethan looks around, and then kneels and fights the vines as he removes the band. The vines have sharp little barbs and pointed tips that make it easier for them to hurt Ethan. But when he unclips the band, he can easily pull away from the vines, though they leave a parting gift of small rips on his sleeves and gloves.

Ethan steps away from the vines and clips the band on his free arm, and studies the device, noting that it is a Master Key Band or MKB. Another product of Arx Corporation, for use on their ships, or other ships if programmed right.

Ethan studies the band for a few more seconds before looking at the locked door. He presses the MKB against the door's orb and it switches from red to green and the door opens. With the door opening, lights flicker on in the room on the other side, and Ethan steps inside.

The room is bare, except for a single black dome camera aimed at a wall of photos with dying candles and melted wax beneath them, and a entwined tree covered by streaks of paint. The door closes, and Ethan approaches the wall of photos, seeing they are of people of all ages and all walks of life; men, women, children; colonists, staff, security; normal humans to spliced humans, or technologically augmented humans. So many varieties are united by their gruesome fate in this vessel of hell.

"You in the room! You aren't Bitson!" says the odd voice from earlier.

The sudden voice makes Ethan jump, and he frantically searches for the source.

"Up here," says the voice.

Ethan looks at the camera.

"There you go! How are you doing, big guy? You like the ship?"

Ethan already hates him. "No. What happened here?"

"Just a freak accident of mass food poisoning. I don't know if I should blame the salad bar or the soup kitchen for this mess."

Ethan sneers.

"But you aren't Bitson. Who are you?" asks the voice.

"Ethan Rifts. I'm with the Association of Assisted Transport and Security… Sir."

"So, the new contestants are with AATS? Neat. And I was thinking you guys were scavengers or smugglers or some other unsavory bottom feeders."

"I promise we are AATS, sir."

"Don't sir me. I'm not a ranking officer. But anyway, I'm glad we finally get to chat. I have been watching you and your team battling those Haunters for a while and I believe we can help each other. I told Bitson to meet you down at the Transit Station, but I'm going to take a wild guess and say that Bitson is no longer a contestant since you are wearing his Master Key Band."

Ethan looks at his MKB, and then at the camera.

"I didn't kill Bitson," says Ethan.

"I never accused you of killing Bitson," remarks the voice.

"So, those things out there are Haunters?" asks Ethan, wanting to divert the conversation from Bitson as quickly as possible.

"Technically, they are Onyx Spore Infected, but they make creepy noises, can change their forms, and are ugly, so we called them Haunters. I didn't pick the name, though. Captain Junjie Ding did, but you and your band of friends are doing good against them so far. So, hats off to you."

Ethan frowns. "If you can see us, that means you're on the bridge, right? That means you have control over the systems."

"Stop. I'm not on the bridge. I'm in the Section 0 Laboratory. I just had to do some creative rearranging and hacking to get the camera feeds to me, which was difficult, but the cameras and intercoms are all I have control over. The rest belongs to Captain Ding, and he does not share power."

"Can you communicate with other ships?" asks Ethan.

"I literally just told you I can only control cameras and intercoms."

"Right." Ethan paces in a circle. "Do you know any way off this ship? Or are we all just contestants to you?"

"I have a plan to get off this ship since I'm tired of this ship's game, and I **was** *trying to get the other contestants to come to me so we can all get out of here, but they decided to do their own thing,"* says the voice. *"But if* **you** *want to help me out of here, I can promise you glorious rewards. Book deals, gift cards, movie passes, money, acting gigs, talk show appearances. You name it, I can get it. Hell, we can even do toy lines, comic books, video games, movies! The possibilities of my rewards are endless! I'll be your genie if you save me!"*

"Okay, okay, relax. But you need to understand that I'm not leaving this ship without my team," says Ethan.

"Of course not! I would never ask a man to abandon his team. That's just mean. But get reunited with your team. Talk it over, and when you have an answer, just wave at a camera and we'll speak again! Bye!"

The intercom clicks off, and Ethan shakes his head and goes to the door, but before he opens it, he pauses, then turns back to the camera and waves at it. When it clicks on, he speaks.

"I didn't get your name," says Ethan.

"You may call me the Voice," says the odd man. *"And by the way, Bitson turned into a Haunter. Good luck!"*

The intercom turns off again, and Ethan looks at the door, paling and taking a step back when he hears shrieking and banging on the other side.

"Crap."

9

The Lurker

A terrible screeching and banging comes from the other side of the door, and as the noise carries on, Ethan levels his rifle and desperately tries to keep his breathing steady. It should not be so hard, because he has done it before.

And he also did something similar back on his home planet, Oros. But those targets were Orosian humans. This is the *Bon Voyage*, where humans become… whatever Haunters are.

The door shakes and its lights flicker, and Ethan steps back. His rifle quivers in his hands and his breathing shakes. Then the door buckles and two sets of claws wedge their way through the middle and begin pushing outward. The door bends and sparks, and the Bitson Haunter appears.

Bitson's arms have burst open from the claws and thorns trailing his bones. Their head is crooked, their eyes are bright yellow, their muscles have bulged on their limbs and chest, and the vines on their back wiggle in the air or grab the broken door.

As Bitson's Haunter passes through the door, it releases an airy yet loud scream, and it rushes Ethan with its arms stretched to him. Ethan backpedals and shoots it in a circular pattern of chaotic gunfire.

The bullets tear through the Haunter's chest and shoulders, and it shrieks while bloody pieces spill to the floor. The number of bullets tearing into the Haunter makes it stumble, and Ethan shoots its legs, bringing it to its knees.

After that, he puts a few rounds into its head and runs past its limp form while its vines try grabbing him. Their grip is weak, but they still lightly tear into his pants.

Ethan races down the hallway in the direction he needs to go. His heart is frantic, and his feet barely touch the floor while the weak clanks and buzzes of electric currents trail him from behind the walls.

The chaos of the noise plus the attack has plagued Ethan with a crushing feeling on his chest and throat. When he rounds a corner, he slides to a stop, to sweep the area while swallowing some spit to soothe his burning throat.

His general observation is more hallway, plus a bathroom and multiple locked doors, one leading into an area labeled "Schedule Chamber."

Ethan continues forward. His steps echo off the walls, and when he is near the bathroom, he hears a loud thud from the direction he came from. Next comes heavy footsteps.

"Ethan," calls Moon.

"I'm here," says the second raspy voice.

Ethan hurries into the bathroom, ducks into a stall, and uses the toilet as a perch. There he waits, listening to the footsteps and the warbling cries of the Moon Stitcher.

The steps continue. They are now outside the bathroom.

Ethan presses his back against the wall and places his finger on his trigger.

The footsteps get closer. Each step creates an echoing thud and sweat scratches Ethan's cheek.

The thumping footsteps reach the doorway, and the light shining into the bathroom from the hallway is blocked out.

"Let me in," slurs a female.

"Ethan," calls Moon again.

"I'm here," says the second voice.

"Let me in," repeats the female.

The shadow passes, with the last of it being vines feeling the air, and the footsteps keep going for a few more seconds before they pause. Then, metal snaps and bangs, followed by metallic screeching, and the footsteps continue and eventually fade out of earshot.

Minutes pass before Ethan dares to exit the stall. With the light from the hallway, he can see broken toilets, sinks, and tiles with blood covering the floor and walls. There is a drain that is covered in a green film with orange veins spreading out, and Ethan stares at the odd sight for a few seconds before he exits the bathroom.

Out in the hallway, he sees a mangled door laying in the middle of the floor. He cautiously approaches it and looks at where it came from. The hallway is shrouded in deep darkness, and with what little light the hallway gives, he sees thick vines and a network of roots sprouting from corpses clinging to the walls and ceiling.

He does not even have a desire to turn on his lights or explore that area, because it not only looks like the tunnel to Hell, but he also knows that is where the Moon Stitcher went, and he does not want to deal with that. So, with the simple decision made, Ethan goes to the chamber door at the end of the hallway and uses his MKB to unlock it.

The door jerks at first, and then it shudders and squeaks as it moves along its rails, with each movement spraying sparks. It stops moving and dims when it is halfway opened, so Ethan wiggles his way through. Once through, he stops and sulks.

There are four marked stairways, and in the center of the room is a tall, circular device with screens and keypads on it. Above it is a flickering holographic projection of the Sculptor constellation of the Federation of Sol Systems. All along the walls are various posters giving health advice, safety tips, legal announcements, as well as large vent shafts.

Ethan shakes his head and goes to the first stairwell, which has a board with all the points of interest on them, including the maintenance quarters and the engine room. As Ethan looks at the board, a sharp tingle runs along his spine and he hears a faint, stuttering clicking, and he looks around but sees nothing.

He also shines his light on the vents but sees nothing, either. He cautiously moves to the next stairwell, which leads to food processing. It is an area he is not interested in, and the tingles along his spine only get sharper. He grips his rifle harder as he scans the area.

As he surveys the chamber, he takes a few steps back, and then sudden, sharp pains dig into his shoulders from a set of claws and a massive weight that pushes him down. Next, he is pulled in the air, and everything shrinks in a blink, and his rifle falls out of his hands.

When he stops, his legs are dangling and blood oozes all over his arms and chest, and he is pressed under a muscular mass. Hot breath blows on the back of his neck and slobber drips all over him, and Ethan slams his head backward.

There is a crunch and a screech of pain as a bit of blood splatters on the back of his head, and Ethan repeats this attack. After the sixth time of slamming his head against the beast, it drops Ethan. During his fall, he grabs the railing to the stairs but is tackled by the new creature: the Lurker.

The two crash onto the floor near the rifle with the Lurker's talons tearing at Ethan's suit. When it has him subdued, it looks down at him and screams with its face split open into four mandibles and a sharp tongue.

Now that Ethan can see the Lurker, he sees its muscles are bulged and pulsing from vines worming beneath the skin, its back has ripped open to create wings, and thick patches of bark cover its shoulder, thighs, and parts of its chest. What is not covered by the bark on the chest is a translucent sack with bug-like abominations swimming inside it. And its head has two thick vines with glowing tips protruding from it, like antennas.

The Lurker brings its talons down on Ethan, and he slams his hand against it, grunting in pain as his weakened state struggles to keep the talon up.

The Lurker lifts its other talons, and Ethan's watery eyes bulge. When it brings those talons down against him hard and fast, he uses his other hand to keep that one up.

Ethan grits his teeth, growling in pain, with tears and sweat soaking him. His arms slowly bend, bringing the Lurker's face closer to his, and as this happens, the creature's tongue coils up. Seconds later, the tongue shoots towards Ethan's skull like a dart.

He tilts his head to the side, making the tongue strike the floor, and the Lurker releases a pained scream. It coils and strikes again, and Ethan shifts and presses his legs against the Lurker's abdomen and flips it off him.

It lands flat on its back, screeching and flailing, and Ethan rolls upright and snatches his rifle. By the time he grabs his rifle, the Lurker is already rushing, so he shoots at its sack, popping it and leading to a wretched stench and goo spraying out, along with the bugs spilling out and scattering.

The Lurker reels back, clutching its destroyed sack, and Ethan shoots its arm and chest. He is about to go for a headshot, but one bug leaps on him and sinks its teeth into his neck.

A burning pain surges through Ethan like a wildfire. It surges through his throat, spine, and lungs, subduing his screams.

Ethan squishes the bug, but more jump on him and he flails around, trying to squish them as they gnaw at him. He wheezes for air as the Lurker regains itself. Blood covers him and the pain is breaking him down to near uselessness. The bugs keep chewing on him, drawing more blood, and ripping apart more flesh and fabric.

The Lurker hobbles towards Ethan, tongue snapping like a whip, and using what energy he has left, he shoots it again, forcing it to stumble back. Then he beats himself to crush the bugs.

The work is quick, but even after killing them, he is having trouble breathing. His throat is sealed and burning, and his eyes are clouded. Slowly, his vision goes to black.

The Lurker rushes Ethan again, and again he shoots it.

His vision is almost completely dark now. He can barely hold his rifle.

The Lurker grabs Ethan and carries him to the ceiling again. Ethan drops his rifle and comes face to face with the Lurker, meeting its antennas and an open mouth with a dazed look.

The Lurker grabs a steel beam with its feet and holds Ethan as its tongue coils with bloody drool dribbling on him.

Then Ethan yanks out his pistol and shoots the Lurker through its mouth. The back of its head pops, splashing the ceiling with its bits, and it goes limp and drops Ethan.

Down they go, falling together.

Ethan feels weightless as the dim metal and emergency lights rush past him. He hits the top of the terminal, shattering the holographic projector, which punctures his suit and burns him with large sparks.

Then he rolls off, bounces off a keypad, and lands on the floor, blacking out instantly.

10

A Deal With the Voice

"Rifts come in."

...

"Rifts do you copy?"

...

"Ethan Rifts, do you copy?"

...

"ETHAN!"

Ethan's eyes snap open with his mouth pooling with blood and some leaking past his lips. He blows through his nose and looks around the room. He feels dizzy, and everything is a blur. From the dimly lit room that he is in, to the twitching Lurker impaled on a broken rail, and Marian's audio box being projected in front of him. Only the projection is flickering, with strands of the audio box breaking into cubes.

"I'm here," says Ethan weakly.

"Thank God," says Marian. *"Where are you? We've been trying to reach you for the past twenty minutes. Are you alright?"*

Ethan's eyes sluggishly scan the room while he lies on the floor. He can barely move from the pain and dizziness, and there is a ringing in his ears. His whole body is aching and cold, and he is covered in a mix of sticky blood and hardened foam and ruptured medical foam cans surround him.

"Not really... but I'll make it. I'm in the schedule chamber... for Section C," says Ethan.

"Riva, where's the alternate route?" says Marian.

"I'm not seeing any good routes," says Riva tearfully in the background. *"There's too much damage to the ship."*

"We can't leave him there! It was a mistake not to get him in the first place!" says Aiden.

"We couldn't go back, and we still can't go back!" says Taksheel.

"So, we're just going to leave him to bleed to death?"

"Aiden, you can save Ethan, right?" asks Riva.

"Give me any route, and I can get to him quickly," says Aiden.

"Aiden don't be stupid," says Taksheel. *"Going back is going to get you killed, and then he'll bleed to death, anyway. We need you here to* **protect us** from whatever those things are!"*

"We're not leaving anybody, Taksheel!" snaps Marian.

Ethan's eyes fall on a syringe of adrenaline, and he extends a shaky hand towards it.

"Riva, if you do not find a way to Ethan in the next sixty seconds, I will beat the shit out of you," says Marian.

"I'm trying, but the ship is wrecked!" cries Riva. *"The corridors are death traps, the transit is not working, and there are those* **things** *running around!"*

Ethan pulls the adrenaline towards him and pops off the cap.

"Find a way! We lost too many already and I will be damned if any more of us die here!" says Marian.

"We can't risk it. We'll die if we try going to him," says Taksheel.

Ethan is in a trance-like state when he injects himself with the adrenaline. The surge brings him to cough out globs of blood. He clutches his chest with his eyes wide and mouth hanging open to swallow air, while his heart bangs against his ribs like a wild animal in a cage.

Strings of blood dangle from his lips, and he rolls on his knees and coughs up more blood. His coughing turns to dry heaves and wheezes, and his arms tremble as they brace him. Then his green eyes widen, and his fingers slide to his blood. He dips his fingertips into the small puddle and holds them to his eyes, seeing an orange tint with some green dots.

"No," gasps Ethan. He sits up and stares at his shaking hands with tears clouding his eyes. "No, no, no. God, no."

Marian and the others are arguing with Taksheel on the other end, but Ethan cannot comprehend their words. He is focused on his problem. He pulls off his MAD and gloves and inspects his hands. His hands tremble, but he cannot see any mutations.

After that, he moves to scan himself using the MAD's manual function. The lines crisscross on his chest, shoulders, and head, and when it finishes, it displays the information.

Cuts, bruises on flesh and bone, medical foam sealant plus disinfectant agents in his system, and last, an unknown contaminant with a request of blood work for further analysis.

Ethan drops the MAD, pushes himself against the terminal, and bangs his head against it. His wet eyes are dead, and his body is limp.

"I'm in charge and we're going to get him! That's final!" yells Marian.

"Don't," croaks Ethan. He coughs. "I mean, don't ma'am."

"What?"

Ethan swallows and blinks tears out of his eyes. "I... I'm almost there. I can get to the Transit Hub. I can save you... All of you."

There is a moment of silence, and the audio box momentarily flickers away before returning as a broken pixelated mess.

"Ethan, we're coming to get you. I don't know how yet, but we will," says Marian.

Ethan shakes his head. "No... It's too dangerous."

"This entire ship is dangerous. And we're coming to get you, so stop arguing about it."

Ethan takes a few large gulps of air, puts on his gloves and MAD, and stands up with the help of the terminal. "Don't come for me... I can get to the Hub. Just please... Please stay there. I only need a few more minutes."

After a heavy moment of silence, Marian speaks. *"Fine. You have thirty minutes."*

Ethan nods. "Roger that. I'll call you when I get there. Rifts out."

Ethan disconnects the call, and then he takes a long, shaky breath and looks at the mix of blood and foam on the floor. He then inspects himself, noting the many bites and scratches all over his body, plus the foam-sealed gashes on his upper body.

After that, he collects his weapons and is about to inspect the last doorway, but he stops himself and inspects his tattered outfit. It might as well not exist with how damaged it is, so he hobbles towards the maintenance quarters. Thankfully, nothing lurks in the stairwell, but the taps of his boots on the metal steps are unsettling for him.

When he reaches the top of the stairs, he finds the door locked, but the MKB opens it without a problem, revealing a long room with rows of broken beds, torn and bloody sheets, and broken footlockers. At the far end of the room are tubes with orange glows and silhouettes of crossing wrenches and hammers painted on them.

Ethan stays in the doorway as he sweeps the area with his rifle. The lights from his rifle and shoulder create shadows that stretch along the walls and floor, fusing with other shadows. He finds a few bodies slumped against a wall with thick roots and layers of pollen covering the area, and bulbs and vines protruding from the consumed corpses. He also shines the lights on the ceiling and finds vines hanging from broken vents.

Ethan cautiously steps into the room and steadily sweeps the area with his lights until he is in front of the cylinder. It has an orb lock next to it, like the others, and Ethan uses his MKB to unlock it.

The doors slide apart with a hiss as the interior light flashes on, revealing a thick, dark blue suit with the Arx Corporation logo stitched on its chest. There are metal-plated gloves, boots, and pads that fit on the user's limbs, spine, and ribs, and on a small platform is a full-faced helmet with a tinted visor. This is the suit of the Arx Corporation certified engineer. In a much better time, only they would work on their ships, which the Federation of Sol Systems love using, whether it be for colonial or more violent uses. But alas, this is not a better time, and Ethan would rather not die in space.

Ethan looks around one last time for signs of danger before he removes his equipment and then peels off what remains of his medical uniform. Each movement feels like his muscles are going to snap, and parts of his suit did not want to come off because of the mix of blood and foam acting like glue. But after a few minutes of struggling, he is finally out of his suit, and he puts on the engineering suit.

Getting in the new suit is a strenuous task, and his movements are wooden when he puts on the armored pads. He needs to adjust the straps to all the pads, and after that, he puts on his devices and then grabs the full-faced helmet.

He holds the helmet in his hands, his thumbs rubbing its visor and cheek. After a few seconds of blank staring, he slips the helmet on, immediately giving him a moment of claustrophobia as the pads press against his skull and the visor gives his vision a red tint that outlines the objects in the room. He pushes a button on the side of his helmet and the visor slides up, putting his vision back to adjusting to the dark with the help of his lights. He doesn't like it, so he puts the visor back.

With the suit complete, Ethan inspects himself and gets a small smile from the thickness of the jumpsuit, plus the protection from the outer armor. He also finds a few slots on the utility belt for batteries plus a holster, which he uses for his pistol. He then slips on the pouches of his supplies and shoulders his rifle. After that, he paces in circles a few times, as well as practices jumping, and he finds that the suit's weight, plus the weight of his equipment, is taking a toll on him. But he also feels safer in it, so it's worth it.

"Looking good," says the Voice suddenly.

Ethan spins in a circle in search of the source and stops when he sees a camera above a poster depicting a large group of smiling maintenance workers from all walks of humanity.

"It honestly surprised me you survived after what happened to you back there," continues the Voice. *"I thought you were going to transform into a Haunter, but you haven't, so it looks like you're clean!"*

Ethan stiffens, and the Voice hums.

"Oh... You're infected, aren't you? That's a shame," says the Voice. *"I guess I should start a timer to see how long it takes for you to go kaput. For research, of course."*

"I have to get the transit system moving," says Ethan quickly.

He walks to the door but stops when the Voice calls him.

"What are you going to do once you get Riva Bonnevue connected to the Section C Transit Hub? Tell them you're infected and can't join them?" says the Voice. *"That would be most unfortunate. Especially for Marian Dartmount. I put a poll up for the boys and it turns out they ship you two like salt and pepper. It's called MariThan!"*

Ethan's breathing shakes with his body, and the hair stands on his neck, but he remains quiet.

"But on a more serious note, you don't have to be left behind, Ethan. I can help you and your team," says the Voice. *"The other contestants have lost ambition, but I want your team to win the game!"*

Ethan turns to the camera. "How can you call this a game!? And how can you help me? It's only a matter of time before I'm like those things out there!"

"I have a vaccine, Ethan."

"You..." Ethan shakes his head in disbelief, paces, and then glares at the camera. "You have a vaccine and you let this happen!?"

Ethan's furious voice echoes in the room, and the Voice remains silent for a few seconds.

"The Bon Voyage *is a Santa Maria Class colony ship,"* says the Voice, his tone heavy. *"This ship held sixteen thousand contestants, and the information*

I had was incomplete until recently, and even then, I do not have the materials to make sixteen thousand doses. I had no hope of saving anybody, but now I can save you. All I ask in return is that you save me from this game."

"Who's responsible for this 'game'?" asks Ethan.

"The Onyx Spore infected. Duh, dinkus! Who'd you think I was behind it? The devil?"

Ethan sighs heavily and opens his helmet to wipes the sweat from his face as he paces again, and he stops with his back to the camera. Or that one at least. There is another one not too far from him, and he only knows it is there because of its little red light.

"Alright, I'll help you. How long do I have before I change?" asks Ethan.

"That depends. I've seen the Onyx Spores transform someone in minutes. For others, hours. Quite a few have lasted days. The factors rely on the victim's health, muscle mass, and fat, plus the quantity of ingested spores. We may never know the full mechanics of this abomination."

"Great," huffs Ethan. "Can you reverse it, even if it is in an advanced stage?"

"Couldn't tell you! But come by anyway to see if we can. It should be fun."

Ethan grunts. "Fine. But just so we're clear, you have enough vaccines for my team and I?"

"I do. But you aren't getting any until we are safely off this ship."

"I figured."

"Good. Now run along. Your team needs you to get the trolleys up and running and I need you at Section 0. Good luck and Godspeed, brave contestant!"

The intercom clicks off after that, and Ethan shakes his head and leaves the room.

11

Section C Transit Hub

"Good luck."

Those words sounded a little too light for Ethan's liking, but he also reasons that the Voice has been isolated and has suffered severe mental and physical trauma. Nobody will be sane after going through the *Bon Voyage* nightmare for any period.

So, taking the Voice's odd tone as a sign of coping, Ethan makes his way back to the schedule room, and upon entering, he keeps his distance from the still-twitching Lurker and the mix of blood and foam spread on the floor. He goes to the last marked doorway and is relieved when he sees that its sign points to the stairwell as the entry point for the Section C Transit Hub.

He goes up the stairs and quickly travels down the hallway with his lights leading the way. His eyes flick to each sign above locked doors, finding broom closets, a break room, a storage room, offices, entrances to hallways, and so on.

As he goes, the vent rattles, and multiple scuffs echo with stuttering clicks, causing him to slow down and aim his rifle up. The trail of rattles and scuffing moves down the hallway, and when it reaches a vent grate, the barrier breaks, and a Haunter drops.

Ethan shoots it on the spot, and it writhes and shrieks as the bullets tear into it. Then two more jump down and Ethan keeps shooting. They screech and roll around with squirts of blood splashing on the walls and floor, and when Ethan's magazine is empty, the Haunters roll or twist upright. Ethan curses and reaches for a new magazine.

Which turns out to be his last magazine.

Ethan slips it in, but by the time he raises his rifle, the Haunters are already on him. He jumps back as the first one swipes at his face. Then he dives away from the next Haunter that swings at him and scrambles underneath the last Haunter's slash. During his scramble, he slips and falls on his stomach, but he quickly rolls upright and shoots the nearest Haunter.

The Haunter is leaping at him when the bullets strike its chest, and as it falls on its back, the other two rush Ethan. He sprays them with gunfire until his magazine runs dry, and the bullets push them back and make them stagger and snarl painfully. But they are quick to recuperate and rush him again.

Ethan flips his rifle and screams as he swings it like a club, striking the first Haunter in the head. Its head pops with bits of skull and brain flying, and it spirals to the ground with orange blood splattering on the wall. He then holds his rifle at both ends and uses it to block the swings of the other two, which leave gashes in the rifle and make his arms buckle.

Ethan yells and pushes against them, ramming into the other and pushing them into the wall. They shriek and thrash, and Ethan jumps back, pulls out his pistol, and unloads on them.

The constant gunfire leaves his ears ringing, and during the barrage one has its head pulverized. As that one slumps to the ground, the last Haunter charges Ethan.

It grabs his shoulders and slams him into the wall. Its claws dig into his shoulders, and its mouth opens wide, revealing slobber-covered fangs and its sharp tongue.

Before it can bite Ethan, he presses his pistol underneath its chin and pulls the trigger, blowing out its occipital bone. Orange blood splatters on Ethan's face, and he sputters and pushes the now limp Haunter off him. It crumbles to the floor, and Ethan spits some more before looking at the three twitching Haunters.

All three still have some human features, but orange veins have popped from their skins and sharp, wood-like claws have sprouted and fused their fingers together. Their jaws have become wide and bark covers parts of their skin. Vines have broken through their skin and are feeling the air, and Ethan shakes his head, grabs his rifle, and hurries away.

As he goes down the hallway, he inspects his weapon and finds that large cuts have dug deep into the rifle's body, but he finds nothing more excessive than that, and when he checks the sights, he finds they are still good. Seeing that his rifle can still work, Ethan turns his brisk walking to a hard run.

As he runs down the hall, the clanking and humming of pipes and failing lights clog his ears. His breathing is heavy, he can barely see straight, his sides and limbs ache, and above him the metal rattles once again. When Ethan rounds a corner, he finds a large, circular door labeled as "Section C Transit Hub".

The door is locked, but that quickly changes with Ethan's MKB's use. The door slides open, and Ethan goes inside with his pistol at the ready. What he finds instead of the demons is a large room with two rows of black computer screens, and there are rapidly blinking lights off to the side, a buzzing over a speaker that sounds like a voice trying to speak, and a long window that has a clear view of *Bon Voyage's* rail system.

Ethan closes and locks the door and steps further into the Hub. The further he goes, the louder the buzzing becomes, and soon Ethan is gritting his teeth from sheer annoyance. When he is in the center of the room, he approaches an elevated desk with a half-ring of terminals and chairs below it, and one large terminal propped on the elevated position. The buzzing is loud now because of the speaker being next to the setup, so Ethan shoots the speaker and gets to work.

When Ethan turns on the computer, it beeps, its fan spins, and the screen flashes to dark blue, with white numbers and letters scrolling across it. A few seconds later, they are replaced with a spinning circle and an ascending percentage. While the numbers go up, Ethan activates his communicator, bringing up Marian's pixel-fractured audio box.

"Commander, I got the computer up," says Ethan. "It is fifty percent loaded, now."

"Close call. You had two minutes left," says Marian. *"Riva, sync up!"*

Riva's audio box appears next to Marian's.

"Are you in, Ethan?" asks Riva.

"Right now, it is sixty-five percent. What am I looking for?" asks Ethan.

"I need the computer ID. It is on the initial loading screen with all the numbers and letters."

"That's already passed."

"That's alright. When it is fully loaded just hit control, alt, F1, and then go down three rows to diagnostics, hit enter, and it will be on the first row."

"Roger that."

Another minute passes before the computer fully loads to a login screen with the Sculptor constellation of the Federation and Arx Corporation's A, and Ethan follows Riva's instructions, this quickly brings him what he needs.

"I have it," says Ethan. "The computer ID is… uh… um… Barn-Victor-Sigma… um, Carlos?"

"You don't know Standard Signal, do you?" says Marian.

"Three-five… three-seven… eight-four-three… one-niner-one-niner-six," finishes Ethan. "Do you have it?"

"I have it. Stand by," says Riva.

Less than a minute later, the screen changes to a desktop menu, and Ethan watches the cursor moves on its own and selects a little train icon. The app opens, showing a schedule and paths of the transit network, and all the lines are red and marked as disabled. However, the screen quickly turns to coding, and in quick movements, the mouse highlights sections of the code, and those sections are swiftly changed.

Once all the codes are changed, Ethan hears a series of loud thuds and whirs, and he looks up, watching lights flashing to life on the tracks. A pleasant chime also echoes in the forsaken ship.

"Attention colonists and crew, the Bon Voyage *Transit System is now active. Thank you for your patience,"* says an automated voice over the intercoms.

"I did it!" says Riva joyfully.

The code screen disappears, and all the transit lines are green and shown as active.

Ethan smiles. "Good job, Riva."

"Thank you! " says Riva. *"Now please hurry to the station, so we can pick you up."*

Ethan gets up, holding his relieved smile, and he goes to the window as a trolley rolls by. But as it passes him, his smile fades. The windows are covered in green film and vines hang out a broken window, while shadows of Haunters move around inside.

"Oh, no." Ethan activates his communicator. "Commander, there's a trolley of Haunters going towards your position!"

"What? Repeat that message," says Marian.

"Haunters! Those things! They're-" Ethan leans against the window and sees the trolley going towards Marian's platform. "They're coming right at you!"

"Oh, shit!" yells Taksheel in the background as dings and metallic screeches fill the air.

"Riva, get back!" yells Aiden in the background.

"Open fire!" barks Marian.

Then comes gunfire and monstrous roars.

"Marian! Riva!" screams Ethan. "Shit!"

Marian and Riva's feeds cut off, but Ethan can see and hear the flashes and pops of gunfire.

"Oh, ho! What do we have here? An unexpected turn?" says the Voice over a speaker at the far end of the room. *"Whatever will Ethan do?"*

Ethan runs to the door, which is locked and by the speaker. He activates his map and selects Marian's location. Then, he uses his Master Key Band to unlock the door and races down the hallway.

"I can't believe it! He's going for it! Run Ethan, run!" shouts the Voice. *"Your team needs you!"*

The hallway Ethan runs down is crowded with abandoned luggage, destroyed carts and battle-damaged scenery. His rapid steps echo off the walls, and his shadow stretches and shrinks from the swirling emergency lights, and when he reaches a brightly lit opening, he skids to a halt.

There is an elevator in front of him, and it is humming and clanging with its up arrow glowing green and a thin stream of light moving through the cracks. Ethan pulls out his pistol and aims it at the door. His muscles lock and sweat trickles down his head, as his heart sounds like it is banging in his ears.

The elevator stops a few seconds later, and when it opens, a man steps out wearing a gas mask with red-tinted lenses. He is wearing a tattered, blackened, and bloodied white robe with gold bands, with a utility belt tight around his waist. Beneath the robe is an engineer's suit, and a sun with wings hangs around his neck. On his back is a pair of fuel tanks attached to a sturdy pipe network and rigged blowtorch head that created the body and barrel of a makeshift flamethrower. There is a flame flickering in front of the barrel, and his finger is on the trigger guard.

Ethan smiles with relief, and steps forward while lowering his pistol. "Thank God. I'm Ethan Rifts of the Association of Assisted Transport and Security. My team needs help and... and..."

Ethan's words fade and the man's steps make heavy thumps as he leaves the elevator in a trance. When the man is out of the elevator, he stops and stares at Ethan.

"Are you okay?" asks Ethan. He scans the man with his MAD, and when it beeps, it displays a large number of cuts, bruises, poor stitching, and large amounts of disinfectants in his system, but no signs of the mysterious infection. Seeing this, Ethan carefully steps forward with his hand raised and pistol holstered. "I see that you're hurt. Let me take you to my team and we can help you."

"Nobody can help me," says the man with a guttural voice while he walks forward.

"I can take you to someone who can."

"Can you take me to God?"

"Uh… No, not yet. But the Voice has a way off this ship, and then we can get you to a church… or something."

"The Voice can't help me. You can't help me. Only God can, and He has forsaken me for my deeds. We run and we hide, and we fool ourselves, but in the end, we all must answer for our sins before we are granted salvation."

Ethan steps back, and the man releases a burst of flame that rolls on the floor.

"You are running, I can see it," says the man. "What are you running from?"

"Me? Nothing!" Ethan backs up. "I'm actually trying to get to my team, and we can help each other get off this ship!"

"And run some more?" The strange man, the Pyro, shakes his head. "No, we can run all we want, but judgment comes for all of us. I still hear them. I see them trashing and burning by my own hands. I hear their torment and feel their pain of damnation. I burned Vagsten, I lied to my flock. I told them I heard God, but now *Bon Voyage* has their souls. I must save them."

Ethan backs up again and holds out both of his hands. "Right, and you can save them by lowering your weapon and calming down."

"No. To save them *Bon Voyage* must burn, and us with it."

12

The Pyro

As soon as the sentence finishes, the Pyro pulls the trigger, and a stream of fire surges towards Ethan. He jumps out of the way and rushes the Pyro as the psycho sweeps the area with flame.

The fire evaporates the moisture in the air and engulfs the scattered luggage, and Ethan rams the Pyro. The two fall to the floor in a tangle, and after some struggle, Ethan pins the Pyro with the help of the flamethrower's barrel.

Ethan puts his weight down, retracts his visor, and leans forward so he can see his reflection in the red-tinted lens. "Stop! I want to help you!"

"You are not God," says the Pyro.

The Pyro headbutts Ethan, and then he throws him off and rolls to his feet the same time Ethan gets up. He aims his flamethrower at Ethan, and he aims his pistol at the Pyro's head. They become still, with Ethan panting and the Pyro silent.

"Enough!" yells Ethan. "You do that again and I will put a bullet in your head!"

The Pyro says nothing, but when the floor shakes, the two look down the hallway and see a large mass shrouded in the darkness with glowing yellow eyes and overlapping clicks. It is still for a moment, and then it charges forward, shaking the hall with each step, its vines snapping the air, with three sets of roars.

As it gets closer, the details become clearer. Its legs are bulky from multiple legs stitched together. It has two massive arms and large clawed hands covered in thorny bark, and it has three heads, all with their mouths wide open and screaming. Two heads rest on top of the shoulders, and the third is in the chest, held in place by vines. Below it is another pair of arms crossed over each other and fused to the body.

The Pyro swings his flamethrower to the Stitcher, while Ethan slides the visor over his face, runs to the elevator and hits its button. The three screams turn to roars of pain as the fire engulfs the Stitcher. The monster charges the Pyro as he keeps burning it, and it swipes him off his feet.

The Pyro hits the wall and crumbles to the ground while the Stitcher thrashes around, throwing bits of its burning body off. The bright orange glow of the fire reflects off the wall, while the screams echo in the hall.

The Stitcher raises its arm to finish the Pyro, but Ethan shoots it with rapid fire. Each shot tears off a piece of its arm, and soon its arm snaps off, where it blackens and crackles and pops from the fire.

The elevator door dings and opens, and the Stitcher rushes Ethan with its other arm raised. Ethan dives out of the way, letting it hit the wall with a loud thud. Ethan shoots its leg until it buckles, which costs him the rest of his magazine, and he holds the door while waving at the Pyro, who is now getting up.

"Come on, you can thank me later!" says Ethan.

The Pyro ignores Ethan, goes to the Stitcher, and sprays it with fire. At first, there are three loud shrieks of agony, but they quickly die down, and the body sizzles and pops, with cracks spreading across its charred body.

The heads pop and the vines thrash before shriveling and breaking apart. Once it is a crackling husk of burnt flesh and plant, the Pyro turns to Ethan.

"Come on, let's go! We can get out of here, then you can find God all you want!" says Ethan.

The Pyro aims his flamethrower at Ethan.

"Oh crap," says Ethan.

The Pyro pulls the trigger, and Ethan dives into the front corner of the elevator as fire rolls on the floor and wall. Ethan hits the emergency close button, and the door shuts with a bang. As the fire eats at the wall, Ethan slams the next floor down.

The elevator descends with the clanks and hums clashing with the fire, and smoke rapidly fills the tiny space and Ethan's lungs. He coughs and sputters, and when the door opens, Ethan stumbles out and falls on his knees, coughing and wheezing, with the light of the flames dancing on his back and smoke spilling into the hallway.

By the time the door shuts, the elevator walls have peeled away to reveal its metal skeleton. Ethan takes a deep, raspy breath and looks up.

His heart briefly stops, and he pushes himself to his knees and stares at what is ahead. The hallway is dark, and the air is heavy with a thick stench of burnt flesh, metal, and wires. Sparks of light break pockets of darkness. They are popping out of destroyed wires and terminals. The walls and floor are burnt, and the area is littered with destroyed carts and shriveled and crumbling corpses.

Ethan pushes himself up and carefully walks down the hallway, trying not to step on the burnt corpses. As he carefully makes his way through the hallway, his eyes are drawn to the bodies, all burnt and twisted.

Some are clawing at themselves, others are hugging, and some are pressed against the wall. There is also a ring of carts surrounding a huddled group. The carts' wheels are melted to the floor, their metal casings are warped, and their screens and sensors have been reduced to the slivers and curled wires. The bodies they surround are indiscernible from one another, and Ethan stumbles back and falls against the wall, hyperventilating with tears in his eyes.

"No, this isn't..." Ethan looks at the burnt bodies and charred walls, the faces with shriveled eyes, the broken bones, and crumbling flesh.

The stench, the pops, all these things are wrong. Ethan opens his visor to rub the sweat and tears from his face. "This isn't right. Why did this happen?"

Ethan remains still for another moment, and when he looks down the hallway, he walks as fast as he can. He needs to get out. He needs to get to his team. They need to get off this ship.

As he goes down the hallway, he passes locked doors, broken doors, and flickering signs for religious services. There is also a sign that points towards a boarding station. His quick walk turns to a run after that, and right as he is about to reach the door to the boarding station, a distant ding catches his attention.

Ethan stops and listens. Heavy steps echo in the hall, and Ethan's jaw tightens. He puts his hand on his pistol and storms down the hallway. He focuses on the figure illuminated by the small fire in front of him, and Ethan draws his pistol, ejects the empty magazine, and slides a fresh one in. Like Ethan, the Pyro's steps become quick, and the pair stop when they are a few paces apart with the ring of carts between them. But Ethan doesn't close his visor. He wants the Pyro to see his rage.

"Did you kill these people!" yells Ethan, his voice cracking.

"Yes," says the Pyro.

"Why!"

"I had no choice. They had to burn. Just like Vagsten. Just like me. Just like you. We all must burn for our corruption. But my flock was innocent; they were misguided by my greed and arrogance. They shouldn't suffer for what I did. So now I am freeing them one soul at a time, then when the time is right, I will destroy *Bon Voyage* and let God do to me as He feels fit. And you will join me."

The Pyro raises his flamethrower and there is a blinding flash of hot light, and Ethan backpedals, tripping over himself as the stream of roaring fire sweeps side to side. The heat washes over Ethan, and his agonizing screams echo in the hall as the flames latch on to him and eat the right side of his face and suit.

Then, there is a sudden snap of metal, the fire stops, and the Pyro growls, along with the raspy scream of a Haunter.

As the fighting happens between the Haunter and the Pyro, Ethan lies on the ground, screaming and struggling to stand as he clutches his face. His legs buckle and he falls to the floor again, with bloody tears and burnt skin falling to the floor. He whimpers and drags himself across the floor, until he reaches a tipped cart.

He uses it to help him stand, and he looks at the Pyro. He can barely see through the wet haze of his exposed eye as his hand shields his burnt face, but through the blur, he can see the Pyro wrestling with the Haunter. Both are rolling around the floor, with the Pyro bashing it, and it slashing and biting him.

Ethan retreats down the hallway, collapsing against the wall, and then falling over again when he trips over a charred body. It is when he hits the floor that the vent overhead breaks open and a Haunter lands in front of him.

Pushing himself up, he runs past it. Dodging its claws, he forces himself to run faster when he hears its scream and its thumping steps chasing him.

Ethan passes through the boarding station doorway and finds himself on a platform with benches and lights, and a trolley is waiting to be boarded. Ethan runs to the trolley, but the Haunter leaps on his back and digs its claws into him. The claws scratch the suit's metal plating, and the sudden weight pushes Ethan to the ground, which leads to him dropping his pistol.

He elbows the Haunter in the jaw, bringing it to loosen its grip, he wiggles out from underneath it and runs to his pistol. But the Haunter tackles him again and twists him on his back. Then it lunges at his face. He puts his right arm between its fangs and his face, screaming as the Haunter's teeth bend the metal pad and pierce the fabric of his suit. Its claws scrape against the metal floor as it presses down on Ethan, and he reaches for his pistol.

The metal pad bends some more, the teeth sink deeper into his flesh, and his screams turn to sobs. When Ethan grabs his pistol, he slams it against the Haunter's head as hard as he can.

The impact breaks its skull and loosens an eyeball, but it still holds on, hissing and shaking its head. Ethan hits it again multiple times and awkwardly knees it. The Haunter growls louder, and it brings its claws above Ethan's head, and he shoots as fast as he can.

The shots rip apart its arm. When the arm snaps off, he strikes it in the head, this time breaking its jaw loose and sending teeth flying.

The Haunter falls off him, spitting out globs of blood. While more blood gushes from the remains of its mangled arm, Ethan fires a few more shots into it that end with its head being blown open.

The Haunter goes limp, its blood pumping all over the floor with the vines protruding from its skin shifting around. Ethan staggers away from it, hyperventilating and blinking tears and blood out of his eye. His bitten arm hangs limp, and his legs almost give out when he backs up. Then he sees a flash of orange coming from the hallway, and he curses and limps towards the trolley, leaving a trail of blood in his wake.

Once inside the trolley, Ethan forces the door shut and locks it, and then he hurries to the control panel. The controls are glowing with a destination selected, but Ethan is in too much pain and panic to care where it is, so he hastily disconnects the brakes and pushes the throttle forward.

"Lock disengaged. Autopilot engaged. Please stay seated," says a computer over the speaker.

Ethan sees the fiery glow flashing out of the corner of his eye, as the trolley gradually pulls forward. He turns and watches the Pyro walking past the burning remains of the Haunter he shot.

The Pyro is covered in fresh blood and scratches, but he also appears to be unfazed by the injuries. He and Ethan lock eyes, and when the Pyro raises his flamethrower, Ethan averts his gaze and braces himself for the coming pain.

However, the pain and fire never come.

The trolley rattles and hums, and Ethan looks back.

Nothing is there.

No fire.

No Pyro.

Just a burning corpse.

The platform is empty and only getting smaller, and Ethan moves to the back of the trolley, leaving a pool of tainted blood in front of the control panel. His whole body is shaking, his bitten arm can barely function, and his whole body is cold.

When he reaches the back of the trolley, he sits down and stares ahead, hands shaking and his heavy eye misting over as his head sways back and forth. Then he looks at his mangled arm and the teeth lodged in it, and grimaces at the sight and the thought of what must happen next.

More pain is coming.

And it will suck.

13

The Entrance

Ethan lifts his bit arm, grimacing at the thick, red, and orange blotches covering it. Heavy droplets drip to the floor, and three teeth are lodged in his arm. The computer's voice is saying something over the speakers, but he cannot understand the words. The scenery is moving by, giving his peripheral vision a bland show of gray and orange.

The trolley rattles on the rail, and Ethan grabs a seat belt, puts it in his mouth, and grabs a tooth. He takes three deep breaths, then pulls. As the tooth rubs against his muscles, with pain pulsing in his arm and radiating from the other teeth, his breathing gets heavier and faster, his hands and legs shake, and bile climbs up his throat.

When the tooth is out, soaked in orange-tinted blood, Ethan throws it down and spits the belt out, heaving and gagging. His throat burns and his vision blurs. His bit arm is numb and limp, and his bloody hands shake as his heart races.

The trolley turns, and Ethan bites down on the belt and grabs the second tooth. He takes a few more deep breaths and repeats the process, growling through the belt as the pain prickles through him once more. When that tooth comes out, his arm goes completely limp and Ethan falls over, puking and clawing at the seat. When he finishes, he is wheezing for air and shivering with his vision pulsing.

"One more," gasps Ethan. "One more… One… One more…"

He winces and pulls himself up, bites down on the belt again, and rests his completely limp arm on his leg. Then he repeats what he did with the last two and throws the tooth aside. He spits out the belt and his wheezing shakes as he looks at the three spots of torn skin and muscle soaked in his tainted blood. Thick beads of sweat move down his face and drip off his nose, and when he tries moving his fingers, he finds all they can do is twitch.

Ethan tears his sleeve, and his hands shake as he pulls out a can of medical foam and sprays the wound. The foam seeps into the three holes in his arm, and the burning sensation makes him from the pain, while the foam changes from white to a mix of orange and pink.

"Yes, yes, burn you bastards," says Ethan. He then grabs his Quick Stitch Kit and presses it against the first hole. "Okay... Okay... You did it once, you can do it again."

SNAP!

Ethan curses and kicks the seat in front of him, but he refuses to give himself a break, so he uses the QSK again, and every stitch he puts out leads to the chair in front getting kicked. Soon his three wounds are pockets of bunched-up skin, like cloth that is sewn too tight, and Ethan tries moving his arm again, but all that happens is his fingers twitching.

Ethan frowns, grabs an adrenaline syringe, and injects it into his arm. What happens next is a rush of energy, plus a pulsing and thick veins throbbing. His hand clenches and his muscles flex with orange traveling through his veins.

Ethan grips his wrist and stares at his hand with a racing heart, as his fingers twitch and curl. Then it ends, and the trolley slides to a stop at a platform, and a wholesome chime echoes in the empty vehicle.

"*We are now at Section D,*" says the computer voice.

Ethan winces and stands up with the help of the seat. He flexes his hand and moves his bitten arm, which feels thicker than normal, much to his discomfort, and his sleeve is now flapping with metal plating. But seeing as there is nothing he can do about that and how his injured arm works well enough, he goes to the door.

"Fuck this ship, and fuck space," says Ethan.

Ethan goes to the door and punches the window, leaving a fist-sized crack in it, and then he unlocks the door and pulls it open.

"And fuck you, Onyx, for giving us these things. Asshole planet," adds Ethan.

Ethan gets off the trolley and sees a sign above the platform's broken door, reading "Section D." The platform and its benches are riddled with bullet holes, scorch marks, and shrapnel damage, and there is a guard laying by the door, and weapons are scattered on the platform.

Ethan quickly inspects the weapons, finding plenty of ammo for his rifle and pistol, and when he takes what he can carry, he approaches the dead guard. There is a large, dark red gash going from his collar down to his pelvis. It has covered his armor in blood and left broken bones and organs exposed, putting him in a large area of dried crimson. Next to the guard is a shotgun.

Looking around, Ethan reloads his rifle, then pokes the guard. Nothing happens, so he pulls him away from the wall and inspects him, finding shotgun ammo, another pistol with some ammo, and a couple of cans of medical foam.

Once Ethan confiscates the shotgun, plus the ammo and the cans, he checks the shotgun's magazine, finds ammo in it, and then inspects the chamber and finds a slug in it. He slips the magazine back in and aims it at the guard. It is at this moment that Ethan realizes two things.

First, the world seems dimmer. The whole environment is already dark with the failing lights and dark colors of the metal, but now there is an extra layer of grayness. Everything also seems flatter.

He did not notice this at first, but now that he is not running for survival, or patching himself up, he runs his hand over the right side of his face, wincing as his fingers brush and accidentally peel pieces of burnt skin and muscle. His fingers brush against bone, and when they reach his eye, a finger dips inside an empty socket.

Ethan's hand jerks away with a sharp breath, then with a shaky hand he brushes around his right eye again, feeling the burnt skin and muscle, feeling the bone and nothing where his eye should be.

"No… No. No. No! NO!" Ethan yanks off his burnt helmet and throws it against the trolley. The window shatters and he screams, stomps, and claws at his hair, marking his dark red hair with his tainted blood. "Damn it! You took my eye, too, you fucking ship!"

He huffs, scratches his hair again, and then pulls out a bandage and shakily wraps the burned portion of his face. As he is wrapping, a loud bang makes him jump and turn to the broken door. He strains his eye to see down the hallway.

Lights flicker in the hallway, and a buzzing grates his ears.

Dark to light. Dark to light. Dark to light.

Ethan squints his eye.

His back can really feel the weight of the new gear, and even with the quick patch job on his arm he still feels the sting of the wounds, and the odd pulsing has also returned.

Dark to light.

There is a message on the wall at the far end.

Dark to light.

Ethan creeps closer to the door.

Dark to light.

The message is simple: *Turn Back NOW!*

DING!

Ethan looks over his shoulder, and he pales when he sees the trolley pulling forward with the door closing and the words "Next Stop: Section E" scrolling across its length.

"Shit!"

Ethan runs towards the trolley, skids to a stop, and grabs a lamppost to stop himself from going over the edge. Half of his body hangs over the edge, giving him a view of the far drop below. His ribs rattle from his racing heart, and his stomach rises to his throat as he looks at the one-hundred-foot drop. Down below is a thick layer of plants covering the floor and pollen rolling from the abominations lumbering around.

Staring at such a drop gives Ethan the feeling that the world is being sucked away, and when he pulls himself back, he falls on his rump and presses his hand against his racing heart, and watches the trolley go with a lump in his throat. Then he presses his back against the lamp-post and covers his face. If his throat wasn't sore from all his screaming earlier, he would scream now, but all he can do is tremble in silence.

Moments later, he drags his fingers down his face, leaving thin streaks of blood on his skin and bandage, and he stares ahead with a bloodshot eye.

His face is burned, he lost an eye, his body is broken, he is separated from his team, and now he missed his trolley because he was an idiot. What a lousy day.

Ethan remains in his spot for another minute or two before he looks down the passage. He can see the red lights of the trolley in the distance, and he takes a deep breath and stands up. He looks at the trolley for another few seconds before he approaches the broken door.

When he reaches the Section D door, he stares down the hallway, watching the lights flicker and hating the smell of rot seeping into his nose. As much as he would like to heed the warning on the wall, he knows he has no choice but to go forward, so that is exactly what he does. However, before he can pass through, Marian's broken audio box suddenly appears in front of him.

"Ethan, can you hear me?" asks Marian hastily.

"I can." Ethan peeks past the projection and is grateful to see nothing is in the hallway. "I'm still trying to find my way to you guys."

"Well, that's going to be hard since I got separated from the others when those things attacked us. I had to crawl through a vent to get away from them. Second, I haven't been able to get in contact with anybody. You're the only one to answer me."

A distant clank jerks Ethan's heart, and he leaps out of the doorway and presses himself against the wall.

"Can I be honest with you?" asks Marian.

"Sure, why not?" replies Ethan.

"I can't help but get the feeling that Bon Voyage *is a portal to Abonyys, and I feel Shavidin watching me. The symbols all over the place remind me of what the Shavidin worshippers did to summon summon demons."*

"So, this is a Shavadin worshipping thing?"

"No. The symbol is different. Shavadin has a crescent star as the symbol. This is some kind of eco-evil thing. I don't know what this is, but Moon was right. There is something evil here."

"I agree... So, who's Shavadin?"

"'Fallen Star' in Wyvinoor. It is Winter 9's devil."

"I take it you're from Winter 9."

"Me and Riva are born and raised, and Abraham moved there from the New Africa Territories."

Ethan forces a light chuckle and slides to the floor as he rests his shotgun against his body. "Right, the amazing slopes and..."

"Hot chocolate," finishes Marian. *"And little villages called Hutchniis. Me and Riva grew up in the same Hutchnii, called Morjeinstej, and it was beautiful. You know, each of those little towns has its own soul, its own... own identity... You need to see them to appreciate how beautiful they are."*

"I will, and you'll show me and everybody else the sights. We're all getting out of here. Just tell me where you are, and I'll find you."

"I'm in Section E. I'm heading to the Medical-" A loud thud and screech echoes from Marian's feed. Then there is faint, but multiple stuttering clicks echoing in the background. *"Oh, shit."*

"Marian?" says Ethan.

"I need to go."

"Marian, what's going on?"

Marian's audio box disappears.

"Marian!" Ethan tries to reconnect, but "Blocked" appears in front of him. "Oh no."

Ethan jumps to his feet and rushes through the door, but skids to a stop when he sees a tall, frail man in an apron with the entwined tree made from blood, swaying in his spot underneath the failing light. He is blocking the message and looking at Ethan with his head tilted to the side. His cheek is cut, his eyes are bright with orange veins bulging under his skin, and his hands twitch with a large knife gleaming in the light. His other hand has sprouted wooden claws, with his fleshy, thorn-wrapped fingers twitching under the sharp wood, and above him is a camera.

"One by one we go," recites the Tainted. He walks forward with heavy steps and his head straightens out. "When it stops, we don't know."

Ethan aims his shotgun at the Tainted. "Don't you dare!"

The Tainted walks faster. "One by one we go."

"Don't come any closer!"

The Tainted is now running with his knife raised. "When it stops, we don't know!"

"Stop!"

"One by one we go!"

Ethan fires.

14

Section D

The blast from Ethan's shotgun blows open the Tainted's chest, splattering the floor with blood and bits of bone and plant. The deafening bang echoes down the hall, and as the Tainted thrashes on the floor, multiple screams and rushing steps overlap as the flailing shadows stretch and shrink on the wall. Ethan curses and swaps his shotgun with his rifle and aims down the hall. As soon as he does this, a group of Tainted rush around the corner.

Ethan sprays them with bullets, and they jerk and collapse with blood splattered on the walls and spreading on the floor. After he guns down the Tainted, he stays put, panting, and snapping his sights over each of the mutilated bodies.

When they do not move, he trudges down the hallway, and to be safe, he fires a burst into each of their heads as he passes them. This empties the last of his ammo, so he discards his empty magazine and slips a new one in without stopping.

The hallway is now silent, save for the faint hum and crackles of electricity, and the heartbeats thumping in Ethan's ears. As he travels down the hallway, he stays close to the wall. He passes more bullet holes, scratches, and shrapnel, and when he reaches the message at the end of the hall, he rounds the corner and finds a locked door.

He uses his Master Key Band to unlock it, and the door's red circle changes to blue. The door slides open, revealing a poster of a smiling family sitting on a checkered blanket with food around them as an advertisement for the Terrarium. But a spider web crack on its Plexiglas shell and a hole in the child's head ruins the pleasant picture. Blood covers the child and is splattered on the parents, and it streaks down and pools on the floor, where it turns to another streak that goes down the hallway.

Ethan trails the blood with his light and finds it stops in front of one of the locked doors (marked D-101). He keeps himself pressed against the wall as he continues down the hallway, carefully stepping over bullet casings, clothes, and bits of rotting flesh and broken bone.

The hallway lights cast a dim orange hue on the locked doors and metal walls, and the red lights on the doors remind him of the eyes of a predator watching their next meal. Or the eyes of the Voice, which has another camera in the middle of the hallway watching him.

Ethan ignores the camera and rounds another corner and finds more locked rooms lining a dark hallway. Red locked lights reflect off the doors, bathing the hallway, scattered clothes, destroyed carts, and open luggage cases in a red hue.

He continues down that path with quick steps and his rifle at the ready. His bitten arm and wounded shoulder throbs, and they feel like they are both growing and ready to tear open.

This brings Ethan to grind his teeth, and he stops to massage his shoulder. But he pauses when he hears a woman's bloodcurdling shriek and cackling coming from one of the locked rooms.

He snaps his rifle left to right, with his light shining on the carnage. The shriek and maniac laughter return, and a series of bangs and thuds travel through the dark, prompting Ethan to take a step back while sweeping the area with his rifle with more fervor.

"Get back!" screams a man. "Stay back!"

There is a loud buzz, and the man's screaming turns into a wet gurgling sound, and the same buzz abruptly silences the woman's cries.

Ethan freezes, and he aims his rifle at the door where the noises came from. The door flashes green and slides open, and a man stumbles out, pressing his hands against a gash across his chest that has soaked his blue-bodied and yellow-banded jumpsuit in blood. His eyes are bulging, tainted blood dribbles from his mouth in thick globs, and his wheezes are wet and weak. Then he collapses on the floor, twitches, and stops moving.

Ethan stares at the man, shaking and watching in silence as the blood spreads across the floor. A moment later, he reluctantly goes forward, keeping close to the wall, and he aims his rifle at the open door.

The light shows the thick trail of blood left behind by the man, and inside the room is a pair of beds pushed together. The sheets are strewn across the floor, and the only light in the room beside Ethan's is a collection of lit candles with their wax melted on the metal dressers and shelves.

Dots and splashes of blood cover the walls, floor, and ceiling, and in the small kitchen, a table is knocked over with scattered food and metal dishes on the floor, with a circular saw blade lodged in the fridge. Next to the fridge is a headless woman lying in a thick pool of orange-tinted blood, and her head has rolled to the other side of the room.

Ethan steps back and looks down when he steps on something. He sees it is a vent grate, and he snaps his rifle directly up and sees a black pit in the ceiling where the vent opening is. He quickly backs away until he hits the bed, causing it to scrape against the floor.

The sound carries down the dead hallway, which brings him to cringe and lock himself in place. Nothing happens, but it is enough for him to return to the hallway with speed. He steps over the dead man while doing so, but he accidentally steps in his blood, which leads to a trail of bloody footprints when he hurries down the hallway.

The trip down the corridor is tense and quiet, with the only sound being the humming lights and scraping and thuds in the ceiling. The scrapes and thuds are a cause of concern for Ethan, so he occasionally tilts his rifle up to the vents, but nothing comes out of them. Soon he reaches the end and rounds a corner, finding a passage with no doors.

The light is at the far end, in an open area with a large sign above the entrance, reading:

◀*Transit Station*

Elevators▶

Sec. D Mess Hall▶

▲*Sec. D 201-299*

▲*Sec. D Supervisor Office*

▲*Sec. D Extracurricular Activities Hall*

CLA-CLANG!

Ethan jumps into the wall, heart thumping and hands shaking as he aims his rifle at the corner where he just came from. A loud screech echoes in the hall, and a Haunter bolts around the corner, flailing its giant claws and its screaming mouth wide open.

Ethan shoots its chest open and shoots off a piece of its head and shoulder, bringing it to fall as a twisted mess on the ground, twitching and pumping blood everywhere, while its vines wiggle around. Then a nearby vent breaks opens, and another Haunter leaps down, followed by two more.

They rush him and he shoots them, brightening the hall with muzzle flashes and sending sprays of blood and broken bark to hit the walls and floor with the clattering bullet casings. Ethan runs past their mutilated bodies as they break apart and the vines stitch them together. As he runs, a flood of overlapping screams, shrieks, and screeches come from down the other end of the hall.

Shadows stretch and snap across the light in the open area, and a couple of seconds later, a swarm of Tainted rush into view, pushing and slashing at each other to get through their door. They get stuck when they bunch up in the doorway.

Ethan continues running, and he runs faster when he hears the warbled, overlapping roar of a Stitcher. Then its lumbering steps shake the floor.

Ethan briefly loses his footing, and he jumps through a door, locks it, and backs up with a burning throat and shriveled lungs. The heavy steps approach the door, then the door bends with a loud thud, and another spot bends, and sparks fly from its edges.

He backs up and jumps when a pair of claws puncture the door, and then his nose tingles uncomfortably from an odd smell. He looks behind him and sees a tipped-over cart with warning labels on it and a lot of spilled chemicals with flammable warning labels. The cart is also next to a wall panel that has been removed, thus exposing pipes, and a blowtorch with fuel cans is next to it.

The claws pierce the door again, and Ethan grins, draws his pistol, and backs up while tapping his trigger.

"Come on, a little more," says Ethan.

The claws pierce the door in multiple parts and begin forcing it open. Ethan's one eye gets a yellow glow mixed with his green eyes, as his smile widens.

"Closer…"

The door sparks as the metal bends, and the swarm behind the Stitcher is more than eager to get through. The metal screeches and sparks bounce off the four heads and bulky shoulders of the Stitcher while its vines whip the air.

"The door is sealed. Save us. Help me. Kill me," says the Stitcher as it lumbers forward with its claws scraping the floor and sharp thorns wrapping around its limbs.

The floor shakes from its fast and heavy steps, and the swarm of Tainted rush forward. Ethan takes a few more steps back, and when the Stitcher is close to the cart, he shoots at the gas canister.

There is a flash of heat and light, and a force pushes Ethan back while fire rolls over the swarm. The lights in the room are blown out, the Tainted are blasted off their feet, and the Stitcher roars as fire eats its body.

The colorful chemical fire is the only light in the room now, and the Stitcher stumbles around, its vines snap sporadically, or shrivel and fall off. Ethan grabs his rifle, and the fire reflects off his yellow tinted green eye as his smile widens from watching the abominations thrash around and scream in agony.

The exposed pipe has its jagged edges facing outward, and the cart is scattered into pieces. A small lake of fire is consuming the Stitcher as it limps forward, with pieces breaking off and parts of the cart embedded in it.

Ethan then goes to gunning them down. One by one they go. Bullet after bullet tears into the Tainted, and the room becomes thick with smoke. The burning chemicals burn Ethan's eye and make his lungs scratchy, and these, plus the stench of burning flesh and plant, tingle his nose.

But Ethan is not done. He must kill them. He must kill them all. So that is what he does, whether it is by shooting them or beating them down. He makes sure they are no longer moving. When the last of the Tainted is killed, he turns to the Stitcher and sees that it is motionless, with patches of fire bursting through its bark, and its heads are now balls of fire.

Ethan chuckles and scratches his head, taking some of his red hair off, and he looks down the corridor. He sees the door is broken with an emergency fire symbol trying to be projected above it. The door is bent and can barely move, but beyond that is a bright light.

His chuckling fades and tears roll from his eye as he walks forward, trying to laugh at the sheer luck of his survival. His chuckling turns to an odd mix of whimpers and cackles, and his damaged arm and shoulder throb more, bringing him to shoulder his rifle and massage his arm.

When he reaches the light, he squints his eye and steps through the broken doorway. He finds himself in an exceptionally clean part of the ship. The area is free of blood, free of any kind of damage, the lights are good, and even a schedule board is displaying everything smoothly. From extracurricular classes to mealtimes, hours of operations for the clinics and section administrators, and even a large bulletin at the bottom that reads, *"Captain Junjie Ding's Birthday Party in Sec. D Mess Hall. Bring presents!"*

Next to the board is a picture of a middle-aged Chinese man with an awkward smile, and his white-and-gold-banded captain's suit seems too big for him. Just looking at him gives Ethan a sense of pity; it is like looking at a boy who is biting off more than he can chew, just to impress somebody or prove a point. Chances are he had a miserable end, just like everyone else on *Bon Voyage.*

With that thought, Ethan shakes his head and goes towards the transit station. It is down yet another hallway, and as Ethan walks, the buzzes and garbled words from the speakers reappear. Their noises flow down the empty hall, and emergency lights shine on crudely painted arrows pointing towards the Section D Transit Station. Someone was also kind enough to use white paint to leave an extensive set of tally marks near one set of arrows; and the tally marks surround a crudely painted entwined tree. Next to all that, in more white paint, is the message, *"FUCK U CPT DING!"*

Said message is in front of a camera that is trailing Ethan, and he ignores it. He has a mission to do, and the camera is the least of his worries. Which, speaking of his worries, Marian's audio box appears, and it is breaking apart into pixels and bars.

"Ethan, can you hear me?" says Marian.

"I can hear you. Are you alright?" says Ethan.

"Where are you?"

"I'm in Section D and am heading towards its transit station."

"So, you're close then? That's good because I still haven't been able to get a hold of anybody else."

"Where are you now?"

"I'm held up in the Section E Medical Facility. I locked myself in the supervisor's office to separate me from those things." Marian chuckles grimly. Then her chuckle turns to a shaky laugh, and there is banging on her end. *"These demons not get me!"*

Marian's laughing ends with a long sigh, and her audio box flickers out for a moment, before it reappears as a scattered mess and her voice warped.

"Ethan, we must get out of here. We need to get out, do you understand?" says Marian.

"I understand, Marian, and I'm coming to get you. Just stay there and remain calm," says Ethan.

"I'm in charge. I. Give. The orders. Me. Me. It is me that's in charge, remember? Do you remember?"

"I remember."

"'I remember, ma'am.' Remember the ma'am. Remember, it's me. I'm in charge. Me. Don't abandon me, Ethan."

"I-"

The feed disconnects.

"Won't."

Ethan is about to contact Marian again but stops when a vent grate crashes in front of the doorway to the transit station. The metallic crash sounds like thunder with its noise being carried through the dead area, and a couple of seconds later, a woman drops with a metallic thud and a large, handheld saw with a battery pack.

She lands awkwardly on the floor, giggling and kicking her legs in the air. Ethan takes a step back, feeling a painful tingle run up his spine and through his infected arm.

The woman makes a cold, shrill cackle and rolls on her hands and knees. Then she grabs her saw and rises in the middle of the doorway. Her lanky form towers over Ethan, and she sways in her spot with the light shining on her back and darkening her features. She gives Ethan a good look and giggles. Her unfocused yellow-tinted and orange eyes glow in the shadows, hiding her face.

"What the hell?" whispers Ethan.

"I know you. I hear you. I see you. I follow you. Now I meet you again," says the woman, her voice low and hissing like a snake.

"What? Who are you?" says Ethan.

The strange woman stalks forward, shifting from one foot to the other as her body dips and weaves slightly, with strands of her hair occasionally covering portions of her yellow and orange eyes. This brings Ethan to step back and raise his shotgun.

"Stay back!" orders Ethan.

"Ethan, Ethan, I follow you from our first vent. I hear you talk to the Voice. I hear you talk to **ugly. Pixel. Box!** It knows, we know, I know, we all know, you're lonely, Ethan. Lonely, lonely Ethan," says the woman.

The woman is now underneath a light, and Ethan sees she is wearing black security armor over a thick gray jumpsuit. Her armor is damaged with scratches and dents, and on her hips are boxes of saw blades. She has long, rough brown hair, and black bags under her yellow and orange reptilian eyes clash with her bone-white, scaly skin, which has orange veins moving beneath it. Her hands are long and bony, her smile is wide, with her cheeks nearly tearing, and she grips her saw tight. It is then that Ethan realizes that he is talking to the spliced human from earlier, and he doesn't even want to scan her. He can tell she is infected with the Onyx Spore.

"But you don't have to be alone, Ethan. Gary needs a friend," continues the woman. "I need friends, too. We all need friends, and *Bon Voyage* wants us. Come with me. Come, come, we'll be friends!"

Hearing that name sparks the memory of the note he read a few hours ago, and cold dread travels through his veins as his bitten arm twitches with the realization of who he is talking to.

"I don't want to meet Gary, or anyone else," says Ethan, taking another step back. "...Carmen."

The woman, Carmen, takes another step forward, hissing and tightening her grip on her saw.

"You said you wanted to be Gary's friend. Gary needs friends. Ethan needs friends. I need friends!" says Carmen.

Ethan gulps and Carmen aims her saw at Ethan, her cheeks tearing as her grin grows and her eyes glow brighter as she revs her saw.

"Let's be friends!" says Carmen.

15

Carmen

The saw whirs to full speed, and Carmen's eyes and mouth open wide with her loud, shrill cackling, and she rushes towards Ethan. The saw blade is launched at Ethan while she runs, and he leaps out of the way.

The circular blade is impaled into a wall with a shower of sparks. Ethan shoots Carmen, but the slug hits an invisible barrier that ripples with bright blue light, and with that comes a blue glow on her back from a device that looks like metallic vertebrae.

This catches Ethan off guard, which gives Carmen enough time to draw another saw blade and swing it at him like a knife. Ethan evades it, and she slides the saw blade into her device and brings it down on him while revving it. Ethan has just enough time to grab Carmen's arms, and the two lock eyes, while the saw slices the air above his forehead.

He can feel the sharp wind against his skin. His arms quiver, his bitten arm throbs and tightens, and he grits his teeth while Carmen grins and puts more force in her attempt.

She flicks her tongue out, revealing its forked appearance and her sharp teeth, and Ethan twists his body and forces the saw into the wall. Sparks fly and screeching, snapping, breaking metal echoes in the chamber.

Ethan's vision is knocked out of focus when Carmen headbutts him. Ethan retaliates by kicking out her footing and slamming her head into the wall.

Then he yanks out his pistol and tries shooting her in the head, but Carmen kicks him back, leading the shot to fly off far away from them. She yanks out another saw blade from her belt and swipes at Ethan.

Ethan jumps back, and Carmen disconnects her saw from the blade in the wall, slips the new one in, and takes large steps towards Ethan. He runs from her as fast as he can, and her steps pick up speed, and her hissing turns to cackles.

"Where are you going, Ethan? You troublemaker, you!" laughs Carmen.

Her rapid steps trail Ethan, and he is too scared to look over his shoulder as the running, crazed cackling and saw's buzzing get closer. The hallway has a straight shot to the mess hall, and the closer the door gets, the faster Ethan runs, despite the pain in his legs and the burning in his throat and lungs.

At the last push, his feet are barely touching the ground, and as soon as he passes through the mess hall door, he slams his palm against the door lock. His band flashes red, the green holographic circle turns red, and the door slams shut, cutting off Carmen right as she leaps from the darkness. Immediately after the door closes, there is a thud and a scream of pain.

The saw stops, and Ethan steps back, chest heaving, throat and lungs burning, and hands shaking. His legs collapse and he falls to the floor, pressing his hand against his chest as he watches the door. He jumps when there is another thud, and then the saw revs and the door vibrates with sparks flying and a saw blade poking through several seconds later.

Ethan swears and aims his rifle at the door, but as soon as he does this, the cutting stops, leaving a piece of the dull and broken saw poking through with a thin cut in the metal. Nothing else happens after that, but the hair on his neck still stands, and a sharp tingle runs through his spine and his wounded arm. He takes a couple of steps away from the door, watches it for a few more seconds, and then turns around and jumps from the carnage before him.

The tables of the mess hall are tipped over and pushed together to make barricades, and most of the barricades are sliced, crushed, or riddled with bullet holes. Bullet casings litter the floor with bits and pieces of the creatures, as well as severed parts of the humans that once occupied the ship. At the far end of the mess hall is a set of plastic swing doors, a metal door marked "Kitchen Garden," and far across from those is a crushed food bar with its jagged edges and broken glass coated in blood.

Ethan looks around without moving, half-expecting Carmen to re-start sawing or for a Haunter to break through one of the many large vents in the room. But after nothing happens for a couple of minutes, Ethan goes further into the room, stopping at a rotten arm that has been ripped from its socket, leaving a white bone tip poking past the torn skin and muscle.

He grimaces and continues his walk, passing damaged pillars, torn Federation flags, shattered dishes, and an evacuation message on a broken screen advising everybody to remain calm. It is during his walk that he finds a circle of trampled presents, broken glass, and crusty cake splattered all over the floor. The table that the presents and cake were on is also smashed. Above it is a banner from the ceiling with speckles of blood. The banner reads, "Happy Birthday, Captain Ding!"

Ethan continues across the mess hall and checks his map, finding he needs to go through the Garden. So that is where he goes. When he opens the door, he immediately coughs and covers his mouth and nose.

The atmosphere is an odd tint of orange and green, and a thick carpet of pollen covers the floor with a thin amount floating in the air, much like on Oros after a pollen storm. His feet slide across the floor with his steps, kicking up the pollen, and stretching from floor to ceiling almost thirty feet high are thick vines that are fusing to masses that resemble trees; many, many trees.

These trees have taken over the equipment, covered the pipes, carts, crates, and tools. All of them have been consumed and fused to them are dozens upon dozens of bodies. From mangled to intact; sullen faced to agony; mad to horrified. The skin on these faces has been stretched and has turned green with patches of bark, and branches, and bulbs protruding from their heads and twisted limbs. Their torsos have fused to these thick vines, and roots have sprouted from their fingers and toes, locking the vines to the floor, wall, and ceiling.

Ethan's eye waters and darts between the many faces in the trees. The faces' mouths are wide open, but they have no eyes, yet he feels like they are looking at him, *screaming* at him. Screaming, crying, begging, he hears it all.

His heart races, and he steps back with heavy breaths and his bitten arm twitching. Then, thick drool splatters in front of him with stuttering clicks, and he slowly looks up, and his blood freezes.

Hanging upside down from the ceiling rafters is a Lurker, staring at him with its sack of flesh-eating bugs pulsing from its breathing.

The Lurker launches itself at Ethan, and he scrambles back, slipping on the pollen as the creature lands where he was just seconds earlier. A thick cloud of pollen is kicked up from its landing, briefly shrouding the Lurker, and it roars and charges Ethan while he runs out of the garden.

When Ethan returns to the mess hall, the vents break open and Haunters drop in. Ethan skids to a stop and takes a sharp turn as the new group rushes him with the Lurker joining them.

Ethan quickly swaps his pistol for his rifle and shoots the Lurker, just to be rammed by a Haunter. It pins him against the wall and lifts him up, scraping his back against the metal. It raises its claws for a killing blow, but Ethan uses his infected hand to punch it in the face, breaking off its lower jaw.

It staggers back, gurgling with vines slithering out of its throat, and Ethan shoots it in the upper chest and head with his rifle, pulverizing its head. The Haunter stumbles and collapses with a thick layer of blood coating it, Ethan, and the floor.

He snaps to the others and unloads on them. There is no aiming involved, only screaming, and shooting as many as he can.

Each gunshot is deafening, and the recoil is like a punch to Ethan's shoulder, but it keeps them back and punches plenty of holes in them. Some drop and stop moving, and others fall to the ground, just to crawl to their fallen comrades.

Ethan is about to shoot those, but the Lurker tackles him and drags him across the floor. As they go, Ethan punches the abdomen, popping its sack. The bugs crawl all over Ethan, and the Lurker roars, slams him down, and stabs his chest, piercing just enough of the engineering suit so he can feel the tips of its claws poke his skin.

The Lurker's claws get stuck in the suit, and it lifts Ethan and swings him against a table. The table breaks on impact, and all air is forced out of Ethan's lungs with a ringing in his ears and a sharp pain going through his back.

The Lurker then leaps on top of him and raises its talons, but right as it is about to gut him, he draws his pistol and empties his magazine into it. The creature jerks with each shot and then goes limp when the top of its head is shot off. It collapses on top of Ethan, which not only squishes the bugs gnawing on him, but also pushes all the air out of him again.

Ethan winces, pushes the Lurker off, and then he grabs his rifle and shoots the Haunters that are trying to stitch themselves together, being sure to aim for their heads. And for good measure, he hawks a tainted, bloody glob of spit on the closest one and kicks another.

Then he hears a loud thud echo from above his head, followed by quick and rough scrapes and shuffles that travel towards a vent grate. The vent grate dents with a loud bang, and Ethan stiffens.

There is another bang. The dent grows, and Ethan swears and runs to the swing doors. The doors bang against the walls as Ethan passes through them, and right as he enters, there is a pair of thuds. One metallic and the other heavier, with Carmen's eerie giggles coming soon after.

The backroom is filled with rows of dirty make-lines, dead screens, mechanical humming, and a buzzing over the speakers. The air reeks of spoiled vegetables, rotten cheese, and burnt meat, with some grills burnt-out entirely, and some of the make-lines still having partially made meals on their platforms. The backroom is also shrouded in darkness with bands of light sweeping back and forth, stretching and shrinking the shadows as the doors swing. Carmen's giggles float through the air, as her steps get closer.

"Where are you, Troublemaker?" calls Carmen.

Ethan slides behind one of the make-lines, biting his lip and breathing heavily through his nose as he clutches his rifle close to his chest. The swooshing of the doors mixes with Carmen's steps and Ethan's heart, and his eye lifts to look at the light swaying on the wall.

The swaying abruptly stops with Carmen's shadow taking up the middle with her hand holding the door open. There is no movement for a few seconds, but Ethan does not dare peek out. His eye is focused on the shadow, and when it moves, he squishes himself further into the make-line.

"I know you're in here..." sings Carmen.

Carmen's hissing voice floats through the abandoned room as she slowly walks in, and the doors finally shut, with only two circles of light shining through the windows. Ethan sucks in his breath and peeks around the corner.

Carmen's body is a silhouette in the dark, but Ethan can see that her back is turned, and her fingers tap against her saw as she shifts from one foot to the other, body dipping and weaving with each step. When she rounds the corner of a make-line, Ethan creeps across the floor, freezing when the steps take a sudden turn closer to him.

"Playing hide and seek, are we, Troublemaker?" says Carmen.

She revs her saw, and Ethan's heart almost jumps through his mouth. His fingers rapidly tap against the trigger guard from their trembles, and his face hurts from keeping his jaw shut, while beads of sweat claw at his skin. It drips off his nose, and his nostrils flare from his suppressed breathing as his heart thumps hard against his ribs.

Carmen's silhouette moves further down. Ethan stays low to the ground as he backs up and slides around the make-lines, blinking sweat out of his eyes and fearful that Carmen will hear his racing heart.

"Where are you?" calls Carmen.

Carmen stops just shy of Ethan's spot, and he bites his lip hard enough to draw blood. He lays flat to look beneath the line. Carmen's feet are pointed to where his head is, and as soon as they turn so her back is facing him, he slowly shifts into a crouching positing, cringing as his pads scratch the metal floor. But the buzzing and the ship's humming seem to be enough to shield him.

"Sneaky, sneaky, Troublemaker," says Carmen. "Yes, yes. Sneaky."

Carmen leaves her spot, and her steps get fainter by the second. A door opens and shuts on the other end, leaving Ethan with the buzzing and humming, but he refuses to move from his position.

He strains his eye and ears for any sign of Carmen trying to pull a fast one on him, but even when he does not hear her, he does not move for some time. He only moves when his limbs cramp, and even then, he stays crouched and moves slowly, stopping at the end of his make-line when he hears snapping and multiple screams overlapping screeches and thrashes that make loud bangs, and then heavy running followed by silence.

With the return of silence, Ethan stares in the dark with a wide eye and a tense throat When nothing happens for a few more minutes, he crouch-walks towards the mess hall, and gives one more scan in the kitchen before he carefully stands up and looks outside. The Haunters and Lurker are missing.

Ethan takes a deep, shaky breath, checks his ammo, and then gradually pushes the door open. He slips out, guides the door shut to minimize its noise, and then he hurries towards the door leading to the transit station, which has been torn open.

He keeps his light off as he passes through. His senses are heightened in the darkness while he moves down the hallway, only stopping to pick up his shotgun.

When he reaches the platform, he is both angry and not surprised to see that the trolley has left. So, he shakes his head and goes back to the mess hall. He can use the Garden to get to where he needs to go, anyway.

"Damn space shit," grumbles Ethan.

16

Reunion

Nothing happens during Ethan's return to the Garden, and during his walk, he checks his map just to be sure he is going the right way for the alternate route. Fortunately, he is.

Upon entering the Garden, he covers his mouth with his hand and looks at the ceiling. He is grateful to see nothing hiding up there, so he hurries through the large room. When he is about midway through the room, Marian's broken audio box appears in front of him.

"Do you see them?" asks Marian, still out of view.

"Marian," starts Ethan hesitantly, "I can't see anything, There's just an audio box."

Ethan exits the Garden and enters a hallway. Marian's audio box flickers and Ethan sweeps the area with his rifle, finding nothing trying to kill him.

"They're there. They're hiding, but they aren't fooling me," says Marian. *"And neither are the others. They play nice, but don't be fooled. They are **raviks!** They sneak and steal more of the cuts behind your back."*

"Hold on, what are you talking about?" asks Ethan.

"I'll see you soon. Don't let those raviks bite you."

Marian's feed ends, and Ethan quickens his steps to a run, but as he runs, he steps on a vent grate in the middle of the floor. Immediately, a large vine with slimy mandibles slams him into the floor with an echoing thud.

His ears ring, his body becomes stiff from shock. Then he is pulled into the dark vent, leaving just his screams to carry down the hallway, without a body.

The vent opening rapidly shrinks, and tiny lights fly past Ethan. The vine's mandibles hold Ethan tight, and he grits his teeth and presses his hands and feet against the vent walls. Sparks fly and the scraping of metal and popping of tiny lights ring in his ears, but his gloves and boots do nothing to stop the pull.

The vine takes a sudden turn, rattling Ethan's insides and slamming him into the shaft's ceiling. He releases another scream as it continues its pull, making sure he bounces off the vent's surface.

The next thing he knows, he is pulled into a large chamber and dangles upside down. His blood rushes to his head and his eye tries to focus on the beast in front of him as he sways in the air. When he sees what has him, his thrashing becomes more desperate, and his screams and curses become louder.

In front of Ethan is a massive plant creature with thick roots, locking it into the walls, floor, and ceiling. Its bulbous skin is covered in bark, and branches and thorns protrude from it, while its vines dig into the vents or snake across the floor. There are also faint faces and bodies fused to it, and many of those bodies have mutated into bulbs that eject pollen into the air, which linger for some time before settling on the floor to create a carpet. In its center is a circular mouth filled with sharp teeth, and around the mouth are a multitude of eyes, all looking in different directions and shining from the lights overhead.

The vines take Ethan closer to the ring of teeth, and he yanks out his pistol and shoots at the vine holding him. A few shots pass before the appendage snaps with a spray of orange blood, and the beast shrieks in pain, as Ethan falls with the vine.

The impact of the landing, plus the weight of the vine, leaves him wheezing for air, but he quickly finds the strength to pull himself out of the mess, leaving him covered in goo, orange gore, and scrapes and rips in his engineer suit. Once free, he aims his rifle at another vine that is snaking its way towards him.

The bullets rip off chunks of the vine, and the Beast's cries of pain shake his bones. The vine he shot writhes and snaps around, and he keeps shooting it until the vine snaps. The Beast roars again and slams another vine towards Ethan. He leaps out of the way, stumbling and tripping over a severed vine, and the room shakes when the Beast's vine hits the floor.

As Ethan gets up, he notices an open door not too far from him, so he runs towards it, grinding his teeth as his battered muscles burn. Another vine snakes across the floor and swings at him, and he takes a flying leap to the door, but the vine clips him and sends him spinning.

Ethan hits the door frame, bounces into the hallway, and skids on the floor, with his rifle sliding out of his reach. When he stops, he groans and turns on his side as pain radiates through his ribs and spine.

The vine slides towards him, and he draws his pistol. The vine coils for a strike, and right as it is about to grab Ethan, somebody with a rifle shoots it. The firepower reduces the appendage to bloody ribbons, and the Beast howls and retracts its mangled vine with floppy motions, splashing Ethan, the other person, and the surrounding area in orange blood.

The figure then quickly limps past Ethan and closes and locks the door. The roar still shakes the door, and the figure jumps back and Ethan hurries to his feet with his rifle in hand when the Beast bangs against the door. The attack dents the door, and the Beast strikes the door again, warping it and sending sparks flying.

Ethan aims his rifle at the door, waiting for a third hit, but it never comes. The two remain still, and the only noise they make is their heavy breathing. Seconds later, Ethan swallows and flashes a weary smile at his companion, who is frazzled with blood staining her hairline, and her suit is crudely patched, and covered in blood and scorch marks. Her left hand is bandaged with blots of pink and orange dotting it, and her light-brown makeup has run down her cheeks like streaks of tears.

"Obrigado," says Ethan.

Riva Bonnevue snatches Ethan in a tight hug, and he briefly loses all movement because of his muscles locking. When Riva backs away, her hand is trembling, and her brown eyes shimmer as she smiles with tears trickling down her cheeks.

"Thank God you dropped in. I was worried you didn't make it," says Riva, her voice airy and weak. She sniffles and wipes her eyes, and then she adjusts her grip on her rifle and tilts her head down the hall. "Follow me. Taksheel is close by."

The two walk, and Ethan notices Riva's hand is clutching her chest. Her steps quickly devolve into a stumbling cadence, with her eyes losing focus.

"Riva how far is Taksheel?" asks Ethan.

"He's in a break room just down the hall. He asked me to scout ahead for… for…" Riva slumps against the wall and swallows, as she clutches her chest tighter.

"Riva!" Ethan gets in front of her and puts his hand on her shoulder, while trying to look into her brown eyes. They are wide and shifting and tainted with yellow veins, and they shimmer as new tears trail down her cheeks. "Riva, look at me. Stay calm and look at me."

Riva swallows again and tries with little success to meet Ethan's eyes. "Don't worry, it is just *kriettejs.*"

"No, it's not. You should have never been out here," says Ethan.

"But we need to find a way to the communication relay."

"Forget about the relay. Why did Taksheel send you out here alone?"

"We need to…" Riva stops and searches Ethan's face. "Your eyes… Your eye… It's different."

Ethan's throat tightens.

"You're dying," says Riva.

"I'm not dying here, and neither are you." Ethan helps Riva up, slinks her arm over his shoulder, and helps her walk down the hallway. "Where do I need to go?"

"Straight down."

Ethan follows her direction. "Why did Taksheel send you out here alone? And where is Aiden?"

"Taksheel needs to make the bomb, and we don't know where Aiden is."

"Taksheel makes bombs?"

"Aiden taught him. We were… It was when we were on a vacation on Aarde."

"Sounds like an exciting trip."

Riva smiles. "It was, but I think I'll put in my notice after this."

Ethan forces himself to smile. "I don't blame you."

A couple of minutes later, Riva tells Ethan to stop. They are in front of a locked break room, and Riva pulls away from Ethan and plugs in her wrist-top computer. As she types in the command, Ethan scans her with his MAD. At first the device flickers and crackles, but soon the thin green lines move up and down and side to side, and it beeps when it finishes.

SUBJECT: RIVA BONNEVUE

VITALS: UNHEALTHY

>>>Heart Rate: 110 b/m

>>>Bruised Bones: Scapula, L. Fibula, L. Femur, L. Ulna, L. Humerus

>>>Damaged Bones: L. Carpal Bones, L. Metacarpal Bones

>>>Multiple cuts and bruises (click for extension)

MEDICAL FOAM APPLIED

FURTHER MEDICAL CARE NEEDED

>>>WARNING: Unknown infection. Blood examination needed.

Ethan shuts off the MAD, and the breakroom door opens, despite it still being red, and Riva unplugs her computer and motions Ethan inside. Once he enters, Riva follows him in and locks the door behind them.

Ethan stands in the middle of the breakroom, dumbstruck at what he is seeing. Aside from the vent being welded shut, the room is the best room he has seen. The furniture is intact; there's no damage anywhere; not even a speck of blood. There is even a large vending machine in the back near the bathroom that is open, revealing snacks and drinks. Off to the side at a makeshift workstation is Taksheel, hunched over, with a fan plugged into the wall that is blowing sweat off his face. There is a terminal there, too.

Taksheel is carefully working on a bundle of red fuel cylinders and batteries held together by cord and wires, and three more are in a corner next to a cart that is humming and rolling in circles, as if bored or anxious. Nearby are more crates filled with fuel cylinders, batteries, and ammo. Ethan is quick to go there and inspect the ammo.

"Taksheel, I found Ethan," says Riva.

"Cool," says Taksheel without looking up from his work. "Did you find another way to the communication relay?"

Ethan looks away from the ammo and stares at Taksheel, his hand twitching.

"No," says Riva. "We'll have to use the bomb."

"Well, that sucks. At least I am not wasting my time," says Taksheel.

Ethan suddenly grabs Taksheel and throws him against the wall with his tainted green eye flaring and his infected arm throbbing. As this happens, Taksheel draws his pistol and presses it under Ethan's chin, while Riva screams and jumps back.

"What the hell is wrong with you!?" says Ethan, his hands tightening on Taksheel.

"Stop this, please!" begs Riva.

"Do you want to get Riva killed!" says Ethan.

"Interesting eye you got there, Ethan," says Taksheel; his eyes also have a yellow tint. "Nice arm, too."

Ethan pulls and rams Taksheel into the wall again, and Riva tries to pry Ethan off, but Taksheel is not worried. He is giggling.

"Careful, Ethan. I have my gun right under your chin. One slip up and you'll be talking to Yama," says Taksheel.

Ethan is still for a moment, and then he reluctantly releases Taksheel, and Riva steps back while the two men stare at each other.

"Why did you send Riva out alone?" says Ethan.

"Why do you care? She's my girl. You're supposed to be chasing Marian," says Taksheel.

"This is no time for jokes, Taksheel. Riva almost died out there!"

Taksheel huffs dramatically. "If you must know, Riva volunteered. I needed to make this bomb to kill that thing out there, and Riva wanted to see if there was an alternate route to the relay. I didn't argue, and she left."

Ethan looks at Riva. She has taken a seat, is hunched over, and is looking between the two. She says nothing, and Ethan looks at Taksheel.

"Riva has a bad heart. She can't exert herself too much," says Ethan.

Taksheel's thespian demeanor shifts to concern. "What? Are you serious?"

Ethan nods and shows Taksheel his scan of Riva. Taksheel looks at Riva, and she looks down in shame.

"Why didn't you tell me? How long have you had this problem?" asks Taksheel.

"Winter Heart is a common ailment on Winter 9 for clones. It's just... just a thing many of us have from birth," explains Riva, her eyes still on the floor.

"You're a clone?" says Ethan.

Riva nods and shows the three-diamond tattoo on her hand. "I was born on the Three Diamonds Facility on Winter 9. I was an order for an adoption for people who couldn't conceive."

Taksheel slumps in his chair. "Why didn't you tell us about your heart? You've been on so many vacations, so many jobs, and you said you were just having jitters."

"I didn't want to be worthless. On Winter 9 I was just a pretty face. I was just-just a pretty body for my parents advertisement company," says Riva. She sniffles and tears patter to the floor below as she rubs her quivering hands. "But on the *Hook Line*, I was more than a beauty pageant model. I-I-I was more than a face on an ad, or a video stream, or-or a... a..."

Riva kneels further and grips her chest. Ethan goes to her and holds her shoulders while Taksheel stands next to her, looking down at her quizzically.

"Riva, relax. Take deep breaths and relax," says Ethan.

"I learned coding. I learned computers and falsified my records so I can be valuable. I wasn't a commodity, I wasn't a doll to be paraded... On the jobs... On the vacations... I was valuable," says Riva. She suddenly grabs her head and starts tearing out strands of her dark hair. "If you guys found out that I had a bad heart, the AATS would kick me out and I would become a prop again!"

Riva weeps, and Taksheel pats her shoulder while Ethan keeps a firm hold on her, but he looks at Taksheel curiously.

"What do you guys do on these vacations to take them so seriously?" asks Ethan.

"We smuggle stuff," replies Taksheel. He pulls Riva off the chair and has her sit on his lap while she cries on his shoulder. "Drugs, guns, information. You know, stuff."

"Smuggle? Hold on, I signed up for the AATS, not a smuggler gang!" says Ethan.

Taksheel flashes a smile. "We're raviks on the side, Ethan. Smugglers, rats, extreme adventure enthusiasts, whatever you want to call us, but we are more than AATS personnel. Funny enough, we delivered a lot of narcotics from Aarde to the Three Machetes before some nut gunned down a bunch of their guys in a fancy apartment."

Ethan's gut twists into a knot, and he pulls away from Riva.

"Raviks..." repeats Ethan.

"Ravik means 'rat' in Wyvinoor, but it also means 'smuggler.' It is all about the context," explains Taksheel.

Ethan goes to an empty chair and his legs give out, leading him to fall hard and fast on the chair with his one eye staring straight ahead, wide with shock. Taksheel keeps comforting Riva while looking at Ethan.

"You're a trooper, Ethan. I think you've surprised all of us today," says Taksheel. "We can use you on our next vacation. The Good Captain didn't trust you, but you've proven yourself. I would be honored to have you on our smuggling team. But if you don't agree, I'll probably have to kill you, just so you don't tell anybody."

"Please don't," begs Riva.

"Relax. I was joking."

Ethan's eyes are still distant, and a few seconds later, Taksheel gently places Riva back on the chair and begins pacing in a circle.

"But we still have a problem. We have raviks of our own. Section 0 is on our team. I can feel it. They're on this ship, I know it, and they used our ship for a reason. But if we find the ravik, then we can squeeze the information out of them," says Taksheel. "It's not me, it's not Riva, because they won't use someone with a bad heart, and at first I thought it was you, because you're the new guy and a weirdo."

Ethan's hand twitches.

Taksheel scratches his pistol against his head. "But then I realized it wasn't you because you're *not* trying to kill us. Plus, look at you. If you are an agent, you suck at your job."

Ethan inspects himself, and Riva looks at him with sharp flicks of her eyes, both taking in the amount of damage he has sustained over the unknown time they have been on *Bon Voyage*.

"That leaves only Aiden and Marian as Section 0 spooks. They might even be linked!" says Taksheel.

Ethan and Riva look at Taksheel, and Riva wipes her eyes.

"Taksheel, please don't do that. I know Marian. She would never do that to us," says Riva.

"You can't be serious," says Ethan.

"I am!" Taksheel takes a deep breath, and paces in circles again. "You don't know this, Ethan, but it was Marian's idea to smuggle using 'vacation' as the code word, and it is no secret that Aiden worked black ops on Aarde. He was a Tunnel Dragon. He specialized in going behind enemy lines and burning people and underground structures. And those two are close. So think about it: Honey trap or infiltration. Or both."

Taksheel goes quiet and points at Ethan and Riva with an expectant smile. But the two stare at him with annoyance from Ethan and disbelief from Riva. After a few seconds of silence, Ethan shakes his head and stands up.

"That was stupid," says Ethan. "I've wasted enough time. I'm going to get Marian. Then we can find Aiden and get to the bridge."

"Do you know where she is?" asks Taksheel.

Ethan goes to their ammo stash. "Section E Medical Center."

Taksheel smiles. "Oh, that's where she went."

"Yeah. You two stay put. Taksheel, guard Riva, and both of you keep your comms open," orders Ethan.

Then he exits the room.

17

The Stitcher of Section E

'Okay, where am I?' wonders Ethan sourly, as he looks at his map.

He is standing in the hallway... somewhere. All the halls look the same, and after snaking his way through the *Bon Voyage* for an unknown amount of time, killing a few Haunters and Tainted here and there, he has concluded that he got turned around somewhere, somehow. Now he is scanning his map intently, searching for anything that will give him clues where he is, and where he needs to go to reach Marian.

As Ethan studies the map, he finds dorms, offices, a small cafeteria, more halls, and—

His eyes suddenly lock on the "Section E Medical Center," and he selects it with his GPS and backtracks with his eye until he finds his location.

All he needs to do is go straight to the end of the hall, then take a left, then a right, then a left, and another left, then right, then right, then right, then up two flights of stairs, take a left, and go straight. Easy enough.

Ethan sets the directions on his map and goes straight down the hall for a couple of minutes before coming across the main door. The door is locked, but his Master Key Band quickly changes that, and the door slides open with a resounding bang. With the door open, Ethan sees dim lights and a message on the wall directly in front of him.

TURN BACK!

NOT SAFE!

Ethan walks down the hallway, checking his rifle as he goes, and when he gets to the message, he looks to the right and sees a line of broken doors and blood, as well as a tipped-over wheelchair. After that, he looks left and sees a hallway full of windows and doors, all with red lights on them. He goes left.

During his walk, he looks through a window and sees a long room filled with gurneys and bodies that thick vines have completely overtaken. Some bodies have open mouths with their skins stretched out, and others have their limbs extended, with roots spreading out to anchor them to the floor or walls.

Footsteps and scrapping furniture echo from another room, and a moment later, a bald mutant with light green skin and thin bark with green and yellow flower bulbs on its head stumbles out, jerking and twitching. It is wearing a tattered and bloody hospital gown with IVs hanging from its warped flesh. Its mouth is also hanging open as it gurgles, and its ribs have been opened to hold pulsing green bags. It looks at Ethan with its yellow eyes and silently charges him with its clawed hands outstretched, not even screaming, despite its mouth being wide open.

Pat-Pat-Pat-Pat

Ethan backs up and shoots it in the chest, blowing it open and showering the area with its tainted blood, plus a green substance that sizzles and causes smoke to rise as the green liquid eats the metal. This new beast, the Illwalker, stumbles around, bounces off the wall, and then falls on the floor and thrashes around, as its acid melts the metal floor.

When it stops moving, Ethan observes the body, noticing there are no vines, but the pollen from the bulbs has popped out and is now lingering. The acid has also died down, but some of it is still dripping.

It is safe enough to jump over, though, so that is what Ethan does. After jumping across the hole, he investigates the room where it came from and sees more blood, more broken and bloody gurneys. A guard in destroyed armor is laying nearby, with his throat and chest melted open, pollen coating his insides and the blood. The pollen that has clung to his melted bones and organs has grown into small flowers with thorns.

Ethan swallows and carefully approaches the corpse and gives it a light kick. Nothing happens, so he kicks it again, this time harder. Some pollen shakes off, but that is about it, so Ethan kneels and begins searching the body.

During his inspection, he finds that the guard is wearing the same spine shield generator Carmen has, only this one is destroyed, and it has Arx Corporation's logo. There is also a shotgun magazine, a medical kit with some medical foam, adrenaline, and stitches for a Quick Stitch Kit. Ethan takes all of it and quickly explores the rest of the room, finding three more cans of medical foam.

Ethan takes all the cans, goes down the hallway, and takes the first right. The area he enters is littered with vines and bulbs, and his feet kick up pollen as he walks through the area, leaving footprints behind. He also keeps his eyes and ears peeled for any unusual noises as he travels through the area.

He passes a digital screen that is displaying different images of peaceful hills, soothing night skies, and a boat on still waters. But the screen is damaged, so the pictures are warped and pixelated, and their colors reflect off the walls.

Ethan walks on, collecting a spare magazine from a pistol, and raiding a cabinet for supplies. He finds adrenaline, more medical foam, and stitching wire, as well as painkillers. He takes them all, pops some painkillers in his mouth, and resumes walking.

He takes the first left like the map said and finds himself in a bare hallway with the occasional splash of blood. But there are no rooms, only lights and metal walls decorated with informative posters about health and safety. At the end of the hallway is a partially opened door, and when he reaches it, he peeks through the crack.

Ethan cannot see much through the small opening, but what he can see looks about as safe as *Bon Voyage* can get, so Ethan shoulders his rifle, braces himself, and pushes against the door with all his strength. He grunts and his muscles strain as the door scrapes against its railing, filling the hall with a scratchy screech.

It does not move much, and Ethan takes a moment to catch his breath before he pushes again. The door scrapes a little further, which gives him just enough room to wiggle through, and after getting past the door, he stumbles into the middle of the hallway, panting and sweeping the area with his rifle. From side to side, and up to the ceiling, he finds nothing but a dried pool of blood by the wall, and scorch marks, and other battle damage, but no creatures. So, he proceeds left.

After a short walk, Ethan enters another hallway with a line of windows, and peeks through the first one, finding an x-ray picture of a mechanical arm connected to a stubby limb, and two pods, with one that is torn apart with shredded organs and bones thrown everywhere; the body is missing and dried blood coats the entire area in splashes and droplets. The next window has a machine going back and forth between a bed and a smashed cart, with medical tools spilled on the floor.

Out of that room comes an Illwalker that quietly runs towards him, arms outstretched and mouth open.

Ethan shoots it in the chest and head, popping its sacks, which leads to the wall and windows getting splashed with acid. The combination of echoing gunfire and the windows shattering provokes some distant creatures. Their shrieks and banging steps rush down the hallway. Shadows of flailing limbs snap across the wall, and Ethan backs up with a new magazine being shoved into his rifle.

Around the corner comes a pair of Tainted and an Illwalker. Ethan kills them quickly, with the bodies of the Tainted being dissolved while the Illwalker thrashes on the ground. But as Ethan reloads, a deep roar comes from a nearby room, and its window explodes from a gurney being thrown through it. Ethan jumps back and watches a bulky mechanical arm come out of the room; thin vines have wiggled their way through the machinery and help control it.

Next comes a long limb with a scrawny hand made of multiple arms, held together by bent bones, vines and bark, and fingers that have sharp wood protruding from their tips. The warped hand grabs the top of the window, not caring that it is grabbing the jagged glass.

Climbing out a moment later is a Stitcher with an uneven bulbous head, four yellow eyes, a mouth made of multiple jawbones, and a large chest and legs made of various body parts stitched together by the vines. Its covered in sharp bark, and snapping vines poke out of its back. Pulsing green sacks are on its chest, too, but strips of bone and wood cover them. When it marches towards Ethan, it flexes its mechanical hand, and its steps shake the hall.

"Where is it!" yells the Stitcher with a gravelly voice.

Ethan backs up and aims his rifle at it, and when the Stitcher runs towards him, he fires. The bullets chip off pieces of its bark, but it does not stop the Stitcher. Within seconds, it reaches Ethan, swoops its mechanical hand towards him, and slams him into the ceiling, causing him to drop his rifle. Pipes and lights break, showering him with sparks and gas, and when he lands, the Stitcher grabs him with its mutated hand and slams him into the wall.

Ethan's eye rolls, and he feels warm blood trickle down the back of his skull and neck, and when the Stitcher squeezes him, he cries out painfully and grabs its arm to pry it off. His armor groans and cracks and his lungs burn, while his heart becomes heavy and erratic.

The Stitcher then grabs Ethan's head with its mechanical hand and begins squeezing. Ethan's vision quickly becomes dark. Being fueled by the pain of being crushed in two places, he removes his pistol and empties its magazine into the mechanical arm.

Sparks fly, metal snaps, pistons hiss, and then the hand whirs and shudders, and the fingers loosen. With his face freed, Ethan grabs the Stitcher's other wrist with his mutated hand and begins squeezing. The bark cracks and pops into large splinters, and the Stitcher roars and throws Ethan.

He flies across the hall, through an observation window, and hits a bloody gurney with a torn mattress. He falls to the floor with glass raining around him, and he coughs and wheezes with the taste of iron on his tongue, and his abdomen and lungs ache. Ethan then pushes himself up, using the gurney for support. He watches the Stitcher rip off its limp mechanical arm, thus allowing multiple energetic vines to sprout from its stub.

"Where is it!" roars the Stitcher.

It climbs through the window with the vines and hands gripping the windowsill, and its body breaks the last of the glass. When it finishes climbing through, glass crunches under its enormous feet and it marches towards Ethan.

"Where is it!" repeats the Stitcher.

It whips at Ethan, but he dives out of the way, and the vines knock the gurney over. Another swipe sends it crashing into the cabinets across the room, breaking them and spilling their medical supplies on the floor.

It takes another slash at Ethan, and he leaps out of the way, but the small space does not give him enough space to dodge it. A hot slash tears through his hip, and he twirls in the air, crashing to the floor with blood trickling out of his suit.

The Stitcher raises its clawed hand, and Ethan scrambles out of the way as it brings its claws down. He grabs his shotgun and blasts one of its sacks on its chest. It is close to the shoulder, and when it pops, orange-colored blood plus green acid gushes out, and the shoulder is torn apart from the inside out.

Ligaments, bone, and bark are shredded, and the arm goes limp. The Stitcher howls and grabs Ethan with the vines, as a large pocket of the floor dissolves. It slams Ethan down, then to the ceiling, then to the light-board with x-ray pictures. It finishes with throwing him to the floor again and begins squeezing his neck while stepping on his chest.

"Where is it!" yells the Stitcher.

Ethan's vision blurs as the pressure builds in his throat and chest, and through the growing haze, he sees a broken piece of metal near his hand. He snatches it and begins frantically slashing at the vines with his infected hand. One by one, the vines snap off, spraying his face with orange blood, and each vine flops around as it is disconnected. Ethan then plunges the metal into the Stitcher's ankle.

Ethan tears the crude knife out through the side, creating a gash, and the Stitcher recoils with a roar of pain and hops on one foot for a moment, allowing him to scramble away. The Stitcher stomps the floor with its good foot, shaking the room, and the stench of blood and melted metal clogs Ethan's nose. Orange and red blood drops off his face, as his yellow-tinted green eye nearly glows in the dark.

"I found what you're looking for, *seu filho da puta!*" screams Ethan over the Stitcher's rumbling howls.

He plunges the crude knife into the Stitcher's neck, turning its roars into gurgles, its four beady eyes looking into his one bloodthirsty eye. Thick squirts of blood cover its mutated chest and the floor.

Ethan grabs his shotgun and shoots at the acid bags in rapid secession. The floor, walls, and surrounding furniture and equipment sizzle and warp, and Ethan backs up into the door, watching as the pockets of melted metal grow and connect into large openings.

Within a minute, the floor groans and snaps, and the Stitcher drops to the floor below, along with the mutilated gurney and cart, and other equipment. There are metallic crashes and snaps and rattles.

Ethan looks over the edge and sees the Stitcher writhing on the ground with more acid leaking out and melting more flooring. Seeing this, he shakes his head, reloads his shotgun, and exits the room.

Once in the hallway, he grabs his rifle and notices that it's coated in fuel. The stench of fuel is also clogging the air, and when he looks at the creature earlier, he sees that the acid has damaged the Tainted too much, but there is still pollen lingering. He also notices that the fuel has spread to other rooms and is also trickling into the room where he killed the Stitcher.

Ethan frowns, draws his pistol, and goes to the door at the end of the hall. Then, he shoots the wall. The resulting sparks that fall on the fuel lead to a sea of fire that rapidly spreads across the floor and into the rooms, engulfing everything. A weak alarm rings, and Ethan jumps through the door before it closes and rushes down the hall while shaking his head.

"Cabrão."

18

Lost & Found

A short amount of time after killing the Stitcher, Ethan comes across a doorway leading to a flight of stairs dimly lit by red lights. He cautiously climbs the stairs, and upon completion of the first set, he sees a door that has its center bent out with blood and strings of old flesh dangling off its jagged edges.

The door's lights are off, not even sparks pop from it, and it is too bent to move anywhere. Lights from the room beyond flicker through the hole, though, flashing sharp shadows on the wall, and against his better judgment, Ethan peeks inside.

On the wall is a mural of names surrounding various religious icons, and in the center of the display is the Federation flag with "Forsaken" painted across it. There are a lot of scratches and bullet casings on the bloodied floor, and there is a line of shattered observation windows, and broken medical equipment and carts are strewn everywhere.

Ethan shudders, backs away from the door, and goes up the next set of stairs. He comes to a stop at an unlocked door, and after checking his ammo, he takes a deep breath and opens it.

"Attention! All medical personnel, secure the patients! This is not a drill!" says an automated voice on loop.

Ethan sweeps the hall as he steps through the door, grimacing at the sight of shattered windows, carpets of glass, pollen and bullet casings, bloody walls and floors, and broken gurneys, carts, and wheelchairs. Thick vines with bulbs ejecting pollen and snaking roots have claimed many sections, with some creeping into the vents. Arms converted into branches are extended, warped bodies are almost consumed entirely by the vines, and mouths are wide open on the faces barely left on the plants.

The foul stench clogs his nose and causes his eye to water, and faint screams dig into his ears. Ethan closes his eye, grits his teeth, and claws at his hair, tearing strands loose.

"*Keep going, Ethan,*" says the Voice. "*You want Marian to live, don't you?*"

Ethan's eye snaps open, and he finds he is still near the door, and he looks to the side and sees a camera covered in green film.

"*That's right, I see you,*" says the Voice. "*Nice of you to acknowledge me again.*"

Ethan blinks, shakes his head, and hurries down the hall, his boots crushing glass and his breathing heavy.

"*Or you can keep ignoring me. That's fine,*" says the Voice, now coming from another camera. "*Maybe you'll succumb to the Onyx Spores just like everybody else? One by one we go. When it stops, we don't know, right? Will you be next for them to claim, Ethan? How about Marian?*"

"Shut up!" snaps Ethan.

Ethan's voice carries down the hall, and he snaps his weapon around, tense, and wide-eyed, but he does not see anything other than the pollen shifting from the weak air blowing through the vents. With that, Ethan sighs and continues his trek, passing another camera.

"Don't get moody. I'll get to you when I can. I promise," says Ethan.

"*For your sake, I hope it's soon,*" says the Voice.

Ethan freezes, the intercom clicks off, and he looks at the camera for a moment before he continues at a greater speed. He soon comes across an open door with a bright light, and he readies his rifle and peeks inside.

It is an observation room with papers and broken computer pads scattered about. A line of blood stains the wall, and the observation window is cracked. Even with the crack, Ethan can see the unused gurney, which also has straps on it, and four cylindrical lasers hanging from separate arms on a circular device connected to a heavy stand with a terminal. There does not appear to be a way inside, except through a door on the other side.

But that's not what catches Ethan's attention. What has his interest is a brown-eyed, brown-haired, armored security guard with a rifle and pistol. The security officer has a flashlight on his shoulder, a knife on his belt, and an Arx Corporation shield generator on his back. He is going through the lab, tossing aside anything he cannot use for medicine. He stuffed his pouches with medical supplies, and he is covered in bandages and poorly applied stitches.

As the guard scavenges, Ethan carefully approaches the window. He taps it, bringing the guard to jump and aim his rifle at him. Ethan steps back with his hands up. The two look at each other in silence, and Ethan's eye flicks at an intercom box. He slowly goes to it without taking his eye off the guard, and the guard trails Ethan's movements, both with the rifle and his steps, as he, too, goes to an intercom box.

"Don't shoot. I will not hurt you," says Ethan when he reaches the box. He squints and notices the guard's tag says "Simon." That name sounds familiar to him. "I'm a medic. I can help you."

"How do I know you're not one of those Psychos?" asks Simon, aiming his rifle at Ethan with one hand, while his other is on the intercom box.

"I'm not one of them. I'm with the Association of Assisted Transport and Security. My team is nearby. We can get you off this ship."

Simon studies Ethan's face for a moment, then shakes his head and walks backward.

"You're infected," says Simon, his voice muffled by the window. "It is only a matter of time before you turn into one of them."

Simon places his band on the orb next to the door behind him, and the door slides open to a pitch-black hallway. The security guard looks over his shoulder, and then he looks at Ethan.

"Wait! We can help each other!" says Ethan. "There is a vaccine on this ship, and we can all get out of here if we work together."

"The Voice is lying to you. There is no vaccine," says Simon.

Simon then disappears into the darkness, and the door closes and flashes red. Ethan stares at the door for a few seconds before he sighs and heads back to where he came from, giving the door one last look before activating his communicator.

"Marian are you there?" asks Ethan.

"I'm here," says Marian.

"I found a survivor. He's a security guard."

"Neat. Is he going to help you save me?"

"No. He ran away."

"That sucks."

"But I think we should find him as soon as we can."

"Not our mission, anymore. We need to regroup and get to the bridge and get an SOS out as fast as possible."

"But he's a survivor! And he's not homicidal. Maybe he can give us a firsthand account of what happened here. He might even help us off this ship! He must know his way around here."

"One thing at a time, Ethan! I'm still waiting for you to help me out. These things are literally banging on my window, and if I don't get out of this room I'm going to lose my mind! You need to hurry up! You're the only one I can trust right now, so don't leave me!"

Ethan's hand tenses, and after a deep sigh, he nods and speaks evenly. "I'm on my way."

Ethan disconnects and exits the room. He goes as far as he can down the hallway before taking a left and going straight down, being sure to keep himself close to the wall when going underneath the vents. Much to his surprise and relief, nothing happens during this part, and when he comes across a locked door, he uses his Master Key Band to unlock it.

The door flashes green and pulls apart, and he sees a burnt ceiling with popped light bulbs and hanging wires with a crackling over the intercoms. There is also a line of corpses, all twisted, shriveled, and black, like the floor, walls, and ceiling. All of them have their mouths open and eyes shriveled to black pits, with their jumpsuits and lab coats fused to them like burnt shells.

Ethan shines his light down the hallway, expecting to see the Pyro coming towards him, but all he sees is an empty hallway. He cautiously continues his walk, and when he reaches a large, locked door with a "Medical Center" sign barely on, he stops and stares at the door. It looks undamaged, and near the door is a picture of a group of doctors whose faces have been scratched off, all posing with medical equipment.

"Here to Serve!" is what the caption originally said, but it's painted over with, *"LIARS!"*

A clanking above snaps Ethan away from the picture, and he aims his rifle at the nearby vent. When nothing happens, he reluctantly lowers his weapon and unlocks the door with his MKB. The red light flashes to green, and after a series of clicks and whirs, the door slides open.

Ethan steps inside and finds that the room is large and intact. There are pillars displaying evacuation messages, rows of desks with loose paper, writing utensils, and computers with either blue screens, flickering images, or error messages. At the end of the room is a set of stairs leading to the second floor, and at the other end is another room with a thick pane of glass with cracks and scratches, and a damaged door with a red circle.

The intercoms are also buzzing. The buzzing drives Ethan to scratch his head in annoyance, and he wonders if they really are broken or if the Voice is putting out the sounds just to mess with the survivors. His theory is fortified when he sees blinking cameras positioned around the room for optimal coverage. But the buzzing pops out of existence several seconds later.

"Keep going, Ethan. Marian Dartmount is waiting for you," says the Voice.

Ethan walks further into the room and gets an uncomfortable and painful shiver up his spine and infected arm when the door closes behind him. He scans the area and keeps a tight grip on his rifle as he walks deeper into the room.

The evacuation messages flicker away, one by one, and when Ethan reaches the cracked window, he sees Marian standing up in a hurry. Seeing her brings a smile to his face, and he runs to her and puts his hand on the window.

His smile falters when he sees the yellow tint clashing with Marian's vibrant blue eyes. He also sees bandages around her arm, and her armored suit is damaged, burnt, and stained with blood, both red and tainted. Even her hair and face are covered in grime and streaks of blood.

"Marian are you okay?" asks Ethan.

"I'm fine, but you look like shit," says Marian, her voice muffled.

"It's been a day. But let's get you out of here. The others are waiting."

Marian nods and goes to the room's door with Ethan following her, but right as they reach it, the lights suddenly shut off, plunging the room into darkness, and red lights swirl on the walls as a wailing alarm assaults their ears. Ethan tries to use his MKB to unlock Marian's door, but a padlock symbol appears in the red projection, and when he looks at the main doors at either end, he sees the same symbol.

"Warning. Quarantine in effect. Please remain calm," says a computerized voice.

"Oh no," says Ethan.

"Ethan?" calls Marian.

Roars and howls echo from the vents, and metal breaks and clatters to the floor as shadows stretch and snap along the walls from the motions of the swirling lights. Ethan backs away from Marian and sweeps the area while she bangs on the window.

"One by one we go... When it stops, we don't know... one by one we go..." sings the Voice lightheartedly. *"Are you going to be the next one, Ethan?"*

"You bastard! Open the doors!" yells Ethan.

"I can't do that, Ethan. I'm only an observer."

A Haunter roars and leaps over the railing on the second floor, and Ethan shoots its torso and legs, making it spiral out of control and land on its head on the floor. Its neck snaps and its head pops open.

Ethan shoots another Haunter that has jumped down, with more leaping over the railing. He pivots and rams the butt of his rifle into the face of a Haunter that was lunging at him, knocking it off its feet.

Ethan then runs up the stairs with the swarm giving chase. He hears gunfire and glass shattering as he runs, and when he reaches the second floor, a Haunter tackles him. It tries biting him, but he puts his rifle in the way of its mouth, kicks it off, and then jumps up and sprays the crowd of Haunters until his magazine runs dry. When he is out, he draws his pistol and blows the head open of the Haunter that tackled him.

Gunfire echoes down below, and muzzle flashes and the gunshots clash with the swirling red lights, the alarm, and the screams. As this happens, a Haunter leaps on Ethan and begins clawing on his shoulders and back, spraying thick pollen-tainted slobber as it screams.

Some claws pierce the suit, slicing Ethan's skin, and the Haunter snaps at his face, but he pushes against its jaw's underside while the other Haunters try circling him. He turns the clingy monster to the crowd, as strings of blood flick out of his suit from the constant slashes.

Then, he shoots the Haunter in the head. As soon as its body goes limp, Ethan is rammed by another Haunter. The two tumble over the edge, and Ethan lands on a desk, breaking it upon impact, and his pistol slides away from him.

Ethan lays there, coughing and gagging, while the Haunter that tackled him thrashes on the ground, kicking and slashing the air with its claws and vines. The demonic screams get a burst of extra energy, and the Haunters leap over the railing or run down the stairs, all going to Ethan.

The ones that leaped over can barely land before they are gunned down with well-placed shots to the upper chests and heads. More bullets finish the Haunter on the floor next to Ethan. Then Marian slides to a stop next to Ethan and pulls him up.

"Come on, slacker! I can't do all the work!" says Marian.

Ethan is in too much pain to grin at Marian's stupid quip, and his muscles burn as he draws his shotgun. He blasts a Haunter in the chest, spraying him and the floor with bits of gore, and he makes his way to his pistol, firing more shots into the crowd, just like Marian. With Marian covering him, Ethan quickly grabs and holsters his pistol and goes back-to-back with her.

Loud blasts mix with fast, sporadic pops as the pair gun down the Haunters. Ethan's ears are ringing, his nose is clogged with the stench of blood and gunpowder, and his wounds throb like their own beating hearts.

Gunshot after gunshot, second after second, Ethan and Marian fire in sync, each destroying the Haunters and Tainted with bullets or brute strength to beat them down with their weapons. When one reloads, the other covers, and they stay on the move, swapping places in their ever-moving circle like a dance.

Time has become a blur, the rushing bodies innumerable, the floor has become soaked in blood, and by the time the last Haunter drops with its head pulverized by a slug, the two are hunched over, panting, sweating, and their breathing scratchy and painful.

Their hearts are racing and sweat drips off their noses, soaks their attire, and clings to their hair, yet when they look at each other, they smile as two victorious comrades, surrounded by rings of blood and mutilated bodies. And if they are laughing, they can't hear it over the alarm and the ringing in their ears.

However, the more they stand there with burning throats and aching bodies, the quicker their joy fades. The lights have not changed; the doors are still locked, and the alarms are still stabbing their ears.

"What's going on?" asks Marian, her voice raised and hoarse.

Ethan is about to respond, but then he sees movement low on the floor out of the corner of his eye. He turns to it, shining his light on the body, and he sees vines have broken through its skin and its chest has split open.

The vines drag the mangled body towards another body that has also split open. The vines pull their bodies closer together, pressing flesh and bone together, which are then stitched together by smaller vines weaving through the bodies like a thread.

Ethan's jaw drops, and he pushes Marian towards the door he came through. **"Get to the door!"**

As Ethan pushes her, Marian sees the bodies stitching together, and the other Haunter corpses do the same.

"Shit! Shit! Shit! What the fuck!?" yells Marian as she bolts to the door.

She slams herself against the door and presses her band against the orb, but an error message appears with the padlock symbol.

"The door's locked! It won't open!" cries Marian.

Ethan runs next to Marian and activates his communicator. He can hear the multitude of bones snapping, and various screams, voices, and hoarse moans echo in the room. His throat becomes tight, as his words push their way out of his mouth.

"Riva, open the door!" shouts Ethan.

"Where are you!" asks Riva frantically.

The Haunters' bodies continue dragging, splitting, and fusing together. The bones break, the muscles split, and vines snake out to loop through the flesh and pull the broken bodies together. Ethan's heart beats faster, and his eye gets wider as he watches the multitude of bodies collected into one ever-growing mass. Some Haunters and Tainted even climb onto the larger Stitcher and rip themselves open while clinging to it.

"Oh, meu Deus," says Ethan.

"Ethan, what room!" cries Riva.

"E-MH-001!" says Marian. "Now open the fucking door!" She desperately bangs on the door with tears soaking her face. *"Jai ni fookshni aeynik! Jai ni aeynik, Riva!"*

The Stitcher towers over them, Ethan aims his shotgun at it with shaky hands, and Marian reverts to trying to pry the door open with her bare hands.

"What is taking so long!?" screams Marian. "Riva, please open the door!"

"Riva, open the door right now!" shouts Ethan.

"I'm trying!" sobs Riva.

The swirling red lights bathe the growing beast in shades of red and black, and when it takes the last Haunter, it has five heads, each made from multiple heads that have turned bones to jagged fangs. Its multitude of eyes glow yellow with slobber dripping from its large mouths. Its arms are thick at the base, like a gorilla, all made of vines, flesh, and jagged bark, and its spine is lined with sharp vertebrae. On its chest are pulsing bags of green acid, all of which are shielded by thick ribs. Its throats vibrate, as it releases five shaky roars of different pitches that shake the room.

That is when the door flashes green and slides open.

"Run!" yells Riva.

Ethan pushes Marian through the door, and he runs after her. Then the floor shakes as the Über Stitcher begins its chase.

19

The Über Stitcher

The hall shakes as the Über Stitcher chases Ethan and Marian down the hallway. The two run. All their weariness is now gone, and they do not dare to look back. The pair take the first turn they can, and the monster smashes into the wall, bringing the lights to flicker and some bulbs to shatter.

While the Über Stitcher tears apart the doorway, Ethan and Marian run faster down the hallway, unable to feel anything other than panic. They take another turn and run towards a jagged hole that used to be a large door.

Once they enter, they skid to a stop and find themselves in a lobby with dim orange lights, broken benches and carts, and scattered luggage, with pollen in the air. Mutilated bodies are morphed into trees and thick vines, with their roots spreading across the floor and their bulbs spewing more pollen. A gaping hole is in the lobby ceiling, and there are flickering advertisements blocked by cracks and blood splatter. At the far end is a broken door that leads to a trolley platform, which has a trolley with its door open and waiting.

"Next stop. Section F" scrolls across the trolley's message board, and between the pair and the trolley is a crowd of Tainted walking around in a daze, each making their own stuttering clicks, either alone or at

each other. Some of the Tainted are brandishing crude weapons, and others are armed with their sharp claws protruding from their hands and feet.

At first, the Tainted don't see Ethan or Marian, but when the Über Stitcher slams into the door behind them and begins tearing it away, the combination of their screams, breaking metal, and electric discharge catches their attention. The Tainted see the two and immediately scream and charge them.

"Run faster!" orders Marian.

The pair run towards the trolley as metal snaps and a thud echoes in the room. They weave between the Tainted as the creatures swipe at them with their claws or weapons. The pair leap over the benches and rush towards the trolley while the swarm closes in on them and the room shakes from the Über Stitcher.

As soon as they get outside, the trolley dings and starts sliding forward while its door closes. Ethan puts every bit of energy he can into his legs, while Marian zips ahead. She easily makes it to the trolley and holds the door open, bringing the vehicle to stop, and she extends her hand to Ethan.

"Come on! Hurry!" shouts Marian.

Ethan takes a running leap into the trolley, and Marian hits the emergency close button next to the door, bringing it to slam shut as a Tainted runs into it. The Tainted screams and the trolley pulls forward, making a pleasant ding as it goes.

"Next stop. Section F," says the trolley's computerized voice.

The glass suddenly shatters from claws stabbing it, and the Tainted scream and roar as they cram themselves and bully each other to get into the trolley. The vehicle's interior lights snap to red and a screeching alarm sounds as white lights flash inside, clashing with the red.

The trolley comes to a complete stop. Then the vehicle shakes as the Über Stitcher climbs on its roof. The speaker tries to blurt out a message, but all that comes out is a garbled mess of broken words.

Ethan blasts the crowd with his shotgun as Marian runs to the control panel. There, she quickly and sloppily starts pushing every button, turning every dial, and pulling every lever she can.

While the alarm sounds, the lights turn from red and white, to rotating tropical flowers, to dark purple with swirling white stars, and to the rainbow spectrum of a disco ball, with each having matching musical themes to go with them.

Back in the passenger area, the Tainted have gotten inside, but a few incapacitated Tainted lay in front of Ethan while enormous claws tear into the roof. Now Ethan is wrestling with a Tainted that lost one of its arms.

He is keeping the remaining clawed hand from piercing his face. Not too far from him, his shotgun is laying on the floor, getting kicked around by the abominations that are trying to get to him, but he is forcing his current target to block them by sweeping it side to side.

"What are you doing?" yells Ethan.

"I'm trying to get this thing moving!" snaps Marian.

With a sharp twist, Ethan throws the Tainted aside, whips out his pistol, and shoots it in the head. Then he snaps to another Tainted and puts three rounds in its chest and one in the head.

After that, he turns and pistol whips a Tainted in the head, knocking it to the floor. He shoots the next one in the head, before executing the one he whacked.

"Hurry!" screams Ethan as he shoots at another Tainted.

"Hey, I give the orders around here! Not you!"

"Lecture me later! Get this damn thing moving!"

Marian pushes another set of buttons and the trolley lurches forward, causing her to lose her balance, and it rapidly gains speed with warning messages flickering on the control panel. Right as the trolley pulls away from the platform, a Tainted jumps on the window, cracking it with its claws as it latches on.

Marian curses and shoots it with her rifle, knocking it off at the cost of shattering the window. As the trolley passes another platform, two more Tainted leap on it.

The two that leaped on the trolley crawl into the control cabin from the roof, and their clawed hands and feet tear into the panel when they get inside, sending a shower of sparks to scatter all over the area. Marian shoots both, splattering the area with their blood and the force of the bullets knocks them out of the trolley.

Everything is becoming a blur, and the screaming wind bashes Marian's face. When she looks at the sparking control panel, her eyes bulge, and she backs up to the door.

"Ethan, we have a problem!" says Marian.

Back in the passenger area, a Tainted's claws cut through Ethan's armored vest, and he retaliates by pistol whipping it in the jaw, sending it crashing to the ground with its jaw broken off. He then snatches his shotgun off the floor and blows open a Tainted's chest, before beating another back. Then he unloads on what remains of the crowd, while Marian runs in and helps finish them off.

The onslaught of bullets and slugs tear apart the Tainted and splashes the trolley walls and windows with gore. Some windows and portions of the walls have gaping holes in them now, creating a multitude of high-pitched whistles as the trolley zooms along its rail.

With the last of the Tainted incapacitated, Ethan rapidly reloads while looking at the ceiling and feeling sick and cold from the combination of rushing wind, shaking trolley, nerves, and open wounds.

Marian is also looking at the ceiling and reloading her rifle, while vines wrap around her ankle. She tugs herself away from their grip and hops to another spot. While this goes on, the lights flicker, sparks fall off the side, and the outside has lost all definition from their speed.

"Why are we going so fast?" says Ethan loudly over the wind.

"Yeah, about that," says Marian.

She points at the destroyed control panel, and Ethan's shoulder sags.

"*Merda,*" says Ethan.

"Who?" asks Marian.

"What?"

Suddenly, the roof is ripped open, and the Über Stitcher's faces appear and vomit acid on the pair. Ethan and Marian scream and swear as they dive out of the way. The metal floor, and the benches' foamy guts and plastic exteriors sizzle and dissolve.

When Ethan gets in a good spot, he shoots at one of the Über Stitcher's heads with his shotgun. The slug pops one of its eyes, and the Über Stitcher roars and retreats, but its hind legs are still in view of the passenger window, and Ethan shoots the limbs.

The trolley shakes from the shift in weight, and the disco and emergency lights flicker and flash rapidly. The music and alarms turn to disjointed buzzes of various volume levels as sparks fall all around Ethan and Marian. Then another piece of the roof is peeled back and the Über Stitcher's mutated faces return.

Ethan and Marian shoot at the many faces, and bits of bark and mutated flesh fall, and the Über Stitcher shrieks before spraying acid at them. The two jump away as the green liquid splashes on the floor, bodies, and what is left of the windows. The bodies shrivel and screech, the metal bubbles and snaps, and the windows shatter while steam rises. The stench of melting metal and flesh clog their noses.

The wind screams through the holes, and the air becomes thick while pieces of metal and the Tainted plummet down below. Ethan finds his footing on a bench, and he aims his shotgun at the Über Stitcher, but before he can fire, there is a metallic snap and a sharp tilt that knocks him and Marian into the wall.

The trolley shakes and there is a loud groan, which prompts Ethan and Marian to shoulder their weapons and grab the benches. Seconds later, there is another snap that causes the trolley to take a sharp dip backward.

Ethan and Marian scream as they tumble down, bouncing off benches and sliding down the remains of the aisle. But while Marian can grab a bench near the back, Ethan's hand slips when he tries grabbing a bar, and he continues sliding down.

Everything is a blur for him as flickering lights, sparks, and metal and benches rush past him, and then he lands on the emergency exit in the back. Its window breaks on impact and the door snaps open. Ethan can barely hook his arms on the broken frame, and his legs dangle as the door swings from his weight and the trolley's continued path.

"Hang on, Ethan!" yells Marian.

Ethan growls painfully from the burning in his joints and muscles. Some of his stitches have broken, leading to blood oozing out of his shoulder and infected arm. He reaches up, still swinging with the door, and he digs his fingers into the ledge.

As this happens, the screech of ripping metal clashes with the howling wind, and Marian shrieks as the Über Stitcher crawls along the roof. The gunshots are faint against the screaming wind, and Marian's bullets do little to hurt the abomination's thick bark.

Ethan's heart races as he tries to pull himself up, but the hinges snap, and the door takes a sharp, angular dip. The door groans again soon after, and pieces of the remaining hinges pop off, bringing Ethan to grit his teeth and strain himself as he climbs up, battling the rushing wind and the door's swings.

More screws pop out, and another piece of metal snaps. Ethan reaches for a bench's support bar, while his other hand scrapes against the metal floor. Then the door breaks off and tumbles below, leaving Ethan dangling with the wind, determined to push him off.

Ethan's heart races, and everything feels like it is rushing to his throat. Despite the pain ripping him apart and the blood wetting his arm, he pulls himself inside the wrecked trolley. Once inside, he quickly climbs on the bench's back and lays flat, his chest aching from his heavy breathing and his heart going berserk.

As this happens, Marian climbs down and shoots at the Über Stitcher. She leaps to the benches across from her when the large creature sprays a stream of acid at her. Her previous perch dissolves and tumbles out of the trolley.

As this happens, Ethan draws his pistol and shoots one of the Über Stitcher's faces, forcing it to climb out of sight. But with the shift comes a violent shaking for the trolley.

"Ethan!" calls Marian.

Ethan looks at Marian and sees she is climbing towards him, and he begins climbing up. Every move hurts, but he keeps climbing, one bench at a time. He only stops to shoot at the Über Stitcher when it breaks open the side of the trolley and tries to crawl inside. But after getting one of its faces and acid bags popped, it retreats.

The acid quickly eats away at the trolley's side. Through the many openings in the trolley, Ethan sees a steadily moving trolley with its windows covered in green film and vines hanging out. And it is right on their track.

"Marian, hold on!" yells Ethan.

As soon as he finishes the sentence, their trolley hits the other trolley. Metal snaps, glass shatters, fire and sparks fly, and their trolley breaks into pieces as the rail splinters like twigs.

Ethan and Marian are lifted in the air, and they bounce between the benches as metal, wheels, and glass rain past them. Ethan grabs a piece of the broken roof that digs into his gloves as the metal walls zoom *up,* as both trolleys fall, and Marian latches herself onto a bench.

"Oh shiiiiiiiit!" cries Marian.

The end is as sudden as the beginning, and Ethan is flung into the air when the trolley hits the floor. Everything spins, and his terrified screaming is abruptly cut off when he lands far from the wrecks, as the two trolleys are smashed and bounce and skid.

More pieces of the rail network snap loose and crash down or swing into the walls of *Bon Voyage.* During the chaos, Ethan rolls across the floor, his body getting stabbed by sharp jabs of pain.

His vision flashes in and out as a messy blur of gray, orange, and red spins past him. When he stops, he is laying on his side, his mouth hangs open to gobble air, and his lungs and throat feel stuffed.

He wants to move but cannot. He wants to scream, but nothing comes out. His vision is hazy and bloody, and he can only watch as the trolley that he and Marian were on skids to a stop, with its cabin smashed, its mangled wheels facing up, and sparks popping out of the broken wires.

Ethan extends his shaky, bleeding hand. His vision pulses, and his breathing is sharp, while burning, hellish smoke spreads all around him, gradually suffocating and blinding him.

"Marian," gasps Ethan. "Marian, no… Please, no…"

"One by one we go… When it stops, we don't know… One by one we go…" sings the Voice, the tune echoing in the desolation.

Ethan pushes himself up and realizes that his pistol and rifle are gone, so he grabs his shotgun and hobbles towards the wreckage as smoke rolls towards him. He hears the shrill screams and screeches over the crackling fire, and he picks up his pace.

He ejects his spent magazine and slips in his last magazine, and as he does this, a Tainted rushes him with a crude ax. He deflects the ax with his shotgun, then uses his gun like a club to break open the monster's skull.

The Tainted crumbles with vines probing the air, and Ethan continues towards the wreckage, which does not seem to get closer, only farther. After a few paces, he is knocked on his back.

A Haunter has him pinned, and it raises its claws for a killing blow, but Ethan punches it in the throat with his mutated hand and quickly follows with another punch and a kick that knocks it off. After that, he grabs his shotgun and blows apart its collar, leaving its head to dangle.

It struggles to move, and Ethan shoots it again, popping its head. He then resumes limping towards the wreckage.

Ethan sweeps his weapon through the smoke, coughing as he does this. He sees silhouettes of figures and the mangled trolley, and he hears the Haunters and Tainted getting closer with their screams, clicks, and steps. He can also see the blinking red lights of the cameras.

"She's close, Ethan. Don't let her become one of them. It would be a horrible end to my favorite love story," says the Voice.

Ethan's heart races, and his limp turns to hopping run as he races towards the wreckage, which is marked by sparks and flames licking the air. But as he limps through the fog, another Haunter rushes him.

He sidesteps its slash and rams his shotgun against its skull. Its skull pops, splashing the floor with brain and bone. His steps get quicker as he focuses on the wreck with his yellow and green eye glowing in the smoke.

"You're getting warmer," taunts the Voice.

Muzzle flashes appear in the smoke, knocking down a pair of silhouettes, and Ethan sees Marian's figure in the smoke. He runs as fast as his limp will allow. His chest and throat are heavy, his heart thumps in his ears, and his bloody mouth hangs open from his panting.

Every step is a sharp jab, and when he reaches Marian, she snaps to him with her rifle aimed at his chest. He pushes it aside just in time to divert the shots, and she looks into his eye and loses some color on her pale face.

"Careful with that thing!" snaps Ethan. He grabs Marian's arm and quickly looks around before seeing a red door. "Come on, we need to get out of here!"

Ethan pulls Marian towards the door, but she tugs away from him. However, she still follows him, and when they reach the door, Ethan presses his MKB on the orb. The door unlocks, they slip inside, and Ethan locks it while Marian runs towards an elevator, which has a camera watching it.

As she goes to the elevator, Ethan walks backward and keeps his shotgun aimed at the door, which is shaking from the banging. Muffled screams and roars overlap from the other side, too.

There is a ding, and light fills the hallway, stretching Ethan's shadow to the door, and Marian's shadow joins him.

"Ethan, come on," says Marian, her voice wary.

Ethan walks backward, his eyes still on the door, and when he is near the elevator, he looks over his shoulder and sees Marian holding her hand out to him, while keeping the elevator door open.

He looks back at the door they came through. It is still shaking, with claws poking through, and Ethan runs inside the elevator. Marian lets the door close after he gets in, and the room is plunged into darkness.

Seconds later, the door breaks open and the swarm rushes in.

20

A Boring Lift

The elevator's gears clank and streaks of yellow light slide up through the door crack as the elevator rises. Ethan uses his dwindling supply of medical equipment to treat his and Marian's wounds, starting with her.

Hers are not too bad, requiring only disinfectant wipes, gauze pads, and medical tape, plus a shot of adrenaline, which she objected to, but he still injected her. For Ethan, he used one of his last few canisters of medical foam, plus restitched himself with the Quick Stitch Kit, and uses gauze pads, medical tape, and adrenaline shots.

The elevator's rise is slow, and it stops frequently, but each time they are about to climb out, it works again, like a sick joke that is making Ethan nauseous. At one point when it completely stops and goes dark, Marian scoffs and slumps against the wall.

"We probably should have taken the stairs," says Marian.

"It would have been faster at this rate," says Ethan. He looks at Marian and sees her yellow-tinted eyes, her sweat reflecting the dim lights and greasing up her hair. He feels his hair, too, finding it just as nasty.

He sighs, looks at the elevator's display, which shows a clump of numbers meaning absolutely nothing. "Have any of your jobs been crazy like this?"

Marian shakes her head. "No. Some of them got a level of crazy, but nothing like this."

"How about your vacations?"

Marian stiffens, and she looks at Ethan with a bit of unease, and he stares back at her.

"You and your team are raviks, right? You told me that when you were locked in that room," says Ethan. "And Taksheel said that you guys used 'vacation' as a code word for smuggling trips on the side."

Marian looks down.

"Has any of your vacations been like this?" asks Ethan.

"No," says Marian. She groans and rubs her eyes. "I can't believe I did that. I should have kept my mouth shut! Now you know everything! You weren't supposed to know anything until your three-month probation period was up. That way we can evaluate you and decide whether to dump you! Damn it! Taksheel is such an idiot. I'm an idiot. This-This whole stupid ship is an idiot! *Fook nis weshni!*"

Marian growls and paces in circles with her fingers clawing at her hair, tearing some loose, and Ethan stares at his warped reflection with a small frown and a heavy eye.

"I don't know everything," says Ethan. "I know the basics, not the details. I know that the *Hook Line* crew worked as smugglers on the side. I know you were on Oros to deliver the Three Machetes some Aarden drugs, and I know Taksheel wants me on the team. Taksheel also…"

Ethan's voice drifts off, and Marian stares at him critically while the lights flicker on and the elevator hums to life again. After some seconds of silence, her frown grows, and she folds her arms across her chest and hardens her glare.

"Spit it out, Ethan. What did Taksheel say?" says Marian.

Ethan hesitates. "He thinks Section 0 set us up."

The elevator rises, but the numbers remain a mess, and Marian scrunches her brows.

"What? Why would he… Oh no." Marian's demeanor crumbles. She shakes her head, backs into a corner, and grips her head as she slides down, whimpering. "No, no, no, no, no. They found out, didn't they? That must be why they targeted us!"

Ethan sighs and looks at the numbers. Sometimes they go up, sometimes they go down, sometimes they overlap into a mess, and the gears squeak and groan loudly as they ascend the shaft.

"I don't think…" Ethan rubs his face. "This is hard to wrap my head around, but if Section 0 targeted the *Hook Line*, then this was a very elaborate and expensive thing to do when they could have used a torpedo to blow the ship up. It doesn't make sense."

Marian still has her head down. "Right… Right. You're right." She lifts her head and wipes her face with shaky hands. "It doesn't make sense. Taksheel is just being stupid. We're safe. Section 0 isn't after us. We can- We can keep doing vacations on the- No, we can't! We can't! Not yet. Not for a little while. They might be on to us, so maybe we have to chill for a bit."

"Marian…"

"We just need to survive- no, we play dead! Yes, we play dead, lie low-"

"Marian."

"Then rebuild the team. You and me, not those punks. They left me, but you came for me. You're loyal!"

"Marian, Section 0 might have put a ravik in your crew."

Marian stops and looks at Ethan, pale and wide-eyed.

"If that is true, then that means there is an ulterior motive for your team being brought here, and it would have something to do with the scientist we were supposed to pick up," says Ethan. "Think about it-"

Marian shakes her head. "No, don't be a Shavadin's advocate. Don't let Taksheel get in your head! He's been hooked on that conspiracy crap for as long as I've known him. None of this makes sense, you said it yourself."

"Unless there is a ravik with an ulterior motive."

Marian slams her hand on the floor, which makes the lights flicker somehow. "No, Ethan! Nobody on my team is Section 0! They're assholes, but they aren't Section 0 level assholes. Do you understand me?"

Ethan nods, and Marian stares at him with a vicious scowl for a few seconds before she slumps to the floor and rests her head against the wall, with her rifle between her legs.

"Good… You know what? Now that I think about it, I'm hoping this elevator takes longer. I can use a break," says Marian.

Ding!

The elevator stops, and the door opens, revealing a brightly lit hallway with vines poking from the ceiling and potted plants mutated and spreading across the floor.

Marian scoffs. "Well, fine then!"

Ethan smirks.

21

Confrontation

After exiting the elevator, Ethan and Marian have a simple trip back to the break room. Marian is quiet nearly the whole time, and the straggling Onyx Spore Infected did not notice them most of the time, and the pair quickly took out those that did. But they encounter more bodies turning into plants, and in some areas, they have to cover their noses and mouths because of thick pollen. While their trek is easy, it is also long, and when they reach the door to the break room, Ethan is glad to see that the door is locked and has no sign of damage.

Ethan uses his Master Key Band to unlock the door, and when the door slides open, the two slip inside. Ethan quickly closes and locks the door while Marian looks around. In the back, Taksheel is still working on the bomb, but he stops when he sees them, Riva is sitting on a chair and jumps up when they enter.

"Ethan? Marian? You made it!" says Riva with glee. "I was getting worried!"

"You're somehow looking worse. What did you do?" says Taksheel.

Ethan is quiet, and Marian forces a smile and walks forward. That smile leads to the hairs on Ethan's neck standing and his infected arm twitching, and he can tell from the look of the other two that Marian's smile is unsettling.

"There's my team!" says Marian brightly. She stops in the middle of the room and looks around, nodding approvingly. "Wow, you two were busy collecting stuff. I mean, you got food, medicine, batteries... fuel..." She taps an ammo box with her foot. "Bullets... It is like you were too busy to answer my distress calls."

Riva and Taksheel exchange a quick look before Riva speaks cautiously.

"Marian, we didn't hear any distress calls from you," she says. "If we did, we would have come right to you."

"Riva Bonnevue! Oh good, sweet, *Riva!*" says Marian.

Riva shifts uncomfortably in her spot.

"It's hard to believe that we used to be friends, considering that you completely ignored me when I was trapped just down the hallway," says Marian.

"Marian, knock it off. We really didn't hear you," says Taksheel.

"And Taksheel Iyer! Man, I can't believe I had that stupid threesome with you and Riva just because I wanted to be your girlfriend. But I guess I should feel sorrier for Riva, since you're obviously a piece of shit who will leave her when it is convenient. And Aiden, too, since I dashed his feelings for someone more exotic. Boy, that was a bad call for me!"

Ethan looks at Riva, as she whines and hides her face in shame, and Taksheel sneers at Marian.

"Wow. Really?" says Taksheel. "We're stuck on a death ship, and you say that? This is the stuff for bar nights. Right, Ethan?"

Marian steps in front of Ethan and points at Taksheel with a vicious scowl. "Leave Ethan alone! There will be no more bar nights for any of us because you fuckers left me to die!"

"Well, gee, maybe you should send out distress signals next time!" says Taksheel.

Riva holds up her finger. "Taksheel, maybe-"

Taksheel points at Riva. "Riva, there is nothing for you to say. Marian did **not** send out a signal."

"I did!" yells Marian. "Ethan heard them, and he came to rescue me! And the condition he came in, I mean, my God! What the hell is wrong with you two letting him go out alone like that!"

Riva looks down, whimpering and sniffling, and Taksheel glares at Marian.

"Marian," starts Ethan.

Marian lifts her finger at Ethan. "Don't say anything. As for you two, what do you have to say for yourselves?"

"We went out collecting supplies and set out to make a bomb so we can get to the relay tower. You would know that if you didn't abandon us like a coward," says Taksheel.

In a blink, Marian draws her pistol, but Taksheel has his pistol aimed at her head before she could raise her weapon. Riva shrieks, and Ethan lunges forward and pushes Marian's hand down hard and fast, while getting between her and Taksheel.

"You want to say that again!" screams Marian, jerking away from Ethan with her tainted eyes bloodshot and wet. "After all these years, you think I'd abandon you guys. Fuck you! I'll blow your head off!"

"Try it!" shouts Taksheel.

"Enough!" yells Ethan.

"You think you're in charge, quota hire!? You're not in charge of anything! It was you who ran away from us!" says Taksheel. "You locked yourself in a room while me and Riva collected supplies, and we didn't make Ethan get you. He went by himself. Do not blame me for his choices! He went because of *you*. If you hadn't split us up, if you hadn't deserted us, then he wouldn't look like that, and Roger and Calvin and everybody else would still be alive! They're dead because of *you*, and when we get to an outpost, you're done! I'll make sure of it."

The room's atmosphere becomes heavy with silence after that, and Marian and Taksheel glare at each other. Marian's quivering finger taps against her trigger. Riva has stepped all the way in the back and is clutching her chest. Ethan is still between the two, but his throat is dry, and his chest tightens as he holds his hand out to Marian's pistol.

"Taksheel, stand down. Marian, give me the pistol," says Ethan with a soft, but urgent tone.

Taksheel lowers his gun, and Marian's breathing gets heavier. Her mouth is shut tight with shaky breaths going through her nose, and she rubs her pistol against the side of her head. Her eyes and trail of tears shine in the light, and she rubs the pistol harder against her scalp. She is no longer looking at anybody. Her eyes become downcast and unfocused as she paces in a circle, while her other hand claws at her hair.

"HL, Abraham Brown, Han Greqir, Turiv Vulki, Moon Stone, Roger Whirling, Calvin Darwish," recites Marian hoarsely. "I didn't abandon them… I didn't abandon any of you… I… I don't abandon people."

"Marian," says Riva softly.

Marian suddenly ejects her magazine, pops out the bullet in the chamber. Then she throws her pistol and magazine away and goes to the bathroom. When she closes the door, the holographic circle flashes to red with "Occupied" in the center. Seconds later, Ethan looks at Taksheel, who has his finger on his pistol's trigger, but when he realizes Ethan is looking at him, he smiles nervously and holsters his weapon.

"Sorry you had to see that," says Taksheel. "And admittedly I might have hit below the belt."

"That was a terrible thing you said," says Riva.

"Hey, I already admitted it was low."

"You know what she went through before joining the AATS!"

"Look, let's not all-"

"Taksheel, just shut up!"

Ethan's eye widens, and Taksheel frowns.

"Riva don't use that language. It's not like you," says Taksheel.

"Shut up!" cries Riva. "Just… stop."

Riva slumps in a chair and covers her face, and her shoulders buckle as she whimpers.

"I hate this ship," says Riva.

Ethan and Taksheel look at Riva, then Taksheel looks at Ethan's infected hand.

"Don't tell me this shook you up, after everything we've been through," says Taksheel.

Ethan looks down and sees his hand is shaking. He also has some bark growing on his skin, and he grips his hand and sits in a chair next to Riva, staring at the wall with a racing heart and tight throat.

All noise fades and Ethan's mind slowly goes blank. He can hear Taksheel saying something, but he cannot make out the words. He just stares at the wall, and soon there is nothing for him to register.

He is in a void, and that is where he would like to stay.

22

An Explosive End

"Ethan, wake up," says Riva gently.

Ethan's vision snaps to focus and he jerks upright, seeing Riva in front of him with red eyes and nose, and her hand pressed against her heart and one hand on his shoulder; she is also wearing a tool belt.

Marian is leaning against the wall, near the door, checking her rifle.

Taksheel is tightening the straps on his bomb, which is now on the cart. It comprises five bundles of large batteries and red cylinders, all held together by straps, cords, wires, and chains with a rigged blowtorch. A hastily constructed remote control is in his possession, too.

Riva stands back, still rubbing her heart, and she looks at Marian. "He's awake."

"Good. Ethan, we're getting ready to go," says Marian, her voice dead and her eyes focused on her rifle. "If you're done napping, get all the supplies you can carry. We won't be coming back here."

Ethan nods and sluggishly stands up, noticing that everyone is carrying a backpack, with Riva having the lightest of the three.

Ethan goes to their stash, refills his medical supplies, and swaps his rifle and pistol ammo with magazines for his shotgun, which he checks to make sure they are filled. Then he changes out the bandages on his arm, face, and shoulder, and injects himself with more adrenaline.

His right arm and shoulder have become a grotesque mess of blood-streaked, mangled skin, with stitching wire clumping the skin, shells of pinkish foam, thick orange veins, and patches of bark. The orange veins have moved up to his neck, and his face is broken with half his face burned down to the bone, a dark void where his right eye used to be, and half of his dark red hair is burnt.

When these wounds are covered in fresh bandages, Ethan looks at his group with his shotgun held tight. They are staring at him, with Marian horrified, Taksheel grossed out, and Riva worried.

"What?" says Ethan.

"Are you going to be okay, Ethan?" asks Riva.

"I'll be fine, Riva," replies Ethan.

"Be honest. Are you going to snap on us?" asks Taksheel.

"If I do, just shoot me in the head," says Ethan.

"Alright, let's not get morbid," says Marian, fighting to shift her expression to a more neutral look. "We got a job to do. Riva, if we can get to the relay, can you get a signal out?"

Riva nods. "If the relay isn't too damaged, I'll be able to send out an emergency signal. And they should have ports I can use to figure out what the encrypted signal is."

"Good. Taksheel, are you sure your bomb will work?"

"Put it this way, if the bomb doesn't kill whatever that thing over there is, then we'll be in trouble," says Taksheel. "We're looking at fifteen liquid fuel cylinders, plus a dozen Class 1-A batteries that had their safety mechanics disabled. It won't be a clean explosion. It'll be messy, and we better have a good distance between us and this thing, because I do not know what'll happen if I detonate it."

"Are those batteries warp capable?" asks Marian.

"No," replies Taksheel.

"Just checking. I'm point, Ethan, you're rear, and Taksheel and Riva will be center, got it?"

"Yes ma'am," says Ethan.

"Alright, let's roll." Marian presses her band on the door's orb, and it flashes green and slides open. The clangs echo down the hallway, and she pokes her head out, looks left and right, and then slides out with her rifle raised. "Clear. Ethan, you're up."

Ethan steps into the hallway with his shotgun raised, and he aims down the corridor, keeping his breathing steady and his one eye focused. He sees nothing but failing lights, bits of stray trash, and a camera, but no Haunters. With it being as safe as possible, he calls out, "All clear," and Taksheel and Riva move out with the cart.

The cart makes anxious hums and beeps as Taksheel controls it with his remote. The cart's wheels squeak, and it hops and swerves because of Taksheel's less than stellar driving, which adds to Ethan's anxiety like. They might as well be banging pots and pans from how loud the cart is.

When they are halfway down the hall, a faint giggle and light scuffling floats out from the vents above Ethan. He aims his shotgun up, and the group stops and listens. The shifting in the vents returns, and while everyone tenses, Ethan trails the noise with his shotgun until he sees a vent grate on the floor in front of Marian.

Marian sees this, and her eyes snap between the open vent above her head and the door just down the hall.

"Eyes up. Something's in the vents," whispers Marian.

Taksheel and Riva aim their weapons at the vent opening, and Marian motions the group to stay close to the wall. Once they are pressed as close as they can be, they walk forward, and Ethan cringes as the cart makes a ruckus with its movement.

When they are by the vent opening, Ethan peers into the darkness and is greeted by a wide grin and a pair of orange, reptilian eyes, with strands of brown hair hanging in front of it.

Ethan swears and shoots in the vent. Sparks fly from the slug hitting the metal, bright blue light flashes in the dark. Cackles float out of the vent, with some speedy scampering, bringing the others to shoot up into the ceiling as well.

The lights above explode, showering the group with glass, sparks, and wires, and the hallway lights flicker and dim, as explosive pops of gunfire bounce off the walls. By the time they are done shooting, the floor is littered with spent casings, and jagged holes mark the ceiling.

"What the hell was that!?" says Taksheel.

"That was Carmen," says Ethan as he shakily reloads. "She tried cutting me up with a power saw a few hours ago, and she almost jumped me again."

"Great. Now we got a psychopath following us," says Marian, her rifle trained on the vents.

"And the ticking time bomb," adds Taksheel, looking at Ethan.

Ethan and Riva glare at him, but Marian merely rolls her eyes and continues walking.

"Ethan's fine," says Marian. "He just needs some skin grafting and a day on the slopes. But we need to keep going. We still have a job to do."

The group follows Marian in silence, and for the next few minutes, there is no excitement. However, when they reach their destination, they pause and stare at what they can see of the Beast. Seeing the pulsing, green, and fused bodies with a cloud of pollen sends an uneasy tingling throughout Ethan's body and looking at the mangled door brings a sharp pain and hot flash to his back.

The group moves closer until they can see the ring of eyes and teeth taking up much of the chamber walls. The circle of eyes on the Beast moves in different directions, and the tentacles snake around the floor, kicking up pollen, or digging into the vents. The bulbs and their orange veins throb with every breath, and the room vibrates from its groans and hisses. But despite its impressive display of eyes, it does not seem to notice them.

"Taksheel, if that bomb doesn't kill that thing, I'm going to be pissed," says Marian.

"You and me both," says Taksheel.

Marian goes to Ethan, and he has yet to take his eye off the Beast. He wishes he had something better than the shredded armor he is currently wearing.

"Ethan, I need you to guard Riva," says Marian. "Me and Taksheel are going to blow that thing apart."

Another groan and hiss shake the room and their bones. Ethan nods and looks at Riva, who is slumped against the wall and pretending that she is not struggling to breathe.

"Hey." Marian taps Ethan's shoulder, bringing his attention back to her. "If it looks like we need help, help us. I really want to live."

"We all do," says Ethan.

Marian grins nervously, pats his shoulder, gives Riva a quick look, and then goes to Taksheel.

"Let's go, Taksheel. You got a bomb to deliver," says Marian.

"I was waiting for you," says Taksheel while driving the cart forward.

Ethan looks down the hallway, but out of the corner of his eye, he sees Riva slumped against the wall, clutching her heart. Her eyes are wide and unfocused, and her mouth hangs open as she takes heavy breaths.

Ethan turns his full attention to Riva, but before he can reach her, something slimy hits his back, knocking him to the floor. Metal bends and snaps, and crackling sparks fly as gunfire clashes with the Beast's deafening roars.

Ethan scrambles up and turns in time to see one of the large tentacles sliding out of the wrecked doorway. He looks inside the chamber and sees Marian shooting at the Beast's eyes, while Taksheel drives the bomb-cart towards one of its tentacles.

One of the Beast's eyes pops, showering the floor with goo, and the cart makes a high-pitched alarm as it is forced closer to the Beast. The cart's alarms and beeps get louder, the closer it gets, and its lights flash red when a tentacle grabs it. Taksheel runs towards the hallway with Marian close behind, and he waves at Ethan and Riva.

"Get back!" yells Taksheel.

The two get inside the hallway right as the Beast shoves the cart into its mouth. Once it is inside, Taksheel pushes the detonator, and the bomb explodes. There are many pops and crackles, and thick electric sparks of various colors burst through the Beast's hide like jagged needles.

Fire burns through its mouth, rupturing its veins and bulbs, popping its eyes, and tearing apart its cheeks. Its agonizing roars shake the chamber as its plant-flesh sizzles and pops, spraying the room with jets of blood and filling the chamber with foul smelling smoke.

The ruptured canisters ricochet inside its mouth, leading to broken teeth popping out. Chunks of burning flesh, bark, and broken teeth rain down in a gory mess.

It flails its tentacles around, smashing the walls and forcing the group to retreat further into the hallway. The rapid and hard thuds shake the chamber and hallway, leading to the lights overhead to flicker or break, and the metal boards snap or bend, exposing wires, pipes, and the ship's skeleton.

The pipes rupture from the tentacles slamming into them, spraying the area with water, fuel, and other chemicals. A screeching alarm stabs at the group's ears, followed by the damaged door flashing and flickering red.

The flood of chemicals spread towards the group, and the sparks falling on the mixture lead to a surge of flames and red-tinted smoke that engulfs the entire room and rushes towards the group, despite foam being sprayed at it.

"Everybody back!" yells Marian.

The group retreats further down the hall, and when they reach the next section of the hallway, Riva closes the door using an emergency function. An explosion rattles the hallway, and the lights shut off, putting them in pitch black darkness.

Seconds later, red emergency lights start swirling with a screeching alarm. Then, much to Ethan's surprise, the group floats off the floor. Ethan is quiet while the others yell and swear, and he tries grabbing anything to keep him grounded, but he has no luck.

The sealed door they came through also shows "0G" in its display, and the alarm is becoming considerably weaker and dies out with drones and sputters, like the announcement over the intercom.

"W-w-w-w-AR-nnnnnnnn-ING: H-I DamagE – S-C-TIon E-F-01. Hull at 20-3-222-1-1 percent eFF-cee. EVAC-tion maaaaannn-"

POP!

"Your bomb worked a little too well, Taksheel," says Marian. She flicks her lights on and twirls into a new position as she looks down the hallway. "But there is no way that thing lived."

"This should not have happened," says Taksheel as he grabs a door frame. "That thing must have busted a lot of pipes when it flipped out."

"An artificial gravity node was destroyed. We'll be floating like this for a while," says Riva. She swallows hard and swipes her hand aimlessly, trying to grab anything while her eyes lose focus. "Do you think they have a gift shop nearby?"

Marian rolls her eyes and air-swims ahead. "Now is not the time for gift shops."

"I'm just curious," says Riva. "I need to get my sister and my parents something… anything… I always get them something… anything…"

Marian turns back to Riva with a worried look, and Ethan scrunches what's left of his brow while Taksheel remains in the back.

"Riva, you haven't seen any of those people ever since we joined the *Hook Line*," says Marian.

"No. Not true, not true at all!" Riva giggles awkwardly and claws at her hair, tearing strands out. "Wait, it is. It is! I need to make it up. I-I need… Singing, football, cooking. I need gifts like that! They like that they like that they like that."

"Okay, why don't you take a breather?" suggests Marian. "Me and Taksheel will scout ahead. Ethan, you do your medic stuff."

Ethan nods, and Marian floats off with Taksheel, and as they leave, he looks down the hallway for signs of danger. He does not see any, so he uses the wall to push himself to Riva and grabs her shoulder.

Thin red cracks have seeped into yellow and brown eyes, and the tears reflect the emergency lights. Her eyes are darting around madly, her hands tremble, and her breathing is labored as she tries comforting her heart and scratching her hair.

As she does this, Ethan scans her with his Medical Assessment Device. The thin green lines move up and down and side to side on her. When it is finished, it displays her current condition.

SUBJECT: RIVA BONNEVUE

VITALS: UNHEALTHY

>>>Heart Rate: 160 b/m

VENTRICULAR FIBRILLATION IMMINENT

"Riva, relax," says Ethan. "Your heart rate is getting high."

"I need... I need to go home- To go home, where there's snow and snow and-and I can't be here," says Riva. She grabs Ethan's shoulders and struggles to look into his eye, as her tears float between the two. "Morjeinstej has music and happiness. It's been so long! I need to see it again! I need to see my sister and parents again!"

>>>Heart Rate: 165 b/m

"It's going to be okay," says Ethan. "You'll make it home, I promise."

"Don't say that!" cries Riva. "I know how this ends! We're all going to die here! This ship wants us. *Bon Voyage* wants us. These *things* want us. One by one we go."

>>>Heart Rate: 170 b/m

"How could they have missed these things? They had to have known these things were on Onyx! You can't hide monsters like these!" says Riva. "And how are you like them, but not them! What are you, Ethan!? What are you!"

>>>Heart Rate: 175 b/m

Ethan pulls Riva into him and gently shushes her, rubbing the back of her head and shoulder, while she cries into his shoulder. His heart is racing, too, and his eye flicks around, as if hoping there is a clue for his condition on the wall. All he sees is a camera, though.

"One by one we go. When it stops, we don't know. One by one we go," stammers Riva. "One by one, one by one, one by one. I want to go home. I can't be here. I need to see them again. Can you take me home, Ethan?"

Ethan nods. "I can. I'll get all of you home."

>>>Heart Rate: 180 b/m

Riva's sobs float into the void with the blackened foam and rubble, and Ethan keeps his hold tight on her as the two float in a circle. As much as Ethan wants to close his eye and focus on calming Riva down, he is too afraid to do so. He knows the moment he closes his eye is the moment that a Haunter, or Carmen, or the Pyro will greet them.

>>>*Heart Rate: 175 b/m*

As the two drift, Ethan notices Marian and Taksheel looking at them, both quiet, while Riva has not stopped whimpering and sniffling. Ethan looks at them, and Marian nods, gives him a thumbs up, and pushes herself back out the destroyed door. Taksheel looks at them for a few more seconds before leaving.

>>>*Heart Rate: 170 b/m*

Ethan's neck is wet from Riva's tears, and her grip becomes tighter, too, bringing him to wince from the pressure on the many cuts, bruises, and sprains on his body. But he is not complaining. Riva needs him, and so does the rest of the team. He will make sure they all get off this ship and go home.

For the next several minutes, Ethan and Riva are quiet, and while she trembles and cries softly, her heart rate steadily drops to a healthier level. But she is still pale and unfocused, and she continues to hold Ethan tight. But he is not complaining.

Then comes a radio's crackle on everyone's equipment.

"Hello? Can anybody hear me?" asks a familiar voice.

Ethan and Riva perk, and Marian and Taksheel float back in, with Marian smiling wide and a brightness in her eyes Ethan has never seen before.

"Tell me you two heard that!" says Marian.

"Testing. Testing. One-two-three. Testing. Anybody responding will be greatly appreciated," says Aiden Parsen.

Ethan and Riva float to Marian and Taksheel, and when they are all crowded around their commander, she activates her feed, bringing up a holographic display of Aiden's audio box.

"Aiden, we hear you loud and clear! Can you see us?" asks Marian quickly.

"I can hear you, Mary. But you're a little fuzzy. Is everything alright?" says Aiden.

"Taksheel broke an artificial gravity node with a makeshift bomb."

"Nice."

"You taught me well, sensei," says Taksheel.

The group chuckles, but despite the good mood they are now in, Ethan still looks around, paranoid that they will get ambushed by a Haunter. Or worse, one of the Pyschos.

"So, where have you been?" asks Marian.

"I've been trying to get back to you guys ever since we got separated. Them things are persistent, though. They've been chasing me nonstop and popping out of every nook and cranny," says Aiden.

"Yeah, they're a pain in the ass, "says Marian. "But listen Aiden, we're in Section E, and we're about to go to Section F to get an emergency extraction signal out. Is there a safe spot for you to hold up in until we can get to you?"

"Sadly, no. Nowhere is safe on this forsaken ship," says Aiden.

"The safest spot would be the bridge," says Riva hoarsely. "It has the thickest doors and automated security with its own life support, and it will have access to everything we need to plan an escape or hold out until help arrives."

"Great idea!" says Taksheel. "That's probably where Section 0 is hiding, and they can explain to us what happened here."

"Don't start," says Marian.

"He's got a point," says Aiden. *"The bridge is the safest place on any ship, and Section 0 is basically the all-seeing eye, so if they are here that is where they will be, and they will have answers."*

"Look, forget about Section 0! We need to focus on one problem at a time," says Marian. "Our problem is getting a signal out, and your problem is getting to the bridge. So, get to the bridge and we'll meet you there when we can, got it?"

"Loud and clear," says Aiden.

"Good. We'll see you soon. Dartmount out."

Aiden's audio box disappears, leaving the group to float around, feeling lighter than before.

"Finally, some good news," says Riva.

"I honestly can't believe he's still alive," says Taksheel.

"Well, let's not press our luck," says Marian. "We got a mission to finish, and the quicker we get the relay taken care of, the quicker we can get the signal out and get to Aiden. So, let's get going. We're almost home!"

23

Betrayal

The conversation with Aiden has lifted the group's spirits, and with this new boost in morale, they go through the chamber. It is pitch-black, so they use their lights to illuminate small areas of the room.

Their lights slide up and down, and side to side, as they float in the darkness, searching for anything that will want to kill them, as well as the exit. Luckily nothing tries to kill them and finding the exit is easy since it is now a large hole of twisted metal that is surrounded by a ring of charred remains of the Beast.

The team also finds chunks of cooked plant-flesh and blobs of foam floating around the chamber. The walls have been destroyed, the panels either smashed, blown off, or warped from the fire. With many panels gone, burnt wires, warped beams, and broken pipes are exposed to their lights.

The group floats through the debris, and Ethan turns his light to the ceiling, noting a destroyed vent. Even though nothing is inside, he keeps his eye on it if possible, and is the last one to go through the doorway.

The group still must float through the hallway, and the walls are covered in thick strands of burnt plants covered in orange veins. Some of the strands have petrified faces, warped bodies, or limbs fused to them, and charred roots spread across the floor, walls, and ceiling, with thin trails of smoke leaving them. What parts of the wall are not covered by the plants have been destroyed or are barely lit from failing lights.

After a few more minutes of traveling, the group reaches a large door with "Communications Room" barely lit above it. The door is covered in film and thin vines, and Ethan and Taksheel remove these things from the door and its orb. When it is clear, Ethan unlocks it with his Master Key Band.

Taksheel slides in after the door opens, gives the room a quick sweep, and then calls all clear. The rest float in and Ethan finds himself in awe at what he is seeing while Marian closes and locks the door.

The chamber's walls are curved to form a perfect circle. There are blank computer screens in equal increments on the upper level, and said level is guarded by dusty railings, with pipes and steel beams along the ceiling. There is also an observation room overlooking the chamber. Blood, scratches, bullet holes, and floating garbage and bullet casings desecrate the scenery, and when Ethan looks up, he sees a vent network following the circular design of the room with all the vent coverings floating in zero gravity. The room is also being watched by a ring of cameras.

After Ethan finishes looking around, he sees Riva examining a massive pillar surrounded by a ring of blank computers, all connected to it by thick wires. The pillar appears like a series of blocks surrounding a tube, and all the blocks have small dim lights and screens on them, with the Arx Corporation logo at the bottom corner. There is also a holographic projector on a raised platform near the computers, an airlock with a green light at the far end, and a large portion of the ceiling is a thick glass dome, giving a view of space and a relay tower with a satellite dish on it.

Ethan, Marian, and Taksheel watch Riva as she carefully unscrews a panel off one of the cubes, and she inspects the interior for a minute before resealing and moving on to the next one. This method brings Marian to roll her eyes impatiently, and Taksheel taps his trigger guard as he looks at the door. Meanwhile, Ethan scans the area again and is thankful to see that nothing has changed. Despite the impatience, boredom, and anxiety, the group remains quiet. After a long stretch of time passes, of constant unscrewing and screwing with the occasional muttering, Riva sighs heavily and reseals the final cube.

"I hate to say this, but I need to go outside and fix the relay so that way the signal can go further than what it can do now," says Riva.

Marian raises an eyebrow. "Can you even do that?"

Riva glares at her. "Of course I can! It won't be as good as Aiden's repairs, but it will still be enough to get the signal out."

"But what about the encrypted signal? Can you figure that out in here first?" asks Taksheel.

Before Riva can answer, Marian butts in.

"We will not worry about that just yet. We need to get an emergency signal out right now," says Marian.

"Okay, but we don't even know if Riva can fix it. But we know she can figure out the mystery signal. I mean, I hope she can figure it out, anyway," says Taksheel.

"I can fix the relay and decrypt the other signal," says Riva.

Taksheel looks at Riva with a small frown. "How do you know you can fix it the relay, though? Have you ever fixed one before? Do you have *any* sort of training for this model? How about the coding for the encrypted signal? Even you said you were unfamiliar with it."

"Taksheel, I can do this! I have the training, and that relay is maybe unfamiliar, but I can still do it. All I need is a few hours to crack the code. It'll be hard, but I promise I can do it."

"Fine, I'll buy that. But the relay is a problem. How can you work with something you're unfamiliar with? You'll probably hurt yourself if you try fixing that thing."

"I can do this, Taksheel!"

Ethan floats to Riva. "I don't think he doubts you. I think he's worried about your safety."

"No, I doubt her," says Taksheel. "And, yeah, there's some worry, but it's mostly doubt."

Ethan glares at him, Riva huffs, and Marian waves her hand rapidly.

"Okay, hold on. Hold on! I'm in charge. I give out the orders. We don't have time for debates or questioning me. Riva, can you fix the relay? Yes, or no?" says Marian.

"Yes," says Riva. "I said that a minute ago."

"Good. Put on a suit and do it. End of discussion."

Riva nods and makes her way to the airlock but stops when Ethan gets in front of her and gently pushes her back, while giving Marian a condemning look.

"She can't go out there. Her heart is bad," says Ethan.

With that statement, Riva stiffens and Marian frowns while Taksheel floats around, scanning the chamber.

"Uh, no, it isn't," says Marian. "The AATS wouldn't allow her in if she had a bad heart. She'd be doing something else, like modeling or vlogging or advertising."

"You saw what happened to her earlier!" says Ethan.

"What you saw was her having a panic attack, but she always has those and she's fine now." Marian looks at Riva. "Right?"

Riva nods, but also scratches her head.

"See? She's fine now," says Marian.

"She almost died back there!" says Ethan.

"Ethan, I'm fine. It was just a panic attack earlier," says Riva; she scratches her head harder and then runs her trembling fingers through her hair. "I need to do this. I'm not worthless."

"Nobody is saying you're worthless, but you can't go out there," says Ethan.

"For God's sake, Ethan! She's the only one who can fix the relay! If she fixes it then we can go home!" yells Marian.

Ethan narrows his eye, floats to Marian.

"Do you want Riva to get hurt?" says Ethan.

Marian pushes Ethan back. "Get out of my face! You know full well I want all of us out of here, and the only way to do that is to get a signal out, which she can do!"

Taksheel floats next to Ethan, and Riva floats away from them but keeps her eyes on the three.

"Look, Ethan, I hate it as much as you do, but after thinking about it, we really don't have a choice. Riva has more training with relays than all of us, so she is the only one who can do this, and if she does this, she will be the most valuable person on the team. She'll be the big hero of the AATS, too. Think of it like that," says Taksheel.

"So you're switching sides?" says Ethan.

"My position is I want to get out of here, and Riva is confident that she can fix the relay. So, even though I doubt her to an extent, she still has a better chance of getting that thing fixed than any of us, so she gets to make herself useful," says Taksheel.

Ethan claws at his hair. "Does the bad heart not concern you?"

"Riva does not have a bad heart, and she is the only one who has a chance at fixing that relay," says Marian, with more weight on his words. "I hate it, I really do, but none of us want to die here, and if she can get out a signal, then that is what she needs to do. Besides, survival is more important than that encrypted signal."

"There has to be another way besides sending Riva out there," says Ethan.

"Enough with the bullshit, Ethan!" yells Marian. "I'm in charge, and she's going. End of conversation!"

CLI-BANG!

The group looks across the chamber and sees the airlock door now has a red circle projected in front of it with a message displayed. "WARNING: Exterior Maintenance in Progress."

The three rush to the door as fast as they can in zero gravity, and when they reach the door, Ethan presses his Master Key Band against the door's orb, but an error message appears.

"What?" Ethan tries again, and when the same message appears, he bangs on the door and activates his communicator. "Riva, what are you doing? Get out of there!"

A monitor hanging above the door flashes on, and a video of Riva appears. Her shaky hand is pulling away from the camera and she is putting on a thick, white spacesuit with a helmet floating near her. Her eyes shine in the dim light, and her body trembles as she wiggles out of her uniform, revealing the jumpsuit beneath.

"I'm sorry, Ethan, but I have to do this," says Riva. *"This is the only way to save us."*

"Riva, we can figure out something else that doesn't involve you going out there."

"This is the most efficient way to get it done. The inner relay is fine, but there is something wrong with the outer relay, which is why I need to go outside. After I fix it, we can boost Bon Voyage's *signal and go home."*

"At least let me put on a suit to be out there with you," says Ethan. "If you have another attack-"

"You can't come out here. There was only one suit." Riva slips on the spacesuit and offers them an uneasy smile when she grabs the helmet. *"Wish me luck."*

Riva then shuts off her feed, and a minute later, a screeching alarm sounds with red lights swirling above the airlock door, while a loud grinding and popping noise comes from behind it. The three back away, watching the door in total silence, and several seconds later, the alarm stops, but the red lights keep swirling.

Ethan looks at the observation window, feeling sick, watching the relay tower stretch into the darkness of space. A minute later, Riva appears in her white spacesuit with a large air pack on her back, the toolbox attached to her suit, and a cord keeping her tethered to *Bon Voyage*. Taksheel and Marian look away from the door a few seconds later and see what Ethan sees, and Taksheel smiles.

"There she is," says Taksheel.

Marian activates her communicator. "Riva, talk to me. What do you see?"

While waiting for a response, Marian motions Ethan and Taksheel to monitor the area. The two scan the area with their weapons raised. The steel beams cast large patches of darkness all over the chamber, and floating garbage glides past their eyes, but so far there are no signs of any danger, which lifts some weight from Ethan's shoulders.

"The relay has been sabotaged, I'm sure of it," says Riva.

"What do you mean?" asks Marian. "What's wrong with it?"

Ethan risks looking out the observation window and sees Riva holding on to the relay.

"There are clean cuts in the wires, and some circuit boards have been disconnected, but these are easy fixes," says Riva. *"I should have all this fixed enough to get a signal out in a few minutes."*

"Good. Keep me posted," says Marian. She clicks off her communicator and looks at Ethan. "You're supposed to be guarding the perimeter."

Ethan quickly scans the area again, still not seeing anything. This goes on for some time, and if the situation had been the exact opposite, he would have loved the quietness. There is no shooting, no screams, no terrible monsters trying to rip him into pieces. It is just them and the gentle hums and blinking lights. Space is also great to look at for once, with tiny lights dotting the blackness, which is split down the middle by a thick stripe of light brown and dark purple dust that has its own collection of glowing dots.

So calm.

So peaceful.

Yet Ethan cannot help but wonder if there are more of these Haunters or their spores hiding in the galaxy. If there are more, then they are fucked. If not, maybe they can contain them. Provided that they survive to tell the Federation of Sol Systems what happened on *Bon Voyage.*

"Taksheel, you're the closest to the pillar. Can you do me a favor?" asks Riva.

Ethan looks up and sees Riva is putting plating back in place, and the relay tower and its satellite are slowly flashing red.

"What do you need me to do?" asks Taksheel as he takes a position by the pillar.

"I need you to flip the power switch. It is a large lever that is at the base of the relay pillar," says Riva.

After a few seconds of searching, Taksheel finds a large lever at the bottom of the pillar. He pushes against it, and at first, it doesn't move, but after a few seconds of struggle, the lever snaps up with a bright spark and a loud clang.

What follows is a series of hums and lights flickering to life. The lights go from red to yellow, then to blue, and finally green, and then all the computer screens snap to life and a holographic display of a blank map of the Peace System appears, with a loading bar beneath it. The hologram flickers for a moment, but soon enough the image stabilizes, and the loading bar disappears, followed by names appearing and the celestial bodies getting some color.

In the center is a red dwarf star marked as "Peace."

Next to it is "Onyx (Peace I)."

Beyond it is "Onyx Minor (Peace II)."

The last planet is "Ghost (Peace III)."

When everything loads, Taksheel floats away from the pillar with a smile on his face, and Marian gets a small smile, too.

"I got it!" says Taksheel.

"*Very good,*" says Riva, short of breath. "*Everything is green up here, except... The rotatory platform is not moving. I'll have to manually turn it... Go to the main computer, it should be marked as '01,' and let me know when you see an antennae icon.*"

Taksheel floats to the designated computer, and after he reaches the computer, Ethan looks out the observation window again. He can still see Riva floating in the black expanse with the dark red light of the sun and planet behind her, and she is moving fine with the safety cord holding strong. It takes a few seconds for Riva to position herself at the base of the relay, and she makes quick work of unscrewing the cover.

With the cover removed, a network of gears and one large yellow and black-striped crank is exposed. But while Riva works quickly, Ethan can hear her breathing struggle over the communicator, and that alone brings his heart to beat harder. He becomes more worried when he sees her struggling to turn the crank, which leads to the gears and the satellite slowly turning.

"Riva, how is your chest? Is it hurting?" asks Ethan.

"Fine. I'm fine. Fine... Fine... Fine..." replies Riva.

"Are you sure?" asks Taksheel.

"Worry about the computer screen," says Riva. *"Do you see... things? ... Wonderful... things?"*

Taksheel looks at the screen and sees a gray antenna icon appear with "X" in the corner.

"Riva, I see the antenna icon!" says Taksheel.

"Good... Good," says Riva. She chuckles. *"I'm valuable, now."*

"Riva, focus, tell us what to do next," says Marian.

"One... More... One more, one more." Riva rocks back and forth, and her hands rub against her helmet. She floats away from the relay, only saved from going into the expanse by the tether.

"She needs to come back inside, right now," says Ethan urgently.

"We still need to get the signal out," says Taksheel.

"And we have an antenna! Order her inside!" yells Ethan.

"She'll be back inside when she gets the job done!" snaps Marian. "Riva, we have the icon, but it is not connecting. What do we need to do next?"

"You? Nothing... Nothing. Me? I need... I need... I need." Riva's chuckling turns to whimpers, and she swims her way back to the relay and begins pawing at the panels. *"Where is it? Where is it, where is it, where is it?"*

"Riva, relax and focus," says Marian.

"Order her back inside," says Ethan.

Marian bangs on a computer. "Ethan, shut the fuck up!"

"I found it! I found a missing switch! Switches!" Riva's whimpers shift to strained giggles. *"I'll get you home, and then we'll be friends again, Marian."*

Marian's hard expression snaps to shock, and all three look up and see panels floating around, with Riva working on something they cannot see.

"Riva, what are you talking about?" asks Marian.

*"'Riva Bonnevue! Oh good, sweet, Riva! It's hard to believe that we **used** to be friends!' You said that Marian. You! You-you did. You! But we can be friends again after this, right?"*

"Oh... Oh, no, you-you miss understood me! I was just mad. We're still friends," says Marian, with tears welling in her eyes.

The X by the antenna icon disappears and is replaced with one small bar.

"I didn't want to leave you in the room, but Taksheel said that you would be safe in there and that you'd be proud if we collected supplies. It was his idea to pretend not to hear your distress call," says Riva.

Marian and Ethan look at Taksheel, and he looks at them with a nervous smile.

"Come on, guys, don't look at me like that," says Taksheel.

"But you were so angry, and I was scared. Scared-scared-scared. Bars! Do you see bars? Tell me, do you see the bars!? Will this fix things? Am I valuable, Marian?" rambles Riva.

The bars keep climbing, and Marian nods with tears streaking down her eyes, now hot with rage and her hand gripping her rifle tight.

"Come back inside, Riva," says Marian. "We can talk some more when you're in here."

"Marian, I'd like to explain my side," says Taksheel.

Marian snaps her rifle up. "Shut up!"

Taksheel holds his hands up, and Ethan adjusts his grip on his shotgun while Taksheel's eyes flick between the two.

"We got full bars. Make the call, Marian," says Taksheel.

Marian makes her way to computer 01, and Ethan orders Taksheel back, which he obeys.

"How's Riva doing, Ethan?" asks Taksheel.

Ethan tightens his grip on his shotgun, then hesitantly looks up and sees Riva leaning against the crank while rubbing her chest.

"Marian, get Riva back inside," says Ethan.

Marian looks up and stammers into her communicator. "Riva! Riva! Get back inside!"

"I can't... I'm becoming them... I can't come back," says Riva.

"Riva? This is Ethan. There is a vaccine on this ship. It is in the Section 0 lab. We can help you, I promise," says Ethan.

"Oh, so Section 0 is here. Called it," says Taksheel.

"One by one we go... When it stops, we don't know... One by one we go..." recites Riva.

Marian hastily types on the computer, and a command screen appears. She types in another command, and a radio icon appears. She clicks on the icon and an audio bar appears, and when she hits the red circle for recording, it beeps and flashes green.

"Mayday, mayday, mayday. Any available FSSN or AATS craft. This Marian Dartmount of the *Hook Line*. My team is stranded on *Bon Voyage,* and we need priority one evac. Location: System, Peace. Planet, Onyx. Coordinate: plus forty-five North, minus twenty West. Brings lots of guns and medical. Dartmount out!"

Marian ends the recording, and after it flashes red, she types in another command, and the computer beeps.

"Message sent." Marian's message replays, and when it ends, there is another beep. *"Message repeats."*

"Okay, mission accomplished. Come inside, Riva!" says Marian.

The Federation of Sol Systems anthem suddenly plays over the intercoms installed on the cameras, and while the three look around in confusion, a bright flash of white and blue light tears through space. Crackles and pops blind the three, and dark shadows cover them as the new ship glides above them, and over the communicator, Riva's screams are disrupted. When the light disappears, the anthem is still playing, and the three stumble around, trying to regain themselves.

"Jeez, what the hell!?" cries Marian.

"Damn, that was bright!" says Taksheel.

"Riva are you okay?" asks Ethan.

"I-I can't see, and I feel hot!" sobs Riva. *"There are warning alarms going off in my helmet! I-I can't see! What's going on? Why can't I see!?"*

"Oh no," says Ethan.

"Those bastards blinded her!" says Marian.

"Riva, can you feel any breaches in your suit?" asks Ethan.

"I-I don't know. I-I- No. No, no, no, no. I don't feel any tears. One by one we go, when it stops, we don't know!"

"You will not be another one. We're getting you out of there!" says Marian.

"Riva, stay calm and grab the safety cord. Use it to pull your way back inside, slow and steady," says Ethan urgently.

"Okay... Okay... I grabbed it. I grabbed the cord!" says Riva.

"Good. Now use it as a guide to get to the airlock, and I'll get you taken care of, I promise," says Ethan.

"Uh, guys..." Taksheel points up. "We're in trouble."

Ethan and Marian look to where Taksheel is pointing, and Ethan's eye widens. The ship above them is silver, sleek, and has the figure of a sewing needle, which is the design of a Federation of Sol Systems Navy torpedo boat, and there is a glowing dot at the bottom of the torpedo boat. Aiming right at them.

"Get to cover!" shouts Ethan.

There is a flash of light, followed by a loud ***BANG!***

The glass shatters, and Ethan is pulled up with a rush of screaming wind as the communications relay twirls into space, broken into pieces, with the largest pieces scraping against *Bon Voyage's* hull, where it tumbles out of view. The alarm sounds, and Ethan grabs one of the support beams as his lungs shrivel from all the air being sucked out.

His face turns blue, and his eye dries while his heart gets heavy, and then a series of thuds travel overhead, putting the chamber in darkness, piece by piece. When the last metal slab is in place, the room is covered in red swirling lights. All three cling to their beams or rail and gasp for air while air is pumped into the room through nozzles on the wall. As they regain their oxygen, the alarm and Federation anthem play over each other.

"What the hell was that?" says Taksheel, his body barely lit by the red lights. "Seriously, what the hell was that!?"

"Riva?" wheezes Marian; she is lost in the darkness. "Riva, can you hear me?"

There is only static on their communicators.

"Riva, please answer," begs Marian.

More static.

"No," gasps Ethan.

Ethan bangs his head against the metal beam, shaking and swallowing as tears roll down his cheek; Taksheel shakes his head and rubs his sweaty hair; and Marian wails, and a thud echoes in the dark.

"No! No! Why her! Why did it have to be her!" sobs Marian.

"Because the ship needs souls. More souls for *Bon Voyage.* More souls for our new home," hisses a familiar voice.

An icy shiver runs through Ethan's spine, and he looks to the side and sees a shadow slithering out of the vent like a snake with a line of blue lights on its back. His heart races, and Carmen giggles as she unhooks her saw.

"I finally found you, Troublemaker," says Carmen. She revs her saw, which illuminates the crazed yellow eyes, her scarred, scaly skin, and bloody teeth. "Time to play!"

24

Predators

The Federation of Sol Systems anthem blares over the intercom when Carmen's saw revs to life. Ethan pushes himself away and shoots at Carmen with his shotgun. Marian and Taksheel, who are still featureless in the dim room, shoot at her with their rifles.

Muzzle flashes light the dark, and bullets shatter and bounce harmlessly off the rippling energy field covering Carmen. The ricocheting projectiles bounce off the walls and crack the computer screens.

While they shoot at Carmen, her shrill laughter echoes in the chamber, and she fires a saw blade at Ethan. He barely dodges it, and the blade hits the projector, blowing out its lens and flinging sparks and burnt computer pieces twirling in the air, while the projection flickers out of existence.

The group tries to find good footing as they bounce around the chamber, all while Carmen effortlessly launches herself from the ceiling, cackling, and revving her saw again.

"Join us! Gary needs friends!" yells Carmen.

Ethan grabs a metal beam, and after pulling himself into position, he keeps his body pressed against the beam and shoots at Carmen. The shield around her flickers again, but this time with little branches of energy breaking off, which brings her to launch another saw at Ethan before retreating behind one of the beams.

Ethan dodges the blade again by pushing himself off the beam. The saw blade breaks against the metal, sending metal fragments spiraling into the darkness.

"Where are you going!" yells Marian as she hops after Carmen.

Marian shoots some more, but her rifle quickly clicks to signal an empty magazine. While she works on reloading, Carmen leaps towards another beam, turns herself upside down, and grins at Marian.

She has one hand latched on to the metal beam, and she is revving her reloaded saw with her other hand. Carmen's grin widens and her pupils appear to pulse, and Ethan's eye snaps between Marian and Carmen as he coils himself for a launch.

"Come on! Here I am!" yells Marian, her blue eyes nearly consumed by the yellow taint. "Come get me!"

"I don't want you. I want Troublemaker!" says Carmen.

"Tough shit. Let's dance!"

Carmen's grin widens, tearing her skin from lips to ears. She curls her body and then lunges at Marian. As this happens, Ethan rockets to Carmen and rams her, sending them spinning in the weightless room.

They bounce off the metal walls, and Carmen kicks Ethan into a doorway, causing him to hit his head on the frame. A sharp pain explodes through his skull, and a ringing blocks out all noise as his vision blurs.

Ethan winces and holds his head as he twirls, and his eye struggles to focus as he sees Taksheel shooting at Carmen. Despite his best efforts, the bullets are still harmless against Carmen, and her shield has become ripples of bright blue energy.

After the ripples clear, Carmen shoots a saw blade at Taksheel, forcing him to jump out of the way. But while Taksheel distracts Carmen, Marian shoots her in the back, but the shield still holds, and Carmen bounces towards Marian with a crazed grin as she reloads.

Marian tries backing up, and Carmen becomes a walking figure of bright sparks and maniacal cackles. Then Carmen revs her saw and Marian deflects the first swipe, but the second swipe slashes her abdomen.

"No!" screams Ethan.

He bounces towards the two women, vision red and hands gripping his shotgun tight as his infected arm and eye pulse. Orange-tinted blood floats around Marian through the jagged cut across her abdomen, and her eyes water as she tries aiming at Carmen, but the Pyscho brings the saw against her arm. Marian starts screaming after that, and Carmen's cackles turn to shrill laughter.

Marian's screams are crisp in Ethan's ears, and every step brings him deeper into the red. Carmen pushes Marian down, and her laughter gets louder as sparks and blood fly. Marian's legs buckle with flesh, bone, metal, and cloth tearing and popping up and off from her arm.

When her arm snaps off, Ethan shoots Carmen in the head. The shield protects her, but the blast knocks out her footing and she loses her grip on her saw, and when she tries to regain herself, Ethan swings his shotgun like a club against her, and keeps beating her, pushing her further away from Marian.

The shield does not protect against the blunt force of the shotgun, and Carmen's face becomes bloody with some teeth floating around. Ethan goes for another swing, but Carmen grabs his weapon, headbutts him, and then slams him into a computer.

The computer breaks, showering the two with sparks, and Carmen presses the shotgun down on Ethan. The two lock eyes while the anthem repeats, and Ethan twists his body, putting the two in a spin that leads to them hitting and breaking another computer.

Ethan kicks Carmen in the gut, but while she is floating away from the force, she keeps her hold on the shotgun, thus taking him with her. While they struggle for the weapon, one of them pulls the trigger, which pushes the pair further in the air.

When they are in the center of the room, Carmen kicks Ethan away while releasing the shotgun, and while he spins around, she coils herself against the pillar and then launches herself at his chest. The hit pushes the air out of his lungs, and the pair break through the observation room's window.

They twirl with shards of glass floating around them, and Carmen punches Ethan in the face. The punch sends him bouncing into a wall next to a large screen displaying a map of the system and its routes, as well as a signal marked as classified.

Marian's screams continue, and Carmen leaps at Ethan again, now armed with a saw blade that digs into her hand. She tries slashing Ethan with the blade, but he grabs her wrist with his infected hand and holds it back.

Then he grunts when Carmen grabs his throat and starts squeezing. He tries prying her off while keeping the saw from cutting his face open, but it is not working. Her grip is tight, the jagged saw blade is getting closer, and he can feel vines wiggling beneath Carmen's skin.

The blade is near the tip of Ethan's nose, and Marian's screams die with a sudden gunshot. Hearing that, Ethan suddenly releases the hand choking him, and he punches Carmen's face. Her nose shatters and she jerks back, with globs of tainted blood flowing from her flat nose.

Her grip loosens, allowing Ethan to turn her body and smash her into the screen. The screen shatters and bright sparks explode from the display. The surge goes through Carmen and hits Ethan.

His bloodthirsty eye locks on to Carmen's surprised eyes, his jaw and muscles tighten, his heart races, and the two twitch violently as electric currents tear through them. After a few more pops and flashes, the two float away, with Carmen being stiff, and Ethan struggling to breathe with his hair standing and smoke rising from him.

Moments later, he pushes himself away from Carmen and grips his chest as he gulps for air. His skin is hot, his vision is blurry, and his suit has fresh burns and cracks on it. When Carmen does not move, Ethan collects his shotgun and floats out of the observation room.

"Marian! Taksheel!" calls Ethan.

Ethan scans the dark room, feeling sick as swirling red lights stretch the shadows and the Federation anthem plays over the intercom. His heart races, and he coughs as he moves in the dark, wanting to call Marian again, but his gut is telling him not to.

He travels further in the dark, and when he is near the relay pillar, he goes still. Marian is floating in the dim red light, occasionally disappearing in the shadows.

Ethan swallows and makes his way to Marian's limp form. Her eyes are wide and wet, her mouth is open, and her body slowly turns to Ethan. Her severed arm floats nearby with a trail of orange-tinted blood, and a cloud of blood coming from her slashed abdomen and the hole in her head surrounds her body. Vines are wiggling around from where her arm was severed.

Ethan's hands shake as he grabs Marian to hold her steady, and he gives her a quick inspection. Her ammo is gone, but her communicator is still on her shoulder. Ethan checks his and sees that it no longer works. It is charred and its lens is shattered.

So, he removes his communicator and replaces it with Marian's. Then he checks his Medical Assessment Device and finds that it is also useless; it has been destroyed by his stunt to defeat Carmen. Then he checks his Master Key Band and finds the same thing, so he discards them and activates Marian's communicator. It has trouble turning on, so he straps it to his forearm and reboots it. Once it is fully rebooted, he finds Marian did not have it password protected, so he goes to the contacts list and selects Taksheel Iyer.

The connection locks on, but "Blocked" appears on the display, so Ethan cuts the connection and looks at Marian's body. His breathing is heavy, his hand twitches, and his jaw tightens. He feels his one eye pulsing, too, and his muscles are still tight and tingling.

Ethan sighs, closes Marian's eyes, and then looks at the metal slabs covering what used to be the observation window. Tears clean the grime off his face, and his throat becomes tight as he bows his head and digs his fingers into his scalp.

"One by one we go," whispers Ethan.

Ethan looks up again and swallows as he struggles to remember the words he heard at the funerals he's been to. He wants to remember those words, but his mind is clogged with the faces of the departed. He cannot even think about his team's faces when he first met them. They are all dead, bloody, terrified. He hears their screams, feels their blood, their cold skin, he sees the light fading from their eyes. They are dying and he can't save them.

Ethan bows and screams as he claws his hair, ripping some of his scabs and hair out. He screams again and drags his fingers down his face. Marian's blood clings to him, and his screaming turns to cracking whimpers and he rubs his face, smearing blood and tears on his skin.

"Damn it! Damn it! Damn it! I fucked up. I fucked up. I fucked up. *Porquê Deus, porquê?*" whimpers Ethan. *"O que nós fizemos?"*

As soon as those words finish, Ethan's voice trails off and he stares ahead at nothing. He does not need God or anybody else to tell him what he did. He knows what he did; he knows what they did, and he knows what this is, but with this realization, he also remembers the words from the many funerals he attended, because often their deaths were retaliation either by man or by God

Everyone in his Oros circle always tried to get on God's good side when one of them was struck down. But they always went back to their ways in a couple of days, just like Ethan did. Now here he is, torn up on *Bon Voyage* with his dead eye reflecting the red lights. The Federation anthem is also no longer playing, so it completely quiet, and Ethan takes a deep, shaky breath, then recites in an uncertain voice.

"R-Requiem æternam... dona eis, Domine... Et lux... Et lux perpetua luceat eis. Reuiescant in pace... Amen."

Ethan shakily lifts his hand, hesitates, then makes a cross across his chest. Then the entrance to the communications room opens. The whirring and thuds ripple through the chamber, and a small glow reflects off the metal near Ethan. He stiffens at the sight, then turns around and freezes.

The Pyro is looking right at him.

The Pyro and Ethan stare at each other for only the briefest of seconds before a spark of energy gets Ethan moving. He jumps towards the relay pillar as flames shoot towards him, engulfing Marian, which causes her body to thrash with a strangled cry and vines bursting out of her body, just for them to dissolve in the fire.

The Pyro bounces forward and shoots another stream of fire at Ethan. He pushes himself off the pillar and aims for the vent Carmen came from.

The fire crashes against the pillar, and the lights and monitors crack and flicker. The fire moves up the pillar's length, eating it piece by piece as it climbs to the ceiling.

Ethan pedals as fast as he can towards the vent, his teeth grinding against each other and tears fogging his vision. He can feel the heat on his feet, and when he reaches the vent, he quickly pulls himself inside and crawls with his shotgun scraping against the roof, and his gear scraping the walls. As he crawls, the fire reflects off the vent's walls, and blistering heat rolls over his legs.

Ethan curses and crawls faster. The air is pulled away from him, and when he reaches a ladder, he scales it, wheezing and trembling. When he reaches the next level, he crawls forward until a vent grate breaks underneath him, sending him crashing to the floor. What little air he has left is knocked out, and everything becomes fuzzy.

As Ethan lays on the floor, coughing and wheezing, a sudden loud bang and rapid steps catch his attention. He looks down the hallway and sees a shadow moving along the wall. The long shadow shrinks as the quick steps get closer with stuttering clicks.

The shadow has wiggling appendages on its back and long claws, and when it rounds the corner, it turns out to be a Haunter. The creature immediately sees Ethan and rushes him with a scratchy scream.

As it runs, the door around the corner opens again, and Ethan's fingers fumble to grab his shotgun as he sits up. By the time he can aim it at the Haunter, a burst of bullets rips through its back and bursts out of its chest, splattering the floor with blood.

The Haunter staggers and turns, and more bullets tear through it, bringing it to its knees. The Haunter struggles to stand, and the newcomer quickly approaches it, draws his pistol, and puts two rounds into its head.

The Haunter crumbles backward, its broken brains splattered in front of Ethan, and its one eye looking straight up, while the vines feel around and attempt to get the body moving.

Ethan recognizes the newcomer, and when they aim their pistol at him, he holds up his hands.

"Wait! Don't shoot! I'm not one of them!" says Ethan.

Simon freezes, and Ethan gets up with his hands still raised.

"I know I look like one of them, but I'm not. I'm also perfectly sane. Hand to God," says Ethan.

Simon stares at Ethan in silence for a few seconds before he lowers his pistol, clearly confused.

"I know you. You're the weirdo I met a few hours ago," says Simon. "How the hell are you still alive?"

"I don't know," says Ethan. His eye is glistening, and his cheeks are caked with flash-dried blood and sweat, and he notices a yellow tint has seeped into Simon's brown eyes. "They got you too, huh?"

"Yeah," says Simon. "I was trying to raid a vending machine for some food when they got me. Blew pollen right in my face… You?"

"I really don't want to talk about it."

"I see." Simon's eyes dart up and down Ethan's body. "Well, all things considered, at least you still somewhat resemble a human."

"Thanks."

Simon awkwardly looks around for a moment, as if expecting a prank to happen.

"So… about that team you were talking about. Where are they?" asks Simon.

"Dead. Except for one. Our engineer, Aiden Parsen. I'm trying to find him," says Ethan.

"I see…"

Simon aims his pistol at Ethan's forehead, and Ethan raises his shotgun.

"The hell you doing!? I'm not one of them!" says Ethan.

"So you say. Give me your weapon and put your hands up and walk in front of me."

Ethan frowns. "Are you serious?"

"Yes. And I've got an Arx Corporation ballistic shield, so don't try shooting me. Just follow the instructions and save both of us the trouble."

Ethan is motionless, and when Simon taps his trigger and clears his throat, Ethan reluctantly turns over his shotgun and puts his hands on his head. Simon then shoulders Ethan's shotgun and orders him to walk forward.

"So, are you going to shoot me?" asks Ethan.

"That depends on your behavior," says Simon.

"You realize how ridiculous this is, right?"

"I don't care. Keep walking."

Ethan sighs and walks in silence. He has no patience for this, but he has no energy to deal with it, so he has no choice but to see what happens next. And all he can do is pray that what happens next will give him a break.

25

A Talk With Simon

Getting from point A to point B is a blur for Ethan. He barely feels his feet moving, and his mind is disconnected from his body. He has been obeying Simon's commands, but without a conversation to distract him, all he can think about was how everything went wrong within a matter of minutes.

The relay was fixed; the signal got out, and then a torpedo boat appeared and killed Riva and the signal. Then Carmen came and maimed Marian, and Taksheel finished her and left him to die. And, to top it off, the Pyro returned and nearly burned him alive.

How did it all go wrong? How did the torpedo boat arrive with pinpoint accuracy above *Bon Voyage*, and why did it destroy the relay and kill Riva? And why did Taksheel kill Marian and leave him for dead? And is Aiden okay?

These questions boil Ethan's blood, and he feels his eye pulsing with rage, but he keeps quiet.

"Stop. Put your hands on your head, face the wall, and get on your knees," says Simon.

Ethan complies and waits, while Simon unlocks a door.

"Alright, get in the room," says Simon.

Ethan gets up and enters a room that has the Unity winged sun on the wall, a desk with a placard that has "Rev. H. Foster" on it, and a few chairs. The desk is completely bare, and near it is a makeshift bed of pillows, cushions, and blankets with stashes of food and bottled water. He also welded the vent in the room shut.

"Sit on that chair," says Simon, pointing at a chair in front of the desk.

Ethan sits on the chair, finding it remarkably uncomfortable, and he looks around the room, hoping to see more clues about what the place is. Luckily, it is not a death trap since there is a stash of medical supplies and lots of ammo boxes between the sleeping area and the desk. If the Haunters attack, they can put up a good fight.

While Ethan scans the room, Simon sets the shotgun on the wall, sits in the Reverend's chair, and aims his rifle at Ethan.

"The good news is that you didn't act like a Psycho or one of those mutants out there," says Simon. "The bad news is that I am having a hard time believing you're AATS."

Ethan swallows nervously.

"What were you doing in the communications room?" asks Simon.

"We were trying to signal for help, but the Federation Navy tried to kill us with a torpedo boat as soon as we sent the signal," replies Ethan. "They killed our computer specialist, Riva Bonnevue, and then a Psycho named Carmen, tried killing us. She maimed our commander, Marian Dartmount, and then tried to kill me. But when I fought her off, I found our guard, Taksheel Iyer, killed her. *And* after that, some crazy guy with a flamethrower that has apparently been stalking me shows up and tried burning me alive!"

"It sounds like you've got bad luck. And you're what? The…?"

"Medic. In training. I don't even have a certificate yet. I mean, I have veterinarian training, but that's about it."

Simon places his finger on the trigger. "AATS doesn't send ships out to space with medics in training. That is illegal. Only certified medics may travel in space."

"Well, the *Hook Line* broke the law. I would tell you to talk to my captain, but he blew up with the ship when we docked on the *Bon Voyage* Section C emergency entrance," says Ethan sourly.

"Right... So, what happened to your guard? Is he dead?" asks Simon.

"I don't know, but Taksheel is no longer part of the team, and I need to find Aiden before Taksheel finds him."

"And Aiden is your other guard?"

"Engineer."

Simon grunts and removes his finger from the trigger, but it is now resting on the trigger guard.

"What are you doing on *Bon Voyage?*" asks Simon.

Ethan sighs irritably and scratches his head. "Look, we weren't even supposed to be here, alright? We were supposed to go to the Onyx Station to pick up a scientist, and then drop him off somewhere, but then we picked up *Bon Voyage's* distress signal, plus an encrypted signal, and went to investigate. When we got here, there was no Onyx Station, and we saw that *Bon Voyage* was wrecked, so we boarded to look for answers and to help in whatever way we could. Now my team is almost entirely wiped out and I'm a freak and you're interrogating me like I'm the bad guy, and I really want off this ship. Got it?"

Simon is silent for a few seconds before he leans back in his chair, but he keeps his rifle aimed at Ethan's chest.

"This torpedo boat. What color was it?" asks Simon.

"Um... silver... Why?" asks Ethan.

"Because a silver torpedo boat destroyed the Onyx Station when its defenses were taken offline. No shield, no guns, one giant sitting duck. I watched the torpedo boat destroy the Onyx Station engines. I watched the Station plunge to the planet while the torpedo boat shot escape crafts. It killed thousands of people there, and it killed thousands here, and millions more on Onyx. The Federation killed us."

Simon's eyes are wet and red, and Ethan swallows as the guard takes a deep, shaky breath and looks up for a moment, while his hands quiver.

"And I might as well tell you this. The two people you described used to be associates of mine," says Simon. "Carmen Crystinmine was in my patrol section, but she went insane when her fiancé died. The guy with the flamethrower is Reverend Harold Foster, and he also went insane after his congregation was killed by those demons."

Simon slides his rifle to his lap and wipes his eyes with an airy sigh.

"Carmen was one of those spliced humans, and people avoided her every chance they could, and our supervisor gave her third shift without the bonus pay, so her interactions were minimal. But she was a sweetheart who just wanted friends. I trained her during her first few weeks, and she fell in love with a janitor named Gary. I didn't know him that well, but he seemed nice. They were going to get married January first as a new year, new life thing," explains Simon. "I was going to be the best man."

Simon wipes his eyes and nods at the placard.

"And Harold Foster was leading his congregation on a 'conversion tour.' Their goal was to convert as many locals as possible to Unity. He and his congregation were always scampering around on the ship, talking, preaching, and even doing a few baptisms." Simon chuckles and shakes his head. "The thing is, though, is that Harold Foster was an atheist who was taking advantage of the easy pay of a religious leader."

"How do you figure that?" asks Ethan.

"He told me when me, Carmen, and Gary, and some other guy named Bitson, shared drinks with him at the Klumsy K's in the Terrarium. He thought it was a fun game. Memorize a few 'holiday card quotes,' speak loud and energetic, and the people flock and donate and get converted. These Unity reverends got bonus pay from their HQ based on the number of converts, too, so Harold was going for a record. I think he was on his way to winning a free interstellar yacht."

Ethan nods, and Simon's smile fades.

"Then the outbreak happened, and Harold saw his congregation slaughtered. He lost it after that. He went from an atheist taking advantage of an easy paycheck to believing God was punishing him, and he must atone to save the souls of those he led astray."

"Jeez," whispers Ethan.

"Yeah," says Simon. "We're all that's left of our circles, Ethan. If we don't get off this ship and tell the worlds what happened here, the Federation will sweep this under the rug."

"They can't hide something like this! This is an entire colony we're talking about!"

"You don't know our government, Ethan."

This statement stuns Ethan into silence, and Simon's expression becomes grim as he leans forward.

"I witnessed our government kill thousands, and only God and the Federation knows what happened on Onyx, but it's not ours or God's anymore. It belongs to the Devil," says Simon. "You and I, we are it. We snag a ship, snag some evidence, and go to that empire that took Greater Arabia, and we can make the Federation pay for what they did to us, to Onyx, to *Bon Voyage*. We cannot let them get away with this."

Ethan is silent for a little longer, then he nods.

"You're right," says Ethan. He clears his throat. "You're right. But we can't get off this ship without Aiden or the vaccine."

"There is no vaccine on this ship," says Simon.

"Some guy who calls himself the Voice says he has a vaccine on the bridge. I also need to find out what the encrypted signal is. For Riva."

Simon snorts. "Yeah, you need a vaccine, but the Voice lied to you. There is no vaccine on this ship, but there might be some on Onyx."

"We have to check the bridge first, just in case."

Simon shakes his head and stands up, and Ethan follows him as he goes to his stash and starts loading up on ammo and medical supplies.

"Aiden is also heading to the bridge. I need to meet him there," adds Ethan.

"Call Aiden and tell him to meet us in the engine room. We're going to need a miniature warp battery if we're going to jump to Oros after getting the vaccines," says Simon.

"Why Oros?"

"Because it is the closest planet. From there, we can resupply, make copies of the evidence, and then make our way to Greater Arabia to talk to the occupiers."

"Damn it."

Simon looks at Ethan with a raised brow, and Ethan meets his eyes.

"Can we at least check the bridge first? That's where Aiden and the vaccine will be," says Ethan.

"The vaccine isn't there," says Simon.

"How do you know?" asks Ethan.

"Because we already used it."

"No, the Voice said that he was making vaccines and that they'll be ready when we get to him."

"The Voice lied, Ethan. They already had a stash, and they used it on us and themselves when things escalated."

Ethan's hard posture breaks and he steps back, his eye wide and darting along Simon's face for signs of deception.

"I was on the security detail when a cargo ship landed in our Section H hangar from the Onyx Space Port," says Simon after some hesitation. "When we arrived at Onyx, we were expecting a spaceport and the usual fanfare, but the spaceport refused to let us dock. Too dangerous, they said. Shortly after, the torpedo boat arrived and shot them down and blocked our signals. That cargo ship was the only one to escape, and it landed here. But I think they were meant to land here, because what you see now started happening soon after that ship arrived. The scientist on that ship had enough vaccines to inoculate the security and crew and ten percent of the colonists, but that didn't stop the spread of whatever the hell this thing is."

Ethan slumps against the wall and drags his finger through his hair as he mentally pieces together what Simon is saying, as well as what he experienced. From the torpedo boat to the distress and encrypted signals, to the Federation anthem playing before the relay was destroyed, and now the revelations of a cargo ship landing on *Bon Voyage*. It is so strange, and yet...

"I survived because of the vaccine, but I need more of it, and I guarantee you that there is more on Onyx in a lab or something," says Simon. He finishes loading up his gear and looks at Ethan. "And you definitely need that vaccine more than I do, and we can get it if we work together."

Ethan stands up and looks at Simon. "Alright, I'll go with you." He activates his communicator. "Aiden... Aiden Parsens, do you copy?"

"Ethan? What are you doing with Mary's communicator? Is she alright?" asks Aiden.

"No. She's dead. Taksheel killed her. And Riva is dead, too. Killed by a torpedo boat that destroyed the ship's relay."

*"What? Why! Damn it! Why did he do that? Why did **they** do that?"*

"We'll find out soon enough, but I need you to meet me in the engine room. I'm going with a security officer named Simon, and we're going to get a miniature warp battery and get off this ship. We're going to need your help, though."

"The miniature warp batteries are in Section G, sub-section five," says Simon.

"Section G, sub-section five. That's where we're going," says Ethan.

"Understood. I'll see you there," says Aiden with a heavy voice.

"Good. Rifts out." Ethan disconnects, and then he takes a deep breath and looks at Simon. "Okay, let's get going."

"I'm all packed up. Just waiting for you," says Simon.

Ethan spends the next couple of minutes replenishing his supplies of ammo and medical equipment, and he also gives himself a shot of adrenaline. He shudders as a burst of life surges through every part of his body. Then the pair step into the hallway and look both ways before heading to the green lights of the elevator.

"For the record, it is bad enough you look like one of those things, but if you really start going crazy, I'm going to shoot you," says Simon.

"If you do, please aim for the head," says Ethan.

"Will do."

After that, they carry on in silence.

26

Section G

When Ethan and Simon reach the elevator after a short and safe trip, Ethan sees a camera looking at them. He stares at the camera, and Simon calls the elevator and steps back, and motions for Ethan to watch the hallway while he aims his rifle at the elevator door.

The two wait in silence, listening to the approaching hums and clanks, with the occasional light flickering. Then, the intercom clicks on.

"There you are!" says the Voice. *"I was wondering where you wandered off to, and you found Simon! Hi Simon! Have you found a way off the ship yet?"*

"I'm working on it," says Simon.

"My offer still stands. Remember, I have the vaccine, and I know a lot of powerful people. Think about it. Ethan's made a good choice. Why won't you?"

Simon flips off the camera without breaking eye contact with the elevator, and the intercom clicks off. A minute later, the elevator dings and its door slides open, greeting the pair with a entwined tree painted on the interior and spilling bright yellow light into the dimly lit hallway.

Simon gives a quick look, calls all clear, and Ethan gets inside the elevator. Simon hits the emergency close button, followed by pushing the floor button they need, and the gears grind. The elevator hums, and light slides up the wall as it descends into the ship.

"Alright, be honest. Do you still plan to go to the bridge?" asks Simon.

"Yeah. That's where the vaccine is," says Ethan.

"For God's sake, I just told you it wasn't there."

"It is there. The Voice has no choice but to be honest about that. Besides, Taksheel is going to be there, and I want to kill him and the Voice."

Simon balks at Ethan. "You serious? We're in this situation and revenge is on your mind?"

Ethan looks at Simon with a cold, yellow eye and deep scowl. "Taksheel killed Marian, and I know the Voice had a hand in killing Riva because the anthem played right as the torpedo boat arrived. For all I know, he could also be responsible for what happened here. They will not live to see tomorrow. I'll make sure of it."

Simon shakes his head. "Okay, whatever, you do what you want, but I'm going to a hangar when we get the batteries. One for me, one for you, and you can do your revenge thing while I try to live."

"Cool. Fine by me."

"Fine."

"Fine."

"Fine."

"...Fine."

Then Aiden's audio box appears, but it is constantly breaking into pixels and discoloration.

"Hey, just a heads up, I had to take a detour," says Aiden. *"And I admit I got myself a little turned around, but I'll be at the engine room eventually."*

"Keep me posted. We've almost reached the engine room," says Ethan.

"Roger that."

"Rifts out."

The audio box disappears, and Ethan and Simon quietly watch the jumble of numbers and symbols slowly change, while the yellow lights streak past the pair. During this time, Ethan injects himself with more adrenaline, and when the elevator jerks to a stop, the pair aim their weapons at the door.

It slides open with a loud ding, revealing a dark hallway with flickering lights illuminating pipes, beams, tubes, and doors. Some lights have quick flashes, and others have long increments of light to dark and back to light, and at the far end of the hall is an emergency exit being lit up by red lights.

Blood, scratches, bullet holes, and dents damage the hallway, and one of the pipes is broken, leading to the floor being flooded with colorful liquid. And nearby, a door slams open and shut, clicking, whirring and banging, with sparks popping out of the sides and its hologram alternating between red and green distorted symbols.

Simon takes a breath and stops the elevator door from closing, and Ethan moves forward without hesitation, scanning the hallway and taking special notice of the vents. Scratches and faint clicks flow through the vents, prompting him to stop, and Simon stands next to him.

The two follow the noise with their eyes and weapons as it moves over their heads and travels behind them, towards the elevator. Simon turns around and continues trailing the noise while Ethan moves his eye between the vent and hallway, and once the noise fades entirely, they remain still and silent. Several seconds of quietness pass, nothing happens, and Simon takes the lead.

"The batteries are this way," says Simon.

The two briskly walk down the hallway, and when they are at the emergency exit, Ethan notices the door has been welded shut and has dents popping *towards* them. That makes him uneasy, and he follows Simon as the officer takes a left turn to go down another hallway.

This one is almost like the others, but what sets it apart is the large hole in the ceiling with dangling wires and pieces of metal soaked in blood and fluids from broken pipes. The walls are completely covered in dried blood, fleshy bits, and bone. Severed limbs, torn organs, and shattered bones lay on the ground, and just ahead is a door that has been forced open. The room beyond the door is the brightest lit, which reveals more carnage on the other side.

The two stare at the destroyed door for a few seconds before cautiously approaching it. Ripples move through the bloody chemical pool, which stings Ethan's nose, and as they walk, a shadow darts by the gaping hole in the ceiling.

Ethan stops and aims his shotgun up, but he cannot see much of anything due to how dark it is up there. When there is no more movement, he resumes following Simon.

Simon leads the way through the broken door and travels through a carpet of bullet casings, makeshift weapons, and large areas of blood. The two sweep the area with their weapons and look up when the scratches in the vents return.

These vents have thin vines hanging from them, and the room is covered in roots and vines spreading across the walls and floors, coming from mutilated bodies. Some have fused together to make little trees or stalks, and some have bulbs spraying pollen. Some bodies still have their eyes, and Ethan cannot help but wonder if they see him.

"Over there," says Simon.

Ethan looks at Simon and sees him pointing at a stairwell at the end of the room. The stairwell is dark, and when they reach it, Ethan sees a thin beam of light at the bottom. He looks up when the vent shakes, with rapid scratches and clangs moving down the stairwell.

"We're almost there," says Simon. "Be ready to use your gun. A lot of colonists and crew fled down here when these things swarmed us."

They go down the stairs, and Ethan finds that the light he saw came from a partially open door with bullet holes and deep gashes covering it. A faint green holographic circle is barely visible, and the orb is flickering.

Simon touches the orb with his band, and the door whines and slides open the rest of the way, revealing a dim room full of scattered, mutilated corpses that have become engulfed by vines, roots, and bulbs.

Pollen and film cover the floor and have spread to the walls, and some corpses have stood up and morphed into stalks or trees that touch the ceiling or reach into the vents.

One corpse is looking at the door with their mouth open, hand stretched towards them. Bulbs cover their head and roots spread from their feet, while thin trees sprout from the top of their head and latch to the ceiling.

Ethan grimaces, and Simon snorts when he sees a tag on the torn uniform.

"I knew that guy. He kept stealing my salads," says Simon. He walks up to the corpse and looks into the shriveled eyes. "That's what you get, jackass."

Ethan stares at Simon with a mix of disgust and horror, and Simon looks at him.

"Let's go. We can't linger in this room," says Simon.

They continue walking, weaving their way through the forest of bodies, and kicking up small clouds of pollen that are making the floor slick. The stench from the alien plants is almost too rancid for Ethan to bear. He almost pukes twice, as the horrid stench feels like it is melting his nose and throat.

After a couple of minutes, they come to a locked door covered by vines and film. After removing these things, Simon unlocks it, and they enter a new area with nearly a dozen locked doors and failing lights. However, one door is wide open, and the sign above it says, "Engine Room Security Office."

Ethan enters the room, ignoring Simon's calls, and he sees a splatter of blood on the wall and a man in security armor laying on the floor. His eyes are closed and there is a hole from the bottom of his jaw through the top of his skull, and a pistol is next to him. There is also a desk with a smashed computer, and near him is an overturned chair and a woman wearing a blue and yellow jumpsuit with a hole in her head, and her eyes are wide with shock. Roots growing from their wounds, mouths, and eyes anchor both corpses to the floor, wall, and chair.

Ethan sighs and approaches the dead security officer. The security suit's normally gray bodysuit has been stained red, and the thick metal plating that is stitched on the limbs is damaged. There are also curved plates that trace his abdomen and hips, and like the ones on his limbs, they are also damaged.

Ethan kneels and turns the body over, and with a quick inspection he finds plenty of ammo, plus medical foam tubes and adrenaline syringes attached to slots on the suit. There is also an Arx Corporation spinal shield generator. The shield generator is dim, but the suit is remarkably like Ethan's build, so he quickly gets to work.

Several minutes later, Ethan walks out of the room wearing the security suit. He has unceremoniously tossed his old suit in the corner, and he is now shifting in his new suit to get a feel for its weight. The shield generator crackles and hums as its lights brighten, and Ethan is briefly covered in a blue shimmer, right as Simon approaches him.

"Nice," says Simon, "but the shield generators are more for ballistic defense. They are basically worthless against claws and blunt weapons."

"Still better than what I had before. Besides, I know I'll need this later," says Ethan.

"Of course you will," says Simon dryly. "Follow me."

Simon leads Ethan down the end of the hallway, unlocks the door, then leads him through a curving hallway bathed in dim red light that creates dark shadows on the pipes and wires. Liquid churns in the pipes and faint hums vibrate their ears while gauges barely flick. The hallway is long, and there are vent grates at even intervals, starting with one directly above them.

Simon hesitates, then goes forward, his steps quick and shaky, and his eyes darting in every direction they can, while Ethan trails him, occasionally walking backward to see if they are being followed. During their walk, the vent shakes again, and Ethan aims his shotgun at the opening as the shakes travel over their heads and down the hall from where they came from.

Then comes a series of bangs, scrapes, and screeches, and the two run.

"Let's go! The next elevator isn't much further!" says Simon.

A faint collection of screams, shrieks, and roars catch their attention. They look over their shoulders and see blobs of shadows stretching along the red-lit pipes, and within seconds, a horde of Tainted stampede around the corner, brandishing crude weapons or using their sharp, sprouted claws.

"Run!" yells Simon.

They bolt down the hallway, and the screams and rushing steps quickly gain on them. Ethan and Simon take a sharp turn and run towards a green-lit door, and after getting on the other side, Simon hits the emergency close button and smashes the orb. The door's lights disappear, and the horde reaches the door several seconds later, and with them comes loud bangs and scratches that shake the door.

"Where's the elevator?" says Ethan, his throat feeling like it is being rubbed with sandpaper.

Simon's eyes dart left and right, and he jumps when the door rattles harder.

"Where's the elevator!" yells Ethan.

Simon looks for another few seconds, then runs to the right. "This way!"

Ethan trails him, cringing when he hears the metal bending. The roars and screams travel through the shaking vents, and Simon takes another right as a vent breaks open and a Tainted lands on Ethan.

The sudden weight knocks him to the floor, but he quickly recovers and sees the Tainted raising an ax made of a chair leg and a jagged metal slag. Ethan kicks it back and grabs his shotgun.

When the Tainted tries hitting him, he deflects it and swings his shotgun against its head, breaking it open. The Tainted crumbles, and the horde rounds the corner.

"Oh, come on!" says Ethan.

Ethan unloads on the crowd, ripping off chunks at a time as each slug strikes a Tainted, but they are getting closer, and when one slashes at him, he retaliates with a swift punch to its jaw using his mutated hand. It staggers back with its jaw shattered, and he shoots it with his shotgun, blowing out its shoulder and part of its neck.

The Tainted collapses with its head barely held on, and Ethan fires what is left of his magazine into the crowd. As he shoots, the slugs pierce the pipes, spraying streams of chemicals and fuel on the Tainted and making the floor slick.

The mixture quickly spreads across the floor, and Ethan retreats as he slips a new magazine in. The Tainted give chase, with the injured splitting open and crawling to one another to reform as Stitchers.

Ethan shoots at the lights above. The bulbs shatter and sparks shower down on the mixture, creating an instant inferno that engulfs the Tainted and Stitchers with a rush of hot air that knocks Ethan off his feet.

Thick smoke, the stench of burning blood and flesh, and agonizing screams clog Ethan's senses, and he stumbles back, slightly hunched. He watches the mutated bodies flail around as towers of fire with pieces of their bodies breaking off, revealing their blackened, twisted bones.

Ethan keeps backing up as the fire eats the walls, and sizzles and pops soon join the agonizing screams. As this happens, a fire alarm sounds, and foam sprays from the ceiling, burying the fire in thick globs of white foam and turning the smoke from black to gray.

Ethan coughs and keeps backing up, while the shriveled bodies become featureless lumps in the foam. When he is at a good distance between himself and the carnage, he collapses against the wall and injects himself with another dose of adrenaline.

It makes his heart ache, but he is getting a boost of energy, which is good since, as soon as he injected himself, a burnt Lurker flies through the smoke and tackles him.

The force is enough to knock the air out of Ethan, and the Lurker pins him on the floor. Its translucent sack pulses and the bugs inside crawl out of sight, just for them to pour out of its mouth seconds later, where they fall on Ethan and begin gnawing on his suit.

Ethan screams and thrashes as the bugs crawl over him, and the Lurker bites on the crook of his neck. The armor is strong enough to block the teeth, and Ethan punches the Lurker on the side of the head with his mutated hand, breaking its skull open.

The Lurker roars and stabs its talons into Ethan's chest, and it rips into his armor while the other bugs crawl on his exposed jumpsuit and begin chewing on the fabric. But before the Lurker can finish tearing him open, Ethan grabs its throat and yanks out its esophagus.

Its head flops and snaps off. Then it collapses on top of him, with the sack popping on impact and covering Ethan with its goo and spilling its blood all over him.

Ethan flips it off and squishes the surviving bugs. Once the bugs are dead, he kicks the immobile Lurker, and when its vines spring out and try grabbing him, he yanks himself away from them and looks down the hallway, panting and trying to swallow what little spit he has left.

The charred bodies lay twisted and cracked underneath the sizzling foam as the gray smoke rolls down the hallway. Several seconds of silence pass before Ethan takes a deep breath and goes the direction Simon went, fuming about being ditched and making a silent vow to deck him in the schnoz when he sees him again.

As Ethan walks down the hallway, the vent rattles yet again and goes in the direction he is heading. He shakes his head and checks his shotgun, then continues at a faster pace until he reaches a locked door with the fire symbol on it.

Seeing this, he huffs, shoots a vent grate off, and then uses the pipes to give himself a boost. When he has a good grip and distance off the floor, he jumps to the vent opening, barely grabbing it, and he pulls himself up and crawls through.

It is dark and cramped, and slick with green film and thin vines clinging to the shaft. When he reaches the next vent grate, he uses the interior latch to pop it open. The grate crashes to the floor, and Ethan jumps down in a dimly lit square chamber.

As soon as his feet touch down, a Haunter lunges at him and sinks its teeth into his shoulder, while its claws scratch at his armor. The sudden weight knocks him into the wall, and he screams in fright as he punches it in the head with his mutated hand. The Haunter's skull cracks open, blood splatters on him, but it keeps gnawing and clawing at him.

"Get. OFF!" snarls Ethan.

He punches it again, putting his fist through its skull. When he pulls out, pulped brain is coating his hand and wrist, and more dribbles out of the destroyed head. Its grip loosens, and Ethan pushes it away.

It crumbles to the floor, twitching with vines sliding out from underneath it or breaching its skin. The vines try to grab Ethan, but he storms off, shaking his head and wiping the brain matter off his hand.

"Tired of this space shit," mutters Ethan.

Ethan then hurries towards the exit, but about halfway there, a Stitcher lumbers out of a room, and when it sees Ethan, it charges him.

"Oh, for God's sake!" yells Ethan as he skids to a stop and backs up.

The Stitcher rushing him has two heads and stingers on its arms made from a mix of popped bones and sharp wood held together by a network of vines weaving in and out of them. Its legs are stitched together with vines, and the first head has missing eyelids. The second head's mouth is open and moving with the control of the vines that have woven their way through the cheeks and jaw.

"Seal the door," wheezes the first head.

"I'm trying," says the second head.

Ethan shoots the Stitcher in the chest, and both heads roar, and the Stitcher swipes at him. He rolls out of the way and shoots its leg. The Stitcher buckles and swings at Ethan again.

He dodges it, but stumbles and dives away when it tries to stab him with the stinger. The stinger shatters on the metal floor, and it roars in pain while the first head sprays pollen in the air.

Ethan curses and runs away from the cloud, and the floor shakes as the Stitcher limps after him. Then Ethan's communicator activates, and Aiden's audio box appears.

"I'm almost at the engine room. Where are you?" asks Aiden.

"Can't talk. Must live," says Ethan.

The Stitcher whacks Ethan in the side, and he flies off his feet and hits a pillar with some screens displaying emergency messages. The screens shatter from his impact, and Ethan pushes himself up, grunting and growling.

"Where are you!? Are you alright?" says Aiden.

"Not now!" snaps Ethan.

The Stitcher charges Ethan, roaring with its remaining stinger raised, and Ethan disconnects and jumps out of the way, causing it to stab the pillar. Sparks shoot out, and it convulses as its plant-flesh burns, and Ethan rapidly shoots at the upper torso and second head while the first ejects more pollen.

The second head becomes flaps of broken bone, bark, and skin hanging on limp vines, with blood and brain staining its body and the pillar. The Stitcher pulls back, its arm smoking and charred, and the remaining set of bulbous eyes lock on Ethan, with a slowly dropping cloud of pollen surrounding it.

"Seal the door," wheezes the head.

The Stitcher lunges, and Ethan shoots it in the head, popping it, and making it go limp. The large creature shakes the floor and twitches, with vines wiggling their way out of the stumps that used to be heads and breaking through the back. All while blood pumps on the floor.

Ethan looks further down and sees the Haunter he took out is now splitting open. He narrows his eye, checks his shotgun, and then goes to the Haunter and shoots into the vine cluster, turning them into pulp. The Haunter goes still, and Ethan runs out of the room.

The vent rattles again as Ethan goes through the doorway. The doorway leads to a flight of stairs, and he runs down the steps, occasionally skipping a few. Once he reaches the bottom, a Haunter breaks through a vent grate on the wall and charges him.

When it is close enough, Ethan ducks under the first swipe, bats away the second with his shotgun, pivots around it, and shoots its spine. Its legs go limp, and it tries crawling, but Ethan pulverizes its head with a close-range shot, and he resumes running while the Haunter lays in its blood.

Ethan goes a little further down and guns down a group of Tainted moving towards him, no doubt drawn to him by the shotgun blasts.

They go down quickly, and Ethan rushes past them, while the vines work to mend the broken bodies.

The next area Ethan enters has tinted observation windows showing a large room with five generators, all dim, and they have an hourglass shape with glowing orbs in their enters. Near them are computer consoles, various walkways, a few doors, thick cables, and rows of sealed lockers that are connected to the generators by thick tubes.

The swirling red lights in the engine room clash with the streaks of shadows and light of the consoles. While Ethan cannot see anybody, a spark of hope brings light to the darkness clouding him.

He hurries down the hallway, and in a matter of seconds comes across a door around the hallway bend. Its light is flashing yellow, and it is partially open, but not enough for Ethan to squeeze through. So, he rolls his shoulders and presses his hands against the door while bracing his legs against the floor. Then he puts all his weight against it with painful results, but injuries be damned!

As Ethan pushes, he grunts and groans and quietly curses the door for not moving. When he shifts his position to get a better grip, Aiden's audio box appears.

"Hey, where are you? Are you okay?" asks Aiden.

"Just peachy," grunts Ethan. The door shifts, and Ethan gives it another push, straining every part of him. "I had to deal with a lot of crap, and now there's a good chance another Stitcher will come after me. We need to hurry and get those batteries!"

"Understood. I'm in the engine room right now," says Aiden.

"Good. I'll see you in a couple of minutes. Rifts out."

Ethan disconnects, and after he gives the door another push, there is a loud snap and long screech, and he stumbles as the door slides the rest of the way open. After regaining his footing, he gives the new area a quick sweep, seeing nothing as his light shines on rows of steel beams, gears, pistons, gauges, and slowly turning turbines behind thick tinted glass.

At the end of the section is an elevator. He runs to it and bangs on the button as fast as he can while looking down the hallway, waiting for the Stitcher to show up.

The seconds are long, but thankfully nothing happens, and when the door opens, he slips inside, hits the emergency close button, and slumps against the wall as the elevator descends. Though, it seems as soon as he sits, the door opens again, revealing a hallway filled with bars of bright lights and dark shadows.

Weak clangs and hums shake his ears, and Ethan exits the elevator while a Haunter stumbles around the corner with burns marking its body. Ethan shoots it until it drops, and fortunately the loud, brutal symphony of moving machinery covers the gunshots.

The elevator closes, and Ethan goes down the hallway. He stomps on the Haunter's head when he passes it, shattering its skull and splattering brain and blood on his boot.

Ethan turns the corner and sees an open door with a chamber on the other side. "G-5" is painted on the wall directly in front of the doorway, and the chamber is filled with rows of rectangular, cage-like devices with glowing batteries in them, all of which connect to the ceiling through thick tubes. Most of the cage devices have blue lights on them, and the humming shakes Ethan's bones as he carefully walks through the rows.

As he walks through the area, he notices that one cage has red warning lights swirling above it, with "M. Warp Battery Disconnected" flashing on a small screen. Ethan approaches it and finds that the cage has been forced open and a battery is missing. He then looks at the lock and realizes that it has been shot off.

Ethan shakes his head and activates his communicator. "Aiden, I'm in the battery room. Row ten, pillar twelve. Where are you?"

"Right here," says Aiden.

Ethan jumps and sees Aiden Parsen aiming his rifle at him. Aiden is bloodied, bandaged, his suit is patched with scrap metal, and his orange and hazel eyes have a faint yellow tint.

"Don't shoot. I'm not one of them," says Ethan, with his hands slightly raised and his shotgun aimed at the ceiling.

Aiden studies Ethan for a few seconds before he tilts his rifle down. "Not gonna lie. I was planning on shooting you since I thought you were one of them, but then you spoke again. I just wanted to make sure I wasn't hearing things. By the way, I could barely hear you on your feed. Either your comm is broken or there's a jam."

"Well, whatever it is, I'm glad you're here."

They exchange a handshake before Aiden pulls him in for a hug. After that, he holds Ethan at arm's length.

"Man, look at you. How did you get so lucky?" says Aiden.

"I'm sure the government can tell me if they nab me," says Ethan with a tired smile.

"They won't get you. I'll get you taken care of when all this is over. I promise. Hell, I'll even let you work with me and Ara on our dairy farm when this is all over. Or when we build the dairy farm. We should be able to afford it after some compensation."

"I'm lactose intolerant," says Ethan. "Also, who's Ara?"

"My wife… Are you seriously lactose intolerant?"

"Yeah."

"Well, shit. I might as well turn you over then, you freak."

Ethan stares at Aiden, and then they both crack a smile and snicker, while Aiden slaps Ethan's shoulder.

"Don't worry, I'll put you in accounting or something." Aiden's smile fades, and he exhales and runs his hand through his hair. "But in all seriousness, we are going to lie low after this. Maybe it is best if we play dead? I got some friends on Aarde that'll help us, but if the Federation gets hold of us, then we'll be in for some bad times. Especially you with you being… well, that."

"We can talk about all that later." Ethan jabs his thumb at the open cage. "Is that supposed to be like that?"

"No, and whoever did it was lucky they didn't damage it further. That would've caused a nasty chain reaction that would've killed us all and that torpedo boat out there."

Aiden inspects the lock, and then he moves up and squints his eyes at some scratches in the slot of a missing battery.

"Damn fool must've used a knife to disconnect the battery, too," says Aiden. "He scratched these batteries here and damaged the wires! This will blow the ship if it is rattled too much. What in the hell were they thinking?"

"It was Simon. He's trying to get to Onyx to get a vaccine, and he needs the battery to leave the system."

"Well, he should've waited."

Aiden reaches into his tool belt, pulls out a small magnetic screwdriver, and begins working on the top battery.

"I'm not risking further damage, so I'm taking the top battery. Keep an eye out for those things, will you?" says Aiden.

Ethan nods and watches the area while Aiden works. A couple of minutes later, Aiden gingerly pulls out the miniature-warp battery from its slot and has Ethan hold it, while he uses pliers to carefully disconnect the wires. Once the wires are off, the battery dims and Aiden puts it in a metal container on his back pouch.

"Alright, let's get out of here," says Aiden. "I know a quick way to the bridge, and we might intercept Taksheel and get some answers out of him."

Ethan nods and follows Aiden, and after some traveling, they come across an open area that leads to various stairs, walkways, and doors, all surrounding one of the hourglass-shaped generators. Aiden takes a moment to scan the area, and when he finds what he is looking for, he motions Ethan to follow him.

They go across the walkway to a locked door, but when they are about to reach the door, six claws suddenly puncture the door, right down the middle, making the two stop and back up. The door's red lights die, and the metal groans and snaps, with sparks popping out of its edges as it is forced open.

When the door is squished enough, a Stitcher marches out of the darkness. When it is out of the hallway, it stands up, and Ethan and Aiden tilt their heads up, both of their jaws hanging open.

It towers over them by three feet, and its thick body is made of many bodies mangled and twisted, all stitched together with vines, and it is covered in thick bark with small pockets of flesh exposed. It has large, glowing yellow eyes without eyelids on all three heads. The Stitcher's arms and legs are made of limbs that have been twisted and wrapped around each other with vines holding them together, and each of its hands has three sharp, curved claws, the forearms split open to allow stingers to slide out. Its back has split open like a flower, with vines waving in the air.

"Ethan. I'm here. Let me in," says the three heads.

"Oh no," says Ethan.

The Moon Stitcher steps forward, shaking the floor, and it stands at its full height. Then heavy, rapid steps come from behind, and Ethan and Aiden go back-to-back.

Another Stitcher with five heads, four arms, and thin vines on its shoulders scampers up the steps. Each of the arms has sharp claws and long talons have broken through the boots. The five-headed Stitcher twitches and its arms and vines snap as it goes towards them, making many, overlapping stuttering clicks.

Ethan and Aiden move to the center of the walkway, and the two Stitchers come closer. When they are in the center, Aiden looks at Ethan.

"So, do you want the four-armed freak or the demon gorilla?" asks Aiden.

Ethan looks over the edge. "I'd rather jump."

Aiden looks over the edge. "Good call."

The two Stitchers charge and Ethan and Aiden leap over the railing to a walkway below. Ethan rolls upon landing and hops to his feet, and then the walkway shakes and bends when the Moon Stitcher lands behind him.

"Ethan. I'm here," says the Moon Stitcher.

Ethan turns around and sees the monster towering over him with a dent in the walkway and the railing broken. It marches towards Ethan, and he backs up.

"Let me in," says the Moon Stitcher.

Ethan runs and the Moon Stitcher gives chase. The walkway shakes with every step, and Ethan turns and shoots it. The slug chips off a bit of the bark but does nothing to slow it down. Ethan runs faster, too scared to curse, and the walkway's shaking becomes more intense as the Moon Stitcher gains on him.

Ethan takes a sharp turn, slings his shotgun on his shoulder, climbs on a railing, and jumps off to grab the next level up. The Moon Stitcher skids past him, and right as he is about to pull himself up, a vine wraps around his waist and throws him into a window.

Glass shatters against Ethan's back and he bounces off the floor and hits the wall of a hallway. His suit injects him with medical foam and adrenaline, and right as he pushes himself up, claws puncture the wall. The Moon Stitcher pulls itself up, with all three heads giggling in their own tones.

"Ethan. I'm here. Let me in," says the Moon Stitcher.

It breaks what remains of the window, forcing Ethan to cover his head as the glass shards fly, and when it climbs in, he shoots it with his shotgun. The slugs only chip its bark, and the three heads laugh as the massive abomination rolls inside. As it does this, Ethan bolts down the hallway.

"Ethan!" calls the Moon Stitcher.

The rapid, heavy stomps start again. Ethan's heart races as his legs struggle to keep him up. He makes a sharp turn, nearly tripping over himself, and runs up a flight of stairs.

The Moon Stitcher's steps get closer with each passing second. Ethan's body burns as he forces himself to go faster. When he reaches the top of the stairs, he sees the light of a service elevator up ahead, and he puts more speed in his steps.

Ethan hears the heavy steps behind him, and when he reaches the elevator, he bangs on the button and turns to face the Moon Stitcher. It is standing in the middle of the hallway, vines snaking in the air and its claws twitching. Behind Ethan, the elevator hums, and the Moon Stitcher taps the wall with its claw.

Tap-Tap.

Step.

Tap-Tap.

Step.

Tap-Tap.

Step.

Ethan flicks his eye to the elevator and back at the Moon Stitcher. It is inching closer, keeping the way blocked.

"Ethan. I'm here. Let me in," says the Moon Stitcher.

The elevator dings and slides open, and Ethan jumps inside while the Moon Stitcher charges him. Ethan pounds the emergency close button, but before the doors can close, the Moon Stitcher barrels through, snapping the doors, squishing Ethan into the wall, and shaking the elevator.

The lights flicker and the elevator jerks down, leaving no space for Ethan to escape. The impact of being squished between the Moon Stitcher and the metal elevator wall knocks the air out of Ethan's lungs and momentarily disorients him.

He regains enough motor function to duck out of the way of the claws coming down on him, leading to them piercing the elevator wall. Then he pivots around and shoots its spine with his shotgun.

The close range puts enough force to make the Moon Stitcher stagger, but it is not enough to stop it. The Moon Stitcher swings around and tries stabbing Ethan with one of its stingers, but he slides out of the way, narrowly avoiding the massive stinger that stabs another wall.

The Moon Stitcher yanks its stinger out. Ethan shoots its elbow, splattering the wall with its fleshy bits.

The three heads cry out in pain, and with that arm limp, the Moon Stitcher swings at Ethan with its other claws. He ducks and shoots the side of its knee, making it stumble and drop.

Orange blood is pooling all over the floor, and Ethan scrambles on top of its shoulders and pushes against the ceiling's emergency exit. It pops open on the first push, but before he can escape, the vines throw Ethan to the floor, denting it.

Pain shoots through his back and limbs, and when the Moon Stitcher tries stabbing him with its stinger, he presses his shotgun against its hand and pulls the trigger. The hybrid of flesh and plant pops as the slug blows apart its hand and arm, with blood squirting from the large cracks.

The three heads howl, and the vines snap wildly, striking Ethan like whips. His face and armor quickly become scratched, and with a lot of struggles, he wiggles his way between its legs and shoots the blob of vines in the middle of its flesh and bone petals.

They explode in an ugly show of gore. While the Moon Stitcher writhes with limp arms, Ethan once again climbs on its back and uses it to climb through the emergency exit.

Once he is on the roof of the elevator, Ethan looks down and sees the Moon Stitcher writhing and howling. Its noise echoes in the dark shaft, and Ethan looks at the cables on the corners of the elevator. There are eight, with two on each corner, and they are connected to four pulley systems.

Ethan quickly wraps his arm and leg around a cable, and then he shoots a pulley. The shotgun blast sounds like an explosion, and the bright sparks fly as the pulley breaks. The elevator jerks to the side, bringing its lights to flicker.

He shoots the second pulley, and the elevator tilts further and scrapes against the shaft. The other two pulleys groan, screech, and pop with metal bending and bolts popping loose. When Ethan shoots the third pulley, the fourth one snaps loose within seconds, plunging the elevator to the darkness below, and with it, the screams of the Moon Stitcher.

As the elevator falls, it bounces against the shaft and leaves a trail of sparks while metallic screeches and scrapes echo. Ethan watches the elevator fade into the darkness below, its failing lights rapidly getting smaller. They disappear in a matter of seconds with a loud thud, followed by silence, save for the creaking cables.

Ethan is shaking, sore, and wants to puke, and after shouldering his shotgun, he looks up and turns on his light to see the elevator door to the next floor is not too far from him. Just above that is a vent.

Ethan has grown to hate them during the hours he spent on this hellish ship but is now glad to see one. So, he takes a deep, sickly breath, and begins a nasty climb.

*****

If times were good for *Bon Voyage* and someone was standing in a Section G elevator lobby waiting for the lift to show up, it would surprise them to hear thuds, groans, and mutters coming from beyond the door. Then, they would be surprised to hear scraping in the vents, and probably scream after Ethan breaks through and lands on the floor, coughing and wheezing and barely able to move. But since nobody is around, and *Bon Voyage* is Hell in space, nobody sees Ethan suffering.

Ethan arches his back and balls his hands into fists as he coughs and wheezes, with a mix of tainted blood and spit hanging from his mouth. Sweat drips off his nose and dark red hair. His eye has trouble focusing on the floor, as all attempts to regain air scratches his lungs and throat. His abdomen and limbs also feel like burning rocks.

"Ethan!"

Ethan looks up and smiles weakly as Aiden runs to him and helps him up.

"There you are. I got you," says Aiden.

"Thanks," wheezes Ethan, grabbing Aiden's shoulder for support. "Where's your Stitcher?"

"I had to shoot its arms and legs off. Yours?"

Ethan nods to the elevator. "I dropped it down the elevator. Do you still have the battery?"

Aiden grins and pulls out the battery, covering both in its blue glow.

"I see you have a miniature warp battery," says the Voice.

Ethan and Aiden look to the source and see the red light of a camera looking at them from a perfect spot to watch the lobby.

"I hope you aren't planning on jumping ship without me. That would make me sad and my friends terribly angry," says the Voice.

"Yeah, we have the battery, but before we come to you, I need to know something," says Ethan.

"Go on."

"Do you really have the vaccine?"

"I'm in no position to lie, Ethan. I have it, and I made enough for your friends. Or what's left of them."

Ethan sneers, and Aiden clips the battery to his back and walks to the camera.

"When we get to you, we won't have much time to escape," says Aiden. "Secure all your documents, all your samples, all the vaccines you have, and be ready to go as soon as we arrive. We'll have to leave as soon as we get you. And when we do, you better be ready to administer and explain to us everything that happened here."

The Voice is silent, and Ethan looks at Aiden while the engineer stares at the camera with icy darkness clouding his eyes.

"You there?" says Aiden.

"I will have everything ready for you when you arrive at Section 0. Just wave at the bridge door and I'll open it. But beware of the contestant on the other side. He's a bit unhinged."

The intercom clicks off after that, and Aiden looks at Ethan.

"Let's get moving," orders Aiden.

Ethan nods and follows Aiden down the hallway.

27

Regroup

Ethan and Aiden's steps echo in the derelict halls of the *Bon Voyage*. The area they are traveling through has red emergency lights, and they are the only sources of light. They pass vines, bulbs, and bodies rooted to the floor, walls, and ceiling. They also pass a message that is underneath a light and facing a camera. That message is, *"**Junjie Ding- GO TO HELL!**"*

The pair keep walking without paying much mind to that, and they are feeling some relief from nothing coming out to rip them apart. After a few minutes of traveling through the deathtrap of a ship, a familiar voice catches Ethan's attention.

"Very good, Officer Simon," says the Voice.

Ethan and Aiden stop.

"Why don't you come to me, and we can get out of here together? You get the vaccine, I escape, we all win!" says the Voice.

"You're lying. You don't have the vaccine," says Simon.

Ethan's eye twitches and his steps become heavy as he marches towards the corner with his shotgun held tight.

"Ethan!" calls Aiden.

Ethan keeps walking, his trigger finger tapping against his weapon, while his other hand scratches his head. Aiden runs after him.

"Ethan!" calls Aiden again.

"Oh, we have company," says the Voice.

Ethan rounds the corner, right as Simon turns away from a camera. He sees the shotgun and aims his rifle at Ethan, but Aiden gets between them and holds out his hands.

"Stand down! Both of you!" says Aiden.

"You left me to die," says Ethan.

"I saw you get swarmed! There was no way to save you!" says Simon.

"You didn't even try," says Ethan.

Aiden gradually pushes Ethan's shotgun down while pointing at Simon.

"Stand down, Ethan," says Aiden. "And you. Who are you?"

Simon partially lowers his rifle. "Officer Arnvin Simon. Who are you?"

"Aiden Parsen. Engineer of the *Hook Line* and member of the AATS."

"I see. Ethan told me about you," says Simon.

"Did he, now?" says Aiden.

Simon nods. "I'm very sorry about what happened to your team."

"I'm used to it." Aiden holds out his hand. "Nice to meet you, though."

Simon shakes his hand. "Likewise."

Ethan glares at the two, and the intercom clicks, bringing everyone to look at the camera.

"Looks like the gang is all together," says the Voice. *"That means you can get to the bridge, claim your prize, and we can all get out of here."*

Aiden looks at Simon. "Do you want to join us, or no? We're going to the bridge and going to wing it after."

"Well..." Simon looks at Ethan. Ethan is still glaring at him. He looks back at Aiden. "I kind of don't, but it is on the path I am heading."

"Understood. Ethan, don't shoot him."

"I won't," says Ethan sourly.

"I mean it," says Aiden sternly.

"I won't!"

"Alright, chop-chop. Get moving! We need to get off this ship as fast as possible!" says the Voice.

"Officer Simon, lead the way," says Aiden.

Simon nods and walks ahead. "Alright, but just so you guys know, we'll be cutting through the Terrarium."

"That doesn't sound too bad."

"Trust me, it's bad."

With that, Simon turns his walk to a jog, and the other two follow him. They spend the next hour going through the maze of destroyed halls and doors and climbing stairs; they also kill some straggling Haunters or Tainted along the way, but the vines, trees, bulbs, and the root networks are growing and absorbing more bodies.

Sometimes, entire walls are covered with bodies fused into the hellish plants. And some doors they go through open properly, while others need persuading, either through elbow grease or removing the plants holding them shut, but they go through them all the same.

During this period, Ethan has not even tried to keep track of where he traveled since he is too focused on getting to the bridge, but one thing stands out in their traveling. That is when they reach a large door with green trim, a large window with dried blood covering it, and fake trees flanking it. Above the door is a dim, flickering sign reading, *"Terrarium."*

"That looks bad," says Ethan.

"Yep," says Aiden.

"Just past the Terrarium is a set of stairs that will take us directly to the bridge, and that is where I'll leave you," says Simon. He tries to peek through the window, but because of the amount of dried blood covering it, he can't see much of anything. With that, he checks his rifle, and then looks at Ethan and Aiden. "We'll have to be careful. This area had a lot of traffic, and I don't have much ammo left, so if it comes down to it, we may have to just book it."

"I'm low, too," says Ethan after checking his supplies.

"We'll just have to make our ammo count," says Aiden as he approaches the door.

Aiden takes one side, Simon takes another, and Ethan aims his shotgun at the doorway. Then Aiden counts to three and starts pulling with Simon. The group cringes as the metal squeaks and groans, and when the door reaches a certain point, it slams inside its slots, creating an echo in the chamber. A few seconds pass before Ethan moves forward, sweeping the area with his shotgun, and Aiden and Simon follow close behind.

The Terrarium's air is stale, and dying trees are wrapped in thorny vines, wilted flowers are being replaced with orange bulbs, and dead grass coated in film covers the area. In front of the Terrarium is a large observation window that has trees with hundreds of bodies clinging to it. Each of the bodies has various faces and limbs twisted in different ways, with more vines, roots, or bulbs sprouting from them. These trees climb to the ceiling, and their branches are interlocked with each other, and with their numbers and thickness, the view of Onyx, its red dwarf star, and the space beyond is blocked.

The three look around, and Ethan notices that the normal trees are roughly cut or damaged with shrapnel and bullets, and the grass and flowers have been trampled before being overtaken by the Onyx Spore. Off to the side are a couple of damaged carts overtaken by vines, and a Klumsy K's diner no longer has any windows, and its chairs and tables are knocked over or destroyed. There is also a large amount of dried blood near what remains of the diner's doorway. Near the Klumsy K's is another entrance to the Terrarium that has been forced open, and there are a couple of other doorways, too.

"That's the one we need, right there," says Simon, pointing directly in front of him.

Ethan and Simon look to where he is pointing and see a broken door with a sign pointing to Section A. Then, some slobber drips in front of the group. It sizzles when it hits the floor, and they slowly look up. When they see what is hanging from the Terrarium ceiling, Aiden's jaw drops, Simon swears, and Ethan cocks his shotgun.

It is time for round two.
And this time he will kill that thing.

28

Showdown in the Terrarium

The Über Stitcher drops from the ceiling, and the group scatters before it lands. The floor shakes upon its landing, and its five massive heads roar, spraying the area with acidic spit.

Ethan rapidly shoots at the Über Stitcher. The slugs chip at its bark, and the creature roars and pukes out a stream of acid. Ethan dives away from the torrent. The acid hits a tree and the floor, bringing the floor to warp and peel apart, exposing soil and roots that quickly burn away, while the tree burns with chunks dissolving in seconds.

Ethan shoots more slugs at the Über Stitcher and jumps out of the way of another stream of acid puke while Simon and Aiden unload into the abomination. Their bullets chip at its bark and pierce some unarmored flesh, and it shrieks at Simon. He dodges its swipe and shoots it some until his magazine runs dry, all while Ethan and Aiden keep shooting it.

The Über Stitcher roars and rushes Ethan. He leaps away when it takes a swipe at him that rips out chunks of a tree he had been standing nearby. Splinters fly and the tree falls over, shaking the floor with its impact, and Ethan runs as the Über Stitcher chases him.

Each step Ethan takes makes his collection of wounds throb, and his heart feels like it is tearing as his breathing becomes ragged. He looks over his shoulder and swears and takes a sharp turn as the Über Stitcher slashes at him again.

The Über Stitcher sprays more acid at him, and after evading the acid, Ethan shoots a few more slugs into it, aiming at the ribs holding the acid bags. The shots mostly do nothing, but one shot shatters a rib, which leads to an acid bag being punctured, and the Über Stitcher screeches and stumbles back as the stream of deadly fluid destroys the Terrarium's flora.

Thick smoke and a rancid stench assault Ethan's nose, and when he is in the middle of reloading his shotgun, something lands on his back, knocking him to the ground. Then comes scratches into his shoulders, and he screams and rolls around as the Haunter latches on to him.

Ethan rolls around until the Haunter breaks loose, and then he quickly gets up and punches it in the face while it tries standing. The Haunter drops, and Ethan grabs his shotgun and shoots it in the head. As it twitches on the ground, he turns his attention to the Über Stitcher but pales when he sees a swarm rushing in from one of the broken doors.

The swarm consists of Haunters, Tainted, and Lurkers, and Simon and Aiden are shooting into the crowd, and bobbing and weaving through the trees, leaving immobile or crawling creatures in their wake.

The Über Stitcher pukes more acid at Ethan, and he registers this just in time to jump out of the way, leading to the headless Haunter getting melted. Its thrashes become more intense as its flesh and bark melts and burns, and its bones splinter.

Ethan runs to the Über Stitcher and slides underneath it with the help of the dead grass and shoots more slugs along its underside. Bones and bark break, bags pop, and the Über Stitcher shrieks and thrashes as the mix of gore and acid falls with chunks of broken ribs.

In hindsight, it was a dumb move since the spilling acid almost gets Ethan. But with the acid bags out of the way, he will no longer have to worry about being melted. Only mutilated like a normal victim.

As the Über Stitcher thrashes, its claws tear apart the floor, flinging soil and metal, and its legs struggle to keep it up as the acid melts everything. Burnt floral and metal sting Ethan's nose and he whacks a Tainted that has run up to him. As it stumbles away, he shoots a couple more Tainted, before returning to his first target and blowing a hole in its chest.

Then, Ethan suddenly goes airborne with pain running along his side, and he hits the upper portion of a tree. He bounces off the branches, taking broken wood with him, and when he lands, the suit injects him with medical foam and adrenaline. Even with that, his side throbs, his heart is heavy, and his throat stings, as he crawls on the ground, watching with a hazy vision as the swarm rushes towards him.

"Hold on!" yells Aiden, his voice muffled by the loud thumps in Ethan's ears.

Ethan pushes himself up, and he shoots into the swarm while the Über Stitcher stomps towards him with sluggish steps, leaving a trail of blood in its wake. Some Haunters and Tainted collapse as the slugs tear into them.

Right as the Über Stitcher raises its massive claws, Simon zips by and pulls Ethan away. The Über Stitcher's claws rip into the dead tree, and then it swipes towards the pair.

Simon and Ethan shield themselves as thick pieces of wood scatter and bounce around them, and after the air clears, a Lurker snatches Simon off the ground. It does not get too far off the ground before Aiden shoots its wings, leading to the Lurker crashing, and it and Simon rolling over and brawling each other. As this happens, Ethan runs towards them, and Aiden shoots at the Über Stitcher and the swarm.

When Ethan reaches the Lurker, it has pierced Simon's hand with its sharp tongue and bugs are crawling all over him. Ethan rams his shotgun against the Lurker's skull, splattering its head, and it flops off Simon.

He shoots it a few times, leaving it to twitch on the ground with vines sprouting from its flesh and its body splitting open to allow more to wiggle out. Ethan then helps Simon fight off the bugs before helping him up.

Once Simon is up, he seethes and grips his hand, now pumping out dark red and orange blood, and Ethan sprays the injury with medical foam before hastily wrapping it in a bandage. All this is possible because Aiden is drawing the swarm away from them.

"I can't feel my hand!" says Simon.

"You'll be fine. We have a few more…" Ethan looks around and sees the bodies splitting and stitching themselves together to make a large Stitcher. "How much ammo do you have?"

Simon looks up and sees the new Stitchers giving chase to Aiden. "Not enough. You?"

"I'll make it work."

Then a burning bottle sails through the air and strikes the ground in the middle of the swarm. Fire spreads quickly, and the creatures shriek and thrash as the flames consume them. Another burning bottle is thrown seconds later, creating another surge in the flame that engulfs more and spreads the fire.

Ethan looks to where the bottles came from and sees a figure in front of the Klumsy K's. He cannot make out the details, but while the creatures scramble and the fire spreads across the field, the newcomer rushes out and starts gunning down the flailing, burning Stitchers. This draws the swarm and Über Stitcher to them and allows Aiden to run to Ethan and Simon.

"Come on, we need to get to cover," says Ethan.

Ethan takes Simon to a large tree, and Aiden slides next to them, panting heavily and shoving a new magazine in his rifle.

"I'm on my last two magazines," says Aiden.

"I'm not much better, and Simon's hand is useless," says Ethan.

The rattling gunfire compels them to poke their heads out, and they watch the figure running and gunning. They shoot the limbs before shooting the heads of their targets with incredible speed and accuracy, and they evade the vines whipping out from the Stitchers being engulfed by the fires.

While watching, the air has become tainted with smoke, and the stench of acid and burning flesh. Fire is climbing up the infected trees, and the Über Stitcher is limping after the newcomer. As the three watch the scene unfold, the air around them crackles, and Ethan's shield flickers and he feels a tug on him.

He looks at Simon and sees he still has his miniature warp battery, but its cracked and sparking, and it is burning Simon's suit. He then looks at Aiden's battery and sees that his battery is still intact. Seeing this, he holds his hand out to Simon.

"Give me your battery and pistol," says Ethan.

Simon quickly unclips his battery and pistol and gives them to Ethan. Before Aiden can ask what he plans on doing, Ethan runs towards the swarm, slides to a stop near a dead tree, and looks at the Über Stitcher. The growing smoke choking the air shrouds the Über Stitcher and the swarm of Stitchers, the fire spreads to the trees and walls, and the newcomer's distance between themselves and the creatures is shrinking.

"TAKE COVER!" shouts Ethan.

He throws the battery as hard as he can towards the Über Stitcher. The glowing, sparking blue battery sails through the air, twirling and burning, and while it flies, Ethan draws Simon's pistol and shoots at it.

Miss.

Miss.

Miss.

Miss!

MISS!

The battery falls just short of the goal, and it bounces across the ground, tearing apart bulbs and pulling off bark from the nearby trees or pieces of the growing vines. However, it is still close to the swarm, and the newcomer gets a fresh burst of speed and turns to lead them to the bad battery.

Ethan takes a deep breath and then fires another shot. There is a bright flash of white and blue light, followed by a crackling of electricity that pulls on every cell in his body and starts *dragging* him towards an orb growing in the Terrarium.

The orb is swirling with white and blue energy, and the sparks shooting out of it disintegrate everything they touch, while uprooting everything around them. Stitchers dig into the ground with their claws and vines, and the Über Stitcher latches on to the floor with pieces of all of them being ripped off. Some Stitchers are pulled off the ground and are sucked into the orb, which flashes upon their impact and completely dissolves them in seconds.

Ethan grits his teeth and strains every part of his body to pull himself behind the nearest tree, and he squeezes his eye shut as the bright light burns him. The tree groans, pieces of it snap off, plants burn, and the Terrarium observation window shatters, showering the area with large pieces of jagged glass and shredded vines.

Wind howls and swirls as it is stirred by the sudden vacuum and intense gravity well, and the alarm wails with emergency lights flashing for only a moment before popping. Then there is a series of fast and loud metallic bangs that clash with a loud pop that leaves Ethan's ears ringing. After that comes an empty silence and heavy darkness.

Ethan opens his eye and pokes his head around what is left of his tree. He gasps when he sees the devastation. The observation window is now thick metal slabs with jagged glass around the edges, and the Terrarium is dark, with only tiny pockets of light being made by a sporadic rain of sparks. There is a giant hole in the center surrounded by warped metal and pipes. The soil, flowers, grass, and bulbs, and vines are also gone, and most of the trees have disappeared. What trees remain are toppled, snapped, or somehow only crooked.

But the Über Stitcher and the Stitchers are no more. There is only darkness in the gaping hole that used to be the Terrarium, and Ethan loves that, but there is another thing…

"Aiden? Simon?" calls Ethan.

Silence.

Ethan's heart races and panic seeps into his voice as he shakily turns his light on and searches the area. "Aiden? Simon? Anybody out there?"

"Relax, I'm right here," says Aiden, poking his head up from behind a toppled tree.

He turns his light on and Simon walks out with his injured hand pressed against his chest, and he also has his light on.

Ethan sighs with relief and hurries to the two, and when he reaches them, Simon pats his shoulder with a smile, while Aiden scans the area.

"You weren't kidding when you said you would make your ammo work," says Simon.

Ethan smiles, returns Simon's pistol, and starts inspecting the officer's hand. It will need more work and some sort of splint and extra padding, but they are also close to the bridge, which always has a surplus of supplies, so the hand issue should not be a problem for long.

"I'll have a better look at it when we get to the bridge, but for now, I would advise you to take it easy. No extreme activities. Just the bare minimum to avoid further injury," says Ethan. "Also, I'm going to prescribe you some ginger ale and crackers, plus bed rest on a sofa."

"I don't want ginger ale or crackers. They're always stale, and the sofa is never comfortable," says Simon.

"Hey, the medic has spoken. Don't make me force feed you those crackers and ginger ale," says Aiden.

Ethan cracks a smile, and Simon stares at Aiden for a few seconds before he snickers, and shortly after, Aiden joins in. The snickering soon turns to laugh of joy and relief, and as they laugh in the dark, random sparks fall, briefly adding some illumination to them. Then, a familiar voice carries through the desolate Terrarium.

"Did that just happen!" yells Taksheel. "Who in the hell thought it was a good idea to shoot a mini-warp battery? I'm trying to live, damn it!"

All three slowly stop laughing and turn around and see Taksheel walking towards them with his light shining from his shoulder and his rifle aimed down but held tight.

"I mean, I know we're all trying to live, but-"

Taksheel stops when he sees Ethan, and his eyes widen, while Ethan simply stares with his tainted eye hardening and his jaw setting. Taksheel's condition has worsened since Ethan last saw him; now his cheek and neck are coated in tainted blood, his suit is torn, burnt, and patched up, and an ammo belt crosses over his chest.

As Ethan stares at Taksheel, the guard smiles nervously and looks at Aiden, who is giving him the same sharp look as Ethan. Simon is keeping a neutral expression, but his finger is resting against his pistol's trigger guard.

"Hey guys, I haven't seen you in a while," says Taksheel.

Aiden tightens his grip on his rifle. "Did you kill Mary?"

Taksheel swallows, looks at Ethan, then back at Aiden, and nods. "Yeah… Yeah, I did, but I had no choice. She was turning into one of those things. And Ethan, man, I'm sorry, but I thought you were dead. If I had known you were alive, I would have come for you, but that crazy lady was a demon or something."

"Well, we are in Hell, so of course she's a demon," says Simon.

"I'm sorry, but who are you?" asks Taksheel.

"Officer Arnvin Simon of the Colonial Security Service. Ethan told me what happened," says Simon.

"He told you his side, but not mine," says Taksheel sourly. He then shoulders his weapon and steps towards Aiden carefully, with his hands up. "Aiden, I know this looks bad, but I had no choice. Marian's arm was cut off and vines were popping out of her. She was in pain and was going to become one of those things. I had to do it."

Aiden is silent, and Taksheel looks between the three.

"You guys can hate me. That's fine. We can even all go our separate ways when this is done, but let's not get hostile right now. We need to get out of here as fast as possible," says Taksheel.

"Hey, no hard feelings from me. I was taking them to the bridge, and I was going to go to Hangar H and get out of here. Do you want to come with us?" says Simon.

Ethan glares at Simon, and he looks at Ethan.

"You heard him. He had no choice," says Simon, "and having to put down a few friends, I know exactly where he's coming from."

"Thank you. I'm glad someone other than me is thinking straight around here," says Taksheel.

"So, do you want to come with me or them?" asks Simon.

"He's coming with us," says Aiden. "We have a lot to talk about, anyway."

"I don't think that's a good idea. Ethan's giving me a creepy look. It almost looks like he wants to shoot me," says Taksheel.

"That's because I do," says Ethan.

"But you won't," says Aiden.

"Alright, it's settled. We should be at the bridge in a few minutes, unless we get caught up in another mess," says Simon.

Suddenly there is a loud whir, and the sound of armor, flesh, and bone breaking, with the shield around Simon flickering out as he jerks forward. Blood seeps past his lips, his breathing becomes struggled wheezes, and Ethan and Aiden's eyes widen, while Taksheel steps back.

"Simon?" says Ethan.

Simon collapses with a circular saw lodged in his back, and Ethan rushes to his side and holds his head on his lap.

"Simon!" Ethan presses his fingers against Simon's neck, and then his ear against his nose. He pulls back a moment later, trembling and balling his hands into a fist. "No…"

"Arnvin was mean. Ethan is mean. They want to leave Gary. They want to leave Carmen. They want to leave us. They want to leave *Bon Voyage*. No. No! You can't leave us! YOU'RE OURS!"

The hissing voice carries through the hollowed Terrarium, and the three survivors of the *Hook Line* look in the voice's direction. Carmen is standing in a doorway leading to a stairwell, and the light above her flickers, flashing her in and out of the darkness. Her scaly skin is covered in electric burns, her yellow eyes are glowing, her teeth are large and sharp. Her cheeks are ripped with vines wiggling out of holes in her suit, and her brown hair is hanging in front of her face.

"Troublemakers, troublemakers, troublemakers. All of you are troublemakers!" cries Carmen.

She revs her saw, and Ethan's vision goes red with his tainted eye pulsing, and Aiden and Taksheel step back with their weapons raised.

"Who the hell is that?" says Aiden.

"That's the crazy bitch that cut off Marian's arm!" says Taksheel.

Aiden shoots Carmen, but the bullets bounce off her shield, covering her in ripples of blue that spark sporadically, and she shrieks and shoots a saw blade at him. The group runs off in different directions, and Carmen reloads her saw while creeping out of the hallway, giggling, and swaying with her eyes shining from taint and tears.

"Don't leave us, troublemakers. Join us. Join us! Give your souls to *Bon Voyage!*" says Carmen as the vines wrap around her arms.

Ethan growls and goes to Simon's body and grabs his knife, and Aiden pokes out from his cover behind a tree stump.

"Ethan, what are you doing!" yells Aiden.

"Hey, get back here! Don't be a hero!" says Taksheel.

"Take care of Taksheel," says Ethan, his grip tightening on the knife and his eye narrowing on Carmen.

Seeing Ethan coming towards her makes Carmen grin, and she beckons Ethan with one hand and giggles.

"What are you doing?" says Aiden.

"I'm going to kill her," says Ethan.

29

One More Body

Carmen cackles and revs her saw as Ethan approaches her. Ethan's march turns into a full run, with a scratchy, psychotic yell and blood-red vision. When Carmen shoots a saw at him, he dodges it, and she giggles and slips another saw blade into her weapon.

Before she can fire, Ethan slashes at her, forcing her back, and he slashes at her two more times before Carmen grabs his hand and twists the knife out while revving her saw. Ethan ducks as the roaring saw is plunged towards his head. Sparks fall and smoke rises from the saw as it strikes the door frame, and Ethan puts all his strength into ramming Carmen.

Carmen's back hits the door frame, still holding Ethan and leaving the saw stuck, and she pulls out another saw blade and tries slashing him. He grabs her wrist and grunts, as his wounded arm struggles to keep the blade up. The two circle each other, with Ethan slowly sliding into defeat.

Then he sees the dark opening leading to the stairs, and he digs his feet into the floor and springs forward. The sudden move causes Carmen to lose her balance, and they travel further into the dark, stopping just shy of the stairs.

They are partially covered in the dark as they struggle, and Ethan kicks out Carmen's footing and punches her. He keeps punching her until she releases his hand, and after that, he punches her in the jaw. Carmen laughs at this, and her laughter sends cold shivers through Ethan's spine.

Then Carmen's arm splits open into vines that wrap around Ethan's waist, and she swings him into the wall, shattering glass and lightbulbs of a display advertising the Terrarium. Ethan flops to the ground, and the vines stretch out and grab Carmen's saw.

They wrap around it like fingers, yank it out of the wall, leaving the saw blade stuck, and it is in each of her other hand. Carmen slips a new saw blade in and charges Ethan with her weapon revving.

Ethan scrambles to his feet and dodges the first swipe, and when Carmen goes for a second swipe, he pushes the weapon up and accidentally hits the eject button. The saw blade launches into the ceiling, showering the two with sparks.

Carmen pushes against Ethan, forcing him backward. There is a sudden drop, and Ethan grabs Carmen and pulls her down with him. The two bounce off the walls and stairs, and Ethan's vision becomes a blur of red lights and dark colors. When they land at the bottom, Ethan shifts and coughs, and Carmen giggles as she flops around on the floor.

Now they are silhouettes in the dark, and Ethan sees Carmen pushing herself up with her eyes glowing and grin wide. He jumps to his feet, but before he can do anything, he is wrapped in a vine and thrown against the wall.

She lifts him again and throws him against the other wall, and then the ceiling, and he lands on the floor. His ears are ringing, and every part of him throbs.

Then he is kicked on his back and Carmen sits on him, laughing, with a saw blade in her grip.

"Say it with me, Troublemaker," says Carmen. "One by one we go. When it stops, we don't know."

Closer and closer it gets, wider and wider Carmen's grin becomes, and Ethan's throat bobs as the blade is mere inches from his jugular, with his arms failing him.

"One by one we go!" says Carmen.

Ethan twists his body, the saw mauls the right side of his face, and he screams in rage and pain and slams his fist underneath Carmen's chin. Her head snaps back and broken teeth fly out, and Ethan shoves her away and rolls to his feet as Carmen giggles with thick ropes of blood dripping from her mouth.

The vines replacing her arms whip at Ethan, and Carmen trembles as she revs her saw and arches her back. Ethan quickly slides behind her, dodging a swipe from the saw, and he grabs Carmen's last saw blade from her belt while she tries standing.

She whirls around, swinging her saw madly. Ethan cuts her wrist, causing her hand to go limp and drop her weapon, and then he slashes her neck when the vines grab his throat.

Carmen's giggles turn to gurgles, and thick globs of blood pump through the jagged gash in her throat. Her legs give out, she falls to her knees, and Ethan yanks the vines off his neck while he glares at Carmen. His chest heaves from his heavy breathing and his tainted eye pulsates. Blood soaks the right side of his face, his right shoulder, and chest, and the bandages covering his burnt scars and missing eye have slipped off, revealing his skull, the charred and cracked skin, and the black pool that used to be his right eye.

Red lights reflect off him, and blood drips off the saw blade as he stares at Carmen, who is staring back at him with dimming yellow eyes and twitching vines. Her throat pulses, and her mouth moves, as though she is trying to speak, but no words come out.

With a vicious yell, Ethan plunges the saw blade into Carmen's skull and kicks her down. Carmen twitches, gurgles, and then falls silent.

"Ethan!" calls Aiden.

Ethan stares at Carmen's corpse, his breathing shaky and labored.

"Ethan!"

The lights above hum to life, and the red lights are replaced with cold white light, and Ethan's hardened expression melts to horror as he looks at the corpse. Steps bang down the stairs, and Ethan stumbles back. He collapses against the wall and hyperventilates as Carmen's lifeless eyes look at him.

Aiden soon runs into view with Taksheel trailing him, and they skid to a stop and look at Carmen's corpse. Aiden then goes to Ethan's side, takes one of his cans of medical foam, and sprays his wounds, before wrapping them with the last bandage in Ethan's inventory.

The foam hardens with a pink and orange tint, and while Aiden works, Taksheel paces around Carmen's corpse, gives her a light kick. Then he kneels to inspect the vines, just to yank his hand away when they try grabbing him.

"Ethan, can you hear me?" asks Aiden.

"Wow, you wrecked her," says Taksheel.

Ethan looks at Taksheel, and then at Aiden.

"I... I liked it." Ethan takes a deep, shaky breath and coughs in his hand. His throat feels like it is going to rip, and his heart is heavy. He blinks tears away, as his eye flicks without direction. "I enjoyed killing her like I enjoyed killing them."

Taksheel looks at Ethan with piqued interest, and Aiden grips Ethan's shoulder tight.

"You mean the monsters?" asks Aiden.

Ethan shakes his head. *"No. Eu os matei nos Apartmentos Luxuosos do Rio Rise. Eu amei."*

"What?" says Aiden.

Taksheel steps closer, and Ethan swallows.

"I killed those people at the Luxury Apartments on Oros, and I loved it. They killed my mom, so I killed them." Ethan looks at Carmen. "She killed Simon, so I killed her... I loved it. It was fun... Painful, but fun... Am I gone?"

Aiden shakes his head. "No, you aren't gone. I promise you; you are not gone. We're all getting out of here, and we'll put this behind us."

"Like how you put Vagsten behind you?" asks Ethan.

Aiden hesitates, then helps Ethan up. "Come on. We're almost at the bridge."

"That's where Section 0 is, too," says Taksheel. "I'm going to love talking to those guys when we see them."

"Yeah, we're going to have a lot to talk about. We need answers about why this happened, and we need them to get out of this forsaken system," says Aiden.

"We can take them hostage and then jump to a random system," says Taksheel.

Aiden nods. "I still have a battery. So, we nab whoever is on the bridge, jump the system, and then tell everybody what happened here. Whoever is responsible will not get away with this. I'll make sure of it."

Taksheel grins and tilts his rifle up. "I like that. We can do some more vacations after this, too. You, me, Ethan, we'd be an unstoppable team."

Ethan shakes his head. "No, I'm done with space," he says tiredly.

"And I want my dairy farm," says Aiden.

Taksheel sighs in feign disappointment. "You guys are no fun."

"Plus, you still have to explain Mary's death," says Aiden.

"And Riva's," says Ethan.

"Why do I have to explain Riva? I didn't kill her," says Taksheel sharply.

Then comes a distant thud that makes all three of them jump. What follows is metal bending and breaking, and they look down the hallway, as heavy steps echo towards them.

Familiar steps.

Steps that drain what little color is left on Ethan's face.

"Run," says Ethan.

30

The Bridge

The three hurry up the stairs with Taksheel in the lead, and when the heavy steps get quicker, the group runs faster towards the destroyed doorway. They seek shelter in the Klumsy K's and take cover behind the bar counter, which has an employee of the month picture of some photogenic guy named Joe laying on the floor.

All three ready their weapons, each cringing as the clicks echoes in the destroyed eatery. When their weapons are ready, the group remains still, with only their racing hearts making a noise. After a few seconds of silence, the heavy steps thump by. The steps stop outside, and two low growls rumble in the dark.

"Ethan. Let me in," says the Moon Stitcher.

Ethan stiffly peeks out, and he quickly pulls back in when he sees the towering silhouette of the Moon Stitcher standing in the doorway, like a shadow in the darkness. Its vines weave in the air, and its enormous claws touch the floor while its form is hunched over.

Taksheel tries to look, but Ethan and Aiden hold him down, and the Moon Stitcher stays in the doorway for a few more seconds before it lumbers away. The thumping steps and growls gradually fade away, but even when the steps are completely gone, none of them make a sound or risk movement. A few minutes later, Ethan pokes his head out and sees nothing in the dark, except for the dark shapes of destroyed furniture and the Terrarium.

"I think it's gone," says Ethan.

Aiden sighs and bangs his head against the counter, and Taksheel leans over Ethan's shoulder.

"What was that?" asks Taksheel.

Ethan nudges him back. "A Stitcher. It killed Moon and took his body."

"Wow."

"I thought you killed that thing," says Aiden.

"I dropped it down an elevator shaft!" snaps Ethan. "Maybe it fused with your Stitcher or another Haunter or Tainted or something."

"Wait, these things fuse?" says Taksheel. "So, they not only take our bodies, but they take their own, too? What kind of messed up biology is that?"

"It is a defense mechanism. I've seen it happen plenty of times. They get injured enough and they absorb another body to stay alive," says Ethan.

"We can have biology lessons when we get to the bridge," says Aiden.

Ethan nods and peeks around the corner. "Coast is still clear. Let's get out of here."

Ethan creeps forward, stops by the doorway, and he looks outside. When he sees nothing, he moves towards the Terrarium's exit. The other two quietly follow behind, and when they are at the door, they find it has been broken open.

Aiden shines his light down the hallway on the other side. They see nothing, so Ethan goes first, then Taksheel, and finally Aiden.

Nothing spectacular happens during their walk, but after crossing through another doorway they find themselves in a hallway with thick, foul air, a long row of shattered windows, broken lights, and charred walls and floors, with flashes of light reflecting off the wall from a damaged screen. Blackened bodies lay twisted on the ground, their uniforms fused to their charred skin, their eyes burnt out, their mouths warped, and their fingers clawing on the walls or the floor with melted carts around them.

Some exposed bones have splintered, and some bodies are hugging each other, and shriveled plants hang from the ceiling and vents. On the wall is the *Bon Voyage* traveling through space with the Federation of Sol Systems flag in tow, but the image constantly flickers and breaks into colorful cubes. On the other side of the windows are desks, chairs, computers, and a holographic projector in the center of the room. They have been torched, with more burnt bodies crowded by a door that is projecting a red lock.

The group quietly walks through the carnage, and Aiden's hands and breathing tremble as he tries to not look at the bodies. Nobody says anything as they go down the hallway, and they stop when they reach the door at the end, labeled as "Section A."

It has a clump of shriveled bodies pressed against it, and the group moves the bodies aside so they can get to the door. Its orb has been destroyed, and it is completely dim.

"I got this. Ethan, watch Taksheel. Taksheel, watch the hall," says Aiden, as he pulls out a small blowtorch from his supply belt and puts on his visor. "And nobody turns around until I say so."

Ethan waves Taksheel away from Aiden with his shotgun, and Taksheel shakes his head, shifts a couple of bodies, and uses them as a chair while he looks down the hallway. He occasionally looks at Ethan out of the corner of his eye while the light and crackling of the blowtorch reflects and echo in the tomb.

A couple of minutes later, a circle large enough for Aiden to go through is cut into the door. He kicks it out, making a ruckus of metallic bangs and screeches that echo in the desolate ship.

"Alright, Ethan, you're first. Then you, Taksheel," says Aiden.

Ethan nods and goes through the hole, followed by Taksheel, and then Aiden. After that, they walk up the stairs, passing a camera along the way.

"You're almost there. Go down the hall, take the first left, and you'll be at the bridge door," says the Voice.

They follow the Voice's instructions, and after a minute of walking, they come across a large, thick door with the Federation's Sculptor constellation on the left side. On the right side is a telescope with a ring of stars and "FCS" beneath it; this is the symbol for the Federation Colonial Service.

The door is damaged with scratches and scorch marks, and it is being watched by four cameras; one is in front of the door, one is above the group's heads, and the other two are above the symbols.

Taksheel goes to the camera by the Federation symbol and tilts his head in question, and Aiden steps in front of the camera above the Colonial Service and waves.

The door pops, clicks, whirs, and slides open, shining a bright light on the group. Ethan watches this scene in a state of joy and disbelief, and Aiden steps back with his rifle raised, while Taksheel tips his rifle up, smiling thinly. When it is all the way open, Ethan is speechless at what he sees.

The circular room is brightly it, computers line the walls, all flashing warning messages, a holographic display shows the blueprint of the ship, with most of it being red or yellow, and the bridge window has a view of the black and red planet and the blood-colored dwarf star in the distance. There is also a captain's chair in an elevated position that has a view of the whole bridge, plus steering mechanics for the ship. One wall is a large screen displaying profiles in red with flat lines for thousands of names. But two have a steady stream of vitals, and their profiles are enlarged.

One profile is for Harold Foster; his occupation is labeled as a certified religious community leader. His rough, light-brown hair is speckled with light tan streaks, and he has a bright smile with a great tan. His vital signatures are steady, with the occasional spike. His profile is outlined in green.

The other profile is Junjie Ding; his occupation being the Captain of *Bon Voyage,* in service of the Federation Colonial Service. His vitals are sharp and through the roof with rapid pulses and heavy breathing, and his profile is outlined in yellow.

"What did you do! Why did you open the door!" cries a man with a shaky, wimpy voice from the captain's perch.

Junjie is of Chinese descent and scrawny, with his oversized, gold-banded captain's uniform open and ripped with patches of sweat darkening the fabric. His black hair is also a mess, and his eyes are bloodshot.

"Whoa, whoa, whoa, relax, we won't hurt you," says Aiden with his hand outstretched, rifle aimed down, and his steps cautious as he approaches Junjie.

"You're with Section 0, aren't you?" Junjie yanks out a pistol and aims it at the group. "AREN'T YOU!"

Ethan aims his shotgun at Junjie, and Aiden snaps his hand to Ethan.

"Don't," says Aiden firmly.

"I won't let him shoot you," says Ethan.

"He doesn't have the guts to do it," says Aiden.

"He might this time," says Taksheel. "He's got nothing to lose. He's in big trouble for getting all these people killed, and if the government gets a hold of him, oh boy, talk about a bad time."

"Shut up, Taksheel!" orders Ethan. "You still have to answer for murdering Marian and Riva!"

"Riva was not my fault, Ethan," says Taksheel.

"None of this was my fault!" cries Junjie.

"But killing Marian was an act of mercy," says Taksheel. "She was transforming and in pain. I had to kill her for her sake. But as for Riva, she did that all to herself. She wanted to be important and loved, and she volunteered to go out there. Now she is important and loved. In memory."

"You son of a-"

Ethan steps forward, but Taksheel aims his rifle at Ethan's head.

"Ethan, bro, my guy, these bullets travel at 370 meters per second. The shield will block the bullet, but the force of the impact from this close of a range will break your skull. Do you want that?"

"I never wanted this to happen," says Junjie.

"What happened here? What caused this?" asks Aiden.

Ethan glares at Taksheel, and Taksheel steps back, his yellow-tainted eyes shifting between the others and his rifle slightly tilting side to side.

"I figured you would want Marian spared of the pain, but you wanted her to suffer, didn't you, killer?" says Taksheel. "You wanted her screams in those little ears. Maybe you really are Section 0, because all of this happened as soon as you showed up, and you didn't want that signal out."

"Riva was too sick to go out there!" says Ethan.

"You hardly talked, always watched us, and you admitted you killed all those people in that apartment, *and* you survived all that crap out there... It all makes sense. It's all your fault."

"None of this was my fault," whimpers Junjie, his face soaked in tears and his legs wobbling, while stepping back, pistol shaking in his grip. "It was all Section 0. They did this... All of this. I never meant to hurt anybody."

"Captain, lower your sidearm. We are here to help you," says Aiden.

"You are the ravik. You are Section 0, aren't you, killer?" says Taksheel.

"I'm not Section 0, you *bastsardo louco!*" screams Ethan.

Suddenly, three bursts ring out, and Ethan fires off a shot while a flash of light blinds him. A hard punch to the heart sends him crashing to the floor with the shield's light and the force of the shots disorienting him.

He curses up a storm and holds his heart while heavy footsteps approach him. He reaches for his shotgun, but it is kicked away from him. Then, Ethan sees Aiden laying limp on the ground, with a pool of blood seeping from his head and neck, and Junjie is slumped against the stairs, gurgling and gasping, with blood pouring out of his chest and mouth.

Taksheel stands in front of Junjie, and the captain barely raises his hand before Taksheel shoots him in the head. The captain's skull is blown to pieces.

Taksheel walks towards Ethan, while a loud bang shakes the room, followed by scraping. The wall of profiles slides open, allowing a figure to enter the bridge.

The figure is wearing a white jumpsuit with gray bands and a white lab coat, and he calmly walks towards Taksheel.

"One by one we go... When it stops, we don't know..." hums Taksheel as he paces around Ethan. He stops and aims at Ethan's head. "One by one we go..."

"Don't kill him," says the scientist, his voice being very familiar.

A few seconds later, Ethan's eye narrows, and his hands ball into fists. The Voice is standing right in front of him.

"Stand up, Ethan. Don't be shy," says the Voice.

Taksheel steps away to grab Ethan's shotgun, and Ethan slowly stands up, glaring at the Voice. He has gray and white hair, a tight face abused by constant plastic surgery, and his teeth are bleached white and have a slight gleam in the light, like his hazel eyes.

There is a moment of heavy silence between them, which is broken when the Voice's grin widens and holds out his hands.

"I finally get to meet *the* Ethan Rifts in the flesh!" says the Voice. "Let me tell you, you took this ship by. A. Storm! My viewers love you, Ethan. You're a freaking gem. Big, beautiful gem, and I want your autograph!"

Ethan glares at the Voice while he pulls out a screenshot of Ethan fighting the Moon Stitcher in the engine room. He gives it to Ethan, plus a marker.

"Just say, 'To: Dr. Arcos Rock. From: Ethan Rifts.' You can put some x's and o's in there, too," says the Voice, also known as Dr. Arcos Rock.

Ethan refuses to take the picture, and Dr. Rock's smile strains as he reluctantly puts the picture and marker back.

"Okay, I get it. You're moody. Maybe later?" says Dr. Rock.

Taksheel grabs the miniature warp battery from Aiden's corpse and gives it to Dr. Rock, and in return, he gets a large zip-tie.

"Bind him and take him inside. I'm almost done packing," says Dr. Rock.

"With these? You serious?" says Taksheel.

"They didn't trust me with handcuffs. Now chop-chop! Time's a-wasting!"

Taksheel shakes his head and looks at Ethan. "Put your wrists together."

Ethan glares at Taksheel.

"Come on. Don't be a prick," says Taksheel.

Ethan keeps staring and trembling with his breathing heavy and eye pulsating.

"Don't make me shoot you again," says Taksheel.

Ethan is motionless for a few seconds, but in the end, he reluctantly puts his wrists together.

"Thank you," says Taksheel.

Taksheel binds Ethan's wrists and escorts him to the door that used to be the profile wall. Dr. Rock is waiting for them, and when they are by his side, he grins and puts his hand on Ethan's shoulder and guides him further inside his lair while Taksheel stays a couple of steps behind.

"Where are you taking me?" asks Ethan while testing the strength of the zip-tie.

"To the next phase of your life," says Dr. Rock. "Ethan Rifts, you are now Section 0 property."

31

Descension

Dr. Rock leads Ethan and Taksheel through the doorway, and Ethan quietly takes in the scenery, which would be nothing spectacular if *Bon Voyage* wasn't a portal to Hell. The gray metal walls and bright lights are standard, and there are undamaged vents lining the ceiling and walls. Also, standard. Overall, a remarkably boring hallway compared to the rest of the ship.

"The bridge is sealed off from the rest of *Bon Voyage*," explains Dr. Rock when he notices Ethan looking around. "Separate air tanks, separate vent network, separate water system, separate everything."

"Can it split off and fly away as a separate ship?" asks Ethan, half-mocking, half-curious. He also tests the zip tie again.

"Not this model," replies Dr. Rock. "But Arx Corporation is working on it. A model should be ready in a year or two, according to Scientific Federation."

Dr. Rock takes Ethan and Taksheel to a large chamber, and he smiles proudly at a collection of computers, each showing graphs and lines of data of some sort. They are attached to three sealed displays. There is also a screen showing a live feed of various cameras being broadcast to a location titled "Harpoon."

The first display has vials of the Onyx Spore pollen, film, severed mutated limbs, vines, surgically removed yellow eyes, and a brain covered in thin orange vines with tiny thorns. The vials of pollen were being moved by a mechanical arm into a padded metal case with a black and yellow biohazard symbol. There are three more cases like it laying on a cart that beeps and whirs when it sees the group.

The second display has vials of blood, ranging from normal to the orange tint, and finally the pure orange. Some of these are also being moved into cases with the same biohazard symbols, but this case has a blood droplet next to it.

The third display has four rows of eight vials with green liquid. These vials are also being carefully placed in a padded metal case, but the biohazard symbol on this one is red and white, and it has a red cross next to it.

The fourth display has artifacts of entwined trees made from metal and bone, and various books written in an alien language.

"What the hell is all this?" says Ethan.

"The mission, Ethan," says Taksheel.

Ethan looks at Taksheel. "Are you serious? You did all this for a science experiment?"

"You have nothing to worry about. They are sealed," says Dr. Rock.

"They are not sealed," says Ethan.

"Well, those out there aren't, but the ones in here are," says Dr. Rock. "Besides, these things are terrible in space. We literally had to sprinkle the Onyx Spore into the food supply to make *Bon Voyage* happen. Oh, and since you're here, I want to show you something."

"Doctor don't show him anything," says Taksheel.

"He's seen plenty, and besides, I think he'll be interested because of some similarities."

Dr. Rock lifts his sleeve and types in a command on a thin wrist-top computer, and a screen rolls out with the Federation Sculptor as a screensaver, and it flicks on, displaying a bird's-eye view of a city with towering structures and winding monorail and road networks.

But thick vines, large trees, and sharp thorns snake in and out of the structures and wrap around the infrastructure.

Rivers of green ripple through the streets as the wind blows the pollen, and bulbs and shrubs populate the streets, overtaking vehicles and rubble. Ethan sees large Stitchers and other creatures lumbering through the hellish forest. But Dr. Rock is right. Ethan sees a lot of similarities between this and Oros. The similarities take his breath away and he steps back, horrified by what he is seeing.

"This wasn't supposed to happen, but it did due to some unexpected events. These things got out, and Section 0 figured why not test them in space?" says Dr. Rock.

"How did they get out?" asks Ethan hoarsely.

"Some archaeologists were exploring a Xeno Civilization Subject Rho vault. The ruins on Onyx match the ruins on Oros, Andromeda, Eqos, and other systems and sectors. When they opened it, the Onyx Spore got out and infected the team. They were a healthy bunch, so the mutations were slow, but it got into the air and cross-pollinated with the flora and the agriculture. Things went downhill after that, and by the time we figured out what was going on, remote settlements were overtaken, refugees were carrying the pollen with them on their clothes, in their hair, and in the food and other stuff, and it just kept multiplying. Within two months, Onyx fell, and Section 0 saw a weapon."

Ethan's eye is wide and focused on the screen. His breathing is ragged, and his mutated arm is twitching.

"Don't look so gloomy, Ethan!" says Dr. Rock. "You, being an Orosian, saved your life. These spores and the ruins tied to them are all over the Prospect and Portuguese Interstellar Sectors, and what we see here is a new field of study for us to harness."

Ethan's eye snaps to Dr. Rock.

"How can you say that? Millions are dead and you want to weaponize this?" Ethan steps back and shakes his head. "You're insane. You're evil. You're both evil!"

"Hey, we're not evil," says Taksheel. "The Onyx Spore is perfect! We're surrounded by enemies on all sides, and when we weaponize this, nobody will even think of touching us. We can even retake Greater Arabia. Besides, think of it like this. We sacrificed millions to save one hundred and thirty billion. We can protect ourselves and our vassals without firing a shot."

"Protecting others? That's rich coming from you," says Ethan.

"Don't be pious, Ethan. You're a killer, too," says Taksheel.

"I didn't kill my team!"

"They were smugglers! They ran weapons and drugs on the side and hold the blame for who knows how much death and mayhem on Aarde and Federation systems! They had to go, Ethan. And now that we got all their receipts and contacts, they are being wiped out as we speak, which includes the Three Machetes, which let me tell you, Section 0 knows you killed a bunch of them in that apartment. The only reason we didn't help the police is because we needed you on the *Hook Line.* But now the Three Machetes are gone! I saved you from retribution, Ethan! So, a little thank you will be nice!"

Ethan and Taksheel glare at each other, and Dr. Rock goes to the displays and puts the metal cases on the cart. Then he straps them down and looks at the two survivors.

"Don't worry. He will thank us in the end, and so will Harvest. He wanted Ethan, and I want to keep my soul, and you, Taksheel, will be rewarded, too. We all win!" says Dr. Rock.

"You don't have a soul," says Ethan, turning his glare to the doctor.

"Ship says otherwise. It really wants me to stay," remarks Dr. Rock.

Ethan sneers, Taksheel rolls his eyes, and Dr. Rock goes to the display of artifacts.

"Do you know anything about Xeno Civilization Subject Rho?" says Dr. Rock.

"No," says Ethan flatly.

"They struck our fancy because their end is a mystery, like the Indus Valley, the Minoans, the Mayans, the Mycenaeans, Nabataeans, so on so on. What we have found from their works was that they believed the galaxy was a system of branches, all connected to a tree in the center, and they believed that the darkness of space was Hell, and it looked for ways to claim travelers. Some of my colleagues wrote this off as their way of coping with space dementia, but I think they were on to something. There must be something out here!"

Dr. Rock points at one of the entwined trees on display.

"We've found these symbols everywhere in the Rho ruins in the Prospect and Portuguese Interstellar Sectors, as well as other sectors, and when the outbreak of Onyx and *Bon Voyage* happened, people drew them. This symbol is connected to Onyx Spore somehow, and I cannot figure it out or harness the Spores if I die on this ship."

Ethan stares at Dr. Rock intently, and Taksheel taps his rifle impatiently.

"We were rats for your experiment. And now you want to unleash these things on our enemies? That's insane. They'll kill all of us!" says Ethan.

Dr. Rock scoffs and waves dismissively. "Don't be silly, Ethan. Unleashing is a recipe for disaster. What I want to do is controlled demolition using these Spores, and I know I can do it with the data I have collected. When we control the Onyx Spore, then we can destroy our enemies and not risk humanity. But you, Ethan, you and the other Orosians are another key to this. Your people have developed a natural defense to it. Granted, it is not perfect, but if we can replicate and fortify that defense, then humanity can be protected while our enemies suffer. One by one they go, but we will remain."

Ethan sneers, and Taksheel steps closer to Dr. Rock.

"Doctor we really have to go," says Taksheel.

Dr. Rock tightens the last strap and lightly kicks the cart's bumper. "Right, of course. Got a little carried away from being cooped up around here. Up and at 'em, NL-2021."

Green lights flash on the sides of the cart, and it beeps and rolls towards a terminal at the back of the room, while Taksheel shoves Ethan forward. Ethan stumbles a bit, but as he walks, he checks the zip-tie yet again and gets a flicker of a smile that the other two do not see.

"You should be glad that Section 0 wants you alive," says Taksheel. "My orders were to kill everyone on the *Hook Line,* but you made quite an impression."

"Why didn't you gun us down when we were on the *Hook Line?* Why toy with us like this?" says Ethan.

"Because I wanted to test my acting abilities. Imagine, going from lotion commercials, to rescuer, to big-time actor with a tragic story. It'll be beautiful and give me lots of deals."

The conversation ends after that, and when Ethan and Taksheel get to the terminal, Dr. Rock types in a command. As this happens, a fiery glow reflects off the walls.

Ethan's eye widens, Taksheel scrunches his brow, and Dr. Rock watches it quizzically while NL-2021 beeps and rocks back and forth.

"Oh no," says Ethan.

There is a whir, and the floor slides open behind the group, followed by a ding and metallic clang as an elevator with its own terminal locks in place. In front of them, a shadow stretches along the wall and footsteps echo from the hallway. Then the Pyro walks into view, with a ball of fire resting in front of his flamethrower.

"Get on the elevator!" shouts Ethan.

The Pyro runs forward, and Taksheel pushes Ethan and Dr. Rock on the elevator before shooting at the Pyro. His target drops from the first burst and then scrambles behind the computers, which spark and burst from the bullets, tearing them apart, and Dr. Rock quickly types in another command.

The elevator goes down, and Taksheel jumps on after them. The Pyro runs towards them, shooting a stream of fire that goes over their heads. The first control panel explodes as fire engulfs it, and Taksheel shoots another barrage of bullets.

Dr. Rock covers his ears, and NL-2021's green lights flash to red with a warning alarm sounding off. Sparks fall from the destroyed terminal, and the elevator roof jams while the elevator itself speeds down. Then, Taksheel reaches for a new magazine and ejects his empty one.

"Come on. Show your face, you freak," says Taksheel.

With Taksheel distracted, Ethan snaps the zip-tie. Taksheel barely looks over his shoulder before he is rammed into the elevator shaft.

Taksheel drops his rifle and attempts to grab his pistol, but Ethan punches him on the side of the head with his mutated hand, leading to his skin getting torn by the wall and the sharp bark on Ethan's fingers. Then Ethan holds Taksheel's face against the shaft and digs his sharp fingers into his head, while his other hand twists Taksheel's wrist.

Blood streaks up the elevator shaft, and Taksheel screams and tries pushing back, and Ethan slams his head against the shaft wall. He does this repeatedly, leaving a splatter of blood and making a loud crack each time.

He keeps doing this until Taksheel stops screaming and his body goes limp. And for good measure, Ethan slams Taksheel's head against the wall a few more times, before he throws him down with broken bone jutting through his shredded skin, his face bloody, jaw shattered, and one of his eyes popped.

Ethan is now panting heavily.

"One more soul for *Bon Voyage,*" says Ethan.

He then grabs his shotgun and looks at Dr. Rock with near-pure yellow eyes and Taksheel's blood splattered on his face and right arm. The doctor is sitting by NL-2021, and he is looking at Ethan with a pale face and eyes wide with horror.

"That vaccine better work," says Ethan.

Dr. Rock flashes a nervous smile. "It'll work. Don't worry."

Then the elevator stops, and the door slides open, revealing "Hangar H" painted on the blast doors separating the hangar from space. Dim lights shine overhead, reflecting off the metal hulls of the other ships. The floor is cluttered with toolboxes, crates, and supplies, and on the upper level are metal pipes stacked and bound.

At the far end is a rectangular ship with stubby wings that have circular engines on their tips, and an orb-shaped cockpit. On its side is "*CV-OS-10924.*"

Dr. Rock goes to its back ramp, opens a cover, and types a command on the terminal. The ramp gradually lowers, and when it touches down, Dr. Rock motions NL-2021 up the ramp.

"Come on. Up, up, up," says Dr. Rock anxiously.

NL-2021 beeps and its engine whirs as it travels up the ramp, with its load held tight by the straps. Dr. Rock follows the cart up, and Ethan follows him, and when all three are on board, he closes the ramp. It takes its time going back up, and Dr. Rock straps NL-2021's wheels to the floor and he locks the miniature warp battery to a storage slot next to it.

Once the ramp is closed, Ethan sits down and buckles up, while Dr. Rock sits in the driver's seat and goes through the motions. Dials are turned, switches are flipped, and the ship hums to life, with the many screens flashing on and the engines roaring.

"Just out of curiosity, how much money does Section 0 pay?" asks Ethan.

"Why? You interested in joining?" asks Dr. Rock.

"No. I'm just curious how much our lives are worth."

"I don't know the details, but I know I can get my student and medical bills wiped out when this is over," says Dr. Rock. "You really should join, though. The Federation can use more resilient people like you keeping us safe."

Ethan scoffs, and the ship lifts slightly off the hangar floor while alarms blare in the hangar and emergency lights swirl. The blast door slides open, revealing Onyx's curvature and its distant star beyond the blue shimmer of the hangar shield.

Dr. Rock carefully turns *CV-OS-10924* towards the opening and moves forward. However, he does not get far before a large body lands on the ship, bending the hull and shattering the window.

The ship dips and turns sharply, and Dr. Rock screams and Ethan grabs his seat while NL-2021 screeches and flashes red lights. The ship scrapes against the floor, and enormous claws break through what remains of the windshield and tear through Dr. Rock's seat, silencing him.

The ship's hull scrapes as it zooms forward, and it hits a support beam for the second level, causing the upper platform to break and for the metal pipes to roll down and impale the Moon Stitcher to the ship, while the others bounce off or stab the ship.

Ethan unbuckles and jumps away from his seat, while some pipes pierce through the roof, stabbing through the passenger chair or the floor near him.

As this happens, the alarms turn to a shrill blare and the blast door slams shut. The light from the outside creates a lump of shadows inside the wreck, but Ethan can make out the vines working on pulling out the metal pipes impaling the Moon Stitcher.

He takes advantage of the situation and makes his way to NL-2021. Dr. Rock's blood seeps towards him while the Moon Stitcher's claws remain motionless, and NL-2021 beeps and screeches as it rocks back and forth.

Ethan hastily unstraps the cases and throws aside the yellow and black cases to reach the red and white one, and as soon as he grabs it, he hears gurgling and shifting.

"Ethan," calls the Moon Stitcher.

Ethan snaps to the Stitcher and sees Moon's pale face looking at him with blank yellow eyes and orange veins under his skin.

"Let me in," says the female head next to Moon's head; her hair is hanging in front of her yellow eyes, and her head is locked in place with bark.

The middle spot is the remains of a jaw and partial skull, but bulbs occupy that area and are puffing out pollen. The Moon Stitcher is nailed to the ship, and the vines are slowly but surely pulling out the pipes.

While this happens, NL-2021's screeching echoes in the ship, and its red lights reflect off the walls. Ethan grabs the vaccine case and the miniature warp battery, and then he runs towards the ramp.

As he runs, glass shatters and the Moon Stitcher yells, "Ethan! Let me in!"

Ethan hits the emergency open button for the ramp, and when glass shatters, he turns with his shotgun raised and sees the Moon Stitcher is tearing apart what little remains of the windshield, while the vines remove the pipes.

Behind him, metal groans and the gears whir as the ramp slowly opens. When it is large enough for him to go through, Ethan wiggles his way outside and falls to the floor. More metal and glass breaks and the ship shakes, while NL-2021's screams and screeches get louder.

Then NL-2021's cries suddenly stop.

The ramp is still going down when Ethan gets to his feet, and he attaches the case and battery to his back and runs across the hangar. Seconds later, heavy thumps chase after him.

The floor shakes, and Ethan rolls over a large crate and takes a sharp turn as the Moon Stitcher's massive claws slash into it. The crate breaks into pieces, and the Moon Stitcher roars and whacks the remains aside before resuming its chase.

Ethan looks over his shoulder, panting as he runs, and when he sees the Moon Stitcher gaining on him, he has his suit inject another dose of adrenaline into him. He gets a new - and painful - burst, and he bolts to the stairs, but the Moon Stitcher is still gaining on him. The accumulation of his injuries burn and tear at once, breaking him from the inside out, bringing his vision to blur with tears, and his limbs to buckle.

Ethan's heart is close to exploding when he is at the base of the stairs, but the Moon Stitcher's shadow looms over him. Before the Moon Stitcher can strike, there is a sudden dip that forces Ethan to take a leap and grab the railing while the abomination rolls away from him.

The dip leads CV-BV-10923 to crash into the hangar door with other ships and loose items sliding down. As this happens, Ethan yells angrily and tightens his grip on the railing, with the ship's dip getting worse and his feet dangling in the air.

He looks over his shoulder and sees the Moon Stitcher's claws get a grip on the floor, leaving a long gash. When it stops, it begins its climb after Ethan.

"WARNING: SHIP IN DANGEROUS DESCENT! SEEK SAFETY IM-MEDIATELY!"

"ARE YOU KIDDING ME!" screams Ethan.

Ethan pulls himself up and gets a footing on the bottom step, but before he can get far, an Illwalker jumps on him, and he loses his grip and rolls down the tilted floor, while the Illwalker claws at him.

The chaotic scenery zips by, and Ethan's shield flickers as it scrapes on the floor. When the Illwalker tries puking on him, he forces its head sideways. The acid leaves a trail, and its skull breaks open from the friction against the floor.

Then the Illwalker takes the brunt of the impact when they hit a support beam. Broken bones and bark pop out, its arm snaps, and acid bursts out and spreads on the support beam and burns Ethan's shield.

Ethan's shield generator fizzles and pops with the shield being destroyed, and his armor smolders, while the metal support beam warps with the second level dipping. Then the Moon Stitcher stabs the floor near Ethan, and he screams and reels back, bringing him to roll down the hangar as the Moon Stitcher crawls after him.

More Haunters and Tainted, and a few Illwalkers, chase after him. Many fall into a roll or lose their footing and bounce down, and when Ethan comes to a stop at a hangar door, he can't feel much of anything besides panic.

It is hard for him to focus with all the metallic crashes from the ships hitting each other or the blast door, the noise of the blaring alarms, and the flashes of emergency lights and sparks from metal scraping on metal.

A cargo ship with a fuel label snaps loose from some chains holding it, and it speeds towards Ethan with a large trail of sparks erupting from its nose scraping against the floor. Ethan swears and scrambles along the crooked floor, punching a Tainted along the way, and he takes a flying leap to a ladder.

The loose cargo ship slams into the hangar door, squishing more of the infected, creating multiple bursts of fire that fling twisted metal and burning body parts everywhere, causing part of the second level to dip further.

But Ethan does not stop to marvel at the chaos. He keeps climbing, and when he pulls himself up, he resumes running, occasionally tripping over himself, and having to use the railing for support.

A large vent breaks open, and a Lurker flies out, followed by a Haunter climbing after it. Ethan shoots one of the Lurker's wings with his shotgun, making it spiral out of control and fall to the burning mess below, which has more ships exploding, making the door and hangar wall groan with the shield generator sparking and shaking.

"WARNING: HANGAR H FAILURE! EVACUATE! EVACUATE!"

The Haunter charges Ethan, and he shoots off its leg, then its head, and then shoves it over the railing. Then there are two overlapping roars, and Ethan turns around and sees the Moon Stitcher breaking the railing to pull itself up with patches of fire eating away at its bark shell.

Some of its vines are damaged, with burns damaging its heads. He shoots the female head and continues running as it tries to keep its grip on the platform.

When Ethan goes through a doorway at the end, there are more explosions, and the colors of fire and blue and white energy clash, flashing warped shadows on the hallway with the lights rotating in failure and reboot.

A deafening howl of wind, plus the tearing of metal and many explosions and roars, ravages Ethan's ears, and a suction pulls him off his feet and drags him across the floor. Ethan's fingers dig into the floor until he grabs a broken door, and he screams as he is pulled up. Then comes a clang, and all the suction disappears, leading Ethan to fall to the floor with a grunt.

His heart is racing, his chest is tight, and his throat is scratchy as he wheezes. But he can't even hear himself, because the alarm is still going on, and the ship is still tilted, so he has a hard time standing.

But that is no excuse. He needs to get to the bridge and stop *Bon Voyage* from crashing!

Ethan races down the hallway, eye flicking up to every sign he can find, which thankfully gives him directions to the bridge. He does not even bother trying to kill the creatures that are pouring out of the rooms and vents.

Run, run, run, run, run. All he can do is run. If he stops, he is dead.

Ethan bobs and weaves through the slashes and charges, and he goes through an unlocked door, closes it behind him, and shoots the orb. The door dims, and the crowd on the other side roars and bangs and scratches against it.

This doesn't faze him, though. He has complete focus, almost tunnel vision of his aim. If he can run on it, if it is stairs or a door, he is using it. If there is a sign pointing to the bridge, he will follow it in the split second he allows himself. Time is a blur, and when Ethan reaches a hallway with scorched walls and charred bodies, he knows he is getting close.

Ethan runs with an extra burst of speed. He can taste blood on his tongue, feel his heart and lungs tearing, and his joints are ready to shatter, but that is no excuse to stop. He goes up another flight of stairs, and when he reaches the top, he finds a familiar hallway with the bridge door still open.

Ethan runs to the door and slides to a stop, gripping the wall for support as he takes wheezy, ragged breaths, while clutching his heart. Inside, the Pyro is sitting on a navigation chair in the captain's ring.

The projector is now displaying *Bon Voyage's* trajectory. The window is tinted, and Onyx's surface is rapidly getting closer. The alarm seems louder on the bridge, and the screens are all flashing warning messages and safety protocols.

Ethan takes a deep breath and then rushes the Pyro.

The Pyro turns just in time for Ethan to punch him in the jaw with his mutated hand. While he is stunned, Ethan slams his head into the console and throws him out of the chair.

The Pyro rolls down the short set of stairs, and Ethan grabs the controls and starts pulling the ship up. The information on the screens shifts from a sharp descent to a path of leveling, but before Ethan can completely level it out, he is pulled off the chair.

His feet kick out of reflex, shattering the screen and breaking the buttons, and when he lands on his back, the Pyro stomps on his gut and head. Then he pulls him up, slams him against a console, and punches him in the jaw before throwing him to the floor. With him on the floor, the Pyro pushes the controls downward.

"I will not let you win!" says the Pyro. "These things cannot spread, and God willing, I will make things right!"

"You'll kill us both!" says Ethan.

"That's the idea."

Ethan gets up and rams the Pyro into the railing and punches him down before going back to the controls.

"I have the vaccine! I can save us!" says Ethan.

Ethan pulls the controls up, and through the cracked screen, he can see *Bon Voyage* leveling out again. Or at least he hopes it is leveling out. It is hard to say with the screen destroyed. Also, the planet's surface is close now, with sharp spires and hills of black ice stretching towards a permanent twilight and a skyline of gray towers.

"No!" The Pyro charges Ethan and pushes him out of the seat and forces him over the railing. After Ethan lands on the lower level, the Pyro grabs the controls. "It must be this way. For the sake of all that is good, *Bon Voyage* must burn. And us with it."

The Pyro then gives the controls a sharp turn and snaps them off.

"No!" yells Ethan.

The ship makes a sharp tilt, and Ethan is slammed into the platform wall while the Pyro grabs the railing. Ethan grabs the stair's railing and swears as everything goes sideways.

The frozen landscape quickly turns to buildings of various sizes, all overrun with large and winding plants, and everything becomes a blur. *Bon Voyage* shakes with broken concrete, glass, metal, and torn plant bits flying past the bridge's window.

Soon the window shatters, spraying the two with broken glass and other debris. Ethan squeezes his eye shut and holds his head down as the screaming of rushing wind assaults his ears, and bright orange, red, and white light breach his eyelid.

Then, metal panels slide over the gaping hole that was once the bridge window, plunging the room into near-total darkness, with only pockets of red lights to provide illumination. Seconds later, there is a loud screech that overtakes everything on the ship.

Metal snaps, multiple explosive pops shake *Bon Voyage*, and there are rumbles, with heavy thuds against the ship's hull. Next comes a sudden stop that flings the two across the bridge.

After the impact, all Ethan feels is pain, and he growls as every bone in his body feels like it has been snapped and glued back together. His fingers are stiff as they claw the floor or scratch his head.

Near him, the Pyro grunts and shifts on the ground. Sparks fall all around them, and the alarm wobbles, going from low to high pitches, and the red lights flicker with the computer screens going dim.

With everything crooked and blurry, Ethan can barely make out the data coming from the holographic projector, which is barely working as it is now. But once it focuses, Ethan's eye widens. *Bon Voyage's* blueprint is on display, and the engine room is black.

And there is a timer counting down.

30:00

29:59

29:58

29:57

29:56

"W-W-W-W-AR-ARN-ING. WARNI-ING: WARP CORE FAI-AIL-LURE. EVACUATE IMMEDIATELY. WA-WARP DESTA-LIZ-TION Immmmmmmm..."

Pop.

"Oh no," says Ethan.

The Pyro rolls upright with a long, drawn-out groan. After he stands up, he and Ethan look at each other, and the Pyro aims his flamethrower at Ethan.

"Now we end this," says the Pyro.

32

Ascension

A surge of flame rushes towards Ethan, and he scrambles over a row of tilted computer panels. The fire crashes against them, burning and warping them. Sparks fly and smoke rolls over as the fire crackles.

Ethan runs across the bridge, swerving and jumping over another row of computers as the Pyro sweeps the area with his flamethrower. Ethan slides to a stop and crouches behind cover, and with ragged breaths, he checks his shotgun.

It is empty.

"Damn it!"

Ethan stands up and throws his shotgun at the Pyro, who deflects it with a swing from his arm, and he returns to trying to burn Ethan alive. The fire rolls across the tilted floor, and Ethan runs around the captain's perch and crouches again as he grips his chest and takes heavy, shaky gulps of air.

With the fire on the floor and on the computers, plus the failing projected blueprint and countdown, warped shadows snap on the wall and various electrical pops sound off with the dying alarm. Despite this, Ethan can still hear the Pyro's heavy, calculated steps getting closer, and the glow of his weapon makes his position more apparent.

Ethan curses again and moves to the other side of the perch, and that is when he sees Aiden's body laying against the wall with his rifle still slung on his shoulder. He runs to his fallen teammate, being speedy and yet careful as he navigates the environment of tilted stairs, rails, and computer consoles.

As he runs, a rolling stream of fire strikes where he was just a few seconds ago. Ethan slides next to Aiden, removes his rifle, and grabs his last magazine. Then, he turns around and shoots at the Pyro when he rounds the perch, forcing him to retreat.

Sparks fly as the bullets ricochet off the perch, and Ethan climbs over a railing and slides to cover behind a row of computers. He pokes his head up seconds later, just to dart down when the fire returns in a long burst.

Ethan stays low and runs along the edge of the level, while straining his ears in the chaos of the weak alarm and the roaring fire. Computers explode and lights fail, and when the fire stops, Ethan turns around and sees the Pyro leap down to his level.

Before Ethan can shoot, the Pyro unleashes another stream of fire towards him. When it crashes against him, he screams and fires blindly, while the fire eats away his suit.

The fire stops, and Ethan runs, blinded by the fire, and he hits a computer and falls to the ground, rolling madly as his suit's fabric and plates burn. With him rolling, parts of his suit fall off as charred flakes and the fire quickly dies out.

After that, he struggles to get up and shakes intensely, as he injects himself with a dose of adrenaline and sprays his new burns with medical foam. Meanwhile, the Pyro is slumped against the wall, wheezing with trickles of blood seeping past his suit and ceremonial robe. Seconds later, the Pyro forces himself to stand, grunting as he does this, and he marches towards Ethan with shaky steps.

"Don't condemn me. I am doing what is right. I am undoing what needs to be undone. You are preserving what needs to die," says the Pyro.

Ethan shoots the Pyro again, making him stumble back, gasping, and his limbs shake in their struggle to keep him up.

"I have to save them," says the Pyro. He lifts his flamethrower again, and he uses his free hand to inject himself with adrenaline. "I can't let them burn for my mistakes. I must make things right. I must kill us all to end this."

"Don't do it," says Ethan, his voice trying to be stern, but his lips are twitching for a smile, his yellow and green eye bright with anticipation.

The Pyro runs forward and shoots a burst of fire, and Ethan scrambles over a railing to get to the upper level. The fire crashes and rolls upward. The last of the computers pop and warp, and Ethan covers his head as the fire sweeps over, blackening the metal and turning the chairs to torches.

He gets up and shoots past the railing. The Pyro grunts and wheezes as he marches forward, leaving a trail of blood while swinging his flamethrower side to side.

The area between Ethan and the Pyro becomes a wall of fire, and Ethan shoots into the fire while backing up. There is a loud pop, a roll of flame, and an agonizing scream, followed by a thud, and Ethan stops and listens.

His heavy breathing and the crackling fire are now louder than the ship's alarm, and the emergency lights have completely failed, leaving only the hologram's light and pockets of fire as guides. Ethan scratches his head and fights to hold back a giggle as he walks along the fire.

He hops down the stairs to get to where the Pyro is. When he finds him, he stops and hides his chuckle with a cough, as the stench of burnt flesh and electronics stings his nose.

He won.

He beat the Pyro. He beat that jerk that burned his face off and chased him all over *Bon Voyage.*

The Pyro's flesh is burned, revealing red muscle and burnt bone, with portions of his outfit fused to his skin. His fuel tank is popped, with pieces of jagged metal embedded into his body, and his flamethrower is a twisted mess. His skull is cracked, and strands of skin are melted with his mask destroyed and his one remaining eye focused on Ethan.

Ethan's coughing turns to a chuckle, and he shakes his head.

"I told you not to do it," says Ethan.

Then, the Pyro wheezes, and Ethan jumps back with a loud curse while the Pyro grabs the wall with his skeletal hand and pulls himself up, leaving a black and bloody handprint on it.

"You did... But I need to make things right," says the Pyro.

Ethan raises his rifle, and the Pyro lunges and pushes the rifle aside when he fires. The bullets shatter on the floor, and the Pyro delivers a couple of good hits before Ethan can block and attempt to retaliate.

The Pyro deflects the retaliation, and Ethan swings his rifle against the Pyro, but he grabs it and makes a hoarse growl as he pushes against Ethan. The two hit the holographic projector, and the Pyro pushes the rifle down on Ethan's throat and leans in close.

His damaged skull, burnt skin, and one eye nearly matches Ethan's face. While he growls, Ethan grins and giggles with an annoying itch on his head and twitching in his mutated arm.

"Die with me. We can make things right," says the Pyro.

"I'm not dying here!" says Ethan.

He kicks the Pyro back and shoots him again, but that only stops the Pyro for a couple of seconds before he jumps at Ethan, disarms him with sharp twists to remove his rifle, and follows up with a punch to his face. He keeps punching Ethan, leaving minor scratches and streaks of blood, and even while Ethan falls, the Pyro follows him down and keeps punching.

Ethan tries blocking, but it is no use. The blocking fails, and the Pyro wraps his hands around Ethan's throat. Ethan gags and tries prying the Pyro off, but even with his mutated hand snapping the Pyro's wrist, he increases the pressure with his other hand.

Ethan presses his hand against the Pyro's face and awkwardly kicks him, but he does not move. Blood drips down on Ethan, and their eyes meet. But despite what is happening, Ethan cannot help but smile, and his head *really* itches. His mutated hand presses harder against the Pyro's head, drawing blood, but the Pyro does not relent.

And right as Ethan's vision goes dark, a massive figure lands behind the Pyro and grabs his shoulders. The Pyro's head jerks forward as bones break and blood pours out of his mouth and nose. Then cracks pop around his skull, what is left of his skin bulges, and bugs pop out, with more crawling out of his mouth or breaking through his skull.

Ethan pushes the Pyro off and scrambles to his rifle. He watches as the Pyro's body is torn apart from the inside out. His flesh snaps open, his bones break, and bugs rip off pieces of his body, leading to torn organs falling out.

The Pyro goes limp in a pool of pure red blood, and standing above him, with its gullet sack empty, is a Lurker with a saw blade lodged in its back.

The Simon Lurker looks at Ethan for a few seconds, and then it roars and charges him with the bugs following its lead. Ethan shoots at them in a wild spray of gunfire. The bullets push the Simon Lurker back, ripping off pieces of its body one at a time and popping the bugs.

When the bullets tear off its limbs, it screeches until its head is pulverized, leaving chunks of brain and bone splattered on the ground while its body twitches. Behind it, flickering and fluctuating, is the timer.

23:35

23:34

23:33

Ethan bangs his head against a burnt-out computer, shaking and laughing as he looks at Simon's destroyed body. And he looks at the Pyro's mangled corpse, too. All that perfect blood. Guy died as a human. Lucky.

23:27

23:26

23:25

Ethan laughs a little more, wipes the soot, sweat, and blood from his face, and then stands up and puts in the last magazine. Then he checks to make sure the vaccine is still on his back. Thankfully, it is. And the battery is still there, but it is damaged from the fire and has some dings on it. But it is not sparking. There is still a chance to escape.

23:11

23:10

23:09

Ethan looks around and sees nothing at first. Just a clash of dying fires and a failing projector giving some shapes to the wrecked bridge. Then he spots it. An opening in the metal plating that is covering the shattered window. It is bent open, and Ethan can see light pouring in from the outside.

He immediately hobbles towards it with his heart thumping in his ears. Glass crunches under his boots, and his hands have a hard time holding his rifle as he awkwardly makes his way across the tilted room.

22:38

22:37

22:36

Ethan pauses when he thinks he hears approaching thumps, and when he turns around, he sees a pair of glowing yellow eyes rapidly approaching him with the steps and stuttering clicks.

22:32

22:31

22:30

"ETHAN!" screams the Moon Stitcher.

The Moon Stitcher swipes at Ethan, and he swears and jumps out of the way. The Moon Stitcher's claws tear apart a destroyed computer, and it howls in rage.

Ethan runs towards the gaping hole in the bridge's plating. When he gets to the hole, he peeks outside and sees that *Bon Voyage* has a slope he can slide down.

Not too far from the colony ship is a destroyed skyline with vines and trees wrapped around the monoliths with mountains of ice beyond them, and closer is a row of hangars. The permanent twilight also has a green tint to it, and clouds of pollen swirl around in the air or slide across the airfield.

The Moon Stitcher runs, and Ethan slips his rifle on his shoulder and wiggles his way through the opening. When he is outside, he looks down and gulps at the long drop, but after he looks over his shoulder and sees the Moon Stitcher is right on him, he releases his hold.

Sporadic sparks trail Ethan as his destroyed security suit scrapes against *Bon Voyage's* hull, and his heart races as everything zips by him. He tilts his body left and right and uses his gloved hand to brake or turn to avoid jagged gaps in the ship's hull.

Out of sheer reflex, he grabs a steel beam that got impaled into the ship. His body dangles, his heart races, and his throat tightens as he stares at a ball of broken rebars and concrete a few dozen feet down.

Ethan winces and pulls himself up, and he takes a deep, shaky breath while he balances himself on the beam. As he stands there, he eyes his next spot. It is another dip that is a long jump away, and while he makes mental calculations, he is interrupted by metal ripping.

He looks to the source and sees the Moon Stitcher sliding after him, using its claws to adjust its speed and direction while its vines snap the air, and the bulbs eject pollen.

Ethan leaps to the next part of the ship, and he bounces and rolls for a moment before he straightens himself out and jumps off the last bit. While in the air, he tucks and rolls across the concrete.

He unrolls and flops on his side, wheezing and struggling to push himself up, and the Moon Stitcher leaps off *Bon Voyage* and lands near him with a loud thud. The bark shielding its ankles snap, and the abomination stumbles a bit before it limps after Ethan, with its claws scraping the ground, and the vines being pulled to the side as its yellow eyes glow.

"ETHAN!" calls the Moon Stitcher.

Blue electric bolts and jets of fire beach *Bon Voyage's* hull, illuminating Ethan and the Moon Stitcher in orange and blue. Burning rubble crashes down, and pollen is dragged towards the ship. Ethan can feel himself getting pulled, and knowing he does not have time to fight, he runs towards the hangars.

Every step feels like it is in a thick liquid, and panic floods Ethan's veins as each hangar he passes is empty or has destroyed ships. When he reaches the last one, he laughs for joy. The hangar door is wide open, and a white, spearhead-shaped ship with gold bands, tinted windows, and two cylindrical engines on stubby wings waits for him. On its side is, "*Nebula Rider.*"

"Ethan!"

The Stitcher's voice is barely heard over the electric storm erupting from *Bon Voyage*, and the stench of burning air clogs Ethan's nose. As Ethan runs to the *Nebula Rider*, he passes some fuel tanks, and he stumbles along until he reaches the ship's backdoor, which is opened with a bloody handprint on the frame.

Ethan sweeps his rifle between the *Nebula Rider's* interior and the hangar entrance, and he sees the Moon Stitcher entering the hangar. He looks at the Moon Stitcher, then at the barrels of fuel, which are groaning and shaking in a cage.

"Alright, time to end this," says Ethan.

He hurries away from the *Nebula Rider* and shoots at the Moon Stitcher while moving towards the fuel tanks. He fires one bullet at a time, and each bullet chips off a piece of its thick bark.

"Hey, you and me! We're through! You hear me!" shouts Ethan.

When the Moon Stitcher roars and starts running towards Ethan, he turns to the barrels and shoots them until they explode. Four large balls of fire erupt and mold into one rolling blob with a shock wave that knocks Ethan off his feet while flames engulf the Moon Stitcher.

As Ethan lies on the ground, he is dragged towards the hangar exit. The Moon Stitcher's body is also pulled, only it is digging its claws into the ground and its vines are grabbing the hangar door. Pieces of burning metal are ripped towards *Bon Voyage's* incredibly bright blue and white lights, while large bolts of energy tear across the sky.

The atmosphere crackles and rips, and pieces of the concrete outside crack, while burnt pieces of the Moon Stitcher break off its body and are tugged away. The damaged parts of the hangar tear off with loud screeches, and Ethan pulls himself up and takes heavy, painful steps towards the *Nebula Rider*.

The light from the warp storm behind Ethan burns his neck and leaves shadows streaking across the hangar floor, and the *Nebular Rider* is pulled towards the hangar exit.

When Ethan gets inside the *Nebula Rider*, he gives it another sweep and then closes the door and runs to the pilot's seat, while scanning the area with a racing heart for a miniature warp battery slot. He quickly finds one by a cylindrical engine, and he slides the battery in without a problem.

The battery hums and glows bright, and Ethan runs to the pilot's seat and sticks the vaccines in a storage slot underneath the seat and locks it in place. After that, he buckles in and starts flicking switches, pushing buttons, and turning knobs, bringing the engines to whir to life.

He looks out the window and sees the Moon Stitcher pulling itself up with charred and burnt pieces of its body being pulled off. It takes a few heavy steps towards the *Nebula Rider*, and then it runs.

Ethan grins and scratches his head, and says with an excited giggle, "Okay, we're doing this, eh? Alright then! Let's go!"

Ethan's giggle turns to a loud yell as he pushes the power lever forward, and the ship's engines whine loudly as the vehicle lunges forward. The Moon Stitcher jumps and grabs the ship, bringing the alarm to sound.

Ethan turns another knob that increases the speed of the ship while he makes a sharp ascension, glaring at the Moon Stitcher as it peers inside with its mouth wide open from its hoarse screams.

The Moon Stitcher's vines bang on the ship while its claws dig deep, and pockets of flame form as Ethan travels further into the atmosphere with the warp storm behind him becoming brighter and more violent, but his smile grows, and his eye narrows on the monster.

Gradually the Moon Stitcher is pulled down, leaving gashes in the *Nebula Rider* that activate the alarms. Then Ethan waves, the Moon Stitcher's arms snap, and it spins out of sight while the *Nebular Rider* is pulled back by the warp storm's gravity well.

Onyx's atmosphere is beaten back by the flashes of blue and white, while electric discharge and rumbling noises pierce through the ship's interior. Parts of the ship break off and one engine catches on fire as the back groans.

Ethan's smile disappears, and he pushes another button that leads to the battery behind him glowing brighter. The energy being released inside the ship tugs at him, while outside the clouds are evaporated.

Ethan grits his teeth and pushes a lever as far as it can go. The ship shakes from the rumbling, electronics and lights flick as electric bolts strike the ship and crack the sky. The bright blue and white light burns Ethan's eye, forcing him to squint while the rampant energy makes what's left of his hair stand.

"*Agnus Dei, qui tollis peccata mundi: miserere mei,*" says Ethan clumsily.

Ethan's eye darts from the window to the flickering monitors and back again. The ship shakes violently and slows down and go backward, while the miniature warp battery hums louder with vicious sparks snapping out.

"Don't you dare do this to me!" says Ethan, his vision going white as the Onyx's surface and the atmosphere are decimated by the warp storm. "I did not come this far just to die! *Deus me salve!*"

Then there is a pop and a bright flash of light, followed by the *Nebula Runner* suddenly appearing in the black expanse of space, and distant stars and a band of white, brown, and dark purple stretching as far as the eye can see.

Inside, the ship's electronics shut off, bursts of sparks breaking through their buttons and screens, and an alarm beeps loudly as red lights flash above Ethan's head. Even the miniature warp battery has popped, sending shards of burnt battery twirling in the zero gravity and turning its surroundings into a twisted, blackened mess, with fire suppressant foam floating around.

However, Ethan is not worried about that. What he is worried about is the *Nebula Runner* is spinning uncontrollably. Everything is a blur, and his insides feel like they are being blended while his vision becomes clouded.

He desperately smacks the control panel until the ship ejects several controlled bursts that slow the spin. A couple more after that put Ethan looking directly at the tiny glowing dots and the spacious band of the never-ending frontier.

"Warning. Life support critical. Emergency signal sent," says a computerized voice.

Ethan clutches his heart, now beating heavy and fast with tightness in his throat and sharp pain in his lungs. His mouth hangs open as he unclips his belt and floats out of his seat. Ethan presses his hand against his chest, wheezing and coughing with the taste of iron and something icky on his tongue, and his vision fades to black.

He shakily grabs the vaccine case, pops it open, pulls out a vial of the green liquid, and grabs the syringe gun. A rough, scratchy cough forces him to double over, and his grip loosens on the gun.

Saliva with pollen mixes with the blood in Ethan's mouth, and his eye throbs as he breathes heavily through his nose. He spits out a glob of tainted spit and blood, tightens his grip on the syringe gun, and presses it against an orange vein on his neck. The syringe empties in a blink as soon as he pulls the trigger, and Ethan's heart and breathing slow, his eye closes, and his body goes limp.

33

Project GREENWIND

To: CPT. R5 Gerald Moore of the FSSN Harpoon

From: OIC Specter of Ghost Outpost

SECTION 0 EYES ONLY

SUBJECT: **Project GREENWIND**

Objective A: Observe Onyx

>>In cooperation with Arx Corporation, samples of recovered material and previously unknown lifeforms from Onyx Archaeological Site No. 23 will be studied at Dynasty Medical Facility.

>>Pollen was accidentally released during exploration. Observe travel patterns and effects of pollen. Classified as: Onyx Spore.

>>Media blackout on discovery mandatory. Use Section 0 assets on Onyx to complete this.

>>Assets involved in Onyx Spore discovery will be in quarantine at Dynasty Medical Center. Blood samples and routine examinations mandatory.

>>Send all data to myself, Harvest, and Pinnacle.

Objective B: Prevent communications from leaving Peace System

>>Onyx Spore is highly dangerous. Use whatever means necessary for containment and information blackout. Lethal methods authorized.

NOTES: *Colony ship* Bon Voyage *is on its way with asset CPT. Junjie Ding for further experimentation on the Onyx Spore. Asset Dr. Arcos Rock will be leading further experiments in accordance with the goals of Project GREENWIND. All information will be broadcast to the FSSN Harpoon for further analysis. (Many vaccine samples are already being crafted on Onyx, including placebos as well as vaccines tainted with Onyx Spores. (*Special care and tracking are to be implemented for this one.))*

Asset Taksheel Iyer has been activated by Harvest. Asset planted in known smuggler ship, Hook Line. Hook Line *is permitted entrance in the Peace System. Taksheel Iyer's orders are to terminate* Hook Line *crew and Cpt. Junjie Ding, retrieve Dr. Arcos Rock and observe the Onyx Spore Infected environment. Retrieve assets when they leave* Bon Voyage. Bon Voyage *is to be destroyed upon mission completion. (*Bon Voyage *data will be scrubbed from the system.)*

Taksheel Iyer and Dr. Arcos Rock are to be examined at Ghost Outpost. If examinations yield favorable results, relocate assets and scrub them from the system. If examinations yield unfavorable results, terminate assets and scrub them from the system.

===
====================

To: OIC Specter of Ghost Outpost

From: CPT. R5 Gerald Moore of the FSSN Harpoon

SECTION 0 EYES ONLY

SUBJECT: **Project GREENWIND** UPDATE

**100% of Section 0 assets on Onyx have been eliminated. Reinforcements requested.*

**Onyx is 100% compromised. Onyx Station has been destroyed, warp barriers have been engaged, and single crafts have been deployed to prevent spread of Onyx Spore.*

Bon Voyage arrived on schedule, and Dr. Arcos has contacted CPT. Junjie Ding. Project GREENWIND *is now active on* Bon Voyage.

==

To: *OIC Specter of Ghost Outpost*

From: *CPT. R5 Gerald Moore of the* FSSN Harpoon

SECTION 0 EYES ONLY

SUBJECT: **Project GREENWIND**

UPDATE

>>>**MISSION FAILURE**. *100% asset loss. 1 small ship of unknown origin escaped with a random warp jump. Contents of ship unknown. Currently searching for leads.*

>>>*Last broadcast of asset Taksheel Iyer was him being eliminated by* Hook Line *crew member Ethan João Rifts in an advanced stage of Onyx Spore Infection.*

>>>*Last broadcast of asset Dr. Arcos Rock was him being eliminated by Onyx Spore Infected, Class 5. Ethan João Rifts was with him.*

>>>*Ethan João Rifts status is unknown.*

==

To: *CPT. R5 Gerald Moore of the* FSSN Harpoon, *Harvest*

From: *OIC Specter of Ghost Outpost*

SECTION 0 EYES ONLY

SUBJECT: **Project GREENWIND**

Mission Failure *understood. Stand by for further instructions.*

==

To: *OIC Specter of Ghost Outpost, Pinnacle*

From: *Harvest*

Subject: **Project GREENWIND/Ethan João Rifts**

I am on my way to the Peace System and will be arriving at Ghost Outpost first before meeting with Moore. Send the FSSN Harpoon *support and* forward me every file regarding Bon Voyage, Hook Line, *Project GREEN-WIND, and Ethan João Rifts. Do not tell Moore I am coming.*

-Harvest

34

Harvest

A group of three needle-shaped ships with orb centers have formed a triangular formation in the upper atmosphere of Onyx. From space, there appears nothing wrong with Onyx, aside from it being a tidally locked planet.

However, these ships know what is really on the planet, and Section 0 has been working diligently to not only keep the Peace System off limits, but to scrub the existence from the memories of the Federation altogether. The first mission is easy, but the second one is very difficult and requires a skill set that Section 0 has mastered with an intricate network of media and academic lapdogs, politicians in their pockets, technological and corporate oligarchs, banks, and teams of hackers and hunters to remove every bit of information on the Peace System (or other problems). So, for the ones witnessing the horror of what is on Onyx, they can take comfort that their job is easier than twisting the minds of over one hundred thirty billion humans.

The lockdown of the Peace System is under Captain Moore's supervision. Part of the mission includes search and rescue teams for the missing assets and research teams to study the Onyx Spore, which includes heavily armed bodyguards to neutralize the creatures or capture them if the researcher desires it.

Captain Moore's ship, the *Harpoon,* also picked up a ping of a warp jump at the upper atmosphere of Onyx, but it was just that one ping before the devastation of *Bon Voyage's* warp engine left a crater on the planet that engulfed all of Onyx City and briefly blinded the ship.

Outside of the crater are settlements that the Onyx Spore has overrun. The former colonists of Onyx have been mutated, and the horror of the aftermath of Greenwind is something that has confused and terrified everyone, and even the most professional of agents have shown spikes in vitals and changes in voice patterns from what they have discovered and engaged.

Often, flamethrowers, airstrikes, and orbital bombardments are used to stop the creatures, and Section 0 casualties have only been climbing. The good news is that they are easily replaceable clones. The bad news is that even an accumulation of cheap things becomes expensive after a certain point.

Near the three ships, a warp hole opens, breaking the blackness, and its bright blue light collides with the red light of the star. Out of the warp hole comes an oval-shaped ship with six tilted fins, each holding a line of engines that are emitting blue light, and on its silver hull is "*AURA.*"

The *Aura* glides towards the three ships, and their response is immediate as they turn to it.

"*You have entered a restricted system. Present identification immediately,*" says the *Harpoon* to the *Aura.*

*****

On the bridge of the *Aura,* there is an upper-aged, dark-eyed, Chinese man with gray hair styled in a comb over. Unlike the crew, who are wearing blue jumpsuits with various colored bands, he is wearing a near-black, dark purple suit that has a pin of a "0" on his breast pocket. He is also sitting in the captain's chair, which is surrounded by a ring of monitors that are displaying forms of information, from graphs to profiles of the deceased assets, to the *Hook Line* crew.

Next to him is a young woman with light brown, scaly skin, with streaks of gold around her eyes and tracing down her cheeks and neck. She is standing stiff in a red, flowery cheongsam with her dark hair tied into a ponytail, hands clamped in front of her, and her amber reptilian eyes locked ahead.

"Hannah. Starlet. Aeon. Lucky. Wayward. Harvest. D-Six," says the captain, his eyes focused on Onyx.

"Password confirmed. Welcome to Onyx, Harvest. However, with all respect given, I cannot allow you on the planet. There is no safe zone set up," says the *Harpoon*.

This voice differs from the one that greeted Harvest. This one is older, sterner, but Harvest is not mad about this news. He fully understands the situation. However, his aggravation is more towards the past than the present.

"To whom am I speaking to?" asks Harvest.

"Captain-Rank Five Gerald Moore, sir," says the stern voice, adding after a pause, *"I am overseeing the Onyx Quarantine."*

"Are you now?"

Harvest mutes the call and types on one of his computers, which brings up information about Captain Moore and the *Harpoon*. What appears are names, birth dates, and records chronicling every year of Moore's life. The schematic for the *Harpoon* also appears, as well as its history and areas that have had repairs. He types on his computer again. The repaired sections are highlighted, and then the edited file is transferred to his gunners, while his bridge crew works on scanning the other ships.

"Nobody fire unless I give explicit orders to do so," says Harvest.

"Yes, sir," says the bridge crew in total unison, which is to be expected, since they are all spitting images of a younger Harvest. Very cheap. Very expendable. But they are also useful and obedient. Overall, good buys. Which, speaking of good buys…

Harvest turns to the reptilian woman. "Susu, prepare for our guest."

Susu nods and walks away, and Harvest unmutes the call.

"Captain Moore, there was a breach in containment and there was total asset loss. Come aboard the *Aura* immediately with explanations," says Harvest.

There is a long pause, and then an uneasy, *"Of course, sir. I'll be there in sixty minutes with the required files."*

"Make sure they are detailed. I would hate to have Pinnacle involved with this."

"They will be up to standard."

"Good."

Harvest disconnects, and he reclines in his seat and looks at Onyx with his fingers tapping against each other. The experiment's outcome had some drawbacks, but there is always a silver lining, and he got his as information gathered by Dr. Rock and the assets on Onyx. Plus, Onyx is fertile ground for research of this new species. They just need extreme caution.

However, the lone ship that slipped through the quarantine is puzzling. Is it luck? Incompetence? Was there a hole in the warp barriers? Was there a divine intervention? Whatever it is, he needs details before he can proceed effectively, and that is what Captain Moore has.

That said, whoever escaped won't be hidden for long, and they will be dealt with appropriately. The good news is that Harvest is no amateur at this sort of thing, so whoever the escapee is, they are running on borrowed time. All he has on Harvest is a head start.

And there is more good news. With the data they have got so far, excluding new data from the ground teams, the sacrifice of *Bon Voyage* and Onyx was worth it. Great things are coming for Section 0, and that makes the man named Harvest smile.

35

The Explorer

The *Nebula Rider* floats in the cold, black, never-ending void of space. Its colors are scorched, its engines have popped, and its hull is tattered with specks of debris surrounding it. The windows are fogged, and there are slow flashes of light making a pattern.

Dot. Dot. Dot. Dash. Dash. Dash. Dot. Dot. Dot.

And the pattern repeats after a few seconds of delay.

Inside the *Nebula Rider*, Ethan Rifts lays limp in his seat, buckled in. His eye is closed, his breathing is shallow, his limbs float in zero gravity, and his body is soaked in sweat. Luggage from the previous owner floats around the ship's interior, from clothes to discs, and even a couple of toy soldiers. When a bright flash of blue light appears, his eyelid flinches but stays closed.

Then, a large craft looms over the *Nebula Rider*.

"Nebula Rider, *this is Captain Sol of the* Explorer *answering your distress signal. Please respond,"* says a grizzled man over the radio.

Ethan slowly opens his eye and looks at the radio. His eye is heavy and droopy, and his breathing is reduced to labored gasps. He looks out the window and sees a long, rectangular ship with a hexagonal back, three rings along the body, and an orb-shaped bridge. It has large lights on its front and sides and painted on it is a four-spoke star and "*Explorer.*"

"*Nebula Rider, this is Captain Sol of the* Explorer *answering your distress signal. Please respond,*" repeats Captain Sol.

Ethan winces and reaches for the radio. The yellow and orange are now gone from his veins and eye, and he presses his mutated hand against his chest while he looks at the *Explorer.*

"This is Ethan Rifts… I read you," says Ethan, his voice raspy.

"*How many are on your vessel?*" asks Captain Sol.

"Just me… I'm the only survivor."

"*Stand by for boarding.*"

The *Explorer* inches closer to Ethan's craft, and when it is above the *Nebula Rider*, there is a thud that shakes the ship. The gravity returns, and Ethan sluggishly readies his rifle before he makes his way to the back, stepping on battery shards, broken electronics, and burnt wires.

When he is at the back of his ship, he takes aim and waits. Several seconds pass before a female voice speaks over the *Nebula Rider's* intercom.

"*Permission to board?*" she asks in a gentle voice.

Ethan hits a red button near him, bringing the back door to slide open. He steadies his rifle and keeps his breathing as even as possible, which is difficult. Just breathing or pumping blood is painful, and every shell of medical foam feels like it is falling apart.

As the door opens, a bright light floods the *Nebula Rider* and reveals shadowy figures. After a few seconds, the shadows gain details, which show them to be scavengers wearing thick gray jumpsuits, save for one; a seven-foot man with large muscles, red eyes, and thick, curly black hair covering his head and chin. He is wearing a black jumpsuit with thick pads and a bulletproof vest, and he is wielding a low grade shotgun that looks like he purchased from a pawnshop.

Both sides stare at each other, with Ethan shaking and flicking his eye over each of them, and the scavengers being confused and worried.

"Are you infected?" asks Ethan.

The crew stares at him, and Ethan steps back with his rifle sweeping them.

"Are you infected!?" screams Ethan.

The crew gasps and retreats a couple of steps, but the guard moves forward and aims his shotgun at Ethan's head. He turns his rifle to him, chest heaving and breathing scratchy, but before anybody shoots, a young female steps forward and gently lowers the guard's shotgun.

"Wait, let me talk to him," she says, her voice matching the one asking for permission to board.

"Are you nuts? Look at him. I've never seen a modified freak like him before," says the guard.

"He's obviously traumatized. Let me talk to him. I can calm him down."

The guard looks at her, then at Ethan, who has yet to lower his rifle. A moment later, the guard reluctantly steps aside, but he keeps his shotgun ready. The female then approaches Ethan, leading the lone survivor to aim his rifle at her.

This brings her to stop for a moment, but that quickly passes as she carefully steps forward with a soft smile and her hands raised slightly. During her approach, Ethan watches her carefully, noticing her thick, braided brown hair and amber eyes, and a light tan skin, and she's his height, so they are eye to eye.

"It's okay, we won't hurt you," says the female gently.

Ethan studies her eyes and looks at her skin. Her eyes have no yellow and her skin is smooth from excessive lotion use, but her arms and hands are covered by the gray sleeves and heavy gloves.

"Show me your hands and arms," says Ethan.

"Venus, don't," orders the guard.

"It's okay, Mars," says Venus.

Venus pulls off her gloves and shows Ethan her fingers and palms, and she turns them slowly, so he can see all of them. All he sees is skin and the small bumps of her metacarpals trailing down to her wrists. Then she rolls up her sleeves as far as they can go and repeats the slow turning motions, so Ethan can see every angle of her arms. After that, she rolls down her sleeves and slips on her gloves with a smile.

"Did I pass the test?" asks Venus.

Ethan nods, and Mars butts forward with his hand out.

"Give me your gun," orders Mars.

Ethan stares at Mars defiantly, but after Venus nods and assures him it will be okay, he begrudgingly relinquishes his weapon.

"You'll find a metal case with a biohazard symbol inside the ship. Take it and guard it with your life," says Ethan weakly. "There's blood, saliva, and sweat aboard, too. Do not touch them under any circumstances. If you can, set charges on the ship or burn it, and then put me in quarantine for two weeks minimum."

"Are *you* infected with something?" asks Mars.

"The case has vaccines for something I cannot describe. I took one, but I don't know how well it worked. I seem okay for now, but my mutations appear to be permanent. But the *Nebula Rider* cannot stay here. It needs to go."

Mars grunts. "Phobes, Deimos, search the ship."

Two short, hunched, and skinny people with long fingers, pale skin, thick black hair covering their heads, and red-tinted goggles covering their pale eyes, skitter past the group. Just yesterday (or maybe two days ago?) such a sight would have made Ethan shudder, but not this time. How fast things change.

"As for you. You're going to see Pluto, and then Sol," says Mars. "But first, we're going to clean you up."

Then Mars grabs Ethan's shoulder and drags him down the hallway, with Venus following close behind. They take him to a shower room. There, he is put under the care of three women named Selene, Pandeia, and Ersa, who are all very nice and gentle with their duties. When they remove his tattered suit, they wrap it in multiple layers of plastic, and with Ethan's strong recommendations, they put it in an incinerator. After that, they clean him.

He doesn't need a mirror to see his condition when they started cleaning him. He can feel everything, from the wet scars to the blood and sweat that stain him, and the medical foam that is caked on him, and the new bark layer that is digging into his skin, from his right arm all the way to his right shoulder and partially up his neck, and the claws that used to be his right-hand digits.

Even his skin on this portion is thicker. The stinging and throbbing from his wounds is only made worse when they put him through a decontamination shower, and he is put through again three more times by his orders.

After they rinse and scrub him, they clean the bark with impressive precision, and when that is done, Venus leads Ethan to a small, sterile room. Waiting for them is a dark, blue-skinned man with blue eyes, wearing a white and red jumpsuit and a wrist-top computer.

"You must be the guest of honor," says the blue man dryly.

"He is," says Venus. "He was the only one on a derelict ship. Poor guy has been through a lot."

"I can see that," says the blue man. "Now, if you'll please leave. And you, sir, have a seat."

Venus pats Ethan's mutated shoulder and leaves the room, and Ethan sits on the lone gurney while the blue man brings a cart over that is carrying a large tray of supplies.

"For pleasantries, I will say I am Charon, and we have work to do," says the blue man.

What happens next is a rigorous session of further inspection and giving him new bandages and a new splint for Ethan's limbs, braces for his ribs and hips, some stitches, a new eye patch, as well as a very long procedure that pumps out all the chemicals in his body.

He also has a sample of his blood taken and has a cast put over his clawed hand, and extra bandages to cover the mutation on his right side. When that is done, Charon hooks an IV to Ethan with universal blood, and he exits the room.

Ethan is left alone for hours in his gown, and during this time, he studies the room. The gurney is comfortable enough to sleep on; the machines are clean, the stainless-steel cabinets shine in the light, and everything is locked.

Then, an old man enters, carrying a clipboard with actual papers and a pencil. He has wrinkled skin, thick glasses, and thin hair, and he is wearing a white and red jumpsuit. Little lights shine from underneath his sleeves and pants, and his steps have heavy thumps to them. That noise is unnerving for Ethan.

The old man smiles, exposing crooked teeth, and his gray eyes twinkle in the light as he pulls a steel stool in front of Ethan.

"I hope I'm not interrupting anything," says the old man.

Ethan shakes his head.

"Very good. Ethan Rifts, I am Julius Seismon, but you may call me Pluto. I'm the doctor of this ship," says the old man.

"Pluto, huh? I'm seeing a trend here," says Ethan.

Pluto chuckles. "It is a quirk of Captain Sol's to give everyone a name based on the Sol System. You'll get one if you decide to stay."

Ethan shakes his head, and Pluto brings his clipboard up.

"I have to say, I'm impressed that you're still alive. And let me tell you why. First, you're missing an eye." Pluto follows up by giving an impressive list of injuries Ethan sustained on *Bon Voyage*, and the ship doctor finishes with, "So, basically you've poisoned yourself with how much medical foam you used, you wrecked your heart and lungs with excessive adrenaline and extreme activities, and they *will* need to be replaced, parts of your tissue and nervous system are destroyed, your bones are barely held together, and with all the blood you lost, you're lucky to be alive. Oh, and then there's the mental trauma, and whatever the hell this is."

Pluto motions to the mutations, but Ethan says nothing, and the doctor sighs and pats Ethan's leg.

"I don't know what happened to you, but you're going to need some therapy, physical and mental. Fortunately, we know people who can... adjust you," says Pluto.

Ethan frowns. "Are you going to amputate me?"

"Oh, yes. Lots of you, and I'm sure Sol will foot the bill to help you out. He's nice like that. But I wouldn't worry about that slicey-dicey-attachy-wachy stuff, right now. Would you like a drink? Or a meal?

We have Aarden melon juice and microwave dinners. Salisbury steak is especially good," says Pluto.

Ethan shakes his head, and Pluto nods. Then the door opens, and a large man with bronze skin and thick, golden hair and golden eyes enters the room. He is clean-shaven and wearing a recycled red jumpsuit with pads sewn into them.

Next to him is a man of similar stature. He also has thick, golden hair, as well as a beard, and his skin is pale. He is also wearing an old gray jumpsuit with purple bands, and his hands are behind his back, while the first has his hands pressed against his sides.

"Ah, Captain Sol, Jupiter, nice of you two to drop by," says Pluto.

"I'd like a word with our guest alone," says the first man, Sol. Ethan recognizes that voice from the radio.

"Of course," says Pluto.

Pluto pats Ethan's leg again and then leaves the room. Before the door closes, Ethan sees Charon waiting outside. When Pluto is out, Jupiter leaves the room and closes the door, leaving just Ethan and Sol.

Sol smiles thinly and walks to Ethan. Once by his side, he tilts his head slightly. In response, Ethan looks at him, quiet, and mostly unflinching. Fatigue and loss have made his body unsteady and given his eye a heavy weight.

"You've been through a lot, huh?" says Sol.

"Yeah," says Ethan.

"Well, Pluto and Charon said that by all rights you should be dead, and yet here you are. Do you know what that tells me?"

Ethan shakes his head.

Sol puts his hand on Ethan's human shoulder and looks him in the eye. "That tells me God's not done with you. But that case concerns me, as do your mutations. Now, be honest with me. Is someone looking for you and that case?"

Ethan hesitates. "I don't know if anybody knows I'm alive, but for safety reasons, we'll say yes for both. So, if you want to drop me off at some outpost or launch me into space to protect your crew, I will understand."

Sol grins and tightens his hand on Ethan's shoulder. "Ethan, you have nothing to worry about. We found you for a reason, and we're here because the divine hand moved us here. You are now a part of my story, and I want to hear how your story became a part of mine. Starting now. Leave nothing out."

Ethan blinks. "You sure?"

Sol nods and pulls out an audio recorder from his pocket. "Positive. It'll go great with my logs."

"Well." Ethan licks his lips. "I think I will need a lot of that Aarden melon juice and Salisbury steak Pluto was talking about."

Sol smiles. "Of course." He looks at the door. "Jupiter!"

His loud voice makes Ethan jump, and the door opens, and Jupiter pokes his head in.

"Yes?" says Jupiter.

"Have Pluto bring me and our guest two of the gallon jugs of the Aarden melon juice and microwave the family size Salisbury steak dinner!" says Sol.

"Sure."

The door closes, and Sol smiles at Ethan and turns on his audio recorder.

"Now then, Ethan. Tell me your story," says Sol.

"Alright." Ethan takes a deep breath and starts with, "I just want to say, before I get too far, I really hate space."

-THE END-

One day JB was born, and he decided to just roll with it. He also aims to have no more second editions, because two seems to be enough for him.

Author of:

- *The Vigilante Chronicles: Book One: Vigilance*
- *The Vigilante Chronicles: Book One: Vigilance (Second Edition)*
- *Bon Voyage*